FRACTURED
Book Two, The Deprivation Trilogy

LM FOX

The Deprivation Trilogy
Book Two, Fractured

FRACTURED

Editor: Kelly Allenby, Readers Together
Proofreader: Cheree Castellanos, For Love of Books4 Editing
Formatter: Shari Ryan, Madhat Studios
Cover/Graphic Artist: Hang Le
Cover Photographer: Wander Aguiar
Cover Model: Dina Auneau

To my children, who love me unconditionally.

Ask, believe, receive and be immensely thankful
for all is possible when we live in gratitude and joy.

Chapter One

Kat

"Okay, I'm losing it, Dr. Miller," I blurt out, unable to calm the chaos swirling within me. It's barely been two days since my date with Mark, and I'm back in my psychologist's office for an emergency visit. Yearning for comfort, I sink lower into this god-awful green velvet low-back chair. It may be worthy of a Home Magazine cover, but it's one of the most uncomfortable things I've ever sat in. Why can't he have one of those chaise lounges like psychiatrists have on tv? "I honestly don't know what's happening to me anymore." Looking up to this kind, handsome counselor, I feel tears start to spill.

He slowly pushes a box of tissues in my direction, a greater sense of concern reflected upon his stunning face. "Kat, why don't you start at the beginning. What's happened since the last time I saw you?"

Grateful for any help putting the pieces of this mind-numbing puzzle together, I begin. "Well, I stopped taking the zolpidem after we last spoke. I can't risk using it until I'm sure I have better clarity on why I'm waking up with things in disarray. I've never had issues with sleepwalking, but I've been alone so long, who knows." Shaking my head at my situation, I try to refocus. "I haven't had much alcohol lately either. I just need to know I'm going to bed with a clear head. I don't want to keep waking up wondering what happened the night before."

"How has your sleep been? Have you reverted to the night terrors?" he asks softly, again just enough concern present to make me feel comfortable in sharing my ridiculous life with this near stranger.

"Oddly, I haven't had a night terror. I mean, not like the ones I had before I started the sleeping pill. Just the crazy stuff I mentioned, which practically borders on erotica. Plus, the occasional visions of punishing old boyfriends. It takes me longer to get to sleep without the zolpidem, but I think it's because I have so much on my mind… I can't shut it off. But I don't wake up screaming anymore." *Well, unless you count waking up from a dream of hot as hell Dr. Barnes inducing a mind-blowing orgasm. But that kind of screaming I'm okay with.*

"Well, what's changed since I saw you last that has you thinking you're losing your mind? Particularly if you've stopped the pills and the night terrors are gone? Are you still awakening in a state of undress?"

"Well, yes and no." Stopping to assess how to share my most recent concern, I begin again. "Dr. Miller, I… well, I had a date the other night and…"

"Go on, Kat. It's okay," he encourages.

Pulling on the long braid draped over my shoulder as if it's my safety blanket, I cry out, "I don't remember most of it." I look up, noticing a blank stare. "He met me at my home, and I remember going to a restaurant downtown. Dinner was okay, just awkward because I really didn't want to be there. I agreed to this date during a moment of weakness and hoped it would pacify him that I went, but I planned to tell him we should stay friends. There's no spark, and he's part of a close circle of friends," I rattle off quickly.

"Anyway, the evening started rather odd, as I found him in my bedroom. I don't know if he was snooping or what, but he was holding a pair of boots I didn't know I owned until I woke up wearing them one morning following one of my crazy dreams. That paranoia coupled with the aggravation of finding him in my room had my nerves on edge. That I'm clear on."

2

Stopping momentarily, I try to scan the recesses of my mind for the last thing I recall from that night. Grateful for Dr. Miller's patience, I continue. "I remember I turned down having a nightcap at home. He then asked if we could walk to a bar a few doors from the restaurant for a drink."

After what seems like long minutes of crickets chirping, I look up from the floor where I've been concentrating on an errant tuft of rug fiber sticking out of an expensive oriental tapestry like it has all the answers. The penetrating blue eyes of this Matthew McConaughey doppelganger look back at me imploring. "What happened next, Kat?"

"That's just it. I have no idea. I have no way to confirm it because I swear, I feel like I lost hours along the way that night. But I'm sure I didn't take a sleeping pill. There was no pill bottle out. No glass of water. The bottle is still tucked away in the back of the cabinet I'd placed it in when I decided to stop using them." I pause, hoping desperately to connect the dots. "I only had a small glass of wine at dinner, which I didn't finish, and a Margarita at the bar. But in the morning, I woke up in my bra and panties from the night before, nothing else. My clothes were tossed on the floor instead of on the bench at the end of my bed as usual. The whole thing is mind-boggling. I don't remember the end of the date at all." Dropping my head into my hands in shame, I try to keep from losing it in his office. I just want to go home and sit in a hot bath and cry until there's nothing left. *What the hell is happening to me?*

"Katarina? Do you think you were assaulted?" Dr. Miller interrupts with a more serious tone. I look up, noticing he's now leaning forward slightly in his chair.

"I don't think so." I admit it had crossed my mind, but it doesn't make sense. I know Mark. And my crazy nighttime antics started long before a date with him. "I didn't have any marks on me. There wasn't any swelling. I didn't feel particularly sore. Plus, would a guy put your underwear back on after he was done? It doesn't make sense. I really am losing it."

"Kat. We will figure this out. The priority right now is to make sure you are safe, and what's more, you *feel* safe and secure. Is there anyone you could stay with for a while?"

"What? No. I don't want anyone else knowing how crazy my life is that I can't stay home alone. Plus, the only people I could call on have small kids. I couldn't impose on them like that. I'll be fine. I probably should take some time off. I never go anywhere, so I have a ton of personal leave."

"Well, I wouldn't recommend going anywhere right now, but the time off is a good idea. Not needing to be at work will decrease the stress contributed by your lack of sleep. Is there a way you could invest in a security camera? Doesn't have to be expensive, something like a Nanny cam. Something to let you look back on the events of the evening to see if you have left your bed?" he inquires cautiously.

"I hadn't thought of that. That might give me some answers." Leave it to me to need a security camera focusing on me instead of an intruder.

"I would encourage you to take as much time off as you need. Try to develop a routine. Try to wake at the same time, get in a workout if that's something therapeutic. Eat right and stay away from alcohol and sleeping pills. You may even want to keep a journal. It might surprise you the things you recall when you write. You may find something triggers your memories," he urges

Gazing at this miracle worker, I reply, "Thank you. I don't know how you did it, but I feel much better, Dr. Miller." *I still feel crazy, but I have a plan, at least.*

"I'm just doing my job, Kat. I think we should set weekly appointments for a while until you feel things have moved to a healthier place. Is that okay?"

"Yes, of course. I'd appreciate that." I give the semblance of a smile. It's the first I've felt for days.

Departing his office door, I greet Delilah and make next week's appointment. She really is striking. They are fucking Ken and Barbie. If I find out there isn't a hot office romance happening here, I'm going to be sorely disappointed.

"We will see you next Wednesday at 3:15." The blonde-haired, blue-eyed receptionist hands me an appointment card along with a kind smile. Leaving the office, I remember I have my volunteer job delivering meals to seniors next Wednesday, but I should be done in time. Contemplating my schedule as I open my car door and slide in, I remember Dr. Miller encouraging a sabbatical from work. This is unlike me. I've never called out sick. It's so last minute. Looking at the calendar on my cell phone, I notice I have a four-day break from the ER after my next shift. I hope one of the part-time people can pick up tomorrow's shift on such short notice. I'll have to call Jake.

Arriving home, I drop my keys in my purse and place them on the entryway bench. Walking to my kitchen, I decide to put on a pot of tea while I prepare to call Jake. Maybe I'll be fine with five days off. I can get my life back together and get back to work. Tossing around various ways to broach the subject with Jake, I finally chicken out on calling and simply send him a text.

2:25 p.m.
Kat: Sorry for the last-minute notice. I'm not feeling well. Can you find someone to cover tomorrow or use the on-call? I don't think I can make it to work.

2:45 p.m.
Jake Harris
Jake: Hey, sorry to hear that, Kat. You got the flu?

2:55 p.m.
Jake Harris
Jake: Sure, Kit Kat. Just feel better. Let me or Mel know if you need anything.

Wow, that was almost too easy. As the teapot begins to whistle, I stand to grab a steaming cup of calming jasmine infusion and walk toward my bedroom. I mentally decide a hot soak before making my to-do list will be helpful. I need to get all these tears out once and for all. Then I can focus on how to get my damn life back on track.

Stepping into the hot, sudsy tub, I slide down so the water envelopes my shoulders like the hug I so desperately need. Lying my head back on the cushion, I inhale the eucalyptus bath salts encompassing me. Once I leave this calming environment, I need to start plotting a daily routine I can adhere to. This may prove difficult given my rotating shifts in the ER, but it's a start. Anything to feel relatively normal. In PA school, I started my day with meditation and yoga. Looking back, I'm not sure why I'd stopped but suspect my crazy night terrors and constant lack of sleep had something to do with it. I should return to running in the morning, outside when I'm able, or on my treadmill when the weather is poor. Switching to decaf coffee and tea would probably help. Since there's nowhere I need to be for the next few days, the caffeine boost shouldn't be necessary. Picturing the state of my pantry and refrigerator, I cringe. Add hitting the grocery store and stocking up on healthy food to the to-do list. My eating has been crap lately due to my crazy work schedule.

Reflecting on my haphazard nighttime habits, going to bed at a decent time each evening is a must. Maybe I'll force myself to listen to calming, relaxing music before bed—no more angry rock, as much as I love it. This could work. We recommend this sleep hygiene routine for patients in the ER that suffer from insomnia. Why have I never considered it myself?

Lastly, I need to find a Nanny cam. *Where the hell do I find one of those? Amazon maybe? Ugh.* What on earth has happened to my life? *Okay, don't go there, Kat.* Trying to return my mind to somewhere soothing, I take another deep inhalation in this tranquil space and try to picture happy thoughts. I attempt to visualize running through wet multicolored leaves on a cool, fall morning. I picture the warm, engaging smile of my last meal delivery client of the day, who reminds me of my dear gran. My mind shifts to thoughts of laughing at my crazy niece and nephew's ridiculous texts to Nick... *Nick.*

My skin instantly overheats and my heart rate picks up as I picture the hypnotic hazel eyes of the man who stars in my fantasies. Recalling how his hot, soft mouth felt against my lips in the Target has my entire body buzzing. I long to feel his searing lips and tongue trail from my mouth into the hollow of my throat. As I contemplate the sensation of his wanton, open mouth kisses along my skin, I find my nipples have tightened to sharp points. Swollen and pulsating, my groin now fights for attention. Attempting to relieve the ache, I start to trail my hand down toward my belly when I hear a buzz from my phone. Turning to locate the rude device, I realize I've left the pesky thing too far to reach safely from where I'm submerged. Time to end this pleasant diversion. I stop the self-indulgent replay of the sexy orthopedist giving me the hottest kiss of my life in the shampoo aisle, stand, and exit the bath.

Padding dry and slipping on my thick, white terry robe, I wander into the bedroom with my phone to read the incoming message. I hope Jake isn't writing back to let me know no one can cover tomorrow. I need this time off. Sitting at the edge of my bed, I open the text.

3:35 p.m.
Mark Snow
Mark: "How are you, Kat?"

Chapter Two

Nick

Entering the emergency room, I look around with a sense of purpose. I'm here to see a post-op patient who's having continued pain. I suspect they're simply in need of more pain medication, as this patient was using large quantities before their surgery and has likely built up a tolerance. I try to ignore the urge to walk to each nurses' station to see if there's any sign of Kat. I haven't seen or heard from her since playing tonsil hockey in the Target aisle two days ago. *Class act, Nick, class act.*

"Hi, Dr. Barnes." I hear a feminine voice greet, looking toward the closest nurse I see. I recognize her as the cute, curly-haired brunette Kat appears to be friends with. She and the other nurse, Jessica, are the two I usually find giggling at her side when I'm here. She must be able to read my questioning look. "I'm Meghan." She says each syllable slowly, like speaking to a toddler.

"Oh, hi, Meghan. Sorry. I'm still trying to learn names."

"It's okay, Dr. Barnes. You have more important things to remember, I'm sure," she replies with a teasing gleam in her eye. I walk behind the nurses' station to log into a computer and locate my patient. "Are you here to see Miss Browning?"

"Yes, actually. Do you know her room number?"

"She's in room twenty-two. She's my patient. She's been asking for a lot of pain medicine since she's been here," Meghan says, confirming my suspicion.

"I was worried about that. I think she may need help recovering from this surgery. I'll try to get her into a chronic pain clinic. Thanks for assisting her until I could get here."

Standing, I see Jake from the corner of my eye. He's looking down at his phone, facial features tenser than I'm accustomed to in this normally easy-going guy. As I approach, I realize he's so deep in thought he hasn't noticed me standing beside him. "Hey, man, what's up? You look like you're contemplating the meaning of life."

"Ah, it's not me. It's Kat. I'm kind of worried about her."

This has my hackles standing firm. Not sure why I feel so protective of this girl who won't give me the time of day. I try to casually push on. "What's going on? She okay?"

"She called out sick. It's just not like her."

Guess that halts my need to speed walk through the department. "Well, everyone gets sick once in a while. What's the big deal?"

"Well, everyone might get sick, but Kat doesn't call out. Ever. She came to work with pneumonia and didn't realize how sick she was. She almost ended up in the ICU. Something's wrong. I can feel it. She's off the next few days, so I think I'll go check on her. I just can't shake this feeling."

"Fuck, man, now you have me worried."

"Oh, sorry, Nick. It's probably nothing. I'm just going all big brother on her, that's all. Hey, speaking of big brothers, how's your application with the Big Brothers, Big Sisters organization going? They find you anyone yet?"

"Ha. Funny you should mention it. I go Thursday. I have to admit, I'm a little nervous about the whole thing. Almost feels like I'm headed on a blind date."

Chuckling, Jake continues, "Oh, you'll be fine. Hopefully, you two will find some common ground, and this will be a good experience for both of you. I think it's great what you're doing…" Jake stops, swiping his hand through his hair nervously.

"Why do I feel like there's a but in there somewhere?"

"It's not my place. But I'm just going to say it. I think it's a great thing you're doing. But don't let this take the place of having your own family. It wouldn't be fair to you or the kid."

Before I can reply, he slaps my upper arm and walks away. Just as well, I'm tired of this conversation anyway. Turning my head, I see room twenty-two. Knocking on the door, I enter to evaluate my patient.

~

Kat

Sitting in my bay window, warming my hands with my cup of tea as I look over my backyard, I recall the text from Mark. Every time I think back on that date and subsequent morning, I feel warier about what might have happened. I'm not sure how to address it with Mark. I don't need to draw attention to the fact I'm losing control of my mind and my life. He's a nice enough guy, but I honestly don't know him well and don't fancy my madness becoming the firehouse joke. I also don't want to insult him in any way. If there's a chance he thinks I'm accusing him of something… well, I think I'll keep my questions to myself for now.

Getting up from my perch, I head to the kitchen for a refill. As I pour the hot water, I notice an email notification. My Nanny cam is on the way. *Great, now I can start taping myself as I sleep.* Gah! Closing the email app, I decide to send Mark a text, trying to make a clean break. The one thing I am sure of, no repeats of that evening are happening in the future. I walk over to my couch and sit as I begin to type.

11:15 a.m.
Kat: Hi. I'm ok. Sorry for the delay getting back to you. Feeling under the weather.

11:18 a.m.
Mark Snow
Mark: Well, I'd love to take you out again once you're feeling better.

11:22 a.m.
Kat: Thank you. I'm not in a good place for dating at the moment. I've got too much on my plate. I'd like to stay friends though. I hope that's ok.

I sit, awaiting a reply. Nothing.

11:30 a.m.

I refresh my screen. Hmm. Nothing.

11:45 a.m.

Refreshing my screen for the tenth time. No response. Maybe he's at work? On a call? God, I hope he isn't upset. *Uh. This is why you don't date your friends.*

Sitting on my floor several hours later, my workout clothes and skin are both covered in a sheen of sweat. I've finished yoga and wish I could say I'm more relaxed, but I still feel like a human pretzel. The tension and lack of sleep are doing nothing to calm my mood. I need to bite the bullet. It's going to take more than four or five days to get me to a place where I can function as a normal person again. Picking up the phone, I hit the contact button and hold my breath.

"Kat?"

"Hey, Jake. I need to ask a favor." I wince at the thought of asking him to assist with my time off, knowing what a hardship this could cause.

"Sure. What's up? You need some chicken noodle soup?"

"I need to take some time off. Could you help me?"

12

"More time off? What are we talking about, a vacation or something?"

"No. I need some time off now. The counselor I'm seeing recommended I take a bit of a sabbatical to get myself together."

"What the hell, Kat?" he blurts. *Man, I knew it was going to be tough to get the time off, but I didn't expect him to get mad about it.* "What's going on that you need extended time off? Are you okay?" He sounds more concerned than angry.

Unable to control my unease any longer, my voice starts to quiver into the phone. "Jake, I'm losing it. I feel like a crazy person. I was hoping I could take these next few days and pull myself together, but I feel unhinged." I start to whimper into the phone.

"That's it, Kat. I'll be there in thirty minutes."

"No..." I realize it's useless to argue as the line is dead, and I'm sure he's already headed in my direction. I walk to the bathroom to take a quick shower and change my clothes before he arrives. This conversation will be uncomfortable enough without the added layer of sweaty gym clothes and body odor.

Approximately forty minutes later, I hear an aggressive pounding at the door. As I approach, I see the troubled face of my dear friend peering into the narrow window that abuts my front door. Opening the door wide, I step back to let him in. Jake is a few inches taller than I am, about 5'11. He has a broad chest, muscular build, and intense dark eyes that are more dramatic when he's in a serious or anxious mood. Even working in emergency medicine, I don't see that side of him often. He's usually a teddy bear. His alarmed state has me feeling a bit agitated. How do you tell someone you love and respect that you're losing your faculties?

"Okay, Kat. Take a seat. Tell me what the hell is going on."

Taking a fortifying breath, I begin as calmly as I'm able. "Okay, where to start. Well, I started to use the pills you wrote for me, and my sleep seemed to be getting better. I wasn't having night terrors any longer, but some of the dreams I had were a bit on the crazy side. At first, I just laughed them off as if they were artsy independent films at the Biograph or something. But crazy stuff started happening." I look up to see if his expression has changed at all.

"What kind of crazy stuff?" he encourages, waving his hand to continue.

"Well, I started waking up, and things weren't like I remembered when I went to bed. Like, once, I woke up buck naked."

"Kat, a lot of people sleep naked."

"Well, I don't, and I would've remembered if I suddenly went to bed that way. Later, I found my clothes on the bathroom floor, and there was water on the tiles like I took a shower in the middle of the night." Scratching my head at the memory, I carry on. "I woke up one day wearing crazy stuff that I had worn in my dream."

"Like what?"

"I had on an entire jogging outfit, including shoes." I leave out the whole Tarzan theme of the dream. Jake doesn't need to know I've been picturing Dr. Nicholas Barnes wearing a loincloth. "Once, I woke up after dreaming I'd been at a strip club as the headliner, wearing the boots and thong I had on in the dream. I didn't know I owned those, Jake."

I watch as Jake's eyebrows quickly jump up to meet his forehead. "Hell, Kat. Did this just happen?"

"No. I'd already spoken with my counselor about it. He was concerned it was either related to the use of the sleep aid or combining it with alcohol, so I decided to quit both to see if the situation resolved itself. But…"

"But what?" Jake asks guardedly.

"Well, I had a date the other night, and I don't remember much of what happened. It has freaked me out." I wrap my arms around myself and refuse to make eye contact with him now.

"What happened?"

"Mark had been asking me out. I'm not at all attracted to him, but after we were both decompressing about the delivery of Katrina's baby, I agreed to go before I realized what I was doing. Anyway, he came to the house and picked me up, we went to dinner, and I think we went out afterward for a drink…" I stop again, dumbfounded that my memories come to a complete halt at this point. "Beyond that, I can't remember a thing. I woke up the next day in my bra and underwear, and I don't recall anything after getting to the bar."

"Holy shit, Kat. Do you think Mark did something to you?" He sits up taller now.

"I don't think so. I mean, it's Mark. Not some stranger. Plus, there wasn't a scratch on me." I get up from where I'm sitting next to him on the couch, feeling the need to pace as I continue. "I swear I don't think I took anything. I don't remember how the evening ended, but I hid the pills because I wanted to see if the weird clothing changes would stop if I wasn't taking them anymore. I didn't have much to drink at all. I just can't figure out where a large block of time went." Again, with the damn tears.

"Kat. Is there a chance Mark could have slipped something in your drink?" Jake asks, distressed.

"But why? We're friends. I had my underwear on when I woke up. What did he do? Rape me, put my underwear back on, but thought, oh, I'll leave her clothes on the floor? Plus, this weird shit was happening before the date. I can't just blame this on him." Full-blown hysterics have taken over now. "I ordered a damn Nanny cam to spy on myself at night, so I can figure out what the hell I'm doing," I choke out, my face covered in tears.

Standing to grab me in a tight hug, I feel his arms around me like bands of steel. "We're going to figure this out, Kat. Shhh." Kissing my head, he pulls back. "I do think you should get tested, just to be on the safe side. You don't have to go anywhere. I think you can get a Rohypnol test online where they use your hair follicles or something. Just don't wait too long. It's worth it to get some answers."

"This is crazy, Jake," I sputter.

"I know. But you need to sort everything out. Once you can scratch the Rohypnol off the list of possibilities, you can move on. Maybe come up with other things that could've caused the way you've been behaving. I'm glad you're holding off on the zolpidem for a while. At least until you can get this figured out better. Probably not sleeping at all now, huh?"

"Nope."

"Well, if it makes you feel any better, I've had some weird shit happen when I was taking zolpidem. So, it might not be you." He laughs. I could tell he was trying to lighten the mood.

"Like what?" I again sniffle.

"Apparently, Melanie thinks I'm a sex god on the stuff. Which would be great if I remembered any of it." He chuckles. "But that could just be Mel pulling one over on me." He grabs the nape of his neck with his right hand and continues, "And some of the guys from the fire department have said they had fun when I was out with them the night before. But I don't remember going anywhere. I just figured they had their days confused, or I was drunk when I saw them. Or like Mel, they were fucking with me."

Jake's phone pings with an incoming text, and he looks down as he reads aloud. "Mel says, 'tell Kat to get better soon and pick up some milk on your way home. Dinner will get cold if you two hang out too long.' That's her passive-aggressive way of saying get your ass back home. I better go." He snorts.

Hugging him goodbye, I walk him to the door, feeling grateful for my dear friends. I know I can always count on them. "Please, don't tell Mel what a basket case I am," I plead.

"Kat, you aren't a basket case. We'll figure this out. Don't worry about work. I'll move some things around. Just stay in touch with this counselor and get yourself together. You're fine. I mean it. We will figure this out." He rubs my arms reassuringly before heading for the door.

As he turns to go down the steps, I look up to notice a large Ford F150 parked on the street. *That's not usually sitting there.* A feeling of unease shrouds me. Is that Mark's truck? Suddenly, the driver's side door swings open, and a gray-haired man exits. *Good Lord, hold it together, Kat. You're really becoming paranoid now.*

Returning inside, I lock my door and head back to the kitchen. Deciding I need a good distraction, I grab my Kindle and start to peruse my library of romance novels while the teapot begins to heat. *If I can't have a real-life hot alpha male like Dr. Nick Barnes, I'll have to settle for a book boyfriend.* Some of the book covers make me laugh. I reflect on what Jake shared earlier. *Ha, Jake, a sex god.* I chuckle to myself.

Suddenly, I contemplate what he said. *What are the odds we've both had crazy shit happen on this sleeping pill?* I guess that's one thing to be said for being terminally single. No chance I've been having hot sex with anyone. Quickly, I think back to my odd mornings in a state of undress...

Is there?

Chapter Three

Nick

I'm on edge as I leave my office, heading toward the physician's parking lot. The sun is bright this afternoon, so I reach into my jacket to retrieve my Ray-Bans. Spotting my Audi, I click my lock and climb inside. *What is wrong with me? I'm a surgeon, for fuck's sake.* Meeting some teenager for the first time to hang out shouldn't be this nerve-wracking. I pull out and head toward the highway. I'm meeting my new 'little brother' in about thirty minutes. I want to make a good impression. This could be good for me. Give me something positive to focus on. Something besides Katarina Kelly.

Driving down the highway, I think back on the last few weeks. Life's been flat without that snarky brazen beauty around. After mauling her in the Target, she's played a vanishing act. *Yep, blew that one.* She must've thought I was a conceited bastard. 'I just wanted you to have something to think about when you were out later.' She showed me. Probably hasn't given me a second thought. I've missed her sarcastic banter in the ER. Hell, I haven't even received a work text asking for help. Of course, the last time she sent one of those, I practically pounced on her in an exam room. *Any wonder why your texts went silent?*

I didn't have the guts to ask Jake if Kat had begun a new relationship. Jesus, with my knack for incorrect assumptions, she probably wasn't on a date at all. It could've been a family function. But somehow, I could tell from her facial expression there was another man involved. Was it that firefighter?

Even though I'm not looking for a commitment, I've never thought of myself as a player. The women I'd been involved with understood the score. So, why is it I suddenly feel like I've been played? The way she could just walk away after the hottest night of my life. I know there's chemistry between us. How could she not feel it too? *You never wanted a relationship in the first place, you idiot.* I need to move on but stay open to possibilities. Dad's right. If there's a chance for this to develop, I'll consider it if and when it happens. Otherwise, I'll focus on work, my new 'little brother,' and possibly see if Calina will agree to go out again.

Walking into the musty-smelling office, I approach the desk. A kind-looking woman looks up from her paperwork and smiles. "What can I do for you?"

"Hi. I'm Nicholas Barnes. I have an appointment with Sandra."

"Oh, certainly. I'll let her know you're here."

I turn and notice a small waiting area next to the front door and lower myself into the worn, yellow vinyl chair. Wiping my hands on my trousers, I fret. *God, why am I so nervous?*

"Dr. Barnes?" A beautiful redhead approaches, arm extended in greeting. "I'm Sandra. It's so nice to meet you."

"Yes, it's nice to meet you too."

"Would you follow me? I received all of your paperwork and matched you with an athletic young man, thinking it'd give you something in common. I know you said you played soccer. I'm not sure if he does, but I know he's quite fond of basketball. He was on his high school team for a while, but I believe his mother's work situation prevented him from regularly attending practices and games. He, unfortunately, had to quit the team."

"Man, that's too bad. I take it she's a single parent?"

"Hence why you're here," she quickly replies. "Many of the parents work long hours trying to provide for their children. With no other adult in the home, many of these kids spend a great deal of time alone or in the company of wayward friends. It'll be wonderful for Gavin to have a male role model he can look up to."

Gavin. I like that name. I can do basketball. This won't be so bad. I realize as we round a corner, she's pushing open a door to the outside. Just to the rear of the building is a makeshift basketball court. Beneath the hoop, a lanky, dark-haired teen stands about five foot seven.

"Gavin, this is Dr. Barnes. He's going to be your 'big brother.' If the two of you would like to get to know each other for a while, I'll send your mom back to collect you in about thirty minutes." Turning in my direction, she continues, "We're happy to assist you in planning get-togethers in the future, or you can work that out directly with Gavin's mom, Ms. McReedy." I watch the attractive woman smile at me briefly before she turns toward the building. I train my gaze on the young man, noting a questioning look.

"Hi, Gavin. I'm Nick," I say, reaching out my hand. I watch as he looks down at it and quickly spins away to shoot the basketball toward the hoop. Trying to rein in my irritation at his poor manners, I watch as the tattered ball easily swooshes through the net. "Nice," I clap. I remain standing motionless as he sinks ball after ball through the net effortlessly, never turning to make eye contact or pat himself on the back. Initially perturbed at his disrespect, I quickly change gears. How would I have felt at his age to have a gift and no one to support me in achieving it? My incredible parents provided one opportunity after another to find what interested me. They were always there, helping me to reach my goals. I never doubted I was the center of their universe. Yet Gavin has obvious talent but was forced to drop out because he lacked the help he needed. "Hey, I'm not nearly as good as you are but, throw me the ball." I challenge.

I've barely finished the sentence before the ball is hurled at me with some force. *Hmm, angry teen. I get it.* I take a shot and thankfully make it. I don't need to give this kid another reason to dislike me. However, I think nothing short of LeBron James offering to be his 'big brother' would soften this kid up.

He gathers the ball and takes another shot. This might be the longest thirty minutes of my life.

"So, what'd you do?" I hear him ask, still facing away from me, sending the ball in repeated trips through the net.

"I'm sorry. What do you mean?"

"I mean, is this some kind of community service?"

"What?" I laugh. "No. I volunteered to be here," I respond, taken off guard a bit.

"You married?" he asks, continuing to toss the ball in the air. I've still not gotten a good look at his face.

"No."

"You hate dogs or something?" he asks casually, turning to shoot again.

"What?"

"Ah, I got your ticket. You're doing this to get married. You're old, but you ain't a complete disaster. I saw the way the ginger was checking you out. You're using me to pick up women."

I stand completely baffled by this conversation. "I'm not looking to get married. And if I was, what has that got to do with hating dogs?"

"Hell, you know it'd be a lot easier to meet chicks with a puppy. I figure you must really hate dogs to have to come and hang out with some punk kid you don't know."

I'm not sure what I was expecting from this meet and greet, but this clearly wasn't it. If I'd known then what I know now, I *really* would've been nervous. But I'm no quitter.

"Gavin, I like dogs just fine. But as I said, I'm not interested in getting married, so no need for puppies."

"So you're gay."

Holy shit, this kid has balls. I cannot imagine talking to an adult like this when I was young. "No. Not gay. I just wanted to volunteer my time to see if I could support a young man who might need an older male's help."

Abruptly, he spins on his heels and shouts in my direction. "Listen, if you're some kind of perv… I ain't letting you do nothing to me. You just keep your distance, and we'll both be good. Got it?"

Blinking slowly, I wonder how on earth this situation has gotten so out of control. "Gavin, I assure you, I'm not a perv. I like women just fine. Not into kids or anyone with a dick." I notice this gets a lift of one corner of his mouth. "I just had a shitty first marriage and don't plan on doing that again, but always wanted kids. I grew up without any sisters or brothers. I thought this could be a way I could give back and feel like I had a connection with someone. Chill, man," I blurt out, hands held out as if I'm surrendering.

The teen turns his back to me and takes another shot. This time the ball hits the rim and bounces off.

"Now throw me the ball, you loser," I jab. The ball sails in my direction without as much force as his previous lob. We continue to take turns, silently tossing the ball into the net until I get the nerve to break the calm. "So, what grade are you in?"

"Tenth."

"You like school?"

"What do you think?" he quips.

"I don't know. You're a sharp kid. You only have a few years left. Any idea what you want to do when you graduate?"

"Besides getting the fuck out of here? No."

Man, I'm going to need a sledgehammer to break through the chip on this kid's shoulder. "Well, you need money and a job to get out of here. There's got to be something you're interested in."

"What difference does it make? I'm never going to college. Hell, my mom barely makes enough to keep me in clothes. I had a growth spurt, and for months I was wearing clothes looking like I was expecting a flood. Shame you ain't looking for a wife. I could hook you up with my mom. You're a little classier than the dudes she usually brings home, but I bet you can afford a few pairs of pants." I watch as he dribbles the ball a few times before sinking it in the net again.

Jesus, this kid. Was he pimping out his mom? Not sure there's much of a relationship with her if he can talk about her this way. "So, your mom works a lot?" I ask carefully, knowing this live wire could come back with almost anything.

"She works temp jobs. Some last a while, others don't. I don't know what she does exactly. Then at night, she works at a bar. She says she makes good tips there, and that's why she works more there than at the day jobs, but I don't see much of it coming home. Hell, some nights, she doesn't come home. I don't care. I can fend for myself."

"Well, there are scholarships out there. If there's something you're interested in, you should start looking into it soon. Ask your guidance counselor at school about it," I encourage, hating that this young man has written off his life before it's even begun. Quickly, I change the subject, not wanting to hear his reply to my 'just hang in there' dad speech. "Do you have a girlfriend?" Trying to hide his smile, I catch the change in his facial features and realize I've stumbled upon something positive.

"I wouldn't call her my girlfriend. She's hot. We talk."

"She goes to your school?" I ask, tossing the ball toward the net and watching as it circles the rim slowly before sinking in. *Yes.*

"Yeah. She's a year older than me. She's pretty smart. She's going to college to be a nurse." There's more pride in his voice than normal for a kid who is 'just talking' to the girl.

"Well, shouldn't you see if there's something you can work toward that'd keep a hot nurse interested?"

"Well, I'm never going to be a doctor, if that's what you mean." He snorts.

"There are plenty of other professions that interact with nurses. But, if she likes you, I bet she'd be happy to see you go after anything that interests you." I hold on to the ball momentarily, trying to make a point. "Come on, man. If you could have any job, what would it be?"

"I don't know. I thought about being a firefighter. Seems cool. I just don't know anything about it." He shrugs, more serious now.

"I can help you find out." I'm hoping I've had a breakthrough here.

"Hey guys, Ms. McReedy is here to pick up Gavin. Why don't you two come in, and you can exchange contact information and plan a time to get together again?"

Looking toward Gavin, I see a single short nod of the head. *Whew, I guess I passed the first phase of this inquisition.* "Sounds good, Sandra," I say, walking alongside Gavin as we cross the cracked pavement.

I gaze back over at him, finding him smirking, carrying the basketball under his right arm. Looking straight ahead, he drops his voice to a near whisper. "Shame you aren't on the market, old man. Ginger has a nice ass."

Back in my car, heading for home, I have to keep from laughing to myself. *Good Lord, that kid. I need a drink.* I was in no way prepared for the likes of Gavin McReedy. I pat myself on the back for getting through this day. I need to see what I can do to assist this kid. Show him someone out there cares about him and his future. But I need to be careful how I show my support... he already suspects I'm a 'perv.' Maybe Jake can get me some contact info for his buddies at the fire department. I bet Gavin could do a ride-along or something. They could give him the low down on what's required to join the department. And those guys won't put up with any of his shit. It'd be like mini boot camp for him.

Slowing for the light, I contemplate future outings with Gavin. Something tells me he won't be into soccer. He seems committed to basketball. But I could toss it out there. Maybe I can score tickets to a VCU basketball game. I need to take this slow, find out how his grades are and carefully offer help with assignments. If he wants to pursue a career with the fire department, I'm sure his transcripts need to be competitive.

As the light turns green, I notice a True Green lawncare truck to my left. Sandra had said Gavin was fifteen. Too young for a work permit, but I could probably interest him in a job doing some landscaping with my dad. If he doesn't have anything on the weekends, I could bring him to help mow the lawn, trim hedges or edge the lawn. I know my dad doesn't really need help. *Hell, the only thing he does all day is work on that damn lawn and watch the news and weather.* But I think bringing the two of them together could be good, and earning an honest day's labor might give Gavin some much-needed spending money without it appearing as a handout. I just need to warn Dad about that mouth before he gets there.

Pulling my car into the garage, I turn off the ignition and sit quietly for a moment. I've truly had a blessed life. I had wonderful, devoted parents who provided for my every need. They gave me the chance to play soccer and eventually go to medical school. It doesn't matter that my marriage didn't last. Dad's right, that ending *was* probably for the best. If only there was still a chance for me to have a successful marriage and kids. *Well, not that kid.*

I try to picture myself tossing a ball back and forth with my own teenage son. Leaning my head against the headrest of my car, I close my eyes and take in the sight. Laughing, sparring with one another as we play one on one in the driveway. Off to the side, I notice a young girl of about ten years of age creating chalk drawings with a younger sister. I can't help the smile that crosses my face. Just as I decide to open my eyes, pour myself a scotch, and call it a day, I notice a beautiful brunette come out to join the girls on the concrete. She lowers herself to the ground, picks up pale pink chalk, and proceeds to draw hearts on the little one's cheeks.

Laughing at myself, I question where my mind has gone and wander into the house. Grabbing my celebratory scotch, I head to the bedroom for a shower. I take a drink of the amber liquid and begin to sputter as it goes down a little too quickly. Bending over the sink, I splash some water onto my face and look into the mirror. An empty expression greets me. *Make up your mind, Barnes. You can't have it both ways.*

Refreshed from my shower, I sit with my leftover Italian food and a glass of Merlot, trying to rid my mind of self-doubt. I stare aimlessly into the dark kitchen while eating my dinner in isolation. *Is this better? Is this better than taking a chance?* Before Katarina, I wouldn't have questioned my choices, but now…

Admitting I've lost my appetite, I throw the remainder of my meal in the trash and rinse my glass. I might as well hit the hay. Ascending the steps, I trudge to my bed and lie back on the crisp, cotton sheets. Staring at the ceiling, the earlier pictures dance in my head. But the young girl is no longer the cherub making chalk art on the drive but a small girl seated in a metal chair. A breathtaking brunette wearing a white lab coat squats down by her side, reassuring the child she's going to be all right.

Question is, will I?

Chapter Four

Kat

"Hey, Mel, come on in." I've wondered how long it would take for her to drop by. It's been five days since Jake was here, and while I haven't awakened wearing strange apparel, I'm no closer to figuring out what happened to me. I'm sleeping better now. I'm sticking to Benadryl, which often has me waking a bit hungover, but I prefer this to wondering what I'd been doing the night before.

Hugging me tightly as she enters, she asks with notable concern, "How ya holding up, Kat? I thought I'd bring you some dinner." She walks toward the kitchen holding a bag of something which smells divine.

"What's that?" I chase after her.

"It's Luigi's Penne ala Vodka. I also have salad and bread. Sound good?"

"Sounds and smells perfect. You're a goddess."

"I have my moments. So, Jake told me about what's been going on. Are you feeling any better?" she asks timidly.

"Well, nothing else odd has happened since I saw him. I'm sleeping a little better, but then again, I take two Benadryl, and it knocks me out. I don't wake up until after 9:00 a.m. each morning. But I don't have anywhere to be so..."

Grabbing a couple of glasses from the cabinet, I fill one with water and place it on the table by the bay window. "Do you want water?"

"Yeah, I'm driving. Water's fine. You aren't having wine?" She looks at me suspiciously.

"No. With all of the craziness, I'm trying to stay away from alcohol for a while. Just need to get my head on straight. It's terrible when you can't trust anything you know. I swear I put those sleeping pills away, Mel. I guess that's why I'm so disturbed about the time-lapse during my date with Mark."

"Well, I think you should listen to Jake. Take the online Rohypnol test. Make sure he didn't Roofie your drink. I know it seems outlandish, but at least you'll know and can take that off of the table and deal with the fact you must've taken a sleeping pill and just can't remember. Just do it, Kat. For your own peace of mind."

"No, you're right." I scoop penne pasta smothered in luxurious pink sauce onto two plates, inhaling the tempting aroma. Walking toward the table with the food, I can barely wait to dig in. Some candles and a good bottle of wine, and this would be quite the romantic setup. *Ha, figures I'm enjoying it with Melanie.* "Hey, Mel, I wanted to ask you something." I approach the topic carefully.

"Anything. What is it?" she answers with a forkful of pasta inches from her mouth.

"Jake mentioned when he uses zolpidem, occasionally weird shit happens. Is that true?" I await her answer with bated breath.

"Ha. I wasn't sure where you were going with this, but yeah. Sometimes he gets completely turned on, and the sex is incredible. Is that what you mean?"

"Yeah. But more the fact he said he doesn't remember a thing about it the next day." I suddenly hear a loud metallic clank and realize she's dropped her fork. "Mel?"

"I'm sorry. He told you he doesn't remember any of it?" she asks astounded, pushing herself back from the table a bit.

Worried I'll upset her, I squeak out, "Yes." Wishing I could take back the decision to question her on this.

"God, I thought he was pulling my leg about that." She answers more to herself than to me, it appears. "Hell. That's some sleeping pill." Her coloring appears a little pale.

"I know. Now you know why I decided to stop taking them. I'm starting to wonder what is real. I question what I could've been doing when I wake wearing strange clothing. Plus, some of the dreams were crazy. I'm trying not to think too much about it, or I'll make myself nuts."

"No. I get it," she answers, taking another forkful of pasta. "Maybe I should pay a lot more attention at home too. When he's taking those pills."

I stand, carrying my plate to the sink to rinse, and then start to put away the leftovers. Rubbing my stomach in appreciation of her generous delivery, I walk back over to the table. "Thank you, Melanie. That was amazing. I just need a soak in a bubble bath, and I'll probably be able to sleep without the Benadryl. I'm so full." I laugh, covering my open mouth as I yawn.

"Go run your bath. I'll get the rest of this in the dishwasher, and poke my head in to say goodbye before I go."

"What? Are you sure?"

"Yes, girl. Go. I'm going to go home and do the same."

Taking her up on her kind offer, I walk into the bathroom and start running the hot water. Finding a nice Lavender bath bomb, I unwrap it and take a deep inhalation before placing it next to the tub. Before I can get my top off, I hear laughing. Curious, I look around the door's edge and shout, "What's so funny?" Jake or the kids are probably texting her.

Melanie walks in my direction, carrying a phone. Just as I suspected. But it isn't until she's directly in front of me that I realize it isn't her phone, but mine. She turns it around to show the text on the screen.

8:45 p.m.
Nick Barnes
Nick: I'm on call tonight. How's the ER look?

8:48 p.m.
Kat: I'm off, actually. About to get into a bubble bath.

"Mel! Really?" I ask, flabbergasted at her antics.

"What? I was just being honest. Look at his answer," she says, giving me a wicked grin. Looking down swiftly, I take in the words.

8:51 p.m.
Nick Barnes
Nick: Is that an invitation?

Glancing back to Melanie and her shit-eating grin, my mouth hanging open, I'm unable to form words.

"You need to take him up on that, Kat." She smiles devilishly.

"What? He was joking." I haven't seen Nick since the panty-melting kiss in aisle eight of Target. Now thinking about him joining me in my bubble bath has suddenly become spank bank worthy.

"All I know, if I was single, that'd be all the invitation I needed. He's hot as hell, Kat. What are you waiting for?"

"All right, you little tart. Give me a hug and head on out of here before you get me into any more trouble," I say, placing the phone on silent and turning it face down onto the bathroom counter.

"Bye, Chica. I'll check on you later. We need to get together soon to plan the Halloween party," she reminds me. She and Jake's yearly Halloween parties are legendary.

"Of course. I'll have to check my schedule. I'm back to work in a few more days." I reach to turn off the water as the tub is two-thirds of the way full, steam rising to meet me.

I stand, hugging Mel tightly, and again thank her for the delicious dinner. Watching as she enters her car and her headlights come on, I give a quick wave. As she starts to back out of the drive, I return to my bath. *If only my life wasn't so ridiculous right now. Dr. Barnes might be shocked to see the reply I'd send.*

~

Several days later, I walk through the ER doors and immediately feel like I'm home again. The time off was necessary, but I'm glad to be back doing what I love. As I settle into my usual workstation, I look at the call schedule and realize none of my favorite physicians are here today. I didn't see Megan or Jess. Just Bobbi. But it's going to be a good day. I can handle this. I sign into the computer to see if anyone is waiting and look up to see the charge nurse coming my way.

"Hey, Kat. There's a lady here in room five that's in a lot of pain. She just got here by rescue squad, so she isn't on the board yet. Do you mind seeing her?"

"Of course. I'll head straight there."

As I walk down the hall toward her room, I notice the EMS stretcher is parked just outside the patient's door. I take two steps into the patient exam room and come to an abrupt standstill.

"Hey, Kit Kat." Mark delivers with a wink. The hair on my arms immediately stands at attention, and I sense my heart begin to pound within my chest. Feeling off kilter, my body is on full alert.

"Hi." Is all I can get out. I try to focus on the patient, hoping he'll leave. I don't like the way this feels. I suddenly feel trapped. "Hi, Miss?" I address the patient.

"Timberlake," she cries, bracing her right shoulder.

"Ms. Timberlake. I'm Katarina Kelly. I'm going to be taking care of you. I want to try and get you some relief. Do you have any medication allergies?"

"No." She sniffs.

"Well, I'm going to order your pain medication and come back to assess you afterward. Just hang on for us, okay?" I attempt to reassure her. Stepping out of the patient room, I hurriedly pass Mark's partner returning to the stretcher with clean sheets. I don't recognize this young firefighter. Without delay, I rush down the ER hallway to the furthest nurses' station to enter Ms. Timberlake's pain medication and an x-ray order into the computer before stepping out of the department. I need to get out of here, if only for a second. *Jeez, am I having a panic attack?*

Walking down the corridor toward the physician's lounge, I fumble with my badge which garners access to the locked area. I must be completely fixated on Mark's arrival to the ER and its effect on me, as I don't realize Dr. Lee is standing at the entrance holding the door open for me.

"Penny for your thoughts," he says, smiling down at me.

"Trust me, they aren't worth a penny," I reply, frustrated I've barely been in the department fifteen minutes, and this scenario with Mark is already rattling me. I need to get my act together before I return. I cannot let him affect my work. I can't let anyone else see me like this.

Feeling a warm, firm hand on my back, I look up. "You okay? You look like you've seen a ghost," he asks with concern. All of the charismatic flirting is off of the table. My anxious state must be worse than I thought if this man is providing counsel instead of pick-up lines.

"Like you've seen a ghost," I mutter to myself. *It's about as mysterious*, I consider. "Something just caught me off guard. I'll be okay. Thanks for asking." I try to reassure him I have it all together.

"Kat, if someone is bothering you—"

"No." I interrupt, laughing, trying desperately to change the subject and begin acting like a professional instead of a freaked-out teenaged girl. "I'm fine. Really. Thank you, though. You're very kind to ask."

Nick

Driving to work, I note the sun has barely broken through the darkness. It's going to be a long day, and I have no time to spare. Planning to round on my inpatients early, I have a full calendar of appointments in the office until lunch and then I'm in the operating room the rest of the day. Additionally, I'm on call until 5:00 p.m., so if I get called to the ER, it'll throw a wrench in my day. Not to mention, it's more than a little depressing when Kat's not around.

Kat. I've really lost control of that situation. So much for avoiding her at all costs. I just couldn't help myself. When I asked how the ER was, I simply wanted some type of interaction with her. *Hell, I've missed that little minx.* So, when I sent the text, and she mentioned heading for a bubble bath, my mind immediately envisioned her naked body covered in shimmery soap suds, and I lost my fucking mind. *Was that an invitation?*

I was supposed to be giving her space, in case she'd started dating someone… possibly Mark, the firefighter she was giggling with the last time I saw her in the ER. But instead, I put my foot in my mouth again. I must've pissed her off as the texts came to an immediate halt. Just face it, Nick, you've met your match. She blew you off after that amazing night behind the club. The kiss in Target and the inappropriate texting just sealed the deal. Walk away while you still have an ounce of dignity left.

Having finished my rounds, I'm heading back to the clinic in time for my first patient of the day. A perk of my office being attached to the hospital is the ability to slide into the physician's lounge to grab a cup of coffee and a granola bar easily. As I step inside the lounge, I immediately feel a shift in the energy of the room. As the door shuts behind me, I see Katarina. Beautiful Katarina talking to none other than Sebastian Lee. *Why is he standing so close to her? Is he… touching her?* I'm sure he's laying it on thick, by the look on his face. But she doesn't seem to mind. Could he? No. Was he her 'other plans' that night? Have they been dating this whole time?

"Nick," I hear him greet.

"Sebastian," I return. I need to get my damned coffee and go before I lose it. She's a grown-ass woman. She can see whomever she chooses. This isn't my place. But for fuck's sake, couldn't she have picked someone else? Anyone else? Hadn't Jake warned her? With what he told me about her dating history, this is the last guy I'd think she'd want to spend time with. I place my cup in the dispenser and load the coffee. I need to focus on something besides my ire. Forget the granola bar, I need to get the hell out of here before they see the effect they're having on me. I hear a door shut and turn to see if they've left, making direct contact with Sebastian.

"Don't worry, Nick. She's not my type."

What the fuck? "I don't know what you're talking about," I bark, turning back to my coffee. Placing the plastic lid carefully on the beverage, I head for the door. "Everyone is your type," I grind out. Grabbing the door, I make a hasty retreat before he can say anything else, which could set off the powder keg of emotions simmering within me. I have no right to feel this way. I have no relationship with this girl. Heading back to my office, I think, *five o'clock can't get here fast enough.*

～

"Dr. Barnes. Your fifth patient of the day is here, but there's a call from the ER about a consult. What should I tell them?" Ava asks, concerned. She's been walking on eggshells around me most of the morning due to my inability to rein in my disappointment at this mornings' physician lounge discovery.

"I'll take it, Ava. Just put them through." I sit back down at my desk, deciding to take the call and then finish my last two office patients. Hopefully, I can take care of whatever they need quickly, and it won't delay my OR cases. "This is Nick Barnes," I snap.

"Uh, hi, Dr. Barnes. This is Katarina. I'm sorry to have to bother you. I have an unassigned orthopedic patient who has a pretty ugly collarbone fracture. I know we typically put these in a shoulder immobilizer and send them to see you in the office, but this one's in the center of the clavicle, and the fractured area is tenting the skin. I thought I'd reach out to you, knowing this is your area. When I found out you were on call today… well, I feel lucky it's you."

Is she kidding with this? Is she just throwing me a bone after I texted her this weekend and walked in on her with Lee this morning? "Yes. I'm on call. But I have office patients here to see, and I'm scheduled for three OR cases today," I continue to snarl into the receiver.

"Oh. I'm sorry. I can just put her in a shoulder immobilizer and advise her to contact your office for an appointment," she offers quickly.

"No. I'll tie things up here and come see her before I head to the OR." I hang up the phone, irritated with myself for letting this woman get to me. This is exactly what I've been trying to avoid all along. I'm a professional but cannot control my temper at the moment. I can't let women affect my work. Standing, I head for my 11:00 a.m. patient and pray the last appointment of the day has arrived early. I need to knock these out quickly so I can squeeze in the ER case before going to the operating room for the remainder of the day.

"Hi, Bobbi. I'm here to see the patient with a clavicle fracture," I advise. I avoid making eye contact with her, having no tolerance for Bobbi's coquettish behavior today.

"Hi, Dr. Barnes. Mrs. Peterson is in room thirteen." Getting my bearings, I look at the door closest to me to figure out where room thirteen might be located. "It's just to your right." I look to Bobbi, who's smiling, pointing at the room closest to me.

"Thanks," I respond, realizing I've become unhinged. About that time, Kat walks up to the nurses' station, and I don't know what possesses me, but I decide to add, "You're always one step ahead of me, Bobbi." Flashing her my best smirk. As Bobbi returns an appreciative smile, I walk past Kat and head straight for the patient's room.

Exiting the patient's room twenty minutes later, I head toward the main physicians' work area to contact the OR to see if there's a chance I can add this patient to the evening's operating room schedule. Once I stopped acting like a sullen schoolboy, I realized Kat did the right thing in calling. Where many might have sent this patient home, she'd certainly benefit from immediate surgical repair.

Walking to where Kat's normally seated I decide to advise her of my plans. The OR will allow me to add her on at 4:30 p.m., and I need to ensure she doesn't have anything to eat or drink. As I turn the corner, I notice she's cradling her head in her hands. Is she tired, or did something happen?

"Hey, you okay?" I ask softly, not wanting to sneak up on her however, she still appears to jump in her seat at my questioning. Gazing down at her wary face, I want desperately to touch her. If only to comfort her in some way.

"Yes. I'm okay. Dr. Barnes, I'm so sorry I had to bother you."

Suddenly, I'm filled with shame. She hasn't felt well and finally returns to the ER, and I treat her terribly because she apparently chose Sebastian over me. "Kat. I'm the one who should apologize. You were just doing your job. I was having a bad morning, and I took it out on you. I was on call, and my treatment of you over the phone was uncalled for. I'm truly sorry." I stop briefly and decide to go all in. "I'm also sorry for the inappropriate text the other night. I shouldn't have done that."

"Oh, that? Ha. You weren't really texting me." She giggles. *Oh, that sound.* It's like a soothing balm.

Wait, what? "What do you mean?" I ask alarmed.

"Yeah, you have a habit of doing that. It's not your fault, but I feel like I should warn you."

"Okay, you're freaking me out a little."

"Well, the first time my six-year-old nephew saw your texts come through after I'd fallen asleep on the couch babysitting." She laughs, placing a hand over her mouth.

"Oh my God, please tell me you were watching *Boss Baby*."

"Exactly!" She hoots. "Then, the other night, Melanie was over for dinner. She interceded the text and told you about my getting into the bath." This beauty's face is bright pink, and she's smiling from ear to ear. Her exuberance is infectious. My face is starting to hurt from the strain of the huge grin that's invaded my recently grim expression. "I'm sorry. I almost texted you back, but…"

Chuckling, I finally probe, "But, what?"

I watch as her face turns more scarlet. "Well, I didn't trust myself to answer," she says softly, looking down at her hands briefly before peeking up at me nervously. She is fucking adorable.

I stand a little straighter, shocked at the direction my day is going. Trying to demonstrate my appreciation for her candor as well as the gratitude I wasn't being completely shut down, I grin down at her in response. "Well, that's refreshing. I quite honestly never know what to think after the way the tree incident ended, Ms. Kelly."

Swiftly, I observe her jubilant face turn blank. Fuck, have I embarrassed her? *What the hell is wrong with you?* I try to prepare for her admonishment of my bringing up our passionate liaison, much less the fact that I did it at work. Perhaps I should hastily apologize for that too. Before I can assemble an appropriate defense of my blunder, I hear Kat's tremulous voice coming out in nearly a whisper.

"Tree incident?"

Chapter Five

Kat

"Kat, could you come to room twenty-one? The docs are all tied up, and the squad just brought in someone who could be a code stroke," the medic asks frantically.

"Sure, Bennett," I reply on autopilot, jumping from my seat.

Looking up at Nick, I toss out, "Sorry. Gotta run." Then I quickly follow Bennett toward the patient's room.

As I enter, I notice Donovan Grant at the patient's bedside. He must have just arrived for the evening. "Hey, Donovan, you got this?"

"Yeah, Kat, but could you put the code stroke orders in the computer and call to get her a CT scan?"

"Of course," I reply, glad to help in any way I can. Swiftly spinning to head for the computer, I collide with a muscular torso. The hard, firm torso of a domineering firefighter.

"Ah, nice to see you again, Kat. Drop-in anytime," Mark lilts into my ear.

Again, feeling more unease than I should around someone I've considered a friend, I try to stay professional. "Hey, Mark. Sorry, I have to attend to the code stroke. Time is brain," I advise and make haste to put distance between us. Every minute counts when you're trying to care for a stroke patient, as early treatment is key to a full recovery. I head for the overcrowded physicians' workstation and choose a lone computer sandwiched between two occupied stations. I spend much longer at this location than needed, hoping Mark will move on when he realizes I'm not in a position to talk. The orders have been placed, but I continue to see Mark's partner nearby, so I decide to text Olivia. I need someone to ground me after this day. Maybe she can meet me later.

1:00 p.m.
Kat: Hi. What you up to? Any chance you're free for dinner? It's been a tough day.

1:05 p.m.
Olivia
Olivia: Sure. I'm free tonight. What time?

1:07 p.m.
Kat: I'm off at 7:00. I'll meet you anywhere.

1:10 p.m.
Olivia
Olivia: How about Luigi's?

Thinking back to my pasta with Mel the other night, I shrug. Why not? It's only calories.

They're the least of my worries right now.

1:12 p.m.
Kat: That's perfect. See ya at 7:30.

~

I've never been so glad to see a shift end. Heading for the parking lot, I jump in my car and head straight for Luigi's. Thank goodness I always keep a spare set of clothes in my locker, so I don't have to go home before heading out for the evening. I'm not usually one for pasta several times in one week, but my interest in meeting Olivia is more for the company than the food.

I pull into the familiar parking lot of the restaurant I've frequented since my youth. There are many Italian Bistros in the area, some expensive, some not. But Luigi's will always be a favorite. The food is fast, inexpensive, and phenomenal. It's always amazed me how comforting the delicious meals are, and yet I never break the bank. It was the one indulgence I afforded myself in college. And the portion sizes guarantee leftovers.

Swinging the door wide, I take in the well-known eatery. Multiple round tables accommodating four people are located in the center of the space, with worn, deep red vinyl booths on either side. Italian murals hang upon walls painted in a golden hue. There are candles and vases with flowers dotted about the dimly lit space. As I inhale the comforting aroma of Italian spices and rich tomato, I notice Olivia waving at me from her table.

Moving in for a big hug as she stands to greet me, I cling a little longer than is customary.

"Kat? You okay?" she asks with apprehension in her big baby blues.

Sliding into the booth across from her, I take a deep breath. "I don't know, Liv. I'm trying to be." I can tell this dear beautiful friend anything without judgment. It's always been this way. "It's been a tough few weeks."

"What's going on?" she asks, picking up her water.

"It's hard to know where to begin. I'd been trying a sleep aid Jake had given me, to try and get more than four hours of sleep a night. It seemed to be working, which was a relief."

"That's great, Kat. I can't remember when you last slept well."

"Hi, ladies. Can I get you something to drink besides water? Something from the bar? We have a lovely Chianti," the waiter inquires.

"I'm fine with water, thank you," I answer. "How about you, Liv?"

"May I have a glass of the Chianti?" she asks, eyeing me in disbelief.

"Sure, Miss. Are you two ready to order?"

"I'd like the chicken piccata with a side salad, please," I respond.

"I'll take the chicken Caesar salad." Olivia beams at the waiter. I've never seen anyone get so excited about a damn salad. I honestly think she's part rabbit.

"I'll get that right in for you," the kind server states before returning to the kitchen. Our food shouldn't take long, given the few patrons here this evening.

"Okay, Kat. Spill it. You aren't drinking, and you look like something is wrong. I know you just came from work, but you're kind of a mess. You look like you've been up for days. Are you not taking that pill any longer?"

"My whole life is a hot mess, Olivia. So, I started taking the pill, and the sleep came at a price. I started having these crazy dreams. My life is so sad, I actually didn't mind them at first. The night terrors I was having stopped, but in their place, I began having wild, irrational visions."

"Visions of what?"

"Well, in one, I was the headline stripper at a club where all of my ridiculous ex-boyfriends hung out. When I got to the part of the stage where they were standing, I hit them all with a whip I was using as a prop!" I watch as Olivia's eyes widen in shock, hand covering her mouth. "Yeah, Paul, Gabe, and even Tyler. Pow, pow, pow." I mimic cracking the whip, giggling all the while. "Some of them are just, well… erotic." I stop, taking a sip of my water. "A lot of them don't make any sense, but they were the best sex I've ever had!"

"Oh good Lord, Kat. That's what it takes to give you an orgasm?" She laughs.

"Stop. I've never had trouble giving myself one of those," I whisper across the table. "It's just with other people I fall short."

"Well, so far, these dreams sound pretty good to me. Why stop the pills?"

"They were fine when it was just bizarre fantasies. But I started waking up realizing things weren't as I left them the night before." I watch as she sits up in her seat a little. "I've had several mornings where I awoke dressed completely different than when I went to bed. One morning, I woke up wearing a tiny excuse for a thong and fuck me boots I didn't know I owned."

"Holy—"

"Here you go, ladies. Can I get either of you some freshly grated cheese or pepper?"

"No," we both blurt in unison.

"Well, please, let me know if there is anything else you need," he utters flatly as he spins on his heel and quickly walks away.

Liv leans forward. "Go on, Kat."

"Well, that's it, really. It's making me crazy that I don't know what's happening. I put up with it and decided to stop using the sleeping aid to see if things would go back to the way they were."

"And?" she implores.

"Well, I had a date. Not one I was excited about. Okay, fine, I was dreading it. I can't remember if you ever met Mark Snow. He's a firefighter in our group of friends. He's quite the player. The last person I should be dating. Plus, I don't want to date someone from our group. Just makes everything awkward." I stop to twirl a few strands of spaghetti. "Anyway, he brought a patient into the ER that we thought had abdominal pain but turned out was in labor. We rushed her upstairs and barely got her on the stretcher before the baby's head popped out."

"Holy crap! There's never a dull moment in your world, Katarina."

"You can say that again. Well, as we came down off of the adrenalin rush associated with that unpredictable situation, he cornered me about a date, and I lamented."

"Was the date that bad?" Olivia asks around a fork full of leafy greens.

"That's just it. I can't remember most of it." Placing luxurious lemony chicken piccata in my mouth, I moan for the briefest of seconds before Olivia's shriek jolts me back to the conversation. I've shared this often enough now, delivering this crazy tale isn't the gut punch it used to be.

"*What*?! What do you mean, you don't remember it? Did he drug you or something?" Alarm present on her sweet face.

"I don't think so. I've known Mark for years. Plus, I was already mixed up about why I was waking up without clothes on and dreaming of Nick Barnes dressed like Tarzan."

Watching Olivia's flat gaze, she exclaims, "Okay, we're definitely coming back to that! But why can't you remember the date? It's not like you took a sleeping pill *before* you went?"

"I honestly don't know. Jake and Melanie want me to take a Rohypnol test. They say you can get one online. If I'm going to do it, I need to do it soon because I think it only goes back a few months. Once I know for sure, I can start looking at other possibilities." I stab a piece of lettuce from my bowl. "I was at work today, and Mark brought in a patient, and I almost shit myself. My skin started to crawl, and I couldn't get away from him fast enough. I feel bad judging him, but I can't shake this feeling there's more to this. Either way, this situation is plain ridiculous." Putting my fork down, I look directly at her. "I had to buy a damn Nanny cam, Liv. To spy on me! My life gets nuttier by the minute."

"I think they're right, Kat. Take the test. You need some clarity." I observe her as she eats more lettuce. "You know what I need clarity on? This whole Nick Barnes in a loincloth situation? Please tell me it was some kinky role-playing thing. God, he's hot. If that guy can't make you come, no one can."

"Shhh. Liv," I scold, looking about quickly to make sure no one has heard her.

"I'm sorry, Kat." She guffaws. "Have you been seeing him?"

"Who, Nick? No. He's way out of my league. He's an incredible flirt. He did ask me out. It was actually quite sweet. He almost seemed nervous. I was at Target. It was the night of the date with Mark. He approached and asked if I'd go out for drinks with him, and I had to tell him I had other plans. He walked away before I could ask for a raincheck."

"Aw, man. Something tells me that date would've gone a lot better."

"You have no idea. I'd turned back to the shelves of shampoo after he walked away, then suddenly, he spun me around and kissed me like something from the end of a hot rom-com. I've never been kissed like that." Stopping, I replay the memory in my mind's eye like I'm watching Pride and Prejudice. "God, sometimes, I still think I can feel the tingle on my lips," I explain, dragging the pad of my index finger back and forth across my lower lip. I notice Olivia is sitting with her chin resting within her adjoined hands, gazing up at me like a child watching the storyteller during reading hour in the library.

"Well, what's stopping you from telling him you want to go out with him now?" she asks hopefully. "You've got to take another chance, Kit Kat. Life will be miserable if you keep shutting yourself off this way. This man clearly has it bad for you. He's a hot, successful doctor. You could do worse… and have!"

"I know. I know. I'm tempted. But my fear keeps getting in the way. When we met, he was so condescending. Between the initial first impression and his good looks, it just worries me he could turn out like Gabe."

"There's no comparison to Gabe. Gabe is a douche canoe. He was a typical salesman. Plus, this guy hasn't done anything shady, has he?"

"No. Not really. He's said some odd things recently, but we haven't really had a chance to have a normal conversation away from the stress of the ER. We hit a few bumps in the road in the beginning. But I haven't felt like this about anyone before. The others all felt like consolation prizes. I mean, Gabe was nice-looking and charismatic. But, with all my misgivings about him being a cheater, I would've left sooner if I thought anyone better might've come along. Nick's different. He makes me swoon. But that's the part that worries me," I offer, biting my lower lip.

Olivia looks at me, perplexed. "What do you mean? I'd think you'd be over the moon to finally feel that way about someone. Much less to have them show such obvious interest in return."

"I'm just scared. Those other guys really hurt me." Continuing to allow people in my life to betray my trust and treat me like a doormat is crippling. It's taken a long time, but I've managed to mend my broken heart and my self-worth. "If my heart were wrecked by Nick… Olivia, I'm not sure I'd recover." Pushing my plate away, I realize the lump in my throat has ruined my appetite. "Besides, from what I've been told, he isn't looking for a relationship. So, unless I can protect my heart enough to enjoy hot sex and nothing more, considering anything with him is pointless. If I were that kind of girl, I hope I'd choose someone I didn't work with."

"No. I get it. You've had some crappy luck with men. I hope you can gather the strength to try again, especially if it's with someone you truly feel something for. But I get why you're so hesitant. Whatever you decide, I've got your back, Kat."

"Thanks, Liv. I don't know why I'm considering anything like that right now anyway. He's a beautiful distraction, but I have to get my shit together before I even consider getting back out there. Heck, what guy's going to want to start a relationship with a nutjob that either sleepwalks or plays dress up in the middle of the night?"

"I don't know, Kat. I think Nick would probably like it if you played dress-up," she remarks, waggling her brows.

"Is there anything else I can get you, ladies?" the server asks as he holds the check in his hands.

"No. I think we're good," I reply. I'm sure Olivia won't eat anything else. Will she even eat her wedding cake? I can't remember ever seeing her eat anything sweet.

As the waiter walks off, Olivia clears her throat. "Don't think you're off the hook on the whole Nick playing Tarzan thing. The next time we're together, I want deets. I can only imagine how that one went." She smirks.

Hugging my dear friend goodbye and watching as she climbs into her car and drives away, I open my car door and sit quietly for a moment. I know Olivia's right. I can't protect my heart forever. But I need to tackle one thing at a time. First order of business is figuring out what kind of nighttime frolics are occurring and get them to stop. There's no going back to that sleeping pill again. I'll sleep when I'm dead.

❦

Walking into my kitchen, I drop my purse and keys on the island. I need a hot shower and bed. I have another day in the ER tomorrow and want to relax as much as possible before that happens. Luckily, I shouldn't have to worry about seeing Mark tomorrow, as they work twenty-four-hour shifts, and his workday should end at 6:00 a.m.

I walk into my bathroom to start my steaming shower and take off my clothes. As I enter the hot spray, I turn my back to the powerful jets and let the tension of the day empty into the drain. Tilting my head back, I reflect on my recent conversations with Jake, Mel, and Liv. I need to trust they all have my best interests at heart. They seem to be united in their effort to help me find closure on my questions regarding Mark and my date from hell. The other common denominator is Nick. Each has encouraged me to pursue this. I trust these three with my life. They wouldn't push me into something they thought would hurt me.

Exiting the shower, I pat dry before slipping into my robe. Toweling my hair dry, I walk to the edge of the bed and notice my phone has a message present.

9:35 p.m.
Nick Barnes
Nick: Would it be okay to tell you I've missed you?

I take a gulp of air. Wow. Did he really text that? This guy.

9:47 p.m.
Kat: Yes. It's more than okay. Thank you for saying that.

9:53 p.m.
Nick Barnes
Nick: The ER isn't the same when you're not there.

Not sure what to make of these texts, I just let them continue. He really can be sweet sometimes.

9:59 p.m.

Kat: You're very kind. I can remember a time when you felt quite different.

10:05 p.m.

Nick Barnes

Nick: I'm sure you're mistaken, Ms. Kelly. I may have made a terrible first impression with my rude behavior, but I assure you, it had nothing to do with you. Just my reaction to you.

10:10 p.m.

Kat: I'm not sure what you mean.

10:13 p.m.

Nick Barnes

Nick: I've been fighting an attraction to you since the moment you pulled that Mario Andretti move in the parking lot. You weren't in my game plan.

I can't believe this is happening. I literally need to pinch myself. I sit and reread the texts. This isn't the playful teasing, near sexting from before. It feels genuine, heartfelt.

10:20 p.m.
Nick Barnes
Nick: Kat? Am I making you uncomfortable?

10:23 p.m.
Kat: No. I'm flattered.

10:25 p.m.
Nick Barnes
Nick: I tried to walk away, esp when I didn't hear anything from you. But I can't stop thinking about you.

10:30 p.m.

Kat: I'm at a bad place in my life right now. If there was anyone I'd let in, it would be you. I just have to focus on myself for now.

I can't believe I've told him this. I hope I don't live to regret it, but given how honest he's been with me, it only seems fair.

10:37 p.m.
Nick Barnes
Nick: So you aren't dating anyone else?

10:40 p.m.
Kat: No. I had a date, the night you asked me to go for drinks. But I'm not dating anyone. You have no idea how much I wish that night had ended differently.

10:43 p.m.
Nick Barnes
Nick: You mean I didn't run you off with that kiss?

10:46 p.m.
Kat: Are you kidding? I haven't been able to stop thinking about it.

10:52 p.m.
Nick Barnes
Nick: Well, that isn't the only thing I can't stop thinking about.

He must be talking about the hot encounter in the patient exam room. I still can't believe how out of hand we let that get.

10:59 p.m.
Kat: If things were different, I'd love to take you up on your drink offer. But I have to settle some things before I bring anyone else in.

11:05 p.m.
Nick Barnes
Nick: I understand. I'm just relieved my crazy texts, rude behavior, and

accosting you in the Target didn't run you off. I don't have plans for a relationship in the future. But if I was to try with anyone, it'd be with you.

11:20 p.m.
Nick Barnes
Nick: Goodnight, Kat. I'm glad you're back at work.

This beautiful man. So unexpected. He seems sincere. God, what I'd give to be able to go on a real date with someone like him. Someone that makes my pulse race and gives me goosebumps at the thought of another heart-stopping kiss.

I'm curious about what happened with his marriage. Why did it end? Did they want different things? Was he the problem?

I flop back onto the bed, unable to contain my ear-to-ear grin. Never have I felt so giddy. This is crazy. I just told him I'm not in a place where a relationship is possible, but all I can think about is how utterly fabulous it'd be to date, Nick. Dr. Nicholas Barnes. I roll into my pillow in a fit of silliness. Suddenly, I remember the quandary I'm in. Jolting myself upright, I think, I can do this. I'm figuring out this mess once and for all. I deserve a beautiful man in my life. One that can kiss like the end of a Hallmark movie. One like Nick Barnes.

I jump from my bed and walk swiftly toward my study. Sitting down at my wooden desk, I smile as I recall its transformation. I'd found it in a thrift shop, painstakingly refurbished it, and painted it with white chalk paint. With pride, I stroke the top of the desk as I reach for my laptop. Opening my internet browser, I begin to search:

Rohypnol test.

Chapter Six

Nick

"Hey, Dad. I was going to drop by later. Do you need anything?" I ask, knowing he'll say no. He always does.

"That's great, son. I don't need anything. You always bring too much when you shop. I'm fine. Just looking forward to seeing you."

"Well, I should be there in a few hours if that's okay? I had a soccer game this morning. Just want to clean up and run a few errands on the way."

"That's fine. I made some chili. Not as hot as you like it, but you can always add some heat. I'll see you soon," he offers, ending the call.

I mentally add picking up some good cornbread to my list of errands. Dad always could make a mean bowl of chili. It'll be nice to spend the evening with him.

~

Pulling into the drive, I grab my cornbread, some limeade I got at the specialty market, and an extra treat for him I found in the bakery aisle. Walking up the drive, I notice the temperature has dropped quite a bit from the soccer game this morning. But then again, my adrenalin is usually pumping so I'm not sure my body is a good thermometer.

As I ascend the steps, the door swings wide. "Nick, come on in. It's getting cold out." Now he'd know the weather. The Weather Channel probably stays on in the background all day.

"Good to see you, Dad. I brought some things to add to your dinner." I pull out the limeade and cornbread and place them on his table. I save the best for last. "And I just couldn't pass this up." I slide up next to him and pull open the white cardboard bakery box, presenting a mouthwatering key lime pie.

He peers into the box, a brilliant smile crossing his wrinkled face. "Oh, man, Nick. That almost looks like Lydie's." He beams.

"I know. I thought of mom the second I laid eyes on it." I grin back at him. Walking into the den, I sit on the couch and wait for him to join. "How've you been, Dad? Anything new with your lady friend?" I tease.

"Nick. She's just a nice person who enjoys my stories. There's nothing to it, so don't let your imagination get away from you," he scolds. "I could ask the same of you." He eyes me with interest.

"Ah. Well, there isn't much to report there. I hadn't heard from her in a while. I assumed she was dating someone else. She just has a lot on her plate right now. I got the polite brush off," I report.

"Are you sure? I mean, did she turn you down?" he asks, surprised. That's my supportive dad to the bitter end. *'How could any woman not want to go out with my son?'*

"I broke down and text her. Told her I'd missed seeing her. She said something like 'I'm not in a good place for dating right now.'" I shrug, trying to appear nonchalant but knowing this old man can see right through me.

"Nick, that wasn't a no. That was a not right now." Tilting his head, he gives me the once over. "You're really smitten with this girl."

"Dad. I honestly don't know what to make of it. I've fought this tooth and nail, and when I finally think I should go for it, she isn't interested. It's like a sign or something. I've never cared if someone I hit on turned me down. I've never given any woman since Sophia a second thought. Hell, I don't know that I would've pursued Sophia like this." I snicker at the reality of what I've just said. "I've been lucky with women and certainly never had to chase one." I regale, not bragging but just stating fact. I'm not looking for a relationship, so why am I so disappointed? Is it my pride? "I think it's just the chase," I muse aloud. "I'm sure I wouldn't feel this way if she was easy prey."

"Nick! Do you hear yourself? Don't downplay your feelings because you hit a bump in the road. And you've always liked a challenge. Soccer, medical school. You always landed on top. But I know you'd never treat a woman's feelings that way. Not the way your mother raised you. There's no way this is about the chase for you. Admit it. You like her. Is that so bad?"

Stopping to take in his serious, honest expression, I know he's right. I just don't want to admit it. "Okay, fine. I like her. Happy, Dad?"

"I'll be happy when I get to say I told you so."

"Not to change gears away from my lack of a love life or anything," I say, rubbing the back of my neck, "but I have a big favor to ask."

"You don't even have to ask. What do you need?" God bless this man. Little does he know what he's in for.

"Well, I met my new little brother with the Big Brothers Association, and I'd like to try and engage him in some weekend tasks. Maybe he could help with yard work or something. He clearly could use the income and would benefit from some of your wisdom. He's a little lost, but honestly, I think there's a good kid in there somewhere."

"I almost forgot about that. I don't really need any help, but if this is simply a way to help him build some work ethic, I'm game. What's his name? How old is he?"

"His name is Gavin. Gavin McReedy. He's in the tenth grade. His mom works a lot, and they still struggle financially. He's an amazing basketball player and made his high school team but had to quit because he didn't have the support he needed. He's pissed at the world in general. More so than the average teen. I'm hoping to earn his trust while he earns some spending money. He isn't very motivated about the future, but I think that's largely due to his circumstances."

"When you've had a good life, you forget how much of a struggle it can be for so many others." Dad reminds me. I gaze at him in awe. This incredible man lost the love of his life and had to raise his teen son alone, but he's convinced he had a good life. I need to be more like him. Appreciate what I have.

"You're right, Dad. But I have to warn you. He's pretty rough around the edges. I never know what's going to come out of his mouth. I've only met him once, so I didn't want to scold him right away, but he's... well, he's a real live wire."

"Oh, all teen boys are like that. We have to start somewhere, right? Bring him by anytime. He's how old? Fourteen or fifteen? He'd probably like to use the riding mower. Now come on to the kitchen. I'm going to get some of that chili."

"Sure, Dad. You just want to get to that Key Lime pie." I chuckle.

"Can't put anything by you."

I follow him into the kitchen and grab two bowls from the cupboard. He ladles a large serving in mine, a smaller one in his. As we eat and converse about his various neighbors and visiting volunteers, I notice he seems more upbeat than I've seen him. I'm not sure what's different, but the last few visits have not been as morose. Could it be he protests too much, and this lady who visits for lunch each month is more than a nice person who listens to his stories? Whatever the source, I pray it continues, for both of our sakes.

Later, I'm making my way toward the door with almost half of the key lime pie in Tupperware for later. "Thanks for the chili, Dad. And the talk. I'll call you once I talk to Gavin and tee up the weekend landscaping job."

"Can't wait to meet him. It'll be nice to have some young blood around here. Think we could interest him in fishing when it's warm enough?" Dad asks optimistically.

"We can try. Maybe get him on the boat." I turn to wave one last time as I walk toward my car and stop abruptly, remembering something. "Oh, Dad. You were right on the money."

"Oh yeah, what about?"

"Boss Baby!" I laugh.

Kat

Walking into the NICU, I follow the signs for the nurses' station. I have to be at work in an hour, but I haven't been by to check on Katrina and the baby and wanted to see how they're doing. I'm not sure Katrina will be here, but it's worth a try.

I approach the first nurse I see in an attempt to gain more information. "Hi. I'm Katarina Kelly. I'm a PA in the ER here and had a patient who delivered a premature infant a few weeks ago and was wondering if there was any way to check on the two of them and possibly leave Katrina my number in case she needs anything."

"Oh, sure. Katrina, you said?"

"Yes. Katrina Knowles."

"Ah, I think she's here with Grace now. She's pretty much moved into the NICU to be close to her little girl," the nurse shares with a slight smile.

Grace. What a beautiful name. I'm kicking myself that it's taken me so long to come and see her. But it's hard to fit in visits to ex-patients when you're dealing with a 'not even mid-life yet' crisis.

I follow the young nurse toward a large plexiglass enclosed area containing multiple incubators, bassinettes, rocking chairs, and various pieces of medical equipment. As I get closer, I spot Katrina wearing a yellow gown, standing over a clear isolette. The NICU nurse pokes her head in the door and advises Katrina she has a visitor, and I watch as her face lights up as her eyes meet mine. This perplexing girl. My heart goes out to her. She almost skips over to the door to greet me.

"Kat. I can't believe you came. Can you come in? I want you to meet her."

I look to the kind nurse beside me, and she just nods. "Washing station is to your left and then grab a gown and gloves, please."

I smile over to Katrina, who returns to her baby while I wash and don my yellow gown and blue gloves. As I enter the quiet space, I walk slowly over to Katrina's side and peer down into the acrylic incubator. This tiny infant is so small, she almost doesn't look real. She's covered in stickers and a sea of wires and has the tiniest oxygen tubing placed in her nose. "Katrina, Grace is a beautiful name. A beautiful name for a beautiful little girl," I tell her, staring down at the frail little one. I watch as Katrina slides her hand through the portal next to the infant and takes her tiny hand. As she gently rubs her gloved thumb over the baby's tiny fingers, I observe as Grace opens her sweet hand and grabs ahold of Katrina's finger. I inhale a gulp of air, amazed at the sight. "How old is she?"

"She's thirty-two weeks today. It's a miracle she's done so well. I know we have a long way to go, but she's a fighter." She glows, demonstrating pride and obvious love for her child.

"She takes after her momma," I say, almost without thinking.

"Thanks, Kat," she replies, never taking her eyes off of her precious miracle. "I'm so scared. I still don't know what I'm going to do. I have no idea how to be a mother. I can barely take care of myself. Then there's my sister and brother. How am I going to take care of a baby?"

"Katrina, I had no idea. You're taking care of your siblings? That's a lot for anyone to handle."

"Well, I have some help. But I'm all they have. And obviously, that isn't much. I love them, but they deserve better than what I can give them. So does Grace," she pauses momentarily. As I turn, I notice a lone tear trickling down her left cheek. "I just don't think I can do this, Kat."

"Oh, Katrina. Have you talked to any of the caseworkers here? They might be able to help. Maybe they can find some assistance for you. Help with food, a place to live."

"Yeah, they've been here. But there's only so much they can do. I guess I have a while before I have to do anything. She won't be able to leave until she's bigger and breathing on her own. I'll keep praying for a miracle."

I feel my heart squeeze within my chest. Suddenly, my troubles seem so insignificant. "Katrina, thanks for letting me meet your daughter. I have to get to work, but I'd like to come again sometime. I'm going to leave my number with the nurse at the desk if you ever need anything. Hang in there, okay?"

"Thanks, Kat. You're always so nice. It means a lot to me that you came by."

I give her a small smile as I walk toward the door, saying a silent prayer for Katrina and Grace as I head down to the emergency room to start my shift.

~

"Jake, I'm going to the cafeteria. You want anything?" It's been seven grueling hours so far, fueled on caffeine, saltines, and peanut butter. The meal of emergency medical professionals most days. There's finally been a lull in incoming patients, so I'm grabbing this opportunity to get some real food.

"Can you just get me a bottle of water and a bag of chips?" Jake shouts back.

"Got it."

As I stroll down the hall, I think back on the texts from last night. I can't keep the smile from taking over my face. Having someone like Nick tell you he's fighting an attraction to you is like a drug. But what if he manages to fight it? What if he moves on because I'm not ready? I want to take Olivia's advice on this one, but I need to prepare myself for the crushing letdown.

Everyone dates until they find 'the one.' If Nick doesn't turn out to be 'the one,' then I move on. Sure, I'll be disappointed. But I need to consider taking a chance... before someone else does. He's so dreamy. Those sexy hazel eyes and soft lips. *Gah! This is torture.* It was bad enough when I didn't know how good a kisser he was. Now I can just imagine those lips all over me.

As I make a quick salad from the salad bar and grab a sandwich from the fridge, I feel my phone buzz in my lab coat. Man, hope it isn't Jake. Looking down, I see it's a text, not a missed call. Opening the app, I look down at the phone with dread.

5:20 p.m.
Mark Snow
Mark: Hey, Kat. Sorry, we couldn't talk yesterday. Glad you're back at work. Wanted to see if I could take you out next week.

Ugh! I thought I'd handled this already. He isn't making this easy. Once I get back to the ER and have unloaded these items, I'll just make it clear I'm not dating anyone right now. I grab two bottles of water and Jake's bag of chips and get in line before heading back to the emergency room.

"Here." I hand Jake his water and chips.

"You okay?"

"I was. Then I got another text from Mark asking me to go out next week. I'd already told him I wasn't in a good place for dating. You know, now that I think about it he never replied to that." I stop to consider whether there's a possibility he never received it. "Doesn't matter. I'm going to be very frank with him this time."

"I think that's a good idea, Kat. Not sure what's going on with him, but maybe making things clearer will help. Thanks for the food," he says, hopping up from his seat. Like chips are food. He probably won't touch it until he's done for the day anyway.

I walk briskly toward the breakroom to quickly eat my dinner and shoot off a text.

5:40 p.m.
Kat: Hi, Mark. I thought I'd text this before, but maybe you didn't receive it. I'm not dating right now. I have too much going on. I enjoy having you as a friend, but I'm not looking for more. I'm sorry. Hope to see you the next time we all get together.

There. I don't know how much clearer I can make that. I tear through my sandwich and decide to save my salad for later. Standing to make my way back to work, I hear the phone ping again. Looking down, I notice the text isn't from Mark but from Nick.

5:50 p.m.
Nick Barnes
Nick: Just got home from my dad's. Eating a piece of pie. It's so good I thought of you.

Um, what? Giggling, I can't help but wonder what on Earth that means exactly. I walk over to the main physician's workspace to see if there are any new patients to be seen and can't help but reply to his text.

60

5:55 p.m.
Kat: That text was befuddling. I'm afraid to ask what exactly made you think of me.

I return my attention to the screen in front of me and see two patients waiting, one with a rash and another with an earache. I click on each and take a glance at my other patients' test results before evaluating the new arrivals.

5:59 p.m.
Nick Barnes
Nick: *I meant this pie tastes so good, it reminded me of your sweet lips, your wet tongue, your silky hair.*

I can feel my face redden. *Man, is it hot in here?* I wasn't expecting that. But now all I can think about is that hot kiss in the Target.

6:10 p.m.
Nick Barnes
Nick: *But I bet your pie tastes good too.*

Holy crap. I take a large gulp of my water and realize I need to put a stop to this before I get myself in too deep.

6:15 p.m.
Kat: Dr. Barnes, I'm at work. Thank you for making me blush, but I have serious business to attend to.

Okay, it's an earache and a rash, but he doesn't need to know that.

Looking at my watch, I note it is 6:30 p.m. Nick hasn't responded to my text. Now I'm worried he won't realize I was teasing. Do I make him sweat or shoot another text so I can regain my focus?

6:32 p.m.
Kat: I'm teasing, by the way.

I head off to see my two new patients and quickly return to type their discharge papers, as both are pretty straightforward. I look over my other patients and discover one has a small bowel obstruction and will need a consult with general surgery. Consulting Dr. Weston, he advises he'll be over to see the patient as soon as he can. Looking down at my phone, I realize there's been no response from Nick, and I'm surprised at how let down I feel. Hunching my shoulders, I push forward with my work.

Several hours later, I'm sitting at the main physician's work area next to Jake and decide to let him in on my news. "Hey, I thought I'd let you and Mel know I have an appointment to do the Rohypnol test," I whisper. "They send me a kit, and I take it to the lab to process."

"Kat, that's great. I think you're making a wise decision. I hope it comes back negative, but I think you owe it to yourself to check. Did you talk to Mark after that text came in?"

"I didn't talk to him. I just texted back and was a lot more direct about it. He didn't reply, but I can't imagine he could say he didn't get either text." Suddenly, it dawns on me I'd been texting Nick around the same time I was sending that text to Mark. Breaking into a cold sweat, I worry I may have sent the wrong text to the wrong guy. Panicking, I grab my phone from my pocket, swipe to open it, and jump when I feel a hand on my left shoulder.

"I'm sorry, Kat. I didn't mean to scare you," sweet Georgia says as she tries to rub my shoulder in apology. Georgia is a new registration clerk in our emergency room. She's shy but very sweet. Her beautiful alabaster skin dotted with freckles is even more striking set against her luxurious red hair. "Someone dropped this off for you," she says quietly. I turn and notice she's holding a plastic grocery bag. Growing a bit nervous, I peer down at it. *What is this?*

"Who dropped it off, Georgia?" I ask warily.

"I'm sorry, Kat. He didn't say. I thought you were expecting it."

"What did he look like?" I push, looking over toward Jake, who also eyes the bag with suspicion.

"Um, I don't know. He was tall, attractive, very fit. He was wearing a baseball hat, so I couldn't tell what color his hair was."

I look back toward Jake. Why am I so worried? Mark wouldn't

send something inappropriate or harmful here where someone else could see, right? I slowly take the bag from her, acutely aware I have multiple sets of eyes on me. As I peer into the bag, I gasp.

"Holy shit, Kat, what is it?" Jake asks.

I break out into hysterical laughter, placing the bag onto the counter before I drop it. Wiping my eyes, I announce, "It's pie."

Finishing up my charting in preparation to head home, I decide to splurge on my surprise delivery and send Nick a quick thank you for one very exciting diversion. Placing my plastic fork into the silky treat, I bring the tart confection to my mouth and almost groan. This is the best pie I think I've ever tasted. This sets me off giggling again, thinking about his indecent texts.

9:50 p.m.
Kat: Thank you for my surprise. I can't tell you what it did for my day!

As I take another bite, I toy with returning some of his inappropriate correspondence.

9:52 p.m.
Kat: I only hope my pie could measure up, winky face emoji.

9:55 p.m.
Nick Barnes
Nick: Well, there's one way to find out.

Holy mother of all pastries. I almost choke on my last bite. This hot man is so freaking bold. Not that anyone has ever tried my pie. And quite honestly, I don't know that I'd ever be relaxed enough to let any man taste my 'Lady Cake' as my patient so eloquently put it. But the mere fact he put that out there... okay, so I'm not going to be sleeping tonight for a whole different reason.

10:10 p.m.
Nick Barnes
Nick: I'm teasing, by the way, winky face emoji

Again, with the face-cracking grin. I need to finish typing these notes and get out of here. I review a few more charts and sign off for the night when I feel my phone buzz again. I'm laughing in anticipation as I pull my phone back out of my pocket and place it on the counter.

10:15 p.m.
Unknown number
Unknown number: I'd reconsider. I know what you do in the dark...

Chapter Seven

Nick

I wake with a smile on my face. On a Wednesday. A big ass smile on my face. I haven't had that much fun with a woman in years. That says a lot, considering the woman wasn't even in the same room with me. I have to admit. It's going to be an uphill battle trying not to fall for this beautiful girl when I'd rather spend a night texting her than sleeping with anyone else.

I stand and head toward the kitchen for a cup of coffee, knowing it'll be a full day in the office, followed by dinner with Gavin. Lord only knows how things will go with him tonight. I wonder if I'll meet his mother? I only briefly introduced myself at the Big Brothers' Association office last week. She's attractive, but time has not been kind to her. Either years in the sun, hard-living, or a stressful existence has given her a tired, sallow look. Her face is overly made up, and her hair is over-processed, but she's maintained a decent figure. I'm curious when Gavin's father left the scene. Was this recent, or has he ever been a part of Gavin's life?

I head back up to my shower, taking two steps at a time. Turning on the hot spray, I shed my clothes and enter. Standing beneath the rain showerhead, I attempt to clear my head of these questions and instead return to the texts of last night. A grin reappears almost instantly.

It was all in fun, but I'd seriously like the opportunity to taste Kat. All of her. I can't help but picture myself devouring her sweet skin from stem to stern as I lather up my body. Kissing her soft lips, her throat, sucking from her pretty pink nipples. As I grip my hardening cock and give it a consolation stroke, I try to imagine dropping to my knees to lick and nibble at that sweet pussy. Hell, that's all it takes. I'm hard as fuck now. I can almost picture her swollen flesh glistening for me. Stroking my swollen dick, I try to calm the pulsating ache. *Ah, I can only imagine how she'd taste on my tongue.* God, I *need* this woman. I want to make her come with my fingers, my mouth, my dick. Tugging more firmly now, I pick up my pace as I visualize her face enraptured in lust as she goes over the edge while I finger her, sucking ravenously on her clit. I moan out my release onto the shower tiles, panting, desperately wanting to see that fantasy come to life.

"Dr. Barnes, your patient scheduled at 1:00 p.m. called to say he was in too much pain to come to the office today." The morning has moved along smoothly since coming to work and focusing on concrete tasks versus fantasies of my favorite PA. "He decided he's going to the ER instead," the receptionist advises. *Yeah, I'd rather be there too, Mr. Dalton.* I guess I have time to grab some lunch until I get a call from the ER about his arrival.

I walk down the hall toward the physician's lounge and unlock the door with my badge. As I step inside, I see several physicians are chatting over lunch. I still don't know many people at St. Luke's, and the ones I do know don't often get a break to eat. I look over the day's lunch offerings and wonder if Kat might be here today. *Shame there's no pie on the menu*, I chuckle to myself.

"Cracking yourself up is the first sign you're losing it," I hear a familiar voice whisper.

Looking to my left, I see Jake Harris snickering in my direction. "You're right. I might need to face it. How've you been?"

"I'm okay. Just a busy time of year with the kids. Between sports, fall festivals, apple picking, and pumpkin patches, I'm exhausted. Hey, that reminds me. Every year Mel and I throw a huge costume party at our house. It's our favorite holiday, and we go all out. You should come. Halloween's on a Saturday this year, so unless you're on call, you should be off."

"I might have a game that afternoon, but otherwise, I'd love to come by. I'm not really the costume type, though."

"Just wear your soccer uniform. You'll blend right in." He snorts. "At least you don't have Melanie planning your outfit. Every year, I hold my breath and hope whatever it is will allow me to still drink and take a leak if I need to." Scratching the back of his neck, he continues, "Yeah, you'll look like some soccer stud, and I'll be dressed as a pregnant nun."

Chuckling, I grab a sandwich and a bottle of water. "Well, on that note, I need to head back. Oh, you might see a patient of mine soon. Apparently, he was in too much pain to come to his appointment, so he may turn up in your ER today. Feel free to call me if Mr. Dalton arrives, and you need any help with him. He needs an MRI of his knee, but so far, his insurance company hasn't issued the approval. I could run down and give him a cortisone injection if he prefers. Just call and let me know." Backing toward the door, I offer a quick wave and head back to the office, proud of myself for leaving Kat out of the conversation. *Hmm, what would that saucy little Minx dress like for Halloween, I wonder?*

The end of the workday has finally arrived and I'm able to leave on time as the rest of my day was pretty uneventful. Heading to pick up Gavin for dinner, I'm thankful not to have the anxiety I had last week. Should be a short visit as it's a school night. I look at the GPS to make sure I'm headed in the right direction. This isn't a part of town I frequent. There's no judgment, as I don't envy the responsibility any single parent takes on, and I'm sure they live as best she can afford.

"Your destination is on your left," the GPS navigator announces. I turn into an older apartment complex and see Gavin standing on the sidewalk. Before I can open my car door, he's headed in my direction.

My passenger door swings wide, and he plops into the seat and whistles. "Nice ride, old man."

"Thanks." I guess my shiny black Audi R8 does seem a bit pretentious, but I work hard, and I love my car. "Your mom didn't want to join us?"

"Nah. To tell the truth, I didn't ask her. I couldn't stomach it if she started putting the moves on you."

Hell, I never considered this. That would be all kinds of awkward. "How hungry are you? Want pizza? Or there's a good Mexican place not far from here?"

"I'm good with anything."

We decide on Julio's and drive to the destination in companionable silence. It's almost too quiet. Trying to break the uncomfortable tension a bit, I attempt small talk. "How was school?"

"Sucked. Thanks for asking. How was work, dear?" he volleys back.

Snickering, I answer honestly. "Wasn't too bad. My days start early, but I was able to get out on time today, so that's something."

He's quiet for a minute. "I take it you make a shit ton of money if you're a doctor. What kind of doctor are you anyway?" he asks, playing with the tattered hem of his sweatshirt.

"I'm an orthopedic surgeon. I specialize in sports medicine, mainly shoulders. I always dreamt of working as the team doctor for a football team one day," I say, shrugging my shoulders a bit.

"So, you operate on people and everything?" he throws back.

"Yeah. It's not as big a deal as you think. Just takes a lot of training." Downplaying my job, I need to narrow the divide between us. "You give any more thought to pursuing a career as a firefighter? I have a friend who hangs out with a bunch of firefighters, and he could probably get you a ride-along. You could get first-hand experience seeing what they do." I put the car in park and look in his direction. When there's no answer to my question, I decide not to push for now. "You ready?"

Walking into the Mexican restaurant, we're hit with the smell of spicy chili peppers, banter from the nearby bar, and Mexican singers from the speakers overhead. I walk to the hostess station. "Two, please."

We're taken to a booth and given menus as we're seated. I encourage Gavin to order whatever he likes. When the waiter returns with tortilla chips and salsa for our drink order, the smart-ass says, "I'd like a Margarita, no salt." As the waiter and I both stare blankly at him in response to his ridiculous request, he states, "What? You said to order whatever I want."

"He'll have a coke, and I'll take a water, thanks." As the waiter walks away, I continue, "It must be hard work being a top-notch smart-ass twenty-four-seven."

"Nah, just comes natural."

Shaking my head at his ludicrous antics, I try to change the subject. "So, do you mind if I ask about your dad?" I tread carefully, hoping not to upset him. Before he can answer, the waiter returns with our drinks and takes our meal orders. Gavin seems to hesitate, and I reassure him he can order whatever he likes and take the rest home.

"Sorry we were interrupted. I was asking about your dad. But you don't have to talk about it if you aren't comfortable."

"Not much to tell. He wasn't around much, then he died."

Almost choking on my water with his flippant response, I put down my drink and take in Gavin's stoic features.

"I still don't entirely know the score. My mom got knocked up when she was young. She was eighteen or nineteen and waiting tables at a dive where a bunch of college kids hung out. She said the guy really swept her off her feet, but they didn't date long or anything. Mom said he had a girlfriend. He didn't find out about me for years."

I watch as he rips his paper napkin into pieces. "He'd visit once in a while, but he lived in another state. From what I remember, he was an okay guy. Sometimes he brought me stuff, and we'd throw the ball around and shit."

Sitting quietly, I wait to see if he'll offer any more detail. I can't get a read on how he feels about his father. I ponder how old Gavin might've been when he died.

Shifting in his seat, he continues. "He didn't talk about what his life was like when he went back home, and he never took me there. It felt like there was this invisible realm he'd return to that we weren't a part of. Then he just stopped coming. I asked Mom about it one day, and it seemed like she was just making excuses for him. Then, a week before my tenth birthday, she told me he wasn't coming back. At first, I thought he just didn't want to see us anymore, but she said he got sick… a while later, she got a call from a lawyer saying he died."

My heart squeezed at this revelation. This poor kid. I don't know what's worse, losing a parent who has spent their whole life devoted to your upbringing or losing the one you yearn to bond with, knowing that chance is gone. "Gavin, I'm really sorry," I recall how difficult losing my mother was at sixteen. I cannot imagine dealing with a loss like that at the age of ten.

"Don't feel sorry for me. It was his loss. I didn't need him anyway."

With perfect timing, the server returns with multiple plates of food, placing the sizzling platters before us in dramatic fashion. Grateful for the interruption, I thank the waiter and ask Gavin if he needs another drink.

"Nah, man. This is awesome." He smiles over his steaming plate.

Deciding an abrupt change in direction is needed, I propose my weekend job offer. "So, my dad lives on several acres. The land backs up to a lake. He has a ton of grass, shrubs, and a garden and could use a hand with it. I was wondering if you'd be interested in a part-time job helping him on weekends when you're available?" The mouthwatering aroma of the food before us has stolen my attention. I wrap my fajita and bring it to my mouth for a large bite before continuing. "We'd be willing to pay you for your help. He said you could use the riding mower if you promise not to take out his garden with it."

I watch as his chewing slows long enough to look up at me. "Yeah? Sure. I could do that." He immediately digs back into his enchiladas.

"I have a soccer game this weekend. Any chance your mom could drop you off, and I could take you to my dad's after the game?"

"She could probably do that. She only works in the evening on the weekend," he answers, popping a tortilla chip into his mouth.

"Good. Dad could use the help," I say, knowing I'm telling a white lie but want to help this kid however I can, and I'm sure he wouldn't take a handout. "If it turns out my friend Jake can get you a ride-along, and it's on a weekend, we'll work around it. I think talking to the guys at the station about what's needed to apply for the fire academy is important."

Gavin doesn't answer as he is too busy shoveling in rice and beans. I begin to worry he might not have enough to eat at home. But then again, I remember what my appetite was like when I was a teen. His mother probably can't keep enough food in the house. I might need to talk to Sandra at the Big Brothers Association about making an anonymous grocery gift card donation as we get closer to Thanksgiving.

Later that evening, I pull up to Gavin's apartment and thank him for joining me. I write down the address for the soccer fields and tell him I'll see him on Saturday afternoon.. I watch as he exits the car and walks toward the stairs. Knowing it's foolish, as this kid spends much of his life alone, I still wait for him to enter his front door before I depart. There's a great deal of his story I'll probably never know. But this smart-ass kid has my respect for handling the lot he's been dealt.

Kat

I trudge through work like a zombie. I'm back to three to four hours of sleep at most. This job is hard enough with a full eight hours. I'm not having the night terrors again, but my sleep is restless, and I can't help but perseverate on my questionable date with Mark, my still unanswered questions regarding my nighttime routine, and now that ominous text.

Unknown number
Unknown number: I'd reconsider. I know what you do in the dark...

I have to assume the text was from Mark. I'd just told him I wasn't interested in dating. Nothing else had happened recently to 'reconsider.' But why send that from an unknown number? And what did he mean, 'I know what you do in the dark'? *Heck, I don't even know what I do in the dark.* Had Jake let it slip with the guys what was happening with me?

I only have a few hours of my shift left, and then I can head home for some much-needed rest. I have tomorrow off, so I plan to take two Benadryl and sleep hard tonight. I may wake up hungover tomorrow, but that's okay. I walk over to the hallway stretcher, where a young male is seated.

"Hi. Mr. Edwards? I'm Katarina Kelly, a PA in the emergency room. What brings you in to see us today?"

"Well, I was working on a ladder and slipped off and fell onto my left foot, and I can't walk on it now."

"How far did you fall?"

"I think it was about ten feet."

"You didn't hit your head or anything? Does your back hurt?"

"No. The only thing that hurts is my foot. I probably just need some crutches."

"Well, let's get some x-rays and be sure nothing is broken first. Do you need anything for the pain?"

"Not right now. I hate taking medicine."

Returning to my computer to order Mr. Edward's x-rays, I see Jake sitting in the breezeway.

"Hey. Are you working tonight?"

"Yeah. Splitting the shift with Donovan. He had plans he couldn't get out of."

"Hope it isn't with that chick he's been dating lately. She's annoying," I huff.

"I didn't ask. But I agree with you. She's pretty overbearing."

"I made the mistake of answering the phone the other night when he was working. She acted like she'd caught his mistress answering his phone. She called the ER phone, for God's sake. It wasn't like I answered his cell phone. I get the feeling she's just trolling for a hot doctor."

"I don't know. I do think he could do better. But I guess so long as he's happy. I've been with Melanie so long... I'm glad I don't have to deal with all of that dating shit."

"Yeah, me either. That's why I just avoid all of it." I laugh.

"Kat, you are single." He pronounces each word succinctly. "You *should* be dating. Hey, you doing anything this weekend?" I think about it briefly and laugh. I'm never doing anything anymore.

"Nope, free as a bird. What's up?"

"Mel wanted to see if you could spend the weekend. We're behind on planning the Halloween party and thought maybe you could come over Friday night and have dinner and drinks and help us plan. Saturday, the kids have a soccer tournament, and I know they'd love it if you came. Then Saturday night, could you stay and hang out with Seth and Ruby so Mel and I can grab a quick bite to eat without kids?" he asks hopefully.

"Sure, Jake. I don't mind. I miss those rascals."

"Great! I just scored some major bonus points with Mel. You never let me down, Kit Kat."

Friday evening rolls around, and I'm nestled up with Ruby on the couch watching some Disney sitcom about a bunch of very extroverted kids at camp.

"You want some more wine, Kat?" Melanie asks.

"No. I'm good."

"Well, you're going to love the costumes I picked this year. You and I are going to dress like black cats. I just got Jake some khaki safari clothes. Oh, and I found a great caterer. We're doing mini barbeque sandwiches and brisket this year."

"Oh, that sounds good. Are we sticking with a DJ since the neighbors complained about the band you had last time?" I laugh.

"Yeah. Old battleax. I'm surprised she could hear well enough to call the cops. Every time I've ever tried to talk to her, all she says is, "huh?" Just our luck, the one night she decides to wear her damn hearing aids."

I pat her arm. "It's okay. A DJ is fine. Do you need help decorating?"

"That'd be great. I asked Jake to make sure you had the day off. I think Dr. Silver and Donovan are working that night."

"Ah, poor Donovan. Suits me just as well. This way, I won't have to see him there with Ashley. She drives me crazy."

"Yeah, Jake said she's a little possessive."

"A little? She's over the top possessive. I hope that doesn't work out long term. He could do so much better."

"Jake said he invited Nick," Melanie adds, waggling her brows at me, a huge smile crossing her face.

"Hmm. That could be interesting. I wonder if he'll bring a date."

"I doubt it since the one he seems to want to date is you."

Unable to stop the grin, I look at my friend. "Mel, I wish I had my shit together. He's so hot and… well, sometimes he's kinda sweet. But I don't want to get him mixed up in my madness right now. Maybe after the Rohypnol test is back, and I have a better understanding of what's happening. Hey, you don't think Jake said anything to any of the guys about that date with Mark or my waking up in different clothes, do you?"

"No, Kat. He wouldn't do that," she assures me.

I didn't think so either. But what did that text mean?

"Well, speaking of sleep. Ruby, it's time for bed. You have a soccer tournament tomorrow and need to be well-rested so you can kick some serious butt!" Mel teases.

"Are you coming tomorrow, Kat?" Ruby asks.

"I wouldn't miss it, peanut."

"Yay. Okay, I'll see you in the morning." She gives me a big hug before heading toward the stairs.

"I'm going up to bed too, Mel. See you in the morning." I walk into the guestroom at the top of the stairs to retire for the evening. Once there, I pull out my overnight bag and grab the Benadryl. I only take one as I've had several glasses of wine tonight. Luckily, their games don't start until early afternoon, so I have time for the Benadryl fog to lift. Let's just hope I can get six hours of sleep.

I awake, forgetting momentarily where I am. As I turn my head toward the window and take in the expensive drapery, I remember I'm staying at Jake and Mel's place. Looking at my watch, it's 8:0 a.m.. *Wow, I must've slept hard.* I consider whether staying with my friends has relaxed me enough the night terrors were abated. As I sit up, I take in the aroma of freshly brewed coffee.

"Good morning," I greet as I enter the kitchen approximately twenty minutes later.

"Good morning," I hear spoken in unison from Mel, Seth, and Ruby.

"When do we head out for your game?" I ask, trying to plan out my day.

"Their game is at noon, so we have to be there at eleven. If they win that one, they'll have to play another around two o'clock."

"Got it. I'm going to hit the shower then." I pinch Ruby's cheek as I walk by.

The day has flown by and it was exactly what I needed. My throat is hoarse from cheering on the kids. They've had quite a successful day. They won their first game and managed to squeak out a win in the last few minutes of their second game. I haven't been able to shake the smile.

"Where are you and Jake headed tonight?" I ask, a bit jealous of their date night.

"We're going to Red Ginger. I can't wait." Mel smiles broadly.

"I've never eaten there, but I heard it's—" Unable to finish my thought, I stand transfixed as I see one Dr. Nicholas Barnes dressed in full soccer gear. *Holy crap, he's hot.* I'm unable to keep from staring at his tight ass and muscular legs in those soccer shorts, shin guards, and cleats. *Good Lord, if I thought I had spank bank material before—*

"Uh, Kat, you're drooling a little," Melanie jabs.

"Um, what?" I ask, incapable of participating in any intelligent conversation when this sight has taken all of my brain's focus.

Hearty laughter now pierces through my brain fog, and I make eye contact with a very amused Melanie. "I know, he has the hottest ass. Don't tell Jake I noticed. I still think you should've said yes to the bathtub invitation."

I punch her shoulder playfully. As I continue to stare, I observe as a woman approaches with a teenaged boy in tow. Nick jogs over to the pair, wrapping his arm around the boy's shoulders as he greets them. *Wow. I never considered he could have a kid.* I continue to stare as the woman speaks briefly and then waves and walks away, leaving the young man in Nick's care. The two converse briefly and then slowly walk to the adjacent field to greet Nick's teammates.

Trying to absorb what I've just seen, I take a step back. It's a good thing I told Nick I wasn't in a good place for dating anyone right now. I honestly don't think I'm stepmother material. The thought has barely left my mind before I look back, locking eyes with the hot hazel-eyed soccer player.

Kat

I'm stunned. Standing here on this gorgeous afternoon, watching my friends' kids kick ass at their soccer tournament. Nick Barnes in a soccer uniform was the last thing I expected to see. I'd just finished gawking at his amazing physique when I was struck with this new revelation. I don't know why I never considered this. He was married and is certainly old enough to have children. We haven't had conversations where personal details have been shared. I guess I thought after all of this time, there would've been some indication he had kids. Quickly turning away, I try to begin a conversation with Melanie to mask the fact I've been staring at Nick and his son.

No sooner have I turned when I hear his voice pierce the air between us.

"Hey, Mel, wait up."

I turn around to see Nick and the young man approach.

"Hey, didn't realize the kids had a game today. How'd they do?"

"They did great, actually. Won both games today." Mel beams.

"That's fantastic. Where's Jake?"

"He's probably handing out snacks to the team and trying to gather all of their stuff, so we don't leave anything behind."

"Man, too bad. I was hoping to introduce Gavin to both of you."

"He'll be sorry he missed you. Nice to meet you, Gavin." Mel smiles at the boy.

"Gavin, this is Kat." Nick appears to hesitate for a moment. "She works in the ER at my hospital," he says. Feeling my face flush momentarily, I look away from his gaze and make eye contact with his son.

"Hi." Is all I can get out, still completely caught off guard by this new information.

"Hey," he answers, seeming a bit bashful. He's a cute kid. Must take after his mom, though, as he doesn't look much like Nick.

"Unfortunately, we can't stay to chat. Headed to my dad's for the rest of the day. Tell Jake we were sorry we missed him." Pause. "It was really good to see you," Nick says. Looking up, I realize he's directed this to me.

Blushing again, I smile back at him, unable to find words. I watch as the pair turn and walk in the direction from which they came.

"Wow," I utter once the coast is clear. "I'm glad I didn't take him up on that date offer."

"What? Why?" Mel asks, seeming shocked at my words.

"Heck, Mel. I had no idea he had a kid. My life is ridiculous. I've potentially been given a date rape drug, or I'm sleepwalking. I had to get a Nanny cam to spy on myself. I was already hesitant about bringing a new relationship into that chaos, I certainly don't want to bring someone with a kid into my fucked-up world."

"Oh, good Lord, Kat. Nick doesn't have a kid. That's his little brother. Well, not his real brother... he doesn't have any sisters or brothers."

"Mel, you aren't making any sense."

Melanie stops walking and places her hands on her hips in exasperation. "Nick signed up for the Big Brothers, Big Sisters Association to mentor a kid without a dad." Shaking her head, she turns and continues walking. "He only met Gavin a little while ago. He was pretty nervous about it at first. It was cute."

I stop dead in my tracks, shocked to hear this. Is this guy for real? I'd never dated anyone with a heart for others. Gabe wouldn't be caught dead spending time with a kid who needed mentoring, even if they worshipped his rich, sorry ass. I turn to look back to where Nick and his 'little brother' are standing. Nick is pointing toward the field as if he's explaining the game to the kid. *This guy is too good to be true.*

"Come on, Kat. Let's get the kids and Jake and head out. I want to get cleaned up before my hot date with my husband." Mel grins. Walking arm in arm, we stroll down the grassy field, and unable to help myself, I turn, my eyes immediately meeting Nick's. My heart quickens a little at the contact. Pushing the stray hair which has fallen from my braid behind my ear, I continue to walk with Melanie, curious about this enigma of a man.

Nick

Standing next to Gavin, I watch as Kat and Melanie walk away toward Jake and the kids. I must've been staring too long as I suddenly feel an elbow jab my ribs, and Gavin clears his throat.

"Man, that Kat is a hot piece of ass."

Before I can stop myself, I've smacked the back of his head. "Watch your mouth, smart-ass. You don't talk about…" I clear my throat and try to get a handle on my irritation. "You don't talk about women that way." I quickly correct, trying to keep my voice down and not let him realize this is about her.

"Ha ha. Chill, man. She's too old for me anyhow. I know you have your mark on her."

"What? What are you talking about?"

"Ah, come on, Nick. I'm not stupid. I've got eyes. You've got it bad for that one."

Jesus. Is it so obvious even this kid can tell? What the hell is happening to me?

"Come on, playa, let's grab my stuff and head out," I say, grabbing him around the neck as we continue to walk.

As we stroll over to grab my things and head for the car, I notice Kat up ahead. She greets both Ruby and Seth with hugs and exuberance. They're all walking toward the parking lot together, Kat with an arm draped over each kid. My smile is back, and I can't help replaying those earlier thoughts of Kat as a mother in my mind.

"Thanks, I'd love to drive," Gavin says heartily.

"What?"

"Ha, you can't keep from staring at her ass. I should've asked you for some money. You would've handed it right over," he guffaws.

"All right, all right. So funny," I quip.

"Man, you need to tap that."

Again, my hand is sailing through the air, connecting with the back of his head. "The fuck, Gav? What did I just say?"

"Oh my god, you're pussy-whipped," he chortles.

"Jeez, Gavin. Were you raised in a barn? What makes you think it's okay to talk about women that way?"

"All women, or just your woman?"

"All women, you little shit," I say, shoving him forward playfully.

"Okay, okay. I'll try to watch my mouth when I'm referring to your girl's ass."

Glaring over at him, I decide to leave things well enough alone. I'm getting nowhere with this kid. I just hope he doesn't talk like this once we get to Dad's.

Approaching the car, I consider Jake's recent invitation to their Halloween party. Clearly, Katarina is very close with this couple. Unless she's working, I'm sure she'll be attending. I'm not daft. I could tell she was admiring me from across the field. With any other woman, this might annoy me, but I'm happy to give her something to look at. I guess I'm coming dressed as the 'soccer stud,' as Jake put it. I just need to bring some extra heat to this party. I'm tired of circling this girl. I'm all for giving her space as she's requested, but there's obviously a connection between us. This isn't one-sided. I need to make it very difficult for her to reject what we're both feeling.

I'm finally home at the end of a long day, showered, and sitting on the couch with a cold lager. The afternoon turned out better than I hoped. Well, after Mr. Potty mouth got his shit together and focused on working in the yard and not on Kat's ass. Luckily, he kept his antics to a minimum around my dad. Maybe money was the driving factor, but he worked hard while he was there and didn't cause me to get in trouble with child protective services for continuing to need to smack the back of his head.

Taking a long pull from my cold brew, I lean my head back against the couch and channel surf for something mindless. Nothing. All of these channels, and there's nothing worth watching. I grab my phone. Not a social media guy, I open my news app to see if anything big happened today that I may have missed. Multiple ads pop up for Halloween-related products, and I think back to Jake and Melanie's party.

8:20 p.m.
Nick: So, are you off for the Halloween Party? I was thinking about coming but won't know many people there.

8:25 p.m.
Katarina Kelly
Kat: Hi. Yes, I'm off.

It suddenly dawns on me that many of these conversations have occurred with someone other than Kat. Hmm, how do I ask if it's really her?

8:30 p.m.
Nick: I'm assuming after seeing you this afternoon, you're off tonight. Didn't know if I needed to make another delivery.

8:35 p.m.
Katarina Kelly
Kat: Yes. I'm watching Seth and Ruby so Jake and Mel could have an adult night out.

8:37 p.m.
Katarina Kelly
Kat: That delicious pie delivery was the nicest thing anyone's ever done for me.

Well, it's definitely her, and it's truly sad that's the nicest thing anyone has done for her. She

deserves to be treated like that all the time. What kind of guys has she dated? Oh yeah, according to Jake, they're all dicks.

8:42 p.m.
Nick: It's been a long time since I've been to a costume party. Not sure what I'm in for.

8:45 p.m.
Katarina Kelly
Kat: It's a blast. You'll have fun. You probably met a bunch of the guys at the club when you came.

8:50 p.m.
Nick: You going to tell me what you'll be wearing, so I know how to find you?

8:55 p.m.
Katarina Kelly
Kat: Nope. Would spoil the fun.

8:59 p.m.
Nick: I could think of another way to have fun.

9:02 p.m.
Katarina Kelly
Kat: Oh yeah? You're relentless, Dr. Barnes.

9:10 p.m.
Nick: I meant dancing, Ms. Kelly. I thought you liked to dance. Why do I feel like your mind is in the gutter?

9:18 p.m.
Katarina Kelly
Kat: Are you going to dance with me?

Hell. I stepped in that one. I hate dancing. But if that will make this girl warm up to me, I'll

consider it. Although, I'm not sure how well I could control myself being that close to her

9:25 p.m.
Nick: For you, Ms. Kelly, I would.

9:30 p.m.
Katarina Kelly
Kat: Well, Dr. Barnes, I look forward to it. Now I've got to run and put these kids to bed. Sweet dreams.

Sweet dreams indeed. I take another pull from my lager and imagine that tight little body

swaying against me as she had in the club all those nights ago. If I can't relive the hot sex against the tree behind the club, I can at least re-enact her dancing against me. I think back to that night of unbridled ecstasy. The night she ran away and never looked back. The night that remains unmentioned, like she's either unimpressed or embarrassed it happened. Do I bring it up? The last time I mentioned the tree incident, she almost seemed confused. Like she didn't have the first clue what I was talking about. This girl is still such a mystery. Hopefully, one that gets a little clearer on Hallows eve.

Chapter Eight

Kat

Hell yeah. Saturday! I love a Saturday off, much less one with a great party. I stretch as I open my eyes to the morning light. It felt like today would never get here. I worked three days in a row this week to have the weekend off. Doesn't sound like a lot unless you work in an ER and realize working three fourteen-hour days in a row is both mentally and physically exhausting. I only needed one Benadryl last night as I was so tired. I might have gotten to sleep without any, but I didn't want to risk waking after three or four hours and not getting back to sleep. I want to enjoy this evening. Jake and Melanie's Halloween parties are infamous, but now that I know Nick will be there... it just got a whole lot more exciting.

I stand and make my way to the coffee pot, trying to jumpstart my day. Once I get to Melanie's, I know I'll be her bitch. She's very particular about how she likes things, and I'm happy to oblige. Heck, I'll get great food, drinks, and dancing out of the deal, so I can't complain. *Dancing... dancing with Nick Barnes.* Now, this could get dangerous. I walk toward the bathroom to grab a shower and try not to contemplate how incredible dancing with Nick pressed against me might feel. *I will not touch myself.*

Deciding to keep my focus on getting ready and not getting off, I put on a little Post Malone while I shower. *Just focus on the music, Kat.* Making quick work of my morning routine, I throw on jeans and a long-sleeved pullover and fill my travel mug with coffee. Grabbing a duffle bag, I throw in some things I might need for later since I may end up spending the night depending on my alcohol intake. My costume and accessories are already at Mel's.

As I start the ignition and back out of the drive, I contemplate the chaos that will ensue upon my arrival. There's no need to call ahead, as I'm sure Melanie will be knee-deep in to-do lists and last-minute errands. I'll find a way to help with whatever she needs once I arrive.

"Thank God you're here," Mel greets, grabbing my arm and tugging me inside. It's like this every year. Every year she worries she'll never get it all done, and every year it's a phenomenal success.

"I'm here. Just keep the coffee flowing, and I'm at your beck and call." I salute.

"Okay, well, the list is on the kitchen island. I'm going to send Jake for all of the alcohol and supplies. Can you walk through the backyard and help me plan how to set up?"

I laugh to myself because there'll be no helping her plan. This is her ship, I'm just an obedient steward. "Sure, Mel. Just point where you want me and what you want me to do."

As we enter the backyard, there are rows upon rows of lights draped down the sides of the fence, separating their yard from the neighbors. Additionally, she has lights placed at the base of each of the large evergreen trees dotting the periphery of her yard. "Mel, I don't think I can…"

"Oh no, don't worry about that. The guys from Huggie's station are hanging all of those."

"Shew, I…" I stop abruptly, feeling a bit sick to my stomach. "Mel?"

"God, Kat, what's wrong? You look pale all of a sudden."

"Did you guys invite Mark? I mean, I don't want any trouble with the group on my account, but I hadn't even considered he might be here."

"No. We didn't specifically invite him, but we didn't tell him he couldn't come either. You're right. It's kind of a tricky situation until we get all of this stuff ironed out. I don't think from talking to Jake that any of the guys know there's an issue with the two of you. Hopefully, we'll get lucky, and his crew is on duty tonight."

"God, I hope so. I've really been looking forward to this. Plus, I told him I wasn't in a place to be dating. So, I wouldn't exactly be able to let loose with Nick if he was here."

"Uh, let loose with Nick, huh?" She smirks.

"Oh, you know what I mean. It's a party. Dance with him and stuff. I just wouldn't want to be looking over my shoulder the whole night wondering if he was watching. God, I never should've gone out with him. I don't know what I was thinking. It's never good to date someone in your circle."

"Well, what's done is done. Let's not worry about that until the time comes. We need to focus. I need you to help hang some of these cool Halloween decorations around the yard. There's going to be two different bars set up, one over here under the tent and another in the back corner of the yard near the fire pit. I've got some decorations that need to go in the tent too."

"Lord, Mel. I don't even want to know what you guys spend on these parties every year. I feel like it gets bigger and bigger. A tent?"

"Oh, we've done it so long it isn't that big of a deal anymore. We reuse most of the decorations. I just rented the tent at the last minute because they were calling for a chance of rain. And quite honestly, I thought it might muddle the sound from the DJ a bit, so we don't get another visit from the police."

"Well, considering you guys have invited half of the police officers to the party, I think you'll be okay." I laugh.

"Yeah, there's always that. There's no dance floor or anything, just the tent, but it's one less thing I need to stress over."

"I get it. Okay, let me get to work. You start tackling your list, and I'll come to grab you if I get caught up."

My stomach is growling. Looking to my watch, it's 6:10 p.m. I can smell the barbeque and brisket as I walk in and out of the kitchen. Reaching over to steal a small sandwich, I look for Mel amongst the catering staff and firefighters offering last-minute assistance with party prep.

"Mel, when do we need to start getting ready?" I ask, my mouth watering around the bite of sandwich. "Man, these are good."

Looking down at her watch, I see her wince. "Probably now. You go ahead and shower in the guest room and meet me in my room when you're done. I'll tell Jake to dress in Seth's room. He got off easy this year, so it shouldn't take him long."

"Okay. Got it. I'll meet you in your room in about thirty minutes."

Walking into Mel's bedroom, a towel wrapped around my body, I sit on the edge of her bed. I was able to blow out my hair and look up at Mel, who is leaning into the mirror, applying cat eyes with her eyeliner.

"Hey, Mel?"

"Yeah?"

"I think I want to wear my hair down."

I hear a sharp gasp as she swings around facing me with a look like she's just seen Santa come down the chimney.

"For real, Kat? I've been waiting for this for so long!" She claps.

I watch as she runs into her bathroom and returns with a small white box. "What's that?" I ask hesitantly.

"Oh, don't you worry. I've got this, Katarina Kelly. You're going to be the sexiest damn kitten that boy has ever seen."

Oh, Lord. What have I gotten myself into?

Nick

I park my car down the road from the address Jake provided, surprised at the sheer number of vehicles parked along the curb. This must be one big ass party. I feel more than a little conspicuous walking in my soccer gear, party or not. I guess I've watched too many movies, but I always fear walking in being the only person dressed in costume. As I stroll the length of Jake's driveway, I see party-goers standing in the backyard holding beers and chatting. I relax, releasing the air I was holding as I notice all of the said attendees are wearing different outfits, some quite outlandish.

"Hey, stud," I hear called in my direction. Looking over, I see Jake wearing a khaki outfit complete with a pith helmet, looking as if he's about to trek an African safari.

"Very funny," I reply, walking toward him as he's carrying wood toward a fire pit.

"Grab a beer. Better yet, get over here and help me with this so I can grab a beer." Laughing, I bend over to do just that. The yard is aglow in orange and white lights, occasional bursts of ornamental purple decorative bulbs displayed on several evergreens about the yard. There's a tent that backs toward the deck with doors flapped open to reveal a bar, a DJ, and some small tables and chairs. About twenty people are dancing in the tent, enjoying the evening's festivities.

"Man, you guys go all out."

"Yeah, Mel loves it. It's the one big thing we splurge on every year. She missed her calling. She should've been an event planner. But then again, she gets so stressed out by all of it, I probably couldn't live with her if she did this full time. Make sure you get some food. The brisket is amazing."

"Holy shit, brisket? That's some party fare. So where is Mel?"

"She's inside, running around. She should be out in a bit."

"Hey, I know this is probably bad timing since you're in the middle of throwing this big bash and all, but would you mind if I asked you something?"

"Sure. Why so serious?"

"Well, you can tell me it's none of my business, but I trust you, and I know Kat trusts you… so…"

"Spit it out, Nick. You and I both know you like her. What's the deal?"

"I do like her. I'm not sure it'll go anywhere, so I'm hesitant to start anything knowing we have to see each other so often at work. But I don't think I can fight this anymore. I tried to ask her out and got shot down. But she's been pretty flirty, so I'm wondering if she's possibly just as nervous about trying this as I am. But, with her being out of work lately and saying she had to work some things out, I wasn't sure what to make of any of it. I don't want to push my luck and upset her."

"Well…" Jake appears to hesitate, scratching the back of his neck like there's something more he's afraid to divulge.

"Well, what?"

"Okay, this is in the strictest confidence. I don't gossip, and I don't like sharing Kat's business, but I think your heart is in the right place, so I'm going to share this with you. I think Kat's nervous about entering any new relationship given her history. I've told you that before. But she went out with someone recently, and it didn't end well."

I'm filled with unease. "What do you mean it didn't end well?" I say a little too assertively.

"Nothing like that. Well, I hope it was nothing like that. She doesn't think she was assaulted, but there are a lot of questions about that night. Plus, she's been having some odd things happen since she started taking the zolpidem I gave her. I feel like hell about it. I'm praying she wasn't doing any of the weird shit I was doing. Anyway, she's stopped taking those pills and is trying to get all of that sorted out."

"Jake, can you come here a minute," I hear Mel call from the back door. I look up to see her head sticking out of the doorway and wave.

"Gotta run. Keep this between us, okay?" Jake runs off toward the house, and I'm left taking in all he's just told me. Jesus, this poor girl. *If that guy laid a hand on her, I swear I'll…* reining in my temper, I try to refocus.

Taking a calming breath, I take a swig of my cold beer and consider Jake's words. *'I'm praying she wasn't doing any of the weird shit I was doing.'* I try to recall some of the stories he shared. Hell, he said there was an incident where the guys were ribbing him about being out with them at a bar one night, and he didn't remember anything. Does that mean he was out driving around like that? Could Kat—"

My reverie is disrupted by whistles and clapping. I look up to see everyone is facing the back door to Jake's home, where Melanie's emerged. She's dressed in a full leather catsuit like the one Halle Berry wore when she played Cat Woman. Man, she looks incredible. She deserves the applause, not only for her outfit but the incredible event she's planned. The DJ starts playing "Pump It" by the Black Eyed Peas, and the party feels as if it has suddenly jolted into overdrive.

Feeling a slap to my upper arm, I look up to see Huggie and the twins, Tate and Tanner. Don't ask me which is which. One is dressed as an inflatable dinosaur, and the other is outfitted in full hunter regalia, multiple nerf guns hanging about his body. Huggie's wearing horn-rimmed glasses and a black cape. Is he supposed to be Harry Potter? "Hey, man," they greet, offering outstretched hands. "Nice to see you, Nick."

"Hey, guys—" I'm suddenly stopped short, speechless. I stand in stunned silence as I take in the vision before me. *Holy fuck.*

Chapter Nine

Nick

Standing in this dark yard illuminated by Halloween lights, I look toward the back door of Jake and Melanie's home, overcome. My mouth is dry as I gulp air into my lungs. She's an absolute vision.

As the Black Eyed Peas continue to play, I watch as this stunning creature slinks out of the door and onto the deck, surveying the crowd. She moves with the grace of a feline as she descends the deck steps toward the ground below. It's almost too much to absorb.

Katarina is dressed similarly to Melanie in a black cat costume, however, there's no leather suit involved. She's wearing a tight black top that clings to her curves and crosses her chest, leaving her shoulders bare. The sleeves are short, just barely caressing the tops of her arms. The bottoms are what one would describe as hot pants. They're the most incredible black short shorts practically painted onto her thighs and perky ass, beckoning anyone with a pulse to admire her long limbs. She's wearing sexy as fuck heels with long black laces that cross up her toned calves. There's not a lot of flashy jewelry, just a little black furry headpiece shaped like a cat's ears. But the showstopper is her hair. I've never seen it down, and it's utterly mesmerizing. It's long, dark, wavy, and flows down her back like a mane. Without the usual updo, her hair falls just above her waist. It's hard to tell from this distance, but she appears to have a few strands that are dyed a deep purple.

I continue to admire her from my vantage point, knowing I should get myself together before it's evident to everyone here, I've become hard just looking at her. *Thinking I should have completed my costume wearing my athletic cup under my shorts now.* I know I'm still standing next to the fire pit, but somehow, the heat doesn't feel like it's originating from the nearby flames. It's all her.

As she reaches the ground level and greets her many admirers and friends, she looks like a supermodel descending a runway to greet her fans. Her smile is infectious, and her poise is addicting to watch. I note a change in music as *Butterfly* by Crazy Town begins to play. In her usual style, she starts swinging her hips seductively as if she's no longer in control of her own body. Watching this minx dance is better than any porn I've ever seen. I'm sure to embarrass myself if I don't find a distraction.

Turning for the bar at the rear of the property, I ask if they have anything stronger than the beer I've been nursing. I know I can only have one as it's a forty-minute drive home from here, but I need to shock my brain away from images of that sultry woman.

"Scotch?" the bartender asks. Throwing him a generous tip and a nod, he pours two fingers and slides it in my direction as I turn back toward the dance floor. I try to sweep the entire group and not just focus on her, *but who the hell am I kidding?* The song changes, and I watch as Melanie approaches Kat, sidling up to her as they dance together to Usher, Lil Jon, and Ludacris singing "Yeah!" I observe Nate saunter over to the two of them. He's dressed like a gladiator and fits the part. Kat continues to sway between her friends, her arms swinging overhead, extending her profile. I watch as she throws her head back, arms up, back arched, long legs moving in sync to the music, and all I can think about is sneaking into Jake's house for a fucking cold shower.

I take another sip of my scotch and look back up just in time to see Kat bend over in front of Melanie, who mimics spanking her to the music. *Holy shit! I'm never going to make it out of this party without coming in my pants.*

"Enjoying the show?" I practically leap from my spot in the grass as Jake interrupts.

"Hell, I might need a cold shower if they keep that up," I tell him, embarrassed at watching his wife in such a way. "I promise I'm only referring to Kat."

"Nah, I'm just ribbing you, man. You should be flattered."

"Huh?"

"I honestly think this is for you."

"What're you talking about?" I turn to look at him, lost by this conversation.

"I've known Kat for years. This is the first time she's ever asked Mel to do her hair and leave it down. It's a big thing for her. Hell, it was a big thing for Mel. I've never seen anyone so excited to do someone's damn hair."

Still lost, I continue to look at Jake with a blank expression, needing a lot more clarification.

"She gets a lot of unwanted attention when it's down. But she did it anyway, knowing you were going to be here."

Turning back to the striking vixen on the dance floor, I contemplate whether there's the slightest possibility this is true or if he's just fucking with me. As if she can read my thoughts, I take her in as she transitions to a slower song and turns her body toward me, looking straight through to my soul. Her face is pale against the dim lighting of the tent. She's not overly made up. Her face is mostly neutral except for dark lashes and lightly stained cheeks. But those lips. Her lush, pouty red lips steal my attention whenever I look at her stunning face. She locks eyes with me as if reminding me I have a promise to fulfill.

"What are you waiting for?" I feel a shove from behind me. *Shit, I've turned back into that awkward teenage boy.* I hand off my scotch and slowly walk in her direction as Nick Jonas starts to croon the song "Close." I'm almost too nervous to speak as I get... well, close.

Standing in front of her now, I look down into her big brown eyes, and it's official. I'm speechless.

"Hi," she whispers up at me.

Fuck. Words. I need some fucking words. "Hi," I manage to reply.

Giggling, she slides her sweet arms around my waist, and I have to check to make sure I'm still breathing. Unable to stop myself, I drop my head into her hair and take a deep inhalation of that delicious Coconut scent I've come to dream about. I try to slowly move back and forth with her but keep my pelvis from coming into contact with her so she doesn't become horrified by the fact something else also wants to dance with her. She probably wouldn't believe me, but this is more than sexual. I'm completely entranced by her. Any attraction I may have had in the past pales in comparison to this moment.

Abruptly, something hits my leg, and Kat starts to fall to the ground. As I attempt to grab her, I hear Melanie screaming behind me. Shock disrupts my euphoric haze, and I look down to see Kat is grabbing at her ankle.

"Murphy!" I hear Mel shout again. "Kat, I'm so sorry, honey. I don't know how he got out. Big oaf. Are you okay?"

She's laughing, but I notice the slight wince on her face as she tries to comfort Melanie. "I'm fine, Mel. The big guy just wanted to join the party."

Bending down, I scoop her up into my arms, ignoring her protests that she's fine. Hell with being gallant, I just need to hold her.

"Nick, I'm fine. Really."

"We'll see about that. Those shoes and that fall aren't a good combination." I would, however, like to save those shoes for later. *I'd give my Audi for a chance to fuck her with those sexy little numbers on.*

Carrying her out of the tent, I recall seeing a bench off to the rear of the firepit. I reassure her I want to check out her ankle and make sure she's okay as the ground is very uneven. I'm trying to be a gentleman, but quite honestly, the thought of putting her down could make this grown man cry.

As I approach the wooden bench, I realize there's a chill in the air. Of course, neither of us has been wearing much at this party. I'm still warm from the effect she's having on me, but I don't want her to be uncomfortable. Shifting gears, I turn slightly, so I sit down, keeping her cradled in my lap. Fuck it if she feels how hard I am, I don't want her to be cold. I push her intoxicating hair behind one ear as I whisper into it, "You okay?"

"Yes. It's probably nothing," she responds, but I can feel her shaking against me.

"I'm sorry, I don't have a jacket to give you. Come here," I instruct as I attempt to tuck her into my side as I begin to undo those sexy laces on her stilettos. "I need to take this off and check out your ankle, okay?"

"Okay," she whispers back. I can feel the warmth of her breath against my neck, and it's making my already hard as fuck dick now harder than fuck. I try to keep my mind on my task and not my growing erection.

"Does anything else hurt?"

She doesn't answer, and I suddenly become alarmed. I look down and wonder what has her so quiet. As I place my thumb under her chin and raise her beautiful face to meet mine, she whispers, "I think I might've hit my jaw on your arm on the way down."

Damn. How'd one dance turn out to be such a mess? Stroking her jaw with my thumb, I look for bruising. "Does it hurt here?"

"Just a little," I can barely hear her response.

Unable to stop myself, I lean down and lay gentle kisses on her jaw. I hear an audible intake of air as my mouth touches her cool skin. Again, my dick thinks this is a signal to sit up and say hello. I refocus on her ankle, which appears to be the safer option at the moment.

As I wrap my large hand around her delicate foot and ankle, I forget why I'm touching her. I'm not normally into feet, but her dainty limbs have almost hypnotized me. I continue to rub and stroke her skin, looking for signs of severe injury. Pretending to check a pulse, it's a ploy to keep touching her.

Turning to reassure her this is probably just a sprain, I'm interrupted as she slams her mouth onto mine. Any restraint I've had has snapped. I dig my hands into her silky hair and caress it as I nip and bite at her lower lip and tease her lips with my tongue, begging for entrance. She opens her mouth for me, and our tongues complete the dance our bodies started before her fall. Thank god it's dark out because there'll be no hiding the sight of my engorged cock now. Never in my life have I been this turned on.

"Nick?" I hear her murmur between kisses. I can't pull away yet. "Nick?" I don't want to stop kissing her, but the polite thing would be to answer.

"Yes?" My voice is strained, gravely.

"Take me home?"

Jumping up with her in my arms as if my pants have suddenly caught fire, I look down to ensure we have her shoes and quickly head for the front yard.

"Where are your car keys?" I ask, thinking I should be the gentleman and drive her car home.

"No, you drive. I can ask Mel to help get my car" she answers against my neck, arms wrapped tightly around it as I practically jog to my car.

"Okay." Stopping briefly, I squeeze her body against me in order to kiss her again. I continue to walk down the road, looking for my car nestled between the fifty others along the curb's edge.

"Where on Earth did you park?" she laughs.

"In Maryland apparently," I snort.

"I can walk, Nick. It's okay."

"No. You're not walking on that ankle," I bark, knowing I'm thrilled to have an excuse to continue carrying her. I finally see my Audi up ahead and squeeze between the cars to place her by the passenger door momentarily. Opening the door, I go to pick her back up, and she places her small hand on my arm.

"Nick. I can hop into the car."

Good Lord, I'm lost to this woman. I grab ahold of her face with both of my hands and begin to kiss her with abandon. I can feel her arms slide up my back as I dart my tongue into her sweet, wet mouth. Dropping my face to her throat, I continue to kiss and lick as I inhale her tropical scent. Pulling back, I rub my nose along hers and place gentle kisses onto her forehead. We stop to catch our breaths, and I watch as she slides into my car. I have to fight to get the door shut before readjusting my junk. I've never been so fucking hard in my life.

Trying not to look too eager, I slow my pace as I walk around to the driver's door. *Keep it cool, Nick.* Opening the door, I slide in and reach for my keys. Jesus, if I can make it to her house without blowing my load, it'll be a miracle. I turn to see her beautiful face in profile, looking down at her hands, a bashful smile across her features. After starting the ignition and backing out, I reach for her delicate hand and bring it to my lips. I cannot stop touching this woman.

We drive in silence for about ten minutes before I can't take it any longer. "You look stunning, Kat. Honestly. You're radiant." Letting go of her warm hand, I reach up and run my fingers through her silky tresses. "God, I love your hair."

She whispers in return, almost too quietly to hear, "I wore it down for you."

Holy shit, Jake was right. Sitting up taller in my seat, I reach for her hand again and almost place it in my lap until I remember the monster that's waiting there. Thinking better of it, I kiss it again and lie our entwined hands across her thigh. I'm almost shaking with want for her. I need to warn her. I'll probably only last mere minutes before I explode. I don't want her to think I'm a one-pump chump, but I've waited and dreamt of her for so long—

"Nick?"

"Yes?"

"I'm a little nervous."

Squeezing her hand a little tighter, I think to myself. *Me too, kitten, me too.*

The car grows quiet as we get closer to the hospital, and I realize I have absolutely no idea where I'm going. "Uh, Kat. I don't know your address."

Giggling, she squeezes my hand. "You're doing fine. I'd tell you if you weren't going the right way. Just take the next exit."

She continues to offer directions, often pointing with the hand I'm holding. I feel like that fifteen-year-old boy holding hands with his school crush. It's almost maddening how happy I feel right now.

We pull into her drive, and she advises she can enter the home through the garage keypad. I scold her not to get out of the car without me and jog over to the passenger side door. As I open it, she grabs her strappy shoe, and I bend down to scoop her back into my arms. As I lock the car, I carry her over to the keypad and allow her to enter her code. Walking into her small single-car garage, I carry her up the steps into her home. It's quaint but stylish. I instantly feel at home here. Finding a comfortable couch as I walk into her den, I again sit with her draped over me. She reaches up to run her fingers through my hair, and I cannot hold back the moan that betrays how very close to the edge I am. I feel her soft lips laying kisses along the stubble of my neck, below my ear. She's breathing into my ear, stroking my other cheek with her soft hand.

Reaching down, I untie the laces and remove her remaining shoe. I can't help but slide my hand up the length of her soft skin from her ankle to the back of her leg, my fingertips teasing the hem of her tiny shorts.

"Nick?"

"Yes?" I breathe into her ear.

"I need you." She sighs.

"Where's your bedroom?"

I lift her in my arms and carry her in the direction of her outstretched hand. It's difficult to maneuver her into the other room as I keep having to stop to kiss her. It's as if I need them in order to breathe, like inhaling from a scuba diver's tank before continuing on my surreal journey.

Once we reach her room, and I'm able to gently push the door open with my foot, I carry her over to the bed and place her atop the plush bedding. Turning, I notice a door.

"Is that the bathroom?"

"Oh, yes."

"I'll be right back." I attempt to splash some water on my face and rinse my mouth of the aftertaste of scotch and desperation. Leaving the light on and the door cracked, I return to her. Standing over the bed, I look longingly into her big brown eyes. "Kat?"

"Yes?"

"I need to see you."

I observe as she swallows hard and nods. I crouch down on one knee and gently place my hands on either side of her tiny shorts, wiggling them down her sexy legs. Standing again, I peer down at her.

Admittedly, I have no clue how to get this tight little black number off of her.

"Snaps."

"What?"

She parts her legs slightly and repeats, "Snaps."

Ah, I see. I climb onto the bed, straddling her, and reach down to locate the *snaps*. The heat radiating from her core is making my hands tremble. *Fuck man, hold it together.* I carefully pull the snaps apart and roll the garment up and over her head. Tossing it to the side, I look back down. I'm awestruck. There's no other way to describe it. Looking down at the perfection before me, I stare open-mouthed at her beauty.

She's lying back, hands resting by her head, gorgeous coffee-colored mane fanned out upon her pillow. Her eyes are bright and beautiful as she allows me to drink her in. Her succulent tits are even more brilliant than I remember. They're somehow more glorious without the distraction of partially removed clothing. My gaze drops to her flat stomach and the sexiest navel I've ever seen. *I can't wait to sip from that cup.* But looking further south, I take in the magnificence before me. She has the tiniest little landing strip of neatly trimmed dark curls leading to the sweetest pink pussy I've ever seen. She's swollen and glistening, and my body is literally shaking with need as I gaze upon her.

"Nick?"

"Yes?" I'm barely able to speak.

"Can I see you?"

As if hearing his name at roll call, my cock practically leaps in my pants. I climb off of her bed and try to remove my shoes, socks, and shin guards. I cannot believe I've been wearing these the whole damn time. Standing upright, I reach behind my neck and remove my shirt. Looking over at the goddess before me, I watch as her eyes shimmer in apparent delight. Placing my hands at my hips, I slowly drag my shorts and boxer briefs down my legs. Watching her as I undress, I see her eyes widen as my engorged cock bounces out, precum already pooling at the tip.

"You're beautiful," she murmurs. "And big."

I say a silent prayer of thanks for the gift of my DNA and unconsciously reach to give my aching cock a congratulatory stroke. I notice she licks her lower lip as I do this, and I try to keep from smiling.

"Is this what you want, kitten?"

I watch as she nods, so I continue to slowly stroke my rock-hard cock as I come closer to the bed. Even this is causing concern, as I fear I'll humiliate myself if I don't calm the fuck down. Returning to the bed, I straddle her once more and kiss her sweet mouth before trailing my lips lower. I kiss from her lips down her neck toward the luscious tits I'm cradling. As I squeeze them in my hands, I lick the underside of one, then the other, and then latch on to a firm nipple. I suck gently before nipping at it and then turn to offer its twin a similar greeting. Unable to ignore my dick any longer, I change my position to put my weight on one of my forearms by her head and slide my hand down to her wet, swollen center.

"Ah, you're so wet." I slide my fingers up and down her pink flesh until I'm coated with her juices. Bringing my fingers briefly to her clit, I rub gently, watching her pelvis undulate under my caress. I can't fight the need to taste her any longer and lift my fingers to my mouth. Looking into her eyes, I drag my tongue over the length of my wet digits, groaning at the flavor. Her head drops back at the sight, and I return to stroking her pussy and clit with my fingertips.

"Kat?"

"Nightstand."

"What? Oh…" Realizing she's directing me to grab a condom, I try not to laugh.

Giggling, she says, "I bought them at Target after you left. In case, well…"

Kissing her on the nose, I press on. "Kat, I was just trying to warn you. I want to go slow, to worship your body. But I've dreamt of this so long… Well, I'm probably not going to last long. I'm too wound up. But I'll return to giving you the attention you deserve afterward. Okay?"

I notice she's giving me a perplexed look. Is she worried since I'm admitting I'm on the edge that I'm not a worthy lover? Jeez, I need to last as long as possible. I don't want her to be disappointed. *No pressure, Nick.*

Reaching over to the nightstand, I open it to find one box of three condoms. I sit up to open and roll it down my eager length and notice she's watching me nervously. Worried, I stop and look directly at her. "Kat, you okay?"

"Just go slow. It's been a while."

And there it is. Fuck. I'm a horrible human being. I should stop right now and tell her what I know. That I've suspected this, but now it's confirmed. That this isn't our first time, but unbelievably she doesn't remember. That she apparently needs to avoid zolpidem like it's poison as Jake isn't the only one plagued with 'weird shit' while taking it. I feel torn, guilty about moving ahead knowing this. But there's no stopping this train now. It's already left the station, and I just don't have the willpower to stop. I'll tell her when we're both dressed, and I can comfort her. *Yeah, that's the story I'm going with.*

"Nick?"

"I'm going to try to go slow, but you're so fucking beautiful, I'm not sure I'm even going to make it inside you before I lose it," I confess.

Watching as a sweet smile crosses her face, I lower myself back down to my earlier position to caress and stroke her body a little longer. I'm praying I can get her a little closer to the edge, so she's as ready to come as I am. Rubbing soft circles around her swollen nub, I start to sit up a bit. I stroke the head of my cock up and down her wet, hot entrance and groan. I cannot wait a second longer to be inside her. Sliding my hands beneath her pert little ass, I arch my back as I push the tip of my cock into her molten channel.

"Holy fuck, Kat." I rock back and forth, pushing in a couple of inches at a time. I almost shudder at the sensation. "You're so tight. You feel incredible," I pant.

I can feel the sensation building and fear this is going to end far quicker than I like. As I push the full length of my swollen dick into her, I stop momentarily as she rotates her hips, as if trying to make room. "You okay?" I breathe.

"Yes. You feel so good."

Changing the angle of my pelvis, allowing me to hit her clit with every stroke, I begin to slowly slide in and out of her. The feeling so overwhelming it causes me to throw my head back in ecstasy. My hips take over, setting their own pace, and I feel a rush of euphoria overtake me. I lean on my forearms as I thrust into her tight heat.

"Your sweet pussy feels so good. I love how wet you get for me, kitten."

I can hear her heavy breaths as she moves her hips to meet mine with each thrust. Nibbling on her neck, just below her ear, I feel her fingernails bite into my ass. The sting pushing me closer to the edge. My pace picks up, and I buck into her wildly.

"Kat, are you close?"

"What—"

"Kat, are you—"

"What is—"

Shit, am I hurting her? Slowing my pace, I look down at her just as she digs her nails a little deeper into my backside.

"What is happening?" she cries out, and I realize she's about to shatter for me. I watch as she throws her head back, eyes closed, mouth open, neck arched in total rapture.

"Open your eyes, Kat," I command. I have to see her.

I watch as her eyes flick open, glassy and full of lust. The most erotic sight I've ever encountered. "Oh my god, Nick," she belts out.

That's it. Feeling her tight little body squeezing my cock has my balls drawing up, and I begin to thrust feverishly into her. *Oh my god, is right.* I'm hovering on the edge. This feeling so intense. I've never felt anything like this. I pound so hard into her I'm afraid I'm going to drive the head of the bed through the wall.

"You ready for my come, kitten?"

"Oh god, Nick, please," she begs.

One, two more strokes, and I just can't hold out any longer. "Fuck. Fuck," I growl. I'm seated deeply into her beautiful body, coming like it's an Olympic sport. My heart is hammering in my chest. Giving in to my body's fatigue, I collapse onto her, knowing I'll probably crush her but unable to keep myself upright any longer. I bury my face in her hair, needing to feel as much of her skin against mine as humanly possible. I never imagined sex could be like this.

I've had plenty and never felt what I experienced was lacking, until now.

As I turn my head into her throat, I place wanton kisses against her skin as I try to regulate my breathing. Suddenly, I feel something wet splash against my cheek. *Fuck, she's crying.* Rolling us both to the side, I examine her quickly.

"Baby, did I hurt you?"

"No. No." I watch as she wipes her eyes with the back of her hand, my heart contracting at the site.

"Kitten, talk to me. What is it?" I try to dry her tears. Tears I placed there.

"I'm just embarrassed."

"What?" I sit up on bent elbow and look down at her. "What on Earth are you embarrassed about? That was the best sex of my life." *Well, except for that time we did it against a tree, but now's not the time to bring that up.*

Smiling a little now, she adds, "That's just never happened before."

Confused, I push on, "What? You've never had an orgasm before?"

"Well, not with anyone else in the room," she whispers, her arm draped over her eyes, self-conscious.

Sitting up a little more to make room for the sudden pride that's widening my chest, I gaze down at her. Hell, she really did date some dickheads. "I'm sorry, Kat." Pulling her arm away from her face, I kiss the tip of her nose. "But I'm glad when you finally had one, it was with me."

I can no longer hide the shit-eating grin on my face and bend down to smother her cheeks and lips with kisses. I roll off of the bed and walk toward the bathroom to dispose of the condom, wondering how it didn't rip under the sheer force of that climax.

After washing my hands, I open the shower door and reach in to turn on the water. After checking the temperature, I return to the bed and scoop a giggling Kat into my arms again. As I approach the shower, I lift her slightly, allowing her legs to wrap around my waist. Standing us both under the warm water, I instruct her to hold on while I look for body wash. As I turn, I see a bottle with a coconut on the front. "Ah, manna from heaven."

Chuckling, she asks, "What are you talking about, Dr. Barnes?"

Laughing, I manage to pour a handful of the tropical soap and begin to rub it across her body and mine. As I stand us both under the spray to rinse the suds, I reach up to wring the water from her gorgeous locks. Turning off the water, I step back out and find a towel to wrap around both of us as I carry her back to the bed. Gently placing her down, I wrap the towel around her and quickly dart back to the bathroom for another. I pad myself quickly and wrap the towel around my waist before returning to her.

"Lie down, kitten."

I watch as the compliant little minx stretches her still damp body across the sheet, so I can dry her off. After her skin seems sufficiently dry, I towel dry her hair. Tossing the towel to the end of the bed and removing my own, I crawl back under the comforting duvet and snuggle up to her. I'm unable to keep my hands to myself and begin to stroke and fondle her at my leisure, now that I'm no longer distracted by my impatient dick.

I slide her long dark hair to the side and place gentle open-mouthed kisses along her shoulder, her neck, and her back. Gently pushing her so that she's lying face down, I run my hand up and down her back. Realizing my cock thinks he's arrived late to the party, he twitches as I hover over her and continue kissing her back and perky little backside. I observe her looking over her shoulder to watch as I take a bite of one creamy ass cheek. Not one to leave anyone out, I bend to offer similar treatment to the other.

As I continue to nibble and kiss her back and sweet little ass, I reach between her legs and begin to stroke. *Oh hell, she's wriggling into my hand.* I lean over her and lift her hips, so she's on all fours before me. Sliding my hands around her, I grip one soft breast with my left hand as I glide my fingers back and forth over her hot, wet pussy. I hear a moan escape as I push two fingers into her waiting heat.

My cock is at full mast now but trying to behave as long as possible. I adjust my position so that I can reach around her hips to rub and pinch her swollen bundle of nerves with my left hand as I drive my fingers into her with my right.

"I need you to come for me."

"Ohhh."

"I need to feel your tight little pussy contracting around my fingers, Kat."

Suddenly, her arms collapse underneath her, and her arms stretch wide, holding on to the bed as I continue to finger fuck her.

"That's it, baby. You're so close." Continuing to rub circles around her clit, I lean down to whisper in her ear.

"Do you need me to pull my fingers out, squeeze your clit while I fuck that sweet pussy with my tongue?"

"Oh my god," she screams, and I instantly feel the gush of fluid as her body grips onto me. Reaching into the nightstand, I quickly find a condom and sheath my erect cock. Lining up with her entrance, I push forcefully into her, holding onto her hips for support. The sounds of wet flesh and the smell of sex in the air as I slam into her gets my cock even harder. I push one hand down onto the center of her back, grabbing a handful of her luscious hair and fucking her like my life depends on it.

"Fuck, Kat, I'm going to come."

"Oh god, Nick, please. Please. Please."

I slam a little harder into her tight body, feeling my balls slap against her with each thrust.

"Oh my god, Nick." I hear her scream out, her body shaking violently as another orgasm crashes into her. Picturing her face, as she came earlier tonight, I feel the familiar sensation build from the base of my spine and travel straight to my cock.

"Kat!" I growl as I buck into her one last time before emptying into the condom. I try to stay upright, catching my breath, but the night's activities are catching up with me. For what feels like an eternity, I lie on top of her, completely spent.

Slowly, I withdraw and stand to take care of the condom. As I return to the bed, I see she's lying on her side, eyes closed, breathing as if she's been asleep for hours. I climb back in, cover us with blankets and snuggle into her. Knowing how difficult sleep is for her, I relish the feel of her slumbering body against my chest, the sound of her breathing lulling me to sleep.

~

Waking to harsh sunlight pouring into the blinds, I squint as I look at the clock. *It* reads 6:22 a.m.. *Holy Shit!* It hits me, I'm on call today. Call that started at six o'clock.

I gingerly slide my arm out from under Kat's sleeping form and roll quietly off of the bed. As difficult as it is for her to sleep, I'm not about to disrupt this tranquil state. I fish around the floor for my clothes and grab my phone and keys. I'll check in with the service once I'm not at risk of waking her. As I get to the door, I quickly turn back to look at her. I feel my heart squeeze. Anxiety starts to build, causing a bit of unease in my stomach. *I'm probably just hungry. I never ate dinner.* I head out the door, hoping I haven't already missed a call.

Kat

I roll over in the bed with a feeling of satisfaction I cannot begin to describe. I can't keep the wide smile off of my face as I greet the day, arms stretched overhead, feeling the sweet ache of my muscles. Souvenirs from my amazing evening. As I roll toward the god who gave me the best night of my life, I slowly open my eyes, wondering if he wakes looking as ruggedly perfect as he does the rest of the day.

As my eyes accommodate for the bright sunlight, I notice he's already up. Sitting up, I peer toward the bathroom door. But it's ajar, and no sounds are coming from that direction. Maybe he's putting on coffee. He's so thoughtful.

I turn, sitting at the edge of the bed, and again stretch my well-used body. *At least I know why I'm waking naked this time,* I giggle to myself. I dart into the bathroom to grab my robe and walk toward the kitchen. *Hmm? No one here.* I pick up the coffee pot, confirming it's empty. I return to the bedroom and sit down. Suddenly, a feeling of déjà vu takes over. *Holy crap, was this another dream?* It felt so real. I start looking about the room for any sign he might've been here. Nanny cam! I think to myself and push myself up from the edge of the bed just as I notice something on the floor.

Bending down, I reach for the item tucked between the bed and the nightstand. Bringing it to my face, I realize it's a condom wrapper. I open the bedside table and take in the sight of the open box of condoms. He was here. As the relief washes over me, it's quickly replaced with rage.

He was here and left. Got what he wanted and left. No kiss goodbye. Not even a note. Just like all the rest.

Chapter Ten

Kat

I stomp around my house, irritated by my mood swings. I vacillate between outrage and hope. It's denial, disguised as hope. I can't believe I fell for this. Again. I should've stuck with my gut. Between the Mr. Hollywood, 'I'm too good for you' first impression, the rude way he treated me at work, and then all of the flirty innuendo, it was all a trap.

I'm not going to wallow in this. I knew going into it, things could end up this way. Every man I've ever dated has treated me like a doormat. Why should he be different? And we didn't even date! He got what he wanted and didn't even have to take me to dinner. Of course, I'm not sure that makes him sound as bad as it does me.

Walking to my kitchen, I put the kettle back on the stove. The hot shower did nothing to improve my mood. I haven't had an appetite after awakening to find Nick gone but know I should eat something. Placing two slices of bread in the toaster, I trudge over to the couch to await the teapot's whistle. As I wrap my steel gray throw about my shoulders, I pull my knees up to my chest and let out a heavy sigh. *Couldn't, just once, things turn out differently? Am I that unworthy of someone who really cares for me?* I feel a tear tumble down my cheek. *Stop it, Katarina. He's not worth one of your tears.* I need to focus on the positive. I finally had amazing sex after a four-year drought. I got my first orgasm delivered by another person. *You aren't broken.* It is possible to enjoy amazing sex with someone. Lesson learned. No need to repeat it. At least not with him.

As the teapot calls to me, I stand and return to the kitchen. Pouring the water into a mug that says *Santa's favorite Ho,* a gift from Melanie, I hold the steamy liquid under my face and inhale. This feels like brainwash. I'm trying to convince myself I got what I wanted, and I'm not the least bit affected by his running out on me. But if brainwash is what it takes, that's what I'm going to do. I'm allowing myself one day to grieve. I have the day off. I'll get any remaining self-pity out of the way before I return to work. I refuse to let him see how this is hurting me. I'm going to be the bigger person in this scenario and do my job and leave all personal issues at home.

Returning to my couch, I sit with my tea and stretch out my legs. It's then I notice my shoes. My mind returns to sitting here, watching as he gingerly removed my strappy shoe and slowly traveled his strong hand up the back of my leg. I was so wound up by that point, having his fingers tease the opening of my shorts was more than I could handle. That taught string snapped, and I was begging him to take me. And take me he did. I didn't have any idea sex could be like that. I'm sure someone like him is well-practiced. I don't even want to contemplate how many women he's seduced before me.

Taking another sip, my mind ricochets. I consider the possible reasons for his disappearing act. Maybe he got called into work. Perhaps he got an urgent text from his dad. He said he was going to see him with his 'little brother' that day at the soccer field. They must be close. Maybe he and his 'little brother' had early morning plans. Maybe he had car trouble. *Heck, Kat, maybe he got abducted by aliens. Use your head, you're a one and done. Face it. This isn't your first rodeo.*

My heart hurts. I admit it. I really wanted him to be different. I think briefly about how Jake, Melanie, and Olivia all encouraged me to open my heart and try again. How I was so eager to get it right this time, I dropped my guard and literally let my hair down. But I don't want them to take the blame after seeing I was hurt by this. I don't want to see any more faces full of sympathy for poor Katarina. If Jake or Melanie ask, I'll confirm we had a great night, but that's all it'll be. *I'll tell them I was just using him for sex.* I have bigger fish to fry with my pending Rohypnol test, continued questions about whether I've been sleepwalking, and now texts from unknown numbers. I don't need to waste any more time or energy on that superficial surgeon. But today, I admit, I may still need to cry a few more times.

Nick

Sitting at my kitchen island, I look down into my coffee cup. Where do I go from here? I'd raced home when I saw the time and realized I could be called into work at any moment. I'm a professional. There's no way I could arrive at work wearing a Halloween costume, soccer uniform, or not. What's more, I smelled like I just left a porn shoot. *Fuck, that was the hottest night of my life.* It made me sad to shower. Like washing away any remaining evidence the incredible night had actually happened. At least she should remember this one. But is that good or bad?

I drove home in a panic, first at forgetting to set an alarm and allowing myself to compromise my work but later at compromising my heart. I'd made a promise to myself a long time ago. I was never going to be hurt by someone like my father was. I married Sophia, knowing there wasn't the insane love between us my parents shared. It was disruptive to my pride and my bank account when we divorced, but I could handle it. But looking back at that sleeping angel in her bed this morning, there was no ignoring the way my heart was feeling. This girl is different. I knew it then, and I know it now. This isn't the after-effects of a night of ravenous sex. I'm falling hard for this beautiful girl, and if I let myself get in any deeper, it could be catastrophic when it ends.

Walking to the counter, I pick up my phone from where it's charging. I had let the battery run dead last night, distracted by all things Katarina. It's a good thing I woke with the sun or no telling what fall out there might've been with my job. I've never been so careless. I'm just getting established at St. Luke's. I don't need a reputation for being a doctor that doesn't return calls or take his job seriously. I admit, this is what triggered my panic, but the more I thought about Kat, the worse it got.

I don't know if I can do this. Risk everything for someone who could simply walk away. We're already on such shaky ground, and she could crush me. Plus, she has some serious issues to work out. Do I really need to take that on? I'm just recovering from a messy divorce. Should I intentionally enter into a relationship with someone who can't even remember having sex with me? After the amazing night we had together, I'm choosing to believe it's the sleeping pill and not a lackluster performance on my part that had her forgetting it happened. *Fuck. She'll surely leave once she realizes I knew she had no memory of that night, and I didn't tell her. That I knew it and slept with her again anyway.* I hate liars, and I've become one. Withholding the truth is the same thing as lying, and I need to come clean with her. As I consider this, the feelings of panic begin to reemerge.

Looking down at my phone, I note there are no missed calls, no texts. This girl is as cool as a cucumber. She's probably unphased by my leaving and just basking in the afterglow of the amazing sex. She's already made it clear she isn't looking for anything right now, and I pursued her anyway. It was just a hot night between two consenting adults. But it wasn't just a hot night. It was *the* hottest night of my life. I never knew it could be that good. Is it because I'm falling for her? Yet, the sex behind the club was just as amazing, and I had guarded my feelings at that point. It's got to be her. But if I willingly go back for more, I'm asking for trouble. Because when she leaves, it'll break me.

I head for the door, grabbing my car keys. I'm picking up Gavin to take him back to my dad's. Last weekend went well, and he didn't tear down the house with the riding mower, so I suspect he'll do fine today in my absence. Dad will look out for him, and I'll come back around dinner as I can't risk taking a call and not being able to get to the hospital promptly. Besides, I think it could be good for Gavin and my dad to bond. It didn't sound like he's ever had the influence of a grandparent in his life.

Driving down the road, I can't help but check my phone again. Nope. Still no calls or texts. But this is a good thing, right? I need to distance myself from Kat, so I have better control over this situation. Pulling into Gavin's apartment complex, I notice he's standing at the curb talking to another boy with a basketball under his arm. As I put the car in park, the two appear to shake hands until I notice the other teen sliding something into Gavin's hand as they shake. *Is this kid buying or selling drugs?*

The car door opens, and he plops into the seat. I look to see if the object in question is still in his hand as I greet him.

"Hey, Gav, ready to get to work?"

"Yeah, sure," he replies coolly.

I see the item is still there, so I take a chance. "What you got there?"

Gavin turns to me, looking as if he's been busted. "What do you mean?"

"I saw your friend hand something off to you. Just wondering what you've got. No big deal." I try to shrug it off but am worried I'm going to have to go all 'big brother' on him if there is something seedy going on.

"If it's no big deal, why're you asking?" Gavin tosses back, seeming annoyed.

"Forget it then. Just making small talk." I watch as he places the item in his nylon basketball shorts and looks out of the window. I decide not to push it. I've got enough angst brewing today, and what's more, I don't want to open this can of worms, and then he's at my dad's house, stewing about it. "You have much homework this weekend?"

Gavin looks back down at his hands and mumbles, "Not too bad. I usually knock it out on Friday."

"That's good. It's great you're disciplined enough to do that. Leaves your weekend to do what you want," I say, a little impressed with him.

"Yeah, I wouldn't call it disciplined. I don't have a computer or internet at my house. If I don't do it at school or the library, I'm usually left without a way to finish. Hell, I don't even have a cell phone." I watch as he turns to look out the window. "I don't know anyone that doesn't have a cell phone," he mumbles.

I never considered this previously. "Well, maybe we can make that part of your earnings for working with Dad."

"What do you mean?" he asks skeptically.

"Well, I have an old cell phone at home I don't use anymore. When I upgraded, I just threw it in my desk and forgot about it until now. We could probably get you a no-contract service that isn't too expensive. You can just upload minutes and data as you go. I think you can buy the minutes at Walmart or Target or something."

He suddenly has a little more enthusiasm about our conversation. "You really think so?"

"Sure. After I drop you off with Dad, I'll go home and see if I can get it taken care of. I can probably upload your first month for about twenty to twenty-five dollars. Considering how hard you worked last week, I was planning to pay you about fifty dollars a weekend. Even after paying for the phone each month, you should end up with about $175."

I watch as his eyes light up. He's never asked how much I was paying him. He seemed to just go along without questioning it. "Shit, are you serious?"

"Yeah. Gavin, you work hard, and you're doing me a favor looking out for Dad. He's getting up there in age, and it makes me feel better knowing someone can help him out once in a while. I think you two could be good for each other."

I quickly glance back over at him and see he's grinning now as he looks out the window. I'm glad I can do something to make things easier on him. He may be rough around the edges, but all in all, he seems like a good kid. I just hope that whatever he's hiding doesn't come back to bite me.

Back at home, I find the old phone. *Hell. He'll shit himself when he sees this.* It was the top-of-the-line iPhone until the most recent model came out. Looking at my phone, I realize I haven't received the first call from the ER today. Or anyone else, for that matter. I have to leave to pick up Gavin in about an hour, so I have time to get some laundry going and order some take-out to pick up on my way back home. *Hmm, maybe I should order some extra food so Gav can take some back home—*

My phone dances on the countertop, and I think to myself, *damn, I spoke too soon.* Looking down, I realize it isn't the service. It's Dad.

"Hey, everything going okay there?"

I hear a bit of panic as Gavin belts into the phone, "Nick, it's your dad."

Chapter Eleven

Kat

I've been ghosted. It's official. It's been a week since I got the complete and total brush off by the over-the-top, attentive, good Samaritan who carried me around all night to protect my ankle. I'm sure it was all part of Nick's come-on. And boy did I fall for it.

I've only had to work one day so far this week, and I managed that without bumping into Nick, or Mark for that matter. Let's see if I can make it two for two. I pull into the physician's parking and decide not to look for his car. It'll only make me crazy if I know he's here. I just pray he isn't on call today, as I don't want to work with a feeling of impending doom.

"Hey, Kat, glad you're here." I look up to see Dr. Silver greet me as I walk through the ER doors a few moments later. "I have a girl with an ankle fracture. She needs a posterior short leg and a stirrup splint. Do you think you can do it, or should I call Ortho—

"No! I got it. I'd be happy to do it, Dr. Silver. Just let me put my things down, and I'll get right on it. What room is she in?"

"She's in room two. Thanks, Kat. Sorry to hit you with it the minute you walk in the door." *Wow, really? He does it all the time. Wonder why he's being so apologetic.*

"It's okay. I don't mind. Rather do it now before I pick up any new patients."

"Great. Thanks," he says as he walks back toward the main work area.

Placing my work bag at my usual station and taking off my jacket, I quickly log in to the computer so I can see how many people are waiting to be seen. Good, only one. I head in the direction of room two and think to myself, *I just need to stay busy.* The busier I stay, the less likelihood of thinking about anyone who doesn't deserve my attention.

Over half way through my shift and I'm feeling like I can exhale. I still have five hours to go, but Nick is not on call today, and his office hours should be done. The likelihood he'll be here is slim at this point. Reaching up to rub my shoulders, I realize the strain of worrying about his arrival has caused my muscles to spasm.

"Hey, Kat." I hear from the hallway. I turn to see Justin. Justin Norton is a physician assistant with Nick's orthopedic practice. He primarily works with Dr. Morgan but will occasionally help with call if they're in surgery. He's worked here for about a year now and seems like a nice enough guy, but often acts like he thinks he has MD behind his name instead of PA.

"Hi, Justin. You have a patient down here?"

"Nah, I did earlier, but they were easy. Having a hip replacement done tomorrow, so I just had to put in some orders and make sure the hospitalist sees them to do pre-op clearance. Hey, you going to the fall PA conference in a couple of weeks? I don't usually go, but I need some extra continuing education credits, so I'm thinking about it."

"Yes. I signed up a few months back. I like to go to the local ones, so I don't have to pay to fly. Plus, this one's in Washington DC, so there'll be plenty to do before and after. There's usually a group of folks that hit a club. I'm looking forward to it. I haven't been dancing in a while." As I finish my statement, I bite my lip. I barely got to dance at all last weekend before Jake and Mel's dog knocked me over. To think, I was considering rewarding Murphy with a milk bone for giving Nick an excuse to dote on me. Now, not so much. But I guess it's not the dog's fault.

"Kat?"

"Oh, Justin, I'm sorry. What were you saying?"

"I just said maybe we could ride up there together."

"Oh, that's sweet. I'm actually going up a day early to do some sightseeing, but I'll look for you at the conference. Maybe we can sit together."

"Sure. I'd like that. See ya then if not before, okay?"

"Okay. See ya, Justin." I wave and get back to my computer. Maybe I can run and get something to eat, and come back. I can't remember the last time I got to get a meal while I was here.

Nick

Man, what a week. It's been nonstop since Sunday. Luckily, I didn't have to respond to any ER consults on Sunday, but when Gavin called to tell me Dad had fallen, I ended up in the ER for a whole different reason. Thank god he didn't break his hip as I initially feared. He'd broken his pelvis, which, although terribly painful, doesn't require surgery. He only needs pain medication and the use of a soft pillow shaped like a donut to take the pressure off of his pelvis when he sits.

There are times I forget how old my dad is, given how independent he's remained. He's pretty spry for seventy-seven, but that type of injury would be hard on anyone. I was so grateful Gavin happened to be there when the fall occurred. He said Dad just missed his footing and slipped. He seemed anxious about it on the phone since Dad wasn't able to get himself up off of the ground. I'd called for an ambulance from my cell phone and met them in the emergency room.

Gavin appeared to hold his own that evening. I was proud of him. He did all of the right things and seemed to keep it together during an otherwise stressful event. He stayed with us in the ER and never asked to see if his mother could come and get him. While we were waiting for Dad's x-rays to be read by the radiologist, I informed him I'd gotten his new phone put together but had run out so quickly once he called, I'd left it on the counter. He never indicated he was disappointed. There was nothing but gratitude in his facial expression. And the mystery over the item exchanged with the young teen in his neighborhood was at least partially solved. As he was waiting with me in the ER, the small slip of white paper fell out of his pocket, and I was able to read a single name on it before handing it back to him. He didn't appear alarmed that I'd noticed it. It simply read, Poppy Danforth. Not sure why that name seems to ring a bell, but there was nothing to indicate anything untoward was going down. There was no dime bag or cash. Maybe he's interested in someone new. In light of his care of my father, I'm not about to question this young man any further.

It was late when I took Gavin home Sunday night, close to eleven o'clock. He assured me he was usually up late, and his mother often wasn't home anyway. This makes me sad. Thanking him again for his help, I shared how I was going to count on him to help with my dad now if he was still willing.

I was able to contact the office manager for my practice and take Monday and Tuesday off to stay with Dad but had to reschedule most of my clinic patients for later in the week. I've been bombarded playing catch-up ever since. But I remember things could be far worse.

The upside to this crazy week was the limited downtime I had to think about Kat. I didn't receive any calls or texts throughout the week. There was a time or two I felt guilty about not reaching out, but I quickly focused on the very long to-do list in front of me and decided to give us a little more space. Truth be told, I hadn't recovered from my panic attack on Sunday. I knew if I decided to pursue something with Katarina, I'd have to be all in. I've already developed pretty strong feelings for her, and if this were to continue, there'd be no turning back. I just hope I still have that option once I get my head out of my ass.

As I pick up my briefcase and head toward the door, Ava approaches.

"Hey, Dr. Barnes, there's a patient of yours who's on the way to the emergency room. I know you aren't on call, but I wanted you to be aware. I'm sorry. I know you were probably going to check on your dad. It's the lady you operated on with the collarbone fracture recently. She said the area has turned red and become swollen. I'm worried it may be infected."

"Hell, if that's the case, I'll have to take her back to the OR. I was worried this could happen." The patient is a pretty heavy smoker and has a history of diabetes, increasing her risk of infection. "Thanks for letting me know, Ava. I'll head down there now." As I change gears to head to the emergency room, I contact the OR on the way to ask if they'll be able to add her on tonight or if she'll have to wait until the morning.

As I turn the corner into the ER, hanging up my call, I absent-mindedly head for the hallway where Kat usually sits before I realize what I've done. The minute I turn the corner, my mouth goes dry at the sight of her. I have a flashback to the first time I encountered her sitting here. My heart rate speeds up, and I instantly know I've made a colossal mistake this week. She's as gorgeous as ever in her black scrubs and white lab coat, hair twisted atop her head as only she can. I instantly want to go to her, hold her, get down on my knees and tell her what a dumbass I was for not calling. But instead, I blurt, "Hey."

She swiftly turns to look at me as if she's going to say hello, but her facial expression abruptly changes when she recognizes who's speaking. Her eyes narrow as she glares at me and immediately clamps her mouth shut. I watch as she turns back to her computer and resumes typing.

"Kat I..."

"Don't," she states emphatically.

"Kat, please, I need to..."

She turns in my direction, cutting off my conversation with her angry stare. I wait for her to speak, but instead, she turns back to her computer as if I'm not there.

Walking closer to her now, I try to reach out to her. Whispering so I don't garner any unwanted attention. "Kitten, I..."

"Don't. You. Dare. Kitten. Me." She says each word as if it is a dagger she's jabbing into my chest.

"Jesus, Kat, please hear me out," I plead.

She stands and looks directly at me. "I am working, Dr. Barnes. I suggest you do the same." Coming closer, I can almost smell her coconut body wash. She quickly snaps her index finger in my direction, forcing me to take a step back. "And this, here," she says, waving her finger back and forth between us, "is never going to happen, so let's just keep it professional, okay?"

Before I can utter a word in response, she's stormed past me. My heart feels like it's in my throat. My pulse is racing, and I start to feel sick. I'm having a panic attack for a whole different reason now. What did I think would happen after not calling all week? She wasn't a booty call. She's so angry. And I did this. I hurt her. I'm sure she thinks I'm like all the other dickheads in her life. *Maybe I am.*

Chapter Twelve

Kat

THE. NERVE. The absolute nerve of that guy. I can't believe he thinks he can just stroll into work and decide to throw me some half-assed apology. Heck, he probably only apologized because I happened to be here. I doubt he even meant it. By his shocked expression, I certainly don't think he came looking for me.

I'm still fuming, even though it's 9:45 p.m., and I only have fifteen minutes before my shift is over. I should be thrilled to be getting out of here. I've managed my time well today and shouldn't have to stay too late to finish my charting. Thank heavens I'm off tomorrow because if I had to come back in here and see him again, I'd lose it.

I'm about to grab my things and go when my phone buzzes.

10:20 p.m.
Nick Barnes
Nick: Kat, when do you get off of work? We really need to talk.

If he thinks I'm going to call him and listen to this dribble, he's lost his damn mind. There's no way I'm letting him smooth talk his way out of this. The self-absorbed asshole.

I manage to make it home in record time. I've been avoiding alcohol and sleeping pills lately, but I deserve a drink after tonight. I'm pouring a large glass of wine, taking a hot shower, and going to bed. Reaching down for my phone, I notice there are several message notifications.

10:30 p.m.
Nick Barnes
Nick: Kat, please. I can explain.

10:47 p.m.
Nick Barnes
Nick: Kat?

11:05 p.m.
Nick Barnes
Nick: I'm sorry. Please let me talk to you. If you won't see me in person, at least let me talk to you on the phone.

11:28 p.m.
Nick Barnes
Nick: I got scared. It isn't you. Well, it is you. You're beautiful and smart and I'm an idiot for not calling you. It was the best fucking night of my life, and I just got scared, Kat. Please talk to me.

Nick

Well, what's the saying? You've made your bed, so lie in it? I had this coming. I'm a thirty-five-year-old chicken shit, and I fucked up the best thing that's ever happened to me. It's been almost two weeks since I saw Kat in the ER. Two fucking weeks of texting her daily without a response. I'm surprised she hasn't blocked me. I'm sure it's because she knows the torture of not getting any reply is worse. Each time I hit send, I sit staring at the phone, hoping she'll send something back just to be met with continued silence. I even sent flowers to her home, but nothing.

I've honestly never had a panic attack before. But that shit is real. I was sweating, nauseated, my chest hurt. There were times I didn't think I could breathe. I wasn't worried I was having a heart attack because I knew exactly why I was feeling that way. I had the opportunity of a lifetime lying in that bed, and I simply walked away. If there was any doubt my symptoms were panic-related, it was made clear when she stormed off that day in the ER. All of those uneasy symptoms returned as I watched her walk away, hearing her voice in my head repeatedly saying, *'This is never going to happen.'*

If my father knew what I'd done, he'd be so disappointed. I'd finally found someone who could make me feel like my mother did for him, and I turned my back on her because I was scared. I ended up losing her anyway, so what did pushing her away solve? The worst part, I hurt her. For her to be that angry, I'm sure I hurt her. She didn't deserve any of it. She's so trusting, giving... I think about that night. How open she was with me. *She wore her hair down. For you, you asshole.* God, how am I ever going to get her back?

Sitting at my kitchen island on a Sunday afternoon, I stare out my window. I'm glad I don't have any plans, given my sullen mood. I've checked on Dad and am picking at a sandwich I've made but have no interest in when my phone buzzes. I notice it's a message from the answering service. I'm on call today, so I return the call right away.

"Good afternoon, Dr. Barnes. This is Margaret with the answering service. I have you on call today, is that correct?"

"Yes, Margaret, do you have a consult for me?"

"Yes. There's a patient at St. Luke's with a shoulder dislocation."

"Got it. Who am I asking for when I call them?"

"Ms. Katarina Kelly."

My heart skips a beat at the name, apprehension filling my chest. "Um, thank you, Margaret. I'll contact them now."

I'm sure the last thing Kat wanted to do was consult me. This shoulder reduction must be bad for her to call, especially knowing this is a procedure she can do on her own. She's needed my help with this once before. Some of these shoulders are tricky. It's no fault of the ER provider. But, to have to admit defeat, unable to get it back into place, and call me of all people must be awful for her. Jesus, this is why I shouldn't have let myself think about anyone I work with.

Wiping my sweaty hands on my pants, I dial the number provided by the service. As the phone rings, I can feel my chest tighten and pulse pick up. *Good lord, calm down.*

"Emergency room, this is Kat."

Clearing my throat quickly, I try to answer in as professional a tone as I can muster. "Hi, Kat, it's Nick Barnes. I got a message you needed me." *Really, Nick?* "I mean, you have a patient who needed an Ortho consult."

"Yes. There's a young patient in room thirty-four with a shoulder dislocation. He's done this multiple times in the past, and neither myself nor Dr. Silver can get it to stay in place." I notice her tone is clipped but otherwise professional.

"Well, I'm sure you've done all you can. I'm happy to come and see if I can reduce this in the ER or take him to the operating room if necessary." I'm trying really hard to play this game, to stay professional. But all I want to say is, please talk to me. I'll come in if you'll just talk to me.

"Thank you. It's actually Dr. Silver's patient, so I'd appreciate it if you'd advise him once you arrive. You two can take it from here."

Before I can reply, the phone has gone dead. "Fuuuck!" I scream into the air. Hanging my head in shame, I ponder how I could've let things get this bad?

On Monday morning, I'm in the office trying to manage my clinic patients. Normally, I'd have the morning off following a call shift, however, I'm still playing catch up after Dad's fall. I have three remaining patients who were rescheduled, then I'll be caught up. I also need to call the patient I saw in the ER yesterday with the shoulder dislocation to see how he's doing. It was difficult, but I managed to get the shoulder back in place and sent him home with an immobilizer. If it pops back out, he'll need surgery. I spent several hours in the ER, and Katarina avoided me the entire time. It was like a heavy weight in the air, knowing she was near, but I couldn't talk to her.

As I pick up the receiver on my office phone to call my young patient, I hear mumbling outside my door. I stop momentarily and notice it's Justin Norton and Dr. Morgan.

"Yes, in fact, I am." I hear Morgan say.

"I decided to go last minute because I need a few extra continuing education credits before the end of the year. I shouldn't have let it get down to the wire, but it's like November just snuck up on me," Justin replies, and laughter ensues.

"Well, I wish I hadn't signed up for this, to be honest. I have a lot going on at home, and giving a lecture at this PA conference is bad timing. I agreed to do this over the summer before my wife decided to invite my in-laws to stay with us for the week leading into Thanksgiving. I know it is just one lecture, but between the DC traffic, the late hour of the lecture, and the kids pushing her to the brink... well, let's just say I hope my wife is still speaking to me when I get home."

"I'm sorry to hear that. I know Kat and I are going to enjoy your lecture."

Suddenly my ears perk up. What? She's going with Justin? Boy, she moved on fast. He's not her type at all. *What type would that be, Nick, dickhead? You're right, you hold that title, not him.*

"I doubt you'll learn anything new. Hell, Justin, you could probably give the damn lecture," Morgan cajoles.

Trying to refocus on my task, I make my phone call and prepare to see the three patients who are scheduled before lunch. The patient doesn't answer, so I leave a voicemail. As I hang up the phone, I begin tapping my pen on my desk. I'm agitated and know what I'm about to do is not wise.

Stepping into the hallway, I see Dr. Morgan must've returned to his office. Walking over to his door, I stop, take a deep breath, and knock.

"Hey, come in, Nick. What can I do for you?"

"Well, actually, it's something I can do for you. I have a proposition for you."

Chapter Thirteen

Kat

It's Wednesday morning, and I've never been so glad to attend a work conference. It's still early, around eight o'clock, and I'm waiting at the Ashland train terminal for Olivia. She's agreed to a quick trip to Washington DC with me before returning home in time for her shows this weekend. Standing at the terminal reminds me of days gone by, traveling with Nate for a quick weekend getaway to visit Olivia in New York.

"Hey, girl. You ready to sightsee?" I hear behind me.

"Am I ever!" I reply, hugging my friend. "You have impeccable timing. We're about to board any minute."

"Well, good, I'm ready to get this show on the road. What'd you have planned today, my dear?" Olivia asks, digging through her purse for her ticket.

"Well, I want to walk around mostly. Just see some things on foot if it isn't too chilly. Then I want to visit the Spy Museum. I've never been and always wanted to go."

"Ooh, that sounds fun. We'll have to get a cab to take us there since we'll be in old town Alexandria. What made you decide to stay there?"

"It's where they're holding the conference. You know me and sleep. I just didn't want to have to take a cab during busy DC traffic in the morning to get to the conference on time. This way, I can just roll out of bed and head downstairs to the conference room."

Tapping her pretty blonde head, she smiles back at me. "Smart."

The line starts moving forward as people board the train. We grab a pair of seats and settle in for the journey, catching up on her most recent production and how wedding plans are coming. I know it's just a matter of time before the conversation turns to Nick, so I'm bracing myself.

"So, how's your mom and dad? And Rachel and the kids? You haven't mentioned them in a while."

"Yeah, funny you should say that. I think they're okay. I've been so busy lately and haven't stayed in touch. I find I need to pull away from them once in a while for my sanity. They've pretty much given up on asking if I'm ever going to date again. I often wonder if my mom thinks I don't like men. This morning I contemplated calling to let them know I'm working Thanksgiving."

"Wow, Kat, do you usually work it?"

"Yeah, I tend to volunteer to work Thanksgiving as often as I can since that holiday seems to revolve around, 'Kat can't cook… Kat can't find a man… Kat will never have kids… blah, blah, blah.'"

"Oh, honey, I'm so sorry you have to put up with that. They're your family. They should be more supportive."

"Well, it is what it is. I've just learned how to best handle them over the years, and avoiding Thanksgiving *is* the best way to handle them. I'll miss seeing Jenna and Luke, though. God, those two… they crack me up." Shaking my head at the memory of finding those texts will never get old. Then my mind drifts to Nick, and I instantly regret going there.

"What's that face for?" Olivia probes.

"What do you mean?"

"You were laughing one minute and then sullen the next. I've known you forever, Kat. You can't hide from me. What has you down?"

"Well, I guess we have some time to kill on this trip. I slept with Nick."

"Oh my god! What?! Why didn't you start with that?" she practically shouts.

I look about the rows of seats nearest us on this portion of the train and turn back to her. "A little louder, Liv. I don't think the squirrels out there could hear you."

"I'm sorry, Kit Kat. I'm just so excited for you. I need details! Was there a loin cloth involved in this hookup?" She giggles.

"No." I laugh back, surprised she remembers. "It was the most incredible night of my life." I beam at her knowingly.

"Oh. My. God. You didn't? You did? Please tell me you finally had an orgasm?"

I just nod, laughing at my inquisitive friend, who's now looking at me like a mom who just watched her daughter ride a bike without training wheels for the first time.

She turns in her seat, pulling her little legs up to her chest, wrapping her arms around them in excitement. "Kat, I need details here. How did this finally happen?"

"It was the night of Jake and Melanie's Halloween party. Their dog, Murphy, knocked me down as we started dancing, and Nick swooped in, picked me up, and carried me off to check on me. Once we were alone, we started kissing, one thing led to another, and…"

"And what. Oh my gosh, I can't believe you didn't tell me before now. He's so flippin' hot. Did it happen just once, or did he go all night?"

"Oh my god, Olivia. Yes, he's insanely hot. Yes, he probably would've gone all night, but after the second go-round, I think I went unconscious."

She wraps her hands animatedly over her mouth and looks up at me with her big blue eyes. Then I watch as she mouths, "How many O's did you have?"

I lift three fingers at her in response, and we both break into hysterical laughter.

"Then why isn't he accompanying you on this trip instead of me?" she suddenly asks.

"Um, because I only attract dicks, remember."

"What? Oh no, Kat."

"Yep! I woke up from the best night of my life, and he was gone. No note, no nothing. I made excuses for him and hoped for the best, but a full week went by and not a word. I didn't speak with him again until he saw me at work, and I could tell it was purely accidental. I tried to keep it as professional as possible, but I basically told him where he could stick it."

Olivia looks at me dejected, mirroring how I feel most days now. "I can't believe it. Really? I thought he'd be different."

"Yeah, me too, Liv. Me too."

We spend the rest of the day enjoying the sights of the nation's capital and a leisurely dinner at the Blackwall Hitch, a seafood restaurant with views of the Potomac near our hotel. Liv has an early morning cab scheduled to take her back to the train station, and registration for my conference will begin at the crack of dawn. We decide it's best to avoid drinking into the wee hours of the night and head back for a good night's sleep. I admit I sleep better knowing someone is there with me.

"Kat, thanks for inviting me to join you. This was so much fun." Olivia hugs me tightly at the door before heading to the lobby to await her cab.

"Oh, Liv. I love you so much. It meant the world spending yesterday with you."

Holding my hands in hers, she looks directly into my eyes. "Please promise me you won't let what happened with you and Nick close you off again." I look at her, stunned. *Why wouldn't I?* "Kat. You deserve that to happen again. Even if it isn't with him. God, I just can't believe he didn't at least try and reach out and give some excuse for why he left. You're right, he is a dick."

"I never said he didn't reach out."

"Wait, what?"

"Yeah, he's been texting for weeks. He even sent flowers. Ha, must have gone to the school of Gabe." I chuckle with indignation.

"Kat. Did you at least hear him out?"

"No. And I'm not going to, Liv. He had all week to reach out. He only apologized when he accidentally bumped into me at work. Then when I didn't swoon all over him like I'm sure all of the other women in his life do, he's been texting ever since. It's a game. I'm sure it's all about the challenge. I've been there. I know how these guys operate. I'm not giving in on this."

"Okay, Kat. I get it. You have to do what you think is best. I just wish it could've worked out."

"You and me both. But this is apparently the way my life is supposed to go. I'm making the best of it. I finally have a night I can replay in my head… I have a great job and great friends." I reach to hug her again, hoping this is the end of this conversation. "Now, I need to go and shower so I can make it downstairs in time. Text me when you make it home, so I know you got back okay."

Waving goodbye, I turn toward the shower. That conversation has churned up emotions I thought I'd managed to get over in the last few weeks. Something tells me the water coming from the rain showerhead won't be the only droplets spilling down my face. I need to get this out of my system before I head downstairs, so my mind doesn't drift if these lectures don't hold my attention.

"Hey, Kat." I feel a hand on my elbow as I am pouring cream into my coffee. These lectures are usually quite dull. The main thing keeping me going during these conferences is the coffee and its subsequent effect on my bladder. Looking up, I see Justin.

"Hi. How was your trip? Did you arrive last night or make an early start this morning?"

"Came down this morning. I had to stay late at work last night since I arranged this trip so last minute. It would've taken me twice as long in the DC traffic had I driven last night. Did pretty well this morning. Have you gotten a place to sit yet?"

"No, you?"

"Yes. I saved you a seat next to me."

"Wow. Thanks, bud."

We walk toward our seats and chat about nothing in particular. Most of the lectures are available via PowerPoint on our laptops and iPads. I've found I don't take many notes unless it's a subject I'm interested in or an area I need to brush up on. I usually just sit back and listen. Looking through the syllabus, I tell Justin, "It looks like the first part of the day will be pretty heavy stuff. Lots of cardiology and neurology lectures. I'm going to have to keep that coffee coming."

"Yeah. But it'll ease up this afternoon with pediatrics and ortho."

Announcements are made, the first speaker is introduced, and I settle in for a long day. Glad I decided not to drink too much with Olivia last night. After working for so long in our busy ER, it's hard to transition to sitting for long periods of time.

Finishing up a brisk walk outside to awaken me for the next lecture, I bend over to stretch my glutes and hamstrings as sitting in this chair all day has made me quite stiff. At least orthopedics is interesting. As I turn and make my way back into the hotel, I see Justin in the lobby and walk toward him.

"Hey, I'm just going to grab a soda to try and keep myself awake. I can't stomach any more coffee," I tell him.

"I know. I forgot what it was like to be in school, sitting in a chair all damn day."

We return to our seats, and I lean into him to show a picture of Olivia I'd taken on my phone in front of the Potomac River as the next speaker is introduced.

"I'd like to introduce our next speaker. He was a last-minute substitute for Dr. Morgan, and we appreciate his willingness to step in to support the PA community by providing a lecture on *Common Sports Injuries in the Adolescent Population*. He's an orthopedist with Dr. Morgan's practice in Richmond, Virginia, specializing in sports medicine. His primary focus in clinical practice is shoulder-related injuries. He graduated top of his class at the Medical College of

Virginia and went on to be the Chief resident in orthopedics at Johns Hopkins. Would you please welcome, Dr. G. Nicholas Barnes?"

My head snaps up from my phone as the audience greets the last person I wanted to see with a round of applause. *What. The. Fuck? Is this really happening?* I look toward Justin and whisper, "Did you know he was going to be here instead of Morgan?"

"I only just found out about it. I don't know much about him, to be honest. He kind of keeps to himself at the office. I guess it's just as well, Dr. Morgan had a lot on his plate and wasn't invested in giving his lecture."

I hear Nick clear his throat. As I look up from where Justin and I have our heads bowed together, whispering about this unwelcome change in speakers, I see he's focused on me. He's sporting a look of ire on his stupid sexy face. *What the heck? I'm a PA at a PA conference. You weren't even supposed to be here. Why're you looking at me like that?* It dawns on me this look could be about Justin.

As Nick opens his lecture, he's dolling out the charm. Giving the women in the front of the room his saucy smile. *Ugh!* He advises he's taken it upon himself to make copies of his PowerPoint since the last-minute change didn't allow his presentation to be uploaded into our syllabus. I watch as he coyly asks a young attractive woman in the front row if she wouldn't mind handing them out for him. I watch as she and many of the women in attendance all start to whisper and giggle. *Yeah, yeah. He's hot. But he knows it, which is not so hot. Plus, he's a dick. So, there's that.*

As he continues to speak, I try to tune out his annoyingly sensual voice and refuse to make eye contact with him. I hear several attempts at humor which, again, have the females giggling. I, for one, cannot stop my eye roll and don't care if he notices. Deciding to test out my theory about Justin, I reach over and lay my hand on his arm and lean into him. I try to think of something to say, but quite honestly, I'm just hoping to irritate Nick.

"Ms. Kelly. Would you mind coming up here to help demonstrate this particular test for everyone?" *What the heck? Yes, I mind. I guess that little move with Justin backfired.*

Not wanting to make a scene, I stand from my seat and make my way to the front of the room. As I approach, I continue to avoid making eye contact and turn toward the audience. He's supposed to be demonstrating a test, so I certainly don't have to talk to him. Suddenly, I notice he's crouched down by my feet.

"Ms. Kelly, would you mind having a seat in this chair so I can demonstrate the Lachman test?" He points to the chair behind me. "The Lachman Test is commonly used in orthopedic examinations to test for anterior cruciate ligament integrity." I watch as he lifts my skirt and places his muscular hands on my leg, rubbing slightly before moving one hand behind my knee as he demonstrates attempting to push it forward. After he's completed the explanation, I notice he continues to leave his hand behind my leg as he speaks, gently squeezing. *Jeez, this guy.* As he returns to standing, he places his hand on my left shoulder. I look up at him with a glare. He quickly turns to me and says, "Thank you, Ms. Kelly." *Ugh!* I'm almost as annoyed at him as I am myself for loving the feel of his strong hands against my skin, for relishing that spark, even for just a few moments.

The rest of his lecture is completed uneventfully. As he's the last one of the day, I begin gathering my things. I cannot wait to get out of here. He finishes speaking, and everyone claps, so I whisper to Justin. "Hey, I'm headed back to my room. I think a bunch of folks are going to the bar later. You want to meet there around 7:00?"

"Sure. I'll see ya there, Kat." Justin smiles at me, and I swiftly make my way for the door. Justin seems like a nice guy. He's a little stiff and full of himself but still nice enough. But I'm not interested in any man I might have to see at my job. Never again.

I get out of the shower, dress for the bar and pick up my phone, surprised Nick hasn't texted. I expected some effort to see or talk to me after coming up here to do that lecture. There's no way his being here is a coincidence. I apply my makeup and hope he's finally gotten the message. *I want nothing more to do with you.* Grabbing my room key, I place it in my cross-body purse and head for the door. I'm wearing dark jeans, a flowy top, and short black leather boots. I had a light snack in preparation for a few drinks tonight, but plan to deadbolt my door. *Wouldn't want to go anywhere. Good lord.* I haven't had any more episodes of waking in disarray since discontinuing the sleeping aid, so I'm leaning toward that being the culprit.

Spotting Justin at the bar, I walk over to him and start to speak until he leans back, and I notice none other than Nick Barnes sitting on the barstool next to him. *Are you freaking kidding me?*

"Hey, Kat. Hope you don't mind. I invited Dr. Barnes to join us for a drink?"

Uh, yeah. I do mind. I mind a lot.

"Ms. Kelly. It's nice to see you. Thanks again for helping me out this afternoon," he says, appearing sincere. He's wearing a starched white dress shirt, the top button undone to reveal a hint of the firm pecs beneath, the sleeves rolled up displaying his magnetic veiny forearms.

"Uh-huh." I'm so irritated, I cannot get anything else out.

"Can I get you a drink, Kat?" Justin asks.

I grab ahold of his arm. "Yes, please. Can I have a greyhound?" I feel like something tart will go along with my current sour mood, so the grapefruit juice and gin should hit the spot. I look around the bar and notice some other conference attendees and decide to take this time to introduce myself. I'm not normally this extroverted, but I have to step away before I lose it.

As I'm chatting with a PA from southwest Virginia, I feel a hand on my back. A frisson of current travels from my back to my groin, and I instantly know who it is. Looking over my shoulder, Nick has his mouth next to my ear. "Brought you your drink." Looking down, I notice he's holding my cocktail.

"Thanks," I answer flatly.

I suddenly feel an arm wrap around my waist, and I tense up. As I turn to say something, I realize it's Justin's. Normally, I'd politely withdraw myself from this situation, but I'm willing to put up with Justin if it'll keep Nick in his place.

"Some of the guys are headed to a club not too far from here. You interested?" I ask Justin. "I really want to dance."

"I'm not much of a dancer, but sure, I'll go."

"Great."

We head for the door, looking for a cab, and I notice Nick has saddled up to a few of the women from the conference. I try to ignore the irritation I feel at knowing I'm being quickly replaced as the target of his affection. They appear to be joining us on this trip to the club as they all stand and follow us toward the door. *Whatever. I can be the bigger person. Let him try his games with someone else.*

Nick

"Come on," Kat says to Justin, pulling him onto the dance floor. "I want to dance." "We Found Love" by Rihanna begins, and Kat starts to move. I lean against the bar nursing my drink, wishing like hell it was me out there. *I hate to dance, but I'd give anything to be holding her.* I excuse myself from this chick that won't stop talking and stroking my arm. It's my own fault. In my attempt to follow the group so I could stay close to Kat, I started chatting up the women who were in the audience this morning. But I can't seem to ditch this one.

"It was nice to see you, Katie," I say as I start to walk away.

"It's Kara."

"I'm sorry. Nice meeting you, Kara." I wave.

Walking to the edge of the dance floor where Kat is dancing with Justin, I stand trying to figure out my next move. She's in her element. I'm not sure why she even brought him out there with her. He's just standing there, putting his damn hands on her while she wiggles around in front of him. I can feel my jealousy getting the best of me. I look on as the chorus starts to build, and Kat suddenly lifts her arms above her head, throws her head back, arches her neck, and her body starts to shake, reminding me of the last time I saw this. *Holy hell.* I can feel my cock twitch at the memory. *No one should be allowed to see that but me.*

Kat opens her eyes and watches me as she's dancing, placing her arms behind her to pull Justin closer. As the song continues, I note Justin's hands begin to move. I'm getting to my breaking point. Standing with my hand in my pocket, about to break this quarter in half to displace my anger, I continue to observe this travesty unfold.

The chorus returns, and the music picks up, and Kat suddenly bends over in front of him.

That's it! I walk onto the dance floor, grab her arm, and tug her along behind me as I walk her over to the other side of the dance floor. Wrapping my arm around her before she can stop me, I put one hand behind her head and pull her against me, slamming my mouth over hers. The feel of her soft, warm mouth on mine temporarily calms my nerves. I need to get my shit together so she'll listen to me.

"Enough is enough, Katarina. I can't take this anymore. You need to let me explain." I feel her push against me, but I manage to kiss her again, sliding my mouth down her neck. Feeling a little moan escape her, I have renewed hope. "Kat, you have me by the balls. Please." I groan into her ear. "Come back to the hotel and talk to me." She pulls back from me a little, looking into my eyes. "I promise, if you hear me out and still want nothing to do with me, I'll leave you alone."

Crossing her arms across her chest, she hisses, "Fine." Spinning on her heels, she abruptly heads for the door. I follow behind her, keeping a safe distance, so she doesn't feel smothered. I don't need to risk giving her a reason to change her mind.

After getting the cold shoulder in the cab, the silence continues as we head to her room. I want to pick her up and hold her against the inside of this elevator. Remind her how great we are together. But I have a lot of groveling to do first.

The elevator doors open, and I follow along behind her to her hotel room door. As she swipes the key card through the slot, I hold my breath hoping she won't change her mind and send me away. She enters the room, stops, and turns to me with a serious look on her face. I stay in the hallway, awaiting an invitation.

"You coming in?" She hurls in my direction.

Walking in behind her, I look about the room for the safest place to have this conversation. I don't want to sit on the bed and have her think there's an ulterior motive for being here. Walking toward the desk chair, I pull it out and sit. I wait quietly while she sits on the edge of the bed and unzips her boots. Once they're removed, she looks at me blankly. "Well, say what you have to say."

Fuck. She isn't making this easy. "Where do I start?" I ask myself aloud.

"How about the part where you left without saying goodbye and then didn't bother to call or text until you accidentally bumped into me at work. If I was just an itch you wanted to scratch, you should've made that clear from the beginning. I'm making it easy on you. Just walk away. We're both adults. Let's agree to be professional around each other and chalk it up to a mistake."

My head is spinning. How do I get control of this conversation? "Kat." I wait for her to look at me, so she can see the earnestness in my eyes. "I made a huge mistake. I woke up and saw it was 6:22 a.m. and realized I was on call. I panicked. I tried to get home to shower and be available to respond if the service called but didn't want to wake you. I know how difficult sleep is for you."

"Oh, yeah. How do you know that?"

Shit. "Jake told me."

Wincing, she encourages, "Go on."

"I was in such a rush, I didn't think to leave you a note. I took one look at you before I left your house, and I started to freak out."

"Thanks. That's a real confidence booster." She rolls her eyes after hurling that statement at me.

"Kat. Please, let me finish." Pausing, I rub my fingers through my hair, trying to calm my nerves. "I've been afraid of getting too close to any woman since my mom died. I was sixteen. My mom and dad were the epitome of star-crossed lovers. I was grateful to have parents who loved each other so much." Stopping again, I try to compose myself. Talk of my mother always makes me restless. "After she died, my dad fell apart. It was awful seeing him so broken. I swore I'd never allow myself to fall for someone who could destroy me if they left. I don't want to end up the empty shell of a man he's become."

"But that doesn't make sense. You were married." She reminds me.

"That's what I'm trying to tell you. My divorce was messy, but not because I lost the love of my life or anything. I don't want to get into the details of my divorce, but… well, this is going to sound crazy."

She scrutinizes my statement with a questioning glare.

"Kat, I'm falling for you hard. I had a full-blown panic attack in my car leaving your house, wondering what would happen if I entered a relationship with you and you walked away." Stopping, I wring my hands, trying to halt the tremble. "I never felt that way about my ex-wife." I look at her, awaiting some glimmer of a reaction. Noting a blank stare, I continue. "After I panicked, I tried to get myself together. I wasn't even sure you'd consider a relationship with me. You'd told me you weren't in a good place for one. But before I could call you to explain how I was feeling, my dad fell, and I got sidetracked. He's seventy-seven and ended up with a pelvic fracture, and I suddenly had to focus on him and moving my patients around so I could have time off to be with him and..."

Unable to continue sitting so far away, I carefully approach and sit beside her. "Kat, there's no excuse. Please don't mistake what I'm saying for an excuse. I allowed the situation with my dad and work to occupy my time because I was afraid. I was afraid of how I was feeling and scared you weren't interested in seeing where this would go. I was equally afraid you'd want to try, and I'd get hurt down the road. I've kept tight control of my life for years, but you make me want to take a chance. Even though I already know I'll be left in ruins once you're gone."

Again, I turn to her and nothing. No hint of what she might be thinking. I decide to put all of my cards on the table. "Hell, Kat, if the last few weeks have been this miserable without you, what would it be like if we were together, and you left me?" I sit quietly, my head hanging, knowing I've laid everything at her feet. There's nothing left I can say. Looking at her face, I see tears falling down her cheeks. *What?* I move to sit at her feet, holding her hands in mine. "Baby, please talk to me." Sitting up on my knees, I wipe away her tears and can't hold back anymore. I lean forward and try to kiss the salty moisture from her delicate skin. "Kat?"

She reaches up to swipe the additional tears trailing down her cheeks. Looking at me with her red-rimmed eyes, she speaks softly. "Thank you for telling me this."

We sit silently staring at each other, both seeming to wait for the other to talk. I stand, attempting to return to sit by her side when she finally speaks.

"Goodnight, Nick."

Chapter Fourteen

Nick

Standing in the lobby awaiting the arrival of the elevator, I look down into my scotch. Still stunned by Kat's dismissal, I hope the burn of this pricey liquid can dull the pain. I left her room about thirty minutes ago dejected and returned to my suite. I didn't have far to go as my room is on the same floor. I felt a little lightheaded and remembered I hadn't eaten much today, so placed an order with room service. Deep down, I think my feeling ill is related to the sensation of my heart being ripped out, *but maybe a steak will help.* Waiting for the food delivery in the stifling silence of my room was driving me mad. Deciding to get a stiff drink, I headed for the bar.

As the doors begin to open, I contemplate whether I should down this drink and run back to the bar to ask for another. The offerings in the minibar do not appear strong enough to dull the ache in my chest. Deciding to push on, I enter the elevator nodding in greeting to the woman inside. As I push the button for my floor, I step back and lean against the wall behind me. I notice the woman has moved a little closer than I'd like, but I continue to stare into my drink. *There's no one else in this elevator, lady.*

Looking for answers in a two-finger pour of scotch, I reflect on the evening. I bared my heart and soul to Kat, and she dismissed me. Granted, she thanked me first but sent me packing, nonetheless. I know I hurt her, but I thought she might be willing to forgive me if she understood why I behaved the way I did. I don't blame her for being upset. She deserved better than the way I treated her. She deserves better than me.

I'm in a daze as the elevator doors open. Looking up to confirm it's my floor, I begin to step out when I see none other than Katarina standing across the hall. The sight catches me by surprise, and I notice she's eyeing the other passenger with me with a questioning gaze. I walk straight out to her, never looking back, so there's no doubt I'm alone. My heart clenches at the sight of her. The adorable girl is dressed in tennis shoes, black leggings, and an oversized gray sweatshirt that says, 'This is my Hallmark Christmas Movies Watching Shirt' with her hair in braids on either side of her angelic face. *Hell, I could eat her up right now.*

"Hi," she says quietly.

"Hi," I return.

I notice she's looking down at my drink. Feeling the need to explain, so she doesn't assume I left her to go trolling for some company like men on business trips are want to do, I blurt, "I needed a drink."

I watch a pained expression cross her features and wonder what she's thinking. She stays silent, and I decide I can't take this torture any longer. Shaking my head, I walk past her toward my room, resolving to take inventory of that damn minibar.

"Nick," she says, again so quiet I almost miss it.

Glancing back, I look in her direction but avoid making eye contact. She slowly walks toward me, and I hold my breath, bringing my eyes to meet hers. As she comes to stand in front of me with tears in her eyes, she says, "I'm scared too."

Before I can answer her, she's on her toes, wrapping her arms around my neck. Not wanting to spill this much-needed libation onto her, I swiftly wrap my free hand around her waist and pull her into me. Burying my face in her neck, I take a deep inhalation to make sure this isn't a mirage.

"Kitten, have you eaten?"

"What?"

"Did you eat dinner?"

"Um, I had a snack before I went to the bar." She continues to cling to my neck, both of us whispering our answers into the other.

"Will you have dinner with me? In my room? I promise to be a gentleman. I just don't want to let you go." I feel her nod into my neck, and I let out a hesitant laugh. Changing my position to tuck her into my side, I walk us back to my room. "Baby, I need to get my key card. Can you hold my drink?" She looks up at me, appearing confused. "Well, it's that, or you can get the card out of my pocket, but I'm not letting you go."

I hear a tinkle of laughter escape her as she reaches for my drink. Reaching into my pocket for my key, I swipe it and usher her inside. I walk us to the couch and pick up the phone. "Yes, I placed a room service order about twenty minutes ago. Could I add a bottle of your best red wine and a large Caesar salad? Oh, and can you add a berry and cheese plate for dessert? Thank you."

"Nick, you didn't have to do that."

"Well, I haven't eaten much today." I bend my head down to kiss her forehead. "I wasn't that hungry after our conversation, but I'm looking forward to sharing with you." I wink. "Can I fix you a drink?" I notice she looks at mine questioningly. "I needed something better than what was in the minibar." I shrug.

"I'll wait for the wine you ordered."

Again, I kiss her forehead, trying hard to restrain myself. I don't want to do anything to scare her away. "Kat?"

"Yes?"

"Thank you," I answer, looking into her eyes. I've never been more grateful for a second chance. I pull her into my lap. "Can I hold you?" I watch as she nods, a slight smile crossing her face. I wrap my arms around her and crush her beautiful body to me. I feel her pull back from me and reluctantly let her.

She looks at me, seeming nervous. "Nick, everyone I've ever dated has betrayed me in some way. And I mean everyone. I've avoided relationships because I can't bear getting hurt again. Then you come along. I tried to fight the way I was feeling. You already mean so much more than any of those others. I know if you hurt me, I'll never recover. Sound familiar?" she pauses, looking down at her hands briefly. "But I put it all out there with you, and you just left."

Overwhelmed with how much I already feel for this girl, I just nod, knowing what a coward I was. Knowing what a coward I still am, holding this secret back a little longer for fear of pushing her away for good. "Kat, I don't know what's going to happen. But I do know, for the first time, I want to try. I've never been as happy as I was that night of the party. It's hard to grasp. Wanting something so much, knowing it could destroy you." I cup her face in my hands, looking into her big brown eyes. "Can you forgive me? If you still aren't ready to date, I understand. I don't want to push you. But when you are, I hope you'll give me a chance."

Suddenly, she's throwing her arms around my neck, leaning into me. Caught off guard, I fall back with her onto the couch. I can hear a little laughter right before there's a knock at the door.

Kat

Rubbing my belly, taking a sip of some of the best Merlot I've ever tasted, I smile over at Nick. "Thank you. This was really good." He shared his steak, potato, salad, and bread. I didn't realize how hungry I was until he lifted that silver dome, and the succulent aromas spilled out. Grateful to be wearing such casual clothing, I'm suddenly aware he's still sporting suit pants and his starched white button-down.

"Do you want to get more comfortable?"

Nick raises a brow, smirking at me.

"I only meant I'm stuffed, but I'm wearing elastic." I pull at the waist of my leggings for effect. "You've been wearing those dress clothes all day."

"You don't like my clothes?" he teases. I can tell he's trying to be extra cautious, not saying or doing anything to make me feel pressured. I don't want him to walk on eggshells around me. Deciding to lighten the atmosphere, I draw my legs up underneath me on the couch and slowly crawl closer to him. As I approach, I sit up, reach for his dress shirt and begin to unbutton it. As I do, I notice his eyes are starting to sparkle. He jumps up from where he's sitting and bends down to pick me up. Holding me against him, my legs wrap around his torso as he strides to the bed. He carefully places me at the edge, and I don't miss the questioning look on his face. The 'are you sure this is okay' look.

Nodding, I continue to unbutton his shirt. I look up into Nick's beautiful hazel eyes. There's so much reverence in them. He reaches briefly to stroke my cheek, trailing his hand down to one of my braids. I barely get the third button undone before he reaches behind his neck and pulls his shirt over his head, and deposits it at the end of the bed. I instantly place my palms onto his pecs and glide them down his torso to his amazing abs. Sitting up to kiss his warm, rippled abdomen, I'm interrupted when I feel Nick bend down to my ear.

"Oh, you beautiful girl," he whispers, nuzzling my neck. "Will you stay with me tonight?"

Nodding slowly, I watch the broad grin that takes over his face. As I start to giggle back at him, I'm startled as he reaches for the hem of my shirt and pulls it over my head. Watching as he drops to his knees, he slowly removes my socks and then reaches for my pants. He peels them down my legs effortlessly, reminding me how skilled he is as a lover and how many times he's probably done this. Trying to focus on more pleasant things, I shift my gaze to his handsome face. I run my fingertips along the stubble on his jaw and smile.

"What do you want, Kat?" His voice is rich and raspy.

Beaming up at him, I answer, "I want you to take these off." Pulling at his suit pants.

"Yes, ma'am." I watch as he removes his shoes, socks, and pants. He places them carefully over the corner chair, along with his shirt. Turning to me, wearing the sexiest black boxer briefs, my eyes travel to the obvious bulge tucked inside.

"Is that for me?" I point and quickly withdraw my finger, chewing on my nail in anticipation.

"Only you, kitten." He walks back over to the bed, slowly

removes his briefs, and climbs onto the bed with me. "Can I take these off?" Playing with the silky black lace bra and panties I'm wearing.

"Yes."

Again, demonstrating the agility of a well-practiced lover, he reaches behind me and unhooks my bra with one snap of his fingers. As he slides the bra off of my arms, I hear him groan. He then moves to my panties, sliding his thumbs into the sides and carefully pulling them down my legs. He abruptly stops and stares.

"What?" Suddenly feeling vulnerable, I attempt to cover myself with my hands, but he stops me.

"You're so fucking beautiful, Kat." He lies down beside me, pulling me into him. Holding me close to his warm body as if he's found a lost treasure. No one has ever held me this way. I wrap my arms tightly around his neck, placing kisses on his cheek. Turning into me, he kisses me passionately. I welcome his warm, wet tongue. He stops momentarily to tug on my lower lip before sliding his tongue back in for another taste.

I'm suddenly aware of how wet I am, as we've been unknowingly grinding against each other as we kiss. He reaches down and grabs my leg, wrapping it around him as our hips continue to undulate. As I cling to his neck, he moves his strong hands to my buttocks and squeezes as he glides his large erect shaft against my aching pussy. No one has ever been able to get me as turned on as this man. I can barely stand the teasing any longer when I feel the head of his cock slide into me. My head drops back in pleasure, and he moves his mouth down my throat, licking and kissing. His hands continue to knead my backside as he thrusts his hard cock into me. "Fuck, Kat. You feel so fucking good."

My eyes spring open as I become acutely aware that we're having sex without any protection. "Nick!"

"What? What's wrong?"

"You're not wearing a condom."

"Shit." He withdraws quickly. "Sorry, Kat, I just got carried away. Are you on the pill?"

"Yes, but..." I don't want to ruin the moment, but one of us in this bed has a lot more experience in the sex department than the other, and I'm done making poor choices in this area.

"Kat. I haven't been with anyone but you. Since the moment I met you, I haven't been able to think about anyone else."

Stunned, I can't help but stare. *Is he serious?*

"I'm very careful. But I'd happily put one on if I had one. I didn't bring any with me. I never even contemplated this would happen."

"Really? You don't have one in your wallet or anything?"

"No. I'm not the player you think I am."

I've already had a pregnancy that happened despite two forms of protection. I can't not use a condom, even if I want to believe him. "I have one in my purse."

"What? What the hell, Kat? Were you planning on hooking up with Justin while you were here?"

"Oh, for god's sake, no. I found it in there when I was on the train. I'm sure it was a prank. Just the guys clowning around." I sit up, trying to figure out how to proceed. *This is kinda ruining the moment.* "It's from a strip club where a girl named Crystal works. She used to ride at the rescue squad Jake, Mel, and I rode with. I'm sure one of the guys thought me finding that would be hilarious."

"Well, neither of us is going to your room to get it like this." Disappointment at the reality of this situation begins to set in. "Hey, wait a sec..." I watch as he jumps out of the bed and walks quickly into the attached bathroom. As he returns, he is wearing a huge smile and waving a small dark foil packet in my direction.

As relief washes over me, I ask, "Where'd you find that?"

"I forgot I had one stashed in my toiletry kit." I'm trying not to think about that too long and remain grateful there's one available tonight. *This hot, sexy man just told you he hasn't had eyes for anyone since he met you. That has to account for something.*

He climbs back into bed, tears open the packet, and rolls the condom on before returning to our previous position. I wrap my legs back around his waist and enjoy the feeling of his rigid length sliding back inside me. He stops momentarily, just holding me against him and occasionally placing kisses along my throat. This time feels different from our first night together. It's unhurried, more intimate.

He's focused on kissing, and holding, and stroking me. It's not the untamed lust from before. It feels like a dance, our bodies learning our own special rhythm. The heat builds between us as he rocks into me. With every slide of his hard cock in and out of me, he strokes a fire within my core I don't want him to put out. Reaching up, he takes my hands and pins them above me. I can feel his pelvis strike my swollen, wet clit with each thrust.

"Oh, Kat. I can't wait to play out every fantasy I've had about you," he pants.

Intrigued, I push for more. "What have you been thinking about?"

"Oh, there are so many things. I want to fuck you wearing those black laced heels you had on at the Halloween party." He pants. "I want to see them up over my shoulders as I pound into you." I grin, picturing the image. Letting go of one of my wrists, he grabs them with one hand as he reaches down to pinch my nipple with the other. "I want to watch you suck my cock wearing that dark red lipstick you had on." He stops long enough to kiss my mouth again, moaning as I bite into his lower lip. Moving his mouth to my ear, he breathes heavily. "I want to eat your sweet pussy until you come all over my face." Picturing each scenario, I hear him groan as he's getting close to the edge. Unbelievably, I know it won't take much for me, so I consider whether I can take him over with me.

As he slowly and deliberately thrusts into me, I try to whisper-pant into his ear. "Would you like to watch me play with myself while I suck your cock, Dr. Barnes?"

"Oh, fuck, Kat." He drives into me, completely lost in the moment, bucking into me with a fury. With my hands pinned overhead, the sensation heightens in my groin. I can't hold back any longer.

"Nick. I... oh, god." I feel myself clench around him, my heart thumping wildly in my chest.

"Kat. Holy..." I watch as he arches his back, his abs rippling before me. Sweat trailing from his chest down the ridges of his abdominal muscles as he stills inside of me, emptying everything he has. As he collapses on top of me, I can feel the aftershocks of his climax... or is it me?

We lie there, wrapped in each other, hot, sweaty, and gasping for air but too tired to contemplate getting up. I watch as Nick rolls to the side, removes the condom, tying it in a knot, and placing it on the floor before returning to me. Rolling me away from him, he snuggles into my back, nibbling on my neck and murmuring into my ear. "Kat?"

"Hmmm?" I exhale.

"What's your favorite color?"

Giggling, I reply, "Blue. How 'bout you?"

"Same. What's your favorite movie?"

"*It's a Wonderful Life*. The black and white version. What's yours?"

Chuckling, he says, "*Boss Baby*." I jab him in the ribs with my elbow, knowing he can't be serious.

"What would be your perfect date?" he asks, giving me a tight squeeze.

"You'll laugh."

"No, I won't." Again feeling kisses along the nape of my neck.

"I want to eat Chinese food out of the containers."

"What?" He sounds confused.

"I watch movies and tv shows where people share a meal, eating out of white containers using chopsticks... there's something so casual, yet personal about it. Having a meal with someone like that. Ha, even Benson and Stabler did it on *Law and Order: SVU*. I've never had anyone I could sit and eat Chinese out the containers with before."

I feel him hug me a little tighter. Trying to reach up and cover my mouth as I yawn, I volley back, "What about you? You'd probably want to go bungy jumping or something."

"Nah. I'd just want to spend it with someone I knew really cared about me. Someone I had a connection with. Doing whatever made us happy." I feel him nuzzle my neck as he whispers, "Okay, that's enough for tonight. Go to sleep, kitten."

That's the last thing I remember as I drift away.

Awakening to a rustling noise, I open my eyes to Nick dressed in suit pants, his dress shirt, and reaching for his shoes. *Is he trying to leave again?*

"Where are you going? What time is it?" I ask, rubbing my eyes.

"Good morning," he whispers. "It's 5:45. I have to get an early start back home. I have clinic patients later this morning and you can never be sure of the DC traffic." He stands and walks over to my side of the bed. Kissing me gently on the mouth, he cups my face. "I'll call or text you later. I promise. Now, get some more sleep if you can. Stay until it's time to get back to your room to get ready for the conference. You don't have to be downstairs for a few more hours."

"I didn't realize you were only here for that one lecture."

"Yes, just the one. Now get some sleep, kitten."

I think about his statement, and it dawns on me how well I've slept when he's been with me. *I'm probably just worn out from the incredible sex.* "Okay," I reply, closing my eyes and slinking back down into the covers, inhaling his delicious scent. Feeling him kiss my forehead, I smile until I hear the door click shut. *God, please don't let this end like before.*

It's been a tough morning. My muscles are sore from yesterday's long day seated in these uncomfortable chairs, coupled with the delicious pounding my body took last night. I've turned off my phone as not to distract those around me but want desperately to reach out to Nick to ensure he hasn't had another panic attack on the way home. Justin has been stoic, not even mentioning the events of the club the night before. I appreciate this as I don't know how I could adequately explain what's been happening between Nick and I.

Lunchtime has finally arrived, and I go into the lobby to turn on my phone. There are unread text messages. I hold my breath and open the app.

8:15 a.m.
Nick Barnes
Nick: I miss you already

9:43 a.m.
Nick Barnes

Nick: I can't stop thinking about you

I cover my mouth to hold in a giggle.

10:17 a.m.
Nick Barnes
Nick: Can I see you when you get back?

11:38 a.m.
Nick Barnes
Nick: Did I tell you I miss you?

My heart skips a beat, reading these digital love notes. How could twenty-four hours look so different?

It's quiet in the hotel room this evening. It's been a long day of lectures, and I decide to order room service and turn in early. I lie back on the bed, taking in snapshots of the night before. Grinning, I sink into the downy covers wishing he was still here. I miss him. This is dangerous. I'm already wishing for another text, praying he won't ghost me again. He seemed sincere. He's not Gabe. He's not Gabe.

As if he's read my mind, my face cracks with the force of my smile as I witness my phone dance across the nightstand. Quickly reaching for it, I pull the cell toward me and click on the text.

10:17 p.m.
Unknown number
Unknown number: Attachment

Disappointment turns to dread as I click on the attachment, and there's a recording of Fall Out Boy playing "My Songs Know What You Did in the Dark." I don't understand. What does this mean?

Chapter Fifteen

Kat

I'm on the train headed south as my weekend away comes to a close. I should make it back home by 11:00 p.m.. It'll be a short turnaround for work tomorrow, but I've survived on far less sleep. Taking a sip from my water, I lean my head against the headrest and gaze out of the window. The train is more crowded than I expected for this time of day but being surrounded by all of these travelers makes me feel lonely. I've been on my own for so long, you wouldn't think times like this would bother me. Is it that I'm getting older or simply that I've done it so long I crave human contact? *Or is it Nick?*

I can't help but reflect on the unbelievable events of the last few weeks. The euphoric highs to the devastating lows. It wouldn't be unique to have to let dreams of a future with Nick go. I'd accepted my fate regarding relationships long ago. The novel thing in this scenario, beyond the ability to have a heart-pounding orgasm with another person in the room, is his honesty.

I don't dismiss the amount of courage it took to bare his soul to me in that hotel room. He'd been trying to explain for weeks, and I shut him out. I wasn't ready for any more head games. But this man managed to trade places with Dr. Morgan, come clean with me about having a panic attack, and share sincere heartfelt feelings of fear regarding a future together. What's more, he seemed to understand my worries for the same.

When Nick first revealed his reasons for ghosting me, I was in total protective mode. I've heard all the excuses. Gabe was a freaking master at deception. All I could do was acknowledge his words and try to guard my heart. But after telling him goodnight and sending him away, I showered and laid on the bed, considering his declaration. Was it impossible to believe someone else could bear the same scars? That he could be just as broken as I was?

Looking at my watch, I notice it's 9:15 p.m. I pick up my phone, deciding I can't put this off any longer.

"Hello?"

"Hey, Mom. I'm headed back home from a conference in DC and just wanted to let you know I won't be able to make it to Thanksgiving this year. I have to work."

"Oh, Katarina. I wish you worked in a doctor's office or something. I feel like you miss out on so much."

Yeah, if she only knew I requested to work. "I know. But this is where I'm called to be for now. Tell everyone I miss them, and I'll try to catch up closer to Christmas. You and Dad doing okay?"

"Yes. We're fine. Rachel said Steven hasn't been feeling well and will likely not come to Thanksgiving either."

"Wow. That's some flu if he knows he's going to be sick that far out."

"No, I think it's his back. It's from all of the traveling he does. Anyway, we'll miss seeing you. Please try to come for Christmas at least."

"I will, Mom. Give my love to Dad." Hanging up the phone, I exhale, having that monkey off of my back. I haven't heard from Nick most of the day, but I certainly don't want to become one of those women. I bite my lip, smiling at the thought of attending Thanksgiving dinner with him. Oh, if my mom thought Gabe was the cat's meow, she hasn't seen anything until she's met Dr. Nick Barnes. I love my mother, but let's just call it like it is. She'd be over the moon to have her daughter dating a successful surgeon. I can't help but laugh out loud at the thought. I can only picture her face. 'Mom, I'd like you to meet Dr. Barnes. He's an orthopedic surgeon at St. Luke's.' *Ah, he'd probably charm the pants off of her. All the while, fondling my lady parts as I try to scoop the mashed potatoes. Ha! You've got quite the imagination, Kat Kelly.*

Do I dare consider what it'd be like to embrace a normal romantic relationship with a guy like Nick? He's beyond swoon-worthy. Heck, the way he talked to me in the hotel room was the stuff my romance novels are made of. I'm pretty sure he's nothing like Gabe. Gabe would've never spoken of feelings or fears of the future. He was a used car salesman in his attempts to explain away his transgressions. But I fell for it. Maybe that's why I'm so worried about Nick's ability to pull one over on me.

Honestly, I think I knew all along Gabe was a scam artist but didn't want to return to a life alone. I've never thought Nick was a liar. Truth be told, I don't think he has it in him. He seems so genuine. I try not to think too much about some of the things he said to me this weekend. Yet, when he said he was more worried about my leaving than when he and his ex-wife split, I was shocked. How could this be? But, deep down, I know how. I feel it too. It doesn't matter that I barely know him. The attraction is unparalleled. As much as I'm trying to fight this feeling to protect myself, I can't. What's more, I don't want to. Why wouldn't I want to feel this way? He's worth the risk. And for the first time, I'm starting to think… so am I.

Flipping through my phone, I decide to listen to an audiobook for the remainder of my trip. Ah, a nice rom-com would be good. I quite honestly can't handle the drama of an angsty page turner in my life right now. I have too much of my own. Tucking my phone back into my purse, I place my earbuds in and lie my head back to enjoy the ride.

∼

I depart the train terminal looking for my car. That's one nice thing about these smaller terminals. There's no big, fancy waiting area surrounded by travel brochures and vending machines, but I can find my car quickly and head home. We made it back ten minutes early. When does that ever happen? As I pull my suitcase behind me, I can feel a vibration in my purse. I juggle my belongings to see if it's a call or a text. Seeing the pending message, I click on the green icon.

10:52 p.m.
Nick Barnes
Nick: Hey. We need to talk.

Chapter Sixteen

Nick

Since leaving Kat's side that morning in my hotel suite, she's never really been far from me. Throughout my drive, at work in my office, and home, with my lonely dinner, I think of her. I marvel at how much better food tastes with her sitting next to me. It's more than spending time with an attractive woman. She's gorgeous, but it's beyond her looks. Her company is... well, its delightful.

My mind trails back to that evening, and I recall how wonderful it was. *Well, once the groveling was over, and she gave me another chance.* I can't help but smile at the thought she might be willing to take a risk with us. I never want to hurt her like that again.

Looking down at my phone, rereading the text I've just sent, I know I've done the right thing, but at what cost? I probably should've said something earlier, but everything about our relationship has been a mess. You need to find the right way to bring up something as delicate as 'Hey, just thought I'd let you know we actually first fucked against a tree, behind a nightclub, not at your place. It was over a month ago. You just don't remember because zolpidem does some weird shit to you.'

Having this between us is making me crazy. I abhor liars. I don't want to be the very thing I detest in a relationship. Any relationship. But especially one with someone who matters. Keeping this from her is bad. She needs to know. I need to tell her right away. Beyond the impact on us, it's important to her general health and wellbeing for her to know and get a handle on it. *Yeah, that's what I need to lead with.* I can help her figure this out. Stay away from that pill and find another way to sleep. I don't want her to put herself at risk again, taking those pills. Even if she isn't getting enough rest. She seems to doze just fine with me. But then again, we've usually had marathon sex right before. *Think she'll buy she needs to have sex with me before bed each night, and she won't need the zolpidem anymore?*

I startle a bit, deep in my thoughts, as the phone begins to ring.

"Hello?"

"Hi. It's Kat." Her voice sounds hesitant.

"I know, kitten," I say, smiling into the phone.

"I'm sorry. You just have me a bit worried. I thought we'd talked everything out, and we were good. So, your text made me a little nervous."

As it should, I guess. "Yeah, I'm sorry. Where are you?"

"I just got to the train station. I'm heading home. Are you okay? Is your dad okay?"

"Yes. We're fine. I'm sorry to worry you." I pause, trying to find a way to make her less fearful. Unable to come up with anything, I continue. "Kat, I know it's late, but can I come over? I won't stay long. There's something I need to tell you, and I don't want to wait. But it needs to be in person."

"Um, okay. Sure. I should be home in about twenty minutes."

"Okay, see you then."

I hang up the phone and know I've probably worried her. I shouldn't doddle, as she'll most likely grow more anxious the longer she frets about this. I grab my keys and head toward the car. *Please, Lord, give me the right words to say to her tonight.*

~

"Hi." Katarina greets me with a concerned expression, hair up in a high ponytail, wearing jeans and a gray sweatshirt bearing the logo of her medical school. Her shoes are off, and I can see bare feet and hot pink nail polish on her toes. God, even her toes are adorable.

"Hi." I step into her foyer and grab her for a hug. I need to comfort her as much as myself right now. Giving her a light peck on the cheek, I take her hand. "Can we sit down?"

"Sure." She looks up at me, eyes wide. "Nick, you're scaring me a little."

I grab her to me again and whisper in her ear, "I'm sorry, kitten. I don't want to scare you." Placing another kiss on her scalp, I pull her toward the couch, so I don't get distracted by her pained expression. I sit down, trying not to crowd her or sit close enough where I'll want to touch her while we're talking. I realize she may need space to fully digest what I'm telling her once I drop this bomb on her. I'm going to watch her closely and follow her lead on this. Taking a deep, calming breath, I decide I need to simply dive in. There's no other way.

"Kat. First, I need you to know how much I care for you. I can't stand anyone who lies or hides things, and I don't ever want to have a relationship with you where we can't be open and honest with one another." I look to her to make sure she agrees with me before I press on.

"I feel the same way," she responds cautiously.

"I need to come clean about something." I watch as she pulls back from me a bit, wrapping her arms around her chest. "There are no other women or anything. I'd never ever do that to you. I meant it when I said you've been the only woman I could think about." I notice she relaxes a bit.

Taking another inhalation, I continue. "I thought the first time we were intimate, you were just a real cool customer. That sex was pretty casual for you." I watch as a look of consternation appears. "But when we had sex after the Halloween party, and you said it'd been a long time, I was confused." *Great, man, try to prevent being a liar by being a liar. You knew full well what the score was.* "Because we'd already been together. Behind that club. Up against that tree."

I stop and take her in. Her face going pale. Her hands starting to tremble. She appears to be in shock.

"Kat?"

"I don't understand."

"Please, baby. Try not to get upset. I'm here, and we're going to figure this out." I pause for a moment, trying to think of the right words to say. "Jake mentioned in passing one day in the physicians' lounge that you've had a long history of poor sleep, just as he has. He mentioned he'd given you some zolpidem. I didn't think much of it at the time, but later in a conversation, he brought up how he'd done some *weird shit*," I use my fingers to make quotes around the 'weird shit,' "on sleeping pills, and I laughed it off." I watch as she sits a little taller now, her concerned facial expression demonstrating her thoughts.

"Kat, I brought up that night a time or two, and there was no recollection on your part. Once, you actually seemed shocked when I mentioned it. I started to wonder if, instead of being a forgettable lover that night, you might've had memory issues related to using a sleep aid. Like Jake did. The night at your house, when you said it had been a while... well, I was pretty sure that confirmed it."

I hesitate, allowing this information to sink in before moving on. By the look on her face, her mind is reeling right now. "Kitten. That night, against the tree... that was the hottest, most incredible night I've ever had. I couldn't stop thinking about it. I was so disappointed when I saw you again, and you weren't swimming in the same afterglow. I didn't know you well and thought, maybe that's just how you roll. I didn't want to seem like a clingy stalker, so I didn't bring it up. But I couldn't forget it. I'll never forget it."

"Please. Stop!" I look up from my reverie and see tears are pouring down her beautiful face. I try to reach for her, and she swiftly jerks back.

"Kat. I don't want to hurt you. Honestly. I want to help."

"Well, stop telling me about how you'll never forget a night I can't remember. That this crazy chick you fucked against a tree can't even remember being there!" she practically shouts, burying her head in her hands.

Fuck. I only wanted her to know how special it was. But this poor girl is wrapped in her own turmoil right now. "I'm sorry. I know this has to be incredibly hard for you. Kat, I don't want you to take that stuff anymore... the zolpidem. I'm sure it's causing you to do things you wouldn't otherwise. I only mentioned how much that night meant because I don't want you to have any regrets about something you had no control over." I can't take it anymore. I have to touch her. Grabbing her shaking hands in mine, I continue. "We're going to figure this out. We've got this."

I watch as she shakes in front of me. *God, what do I do?* "Kat, what can I do? Tell me. I'll do anything to help."

"So, you knew this on Halloween night? When I said to go slow... that it'd been a while for me?"

"Yes."

"But you didn't say anything."

"I wasn't sure what to say. I was still trying to figure it all out." The guilt is now boring a hole in the pit of my stomach. *That's it, lies on top of lies, Nick.*

"Had you figured it out when you came to DC?" Her eyes flash up to me as if she's questioning someone on the witness stand. I can feel my heart rate pick up again. *Don't be a liar, Nick. Just say it.*

"Yes." I gulp in more air. "Yes. I'd figured it out by then." I watch as she again covers her sweet, tear-filled face with her hands. My eyes are drawn to that same pink polish painted on her fingernails. "But I was more concerned with getting you to hear me out. It wasn't the right time to bring it up."

I watch as she starts to open her mouth in retaliation, and I hold up my hand abruptly. "Kat, before you say anything. I admit I should've told you before. I was so caught up in my own grief at losing you, I chose to attempt to repair any chance at a future we had before telling you. I wanted you to see you could trust me. To believe what I was saying was true. Fuck, Kat, I'd give anything if I didn't have to tell you this. I needed to find the right time to say it."

I pause momentarily, hoping she'll drop her defenses and give me a chance. "If you want me to get down on my knees and apologize for sleeping with you again before I told you what I thought was happening, I will. But I won't take back that night with you. We needed to be together. I needed to focus on you and be clear about how I felt about you. I needed you to see how much you mean to me. It wasn't anything underhanded. And it was magnificent. I've never made love to anyone like that before. Only with you."

I continue to watch as she takes everything in. "Please don't push me away. I know this is a lot to contend with. I'm here. I'm not going anywhere. It might help to talk to Jake about this too. I think both of you should put that stuff away and not look back. It's too risky."

We both sit silently, me watching her like a hawk, her staring at her hands. This seems to go on for an eternity.

"Nick." She sniffles, wiping away her tears with her sleeve. "I appreciate you telling me this. Really. I know this wasn't easy. I wouldn't trade what we've had together either. I only wish I could remember the first time…" She wipes at her eyes with the back of her hand, a strangled sob escaping her. "I've started to suspect the zolpidem was the culprit for a while now. I stopped taking those pills weeks ago. But I'm concerned this isn't just a memory thing."

I look up at her, not wanting to interrupt but trying to understand what she means.

"I thought I was having weird dreams. I'd have visions of things occurring in my sleep but would sometimes wake up feeling like they'd really happened. The images were so vivid. Other times I'd wake up wearing clothes I had on in my dreams." She pauses to recover her face with her hands. My heart breaking at the sight of her. Her body continues to shake as she weeps. "Now I don't know how much of what was happening was in my mind and how much was real."

I can't sit back anymore. I grab her into my arms and hold her tight. Her body wracked with sobs. Rubbing my hand up and down her back, I try to comfort her. Holding her for what seems like hours, my heart cracks a little more the longer I sit with her. Slowly, the sobs become whimpers. The whimpers become sniffles.

"Nick?"

"Yeah, baby?"

"I appreciate you being brave enough to tell me. I know this wasn't easy."

Kissing her hair, I keep holding her. I need her to know there's no judgment. That this doesn't change anything between us.

"Please don't be upset. But I think I'm going to need some time to figure this out. I have a counselor I've started working with. I'll call him tomorrow."

I pull back and look directly into her eyes. "Good. I'm glad. And I understand. Take whatever time you need. Just don't push me away, okay? I'm not going anywhere. I'm here, whenever you need me."

She nods back to me, and I place a small kiss on her cheek. I hate the thought of leaving her. "Are you sure you're going to be okay?" I ask as I stand. She offers a small nod, and I have to take her at her word.

As I walk out her doorway into the cool night air, I carry the added weight of my own fear. Fear that she'll let this take her down and won't let me in to help fix it. I know beyond a shadow of a doubt, this woman means more than anyone I've ever encountered. If she needs time, I'll give it to her. I just hope this doesn't break both of us.

Chapter Seventeen

Nick

Thanksgiving morning has arrived, and I awake struggling with my feelings. It's been four days since I saw Kat. I've sent short texts letting her know she's in my thoughts, but otherwise, she's been fairly silent. She did say she'd be working Thanksgiving. She seems at home in the ER. Maybe that's the best place for her today. Hopefully, one day, we can get past all of this drama, and I can learn a little more about her. Like her family. Are they in the picture at all? How does she normally do holidays?

Getting up, I contemplate my day. I invited Gavin and his mother to join Dad and me for a Thanksgiving meal. Dad loves to cook, and he and Gavin have really bonded. Gavin's mother will be the unknown in this situation.

I trudge down the stairs to greet my coffee which I could smell brewing from the second floor. Thank goodness I set the timer last night. There's something to be grateful for. Sophia never claimed ownership of the Cadillac coffee brewing station. It's been my faithful companion in this now bachelor pad, and I wouldn't want to face a day without it. I pour the fragrant java into my mug and head back to my room to shower.

I pre-ordered and picked up everything my dad said he needed from the grocery store to bring with me. I'll head to Dad's and help get things started after I've showered and dressed. Gavin and his mother won't be expecting me until noon.

"Hey, Dad. I've got the groceries. I grabbed the turkey first so we could get it in the oven."

"Hey, Nick. Happy Thanksgiving, son." I notice a slight wince on his face as he comes in my direction.

"How's the pain, Dad? Do you think you're up to this today? Thanksgiving isn't like the old days. We could just go out to eat if your pelvis hurts."

"Nah. If I take some breaks, I'll be okay. I took some Tylenol. We'll just get Gav to help clean up. It'll all work out."

"Okay. Just don't overdo it. I'm going to get the rest from the car."

Two hours later and the kitchen is surprisingly busy for just the two of us. I frequently feel there are three of us in this room and today's no exception. I'm sure my mother is here. This was her holiday. Sure, Christmas was special, but my mom could really cook. Plus, she was always full of gratitude. Every day of the year, but especially Thanksgiving. We'd watch the Macy's Thanksgiving Day parade while she began preparing the big meal. She'd occasionally pop in to see if she recognized anyone on tv and provide samples for us to taste. I tear up a little, remembering all of the little things I'd previously taken for granted.

"You okay, Nick?" My dad is always alert to my emotions. Wiping a tear away, I point the knife toward the chopping board, conveniently blaming it on the onions. Dad isn't buying it and laughs. "I know. I miss her too."

"It's terrible, Dad. How much you realize you had but didn't appreciate until it's gone. I wish I'd told her more… how much I loved all of the little things."

"She knows, Nick. I feel her here with me all the time. If I didn't think I'd see Lydie again, I'd crumble. But I know she's proud of you. For the man you've become and what you're doing with Gavin."

"I don't know, Dad. I've made a lot of mistakes, but I feel like I've wised up in the last few months. I get what's really important." Hesitating a moment, I decide to put it all out there. "I do want it all."

"Nick, does this mean what I think it means?" he asks with hopeful exuberance.

"Dad. I laid it all out there with her. If it's supposed to happen, it will. I'm going to keep trying. I can't make something happen that isn't meant to be. But she has a lot on her plate right now. So, the ball is in her court. But I'm still hopeful."

"I'm really proud of you, son. I know that wasn't easy for you. But you mark my words. Nothing fantastic ever came easy. Ha, look at you. We'd all but given up on having you."

"I know." I smile back at him. "Not to change the subject, but how's your lady friend doing?"

"I actually haven't seen her in a while. She usually only comes one Wednesday a month, but with Thanksgiving, that got turned around. Maybe next month."

"You sure there's…"

"No, Nick. Now open the oven for your dad so I can try to find room for the stuffing."

Arriving at Gavin's apartment, I notice I'm a few minutes early. I wonder how the day will go with his mother along. I've only had a few brief interactions with her. As I park the car, I reach for my phone and send him a quick text letting him know I'm waiting for them.

11:59 a.m.
Gavin
Gavin: We'll be right down.

Reading this text puts a smile on my face. Not sure why, but knowing he has a phone he can use makes me proud. I'm glad I could make him feel more like a typical teenager. At least in this regard. I look up to see the two are approaching, and I open my door to greet them. Gavin's mom is wearing skin-tight jeans and a silk blouse with a very vibrant print. She's adorned in several gold necklaces, bangles, and has multiple rings on each hand. I notice her blonde hair is pinned up with several clips.

"Hey, guys, good to see you. Happy Thanksgiving."

"Same to you, Nick. I made a cherry pie. Gavin's never cared for pumpkin," Gavin's mother says, smiling at her son.

"Well, that sounds great. Let me take that and put it in the back. Gavin, open the door for your mom," I encourage.

"Good grief." I hear him mutter as he reluctantly opens the front passenger door.

As we pull out of the apartment complex, I look in the rearview mirror and notice Gavin's deep into his phone. I decide to give him a break, as he is late to that party. I attempt to make small talk on the drive.

"So, thanks for joining my dad and me this year. It's usually a pretty quiet holiday for us. He loves to cook, so he'll probably have enough food for ten of us. I should've told you to bring some Tupperware to take the leftovers home." I notice this gets Gavin to look up briefly.

"Well, it's nice of you to include us. We've never made a big deal of the holiday since it's just the two of us. I try to make something a little nicer for dinner, but I don't have any family nearby. Sometimes I go to the bar to work in the evening. With football on, it tends to be a busier night with great tips. I think people are more generous knowing you're working on a holiday." I look over at her while she's speaking and notice she's quite attractive. Her light blue eyes seem young, but her skin and hair bear the brunt of a hard life. I'd never ask, but looking at her here, she appears to be my age or a little older. From a distance and prior quick introductions, she seemed much older.

We travel the distance to my father's, making casual conversation. I learn she never attended college. She was never married. She had a few boyfriends along the way, but 'no one who wanted to take on a wild little boy,' as she put it. I try to peer back at Gavin on occasion as she speaks to see if anything she says affects him, but thankfully, he seems engrossed in his phone. It's apparent Gavin's mom and I have very little in common except Gavin. She does seem to care a great deal for him. I'm sure she's doing the best she can.

As we pull into my dad's driveway, I ask Gavin to grab the pie and I watch as his mother steps out of the car with her mouth hanging open.

"Wow. Is this where you grew up?"

"Yes, why?"

"It's just beautiful. It's like something out of a fairy tale. The landscaping is gorgeous."

"Ha. Well, you can thank Gavin for that. He's been helping Dad on the weekends. Once you come in and meet Dad, I'll show you around back. It's pretty spectacular what he's done with the place over the years. My mom loved her roses, and there's a lake that backs up to the property."

"That's amazing. You had a great childhood here, I bet."

"I did." I'm again reminded today of just how good I had it. I'm also aware I know nothing of her upbringing. It doesn't sound like she may have had it as well as I did. She said she had no family nearby. Was that by choice?

Walking inside the house, I'm hit with the overwhelming aroma of Thanksgiving. I can smell the turkey and something with a hint of cinnamon.

"Nick, Gavin, who's this pretty lady?" my dad greets in his usual charismatic style.

"Hi. I'm Shelly. Shelly McReedy." I watch as she reaches out a slender hand to my father.

"Nice to meet you, Shelly. I'm Garrett. I'm thrilled you two could join us."

"Well, I'm happy to be here. Is there anything I can help with?"

Grabbing Gavin's arm, I decide to relax in front of the television for a bit as my dad puts Shelly to work. He'll talk her ear off, I'm sure.

"You want something to drink?" I ask, finding the remote and flipping through the channels, looking for the game.

"Got any beer?"

"Sure," I answer and walk toward the kitchen. I can see him standing up a little taller. I turn back to him before stepping into the kitchen. "But you can have a coke and a smile." I wink at him. Shaking his head, he plops onto the couch.

Two hours later, we're all stuffed and rubbing our stomachs. My dad completely overdid it and has fallen asleep in his recliner. I'm sure he'll feel the after-effects of his active day tomorrow. Gavin and Shelly rinse dishes and place them in the dishwasher as I collect the containers Dad directed me to use for leftovers. I manage to place enough food in to-go containers for Gavin that he and his mom should enjoy leftovers for days. All and all, it hasn't been a bad day. There was only one thing missing.

Kat

It's been a calm day in the ER. The majority of the patients I've taken care of today have either had flu-like symptoms or a kitchen-related injury. I'll forever be afraid of using a mandolin to slice cheese, as these seem to be some of the worst lacerations that present each holiday.

It's four o'clock, and I have six more hours to go. I've been snacking on food items from the nurses' lounge all day, but I'm getting hungry for a real meal. The cafeteria's options are not at all appealing. Why would they serve stuffed peppers on Thanksgiving? Suddenly, I smell something amazing and notice a covered dish is sitting in front of me. I look up to see Jake's smiling face.

"What incredible cuisine is tucked away in this container?"

"Ah, you know Mel. There's probably enough food to feed you for a week in there. She said to tell you Happy Thanksgiving, by the way."

"It's a shame you had to work. I'm sure she made quite the spread."

"Oh, she did. I pulled a Kat and put myself down for the evening shift on purpose." He gets a little closer, whispering, "Don't tell, but I get a full belly without any clean-up duty."

"Ah. I've got your number. Poor Melanie."

"Poor Melanie? You should feel sorry for the kids. I bet Mel has her feet up reading a book right now."

"Hey, now that you're here. Do you mind if I run up to the NICU to check on Katrina and Grace? I brought Katrina a pie to take home. Although from talking to the nurses up there, I don't think she goes home much."

"Sure, Kat. Take your time. When you get back, you should eat, though. Things could pick up once dinner hour is over, and people start drinking too much and fighting with their family."

"Ha. You're right. I'll be back soon."

As I walk to the elevators, I reflect on my week. I've tried to settle down a bit about Nick's revelation. I try not to ponder what I could've been doing without my knowledge under the influence of the sleeping pill. I made an appointment with Dr. Miller, but he couldn't fit in an emergency visit around the holiday. I'm sure his business picks up this time of the year. I know I tend to get a lot lonelier and more depressed once the holiday season has started.

I haven't seen much of Jake since my conversation with Nick Sunday night. I honestly don't want to bring up the craziness in my life while I'm here. Maybe I can make arrangements with Jake to meet up later in the week so we can talk.

Coming around the corner of the NICU, I see Katrina as I approach the nurses' station.

"Hi, Kat. I can't believe you came to visit us on Thanksgiving."

"Sure, Katrina. I brought you a pie. Did you get anything to eat?"

"Yeah. I get all of my meals here now. I've never eaten so well."

I grimace, realizing I've found something to be grateful for. While I complain about the offerings in the cafeteria, this sweet girl is just thankful to have a warm plate of food. I never question where my next meal is coming from, just whether I'll have time to eat it around the chaos that is the ER. I need to be a lot more grateful for the basics I have every day. The other stuff will work itself out. It just has to.

Thirty minutes later, I've returned to the ER, and Jake is sitting where I left him. I tell him I'm going to grab some plastic utensils when I notice a stretcher come through the ambulance bay doors with a small child strapped to it. I'm immediately drawn to the sweet swollen, red face of the child who appears to be kindergarten age.

"Hey, Huggie, who do we have here?"

"Hey, Kat. This is Caden. Caden's mom thinks he must have gotten into something in the kitchen made with peanuts. He has an allergy, and they don't keep nuts in the house, but they had guests over who brought treats."

Caden's mom is holding the child's hand, looking fearful. "I gave him the EpiPen at home, but I didn't want to take any chances."

"No. Of course. You did the right thing. They'll get you and Caden settled, and I'll come to check on you in a bit."

I walk to the nurses' lounge to retrieve my plastic utensils, knowing that most likely we'll be watching Caden for the next few hours to ensure his symptoms have improved and it's safe for him to go back home.

Walking back to where Jake is seated with my care package from Mel, I notice Donovan has arrived a little early for the night shift. He's holding a plate of something and leaning over the nurses' station counter talking to Jessica. *Hmm, she always seems to smile a little brighter when he's around*, I think to myself. Man, I'd give anything if somehow that Ashley chick wasn't in the picture, and these two could make a go of it.

Jess has been on and off again with Holt for over a year, from what I hear. But she can do so much better than that fire academy playboy. She says his behavior is all for show, but I think he still has a lot of growing up to do. I'm not sure he's mature enough for someone like Jess.

As I approach the physicians' workspace, I see Jake sitting there and remember I need to talk to him about this crazy shit with the zolpidem. As that thought comes to me, I practically slap myself on the head. *You need to get your own situation settled and stop worrying about anyone else.*

"Jake, you got any time free next week? I wanted to see if we could grab a drink. I need to talk to you about something, but I don't want to do it here."

"Sure, Kat. I'll look at my schedule and text you. Is that okay?"

"Yeah."

"Everything all right? Did you hear back on the test results yet?"

"No. Not yet. I'm surprised they take so long."

"Can we talk at the house?" he asks with an odd expression.

"What do you mean?"

"You're still coming over Sunday, right? It's our yearly Friendsgiving dinner. Mel has spent more time planning that than she did today's meal."

"Oh, I'd almost forgotten about that. Sure. But I'd rather talk just you and me. Not make a big production. Do you think we could sneak away for a bit to talk without Mel getting upset that she's having to play hostess all by herself?"

Waving a hand at me, he chuckles. "She loves every minute of it. If we have to, we can run to get whatever she forgot. She always sends me back to the store at least twice."

Laughing along with him, I can easily picture that. I'm usually distracted by all of the chaos. They have a large group of friends, and every year I never know who'll be in attendance.

"Kat?"

"Hmmm?"

"Mel wanted to invite Nick, but I told her not to. At least, not until I talked to you first."

Feeling a bit forlorn about Nick, I try to hide the sadness I'm feeling. I want so much to go to him, but I need to take care of some of my baggage first.

"Thanks, Jake. Not this year."

"Oh, so maybe next year?" he jokes, sounding a bit snarky.

"You never know. If I can finally get my ducks in a row, I think there could be something there."

"Well, that's something I can be thankful for!" He beams. I just shake my head at him, giggling. "What? I'd be thrilled to see the two of you finally get together. Not to mention, I can probably parlay that into lots of future babysitting."

"How do you figure that?" I snort.

"Well, since Mel and I have secretly been trying to get you two together for months, that should get us some type of commission on the deal."

"Unbelievable. And to think I thought you were—" I suddenly feel my pocket vibrate and reach down to grab my phone.

9:05 p.m.
Nick Barnes
Nick: I'm most thankful for you.

Chapter Eighteen

Kat

"Kat's here!" Ruby and Seth run screaming down the hall.

"Kat, come on in the kitchen. I could use your help!" I hear Melanie bellow from down the hall. Sunday night at the Harris house and Friendsgiving is in full effect. The house is full of laughter, and aromatic blends of citrus, sage, and thyme permeate the home.

"Hey, Mel. I brought a bottle of Pinot Grigio. What do you need me to help with?"

"Thank god, reliable help. All Jake does is eat half of it and sneak out. Can you help with putting together the appetizers? That tray of bruschetta needs to have the tomato and herb topping on each with some shaved parmesan. That tray needs pesto and grilled chicken placed on the crackers, and the last station there is for building the cherry tomato, mozzarella, and basil skewers. Once they're all together, lay them here, and I'll drizzle them with balsamic vinegar." Melanie turns from barking out orders like a drill sergeant and heads for the oven. As she opens it, the bouquet of herbs and lemon scent the air.

"Oh my god, Mel, you do this to me every year. I'll be so full on your amazing appetizers I won't have room left for the main course. I need to start packing Ziplock bags to carry everything home."

"Well, by the looks of it, you need to eat as much as you want. You've lost weight, Kat. Is something going on?"

I admit I haven't had much of an appetite lately. The stress of learning I've been doing things I'm unaware of has made me both anxious and depressed. I need to find a way to get Jake to the side so I can talk about my recent conversation with Nick. "I'm okay. Just a lot going on right now."

"I was hoping after Halloween, things would be looking up." I look over to Mel and see she is waggling her eyebrows at me. She starts to whisper yell across the kitchen island, "Holy shit, Kat, the way he picked you up and carried you off. It was the stuff of romance movies."

"Ha. Yeah. It was an epic night." I can't help but blush.

"Are you two doing okay?" She seems to tread carefully with this question. "I almost invited him tonight."

"Yeah, things are okay. And Jake told me. Thanks for understanding about not inviting him. I just need to sort things out before I can start anything serious with anyone. I really like him, Mel. And he seems to like me too, which is not something I'm used to. At least, not from someone I have feelings for. But I have to get that Rohypnol test back… figure out that craziness first. I've got too much baggage. I don't need to bring that into a relationship. Not if I finally want a healthy one."

I jump with a start as I hear metal meet granite. I notice Melanie has put down her utensils and is walking toward me with purpose. I'm suddenly crushed against her body, spilling crushed tomatoes and herbs onto the floor. I quickly inspect her top to make sure it hasn't spilled down her back.

"I'm so happy for you, Kat. I know this may be premature, but it's the most optimistic I've ever heard you speak about a relationship." I attempt to warn her I've dropped appetizer topping onto the floor before she steps in it when suddenly Murphy comes around the corner. Now I know why that lovable chocolate Labrador retriever is so overweight.

Shrugging my shoulders, I just return the hug and smile as she pulls away. "It's hard for me to get too excited about it yet, Mel. I let myself get a little giddy when I'm alone, but honestly, I have way too much taking up space in my brain right now. I'll be so glad when I can iron out this craziness. I'm glad you're letting me stay tonight. I find I sleep much better when there's someone else nearby. Plus, I really want to drink tonight."

"Well, we can't have you driving back home after eating and drinking the night away. Have you had any more of the weird dreams or woken up with different clothes on?"

"No. I think I've determined it's related to the sleeping pills. I haven't had any since I stopped taking them. I don't sleep much now unless I use Benadryl and wake up feeling hungover. I've been having a few night terrors again. But I think they might go away once the Rohypnol test is back."

Mel turns to me abruptly. "What kind of night terrors? Kat, I swear, if he hurt you."

"No, it's more feeling like I'm being watched. Little snippets of things that don't add up. Basically, my nightlife in a nutshell. Nothing adding up."

"Hey, Kat. When did you get here?" I watch as Jake strolls into the kitchen, inspecting the various food items on display. "Melanie put you straight to work, huh?" Jake gives me a one-armed hug, grabbing a small mozzarella ball off of the end of one of the skewers.

"Well, I needed help from someone who didn't assign himself as taste tester and then disappear whenever I need something." Melanie rebuffs.

"I'm trying to entertain our guests. Kat, can I carry those trays out for you?" Jake asks, stealing a pesto chicken appetizer off of the silver platter as he's offering. Melanie catches him in the act and swats him with a dishtowel.

"Yeah, so long as they all make it to the table." I laugh. I carry the larger platter with the mozzarella skewers, and he carries the two smaller silver serving trays.

"Kat, you want to grab a drink and head to the study to talk while

Mel's busy? It might be easier to do it now than later when there are even more people... well, and more alcohol on board."

Looking back toward the kitchen, I wince, worrying about the trouble we might both be in if we stray from Mel's to-do list for very long.

"She'll be okay," Jake reassures, grabbing my arm. "Hey Nate, can you give Mel a hand in the kitchen? I'm stealing Kat for a minute, and I don't want her to think we both ran out on her."

"Sure, Jake." Nate hesitates briefly, taking some bruschetta off of the tray before walking toward the kitchen.

We enter Jake's study, and I try to take a calming breath. The room is beautiful. It's appointed in deep mahogany and red velvet furnishings. The back wall is floor-to-ceiling bookshelves with a formal mahogany desk placed anteriorly. There's a beautiful cloisonné world globe on a stand near the large picture window that opens out onto their backyard. Deep red velvet chairs are seated in front of the desk. "Sit, Kat. What's going on?"

"Okay. So, if I sound a little wound up, know I'm not upset with you. It's the situation. I just need to get some clarity on all of this." I notice Jake has a harried expression on his face now. "Nick came to me recently and shared some startling news."

"Jesus, Kat. I honestly thought he was a good guy. I never would've—"

"No. No. Nothing like that. Let me finish. I know you two have talked a bit about me. I'm not upset. But, because of the conversations the two of you have had and the interactions he's had with me... well, he was able to put some things together I might not have discovered otherwise."

"What're you saying, Kat?"

"It's the sleeping pill. I'd determined my weird dreams and waking up in crazy outfits was somehow related to the pill before Nick came to me, but he confirmed it. The scary part... It appears I've been doing things outside of my home on the stuff and have no memory of it." I look up at him momentarily, trying to gather my strength to continue.

"Like what?"

"Well, I don't want to go into too much detail. I'm humiliated enough by all of this. But Nick saw me out one night, and I have no recollection of it. Like, at all. I have some vague pictures in my head of a dream I had that matches some of what he's told me..."

"Fuck, Kat." Jake looks pale as he runs his hand through his short brown hair.

"Nick told me you'd experienced some weird stuff using it too. That's how he put all of this together. I haven't used those pills since before my date with Mark. But I know you take them all the time. Have you had anything happen? Things you couldn't remember doing?"

"Kat. I feel terrible about this. I was trying to help you get some sleep when I encouraged you to take those pills. I had no idea all of this would happen. I've had people say they've seen me out places when I didn't recall the event they were describing. But I chalked that up to drinking. I figured I was plastered, or the combination of alcohol and the pills caused me to be more out of it. Honestly, other than Melanie telling me that I'm all ramped up in bed on zolpidem, I haven't had anything else happen that made me wonder if I'd done something."

We both sit for a few moments, absorbing all of this information. "Jake, I'm not taking that stuff anymore. I'd have to be either desperate for sleep or too far gone to care what happened to me to take them again." I stop to try and gather my words. "I'm not telling you what to do or how to live your life, but be careful if you choose to keep using them. I wanted to make sure you knew what I'd figured out, so you didn't find out the hard way if the pills were having a similar effect on you."

"Thanks, Kat. And again, I'm really sorry. I was only trying to help. You know I'd never do anything to hurt you."

"I know that, Jake. You're more like family than my blood relatives. I trust you and Mel with my life. The only reason I wanted to speak with you alone was so she didn't become overly concerned about you. I don't want to be the cause of anyone else's trouble." Looking down at my hands, I wring them as I think about my personal experience. "I'm afraid to think of what I could've done. If I was out driving around on the stuff and had hurt someone."

"Kat. Don't think about that. Now that you know, it's time to start putting that stuff behind you. There's no sense wasting any more energy considering the could have's." He looks at me with complete sincerity, and I nod in agreement.

Jake leans forward now, prompting me to do the same. "What I do know is if we don't get back out there, Melanie's going to kill me."

There are about twenty-five people sitting around multiple tables in the dining room, den, and front hallway. We're passing enough food around to feed an army between each of said tables and laughing at memories of various squad, fire, and police calls. Melanie's prepared traditional Thanksgiving fare and some atypical side dishes. The libations are flowing, and it feels good to be surrounded by raucous merriment. I'm sitting across from Tate and Tanner Manning. I've known them for years, and I still have a tough time telling them apart. One has a small mole just beneath his right lower lid. I have to look closely to spot it, but it's the tell I need.

"So, no dates tonight?" I ask, knowing they both had girls on their arms last year.

"Nah, flying solo tonight," Tanner says.

"We've had a lot of family drama lately. Our little brother's gotten himself into a bit of a situation with a girl. Stuff like that happens, and you realize spending time with people can get real serious, real quick. Whether you want it to or not." I notice Tate shares this intel in spite of Tanner's apprehensive expression. I'm picking up definite vibes from Tanner. This is a more personal matter than he wants to discuss in this setting. Despite my curiosity, I don't push for more details.

"How's Eve? I feel like I never really get to talk to her. We're always working opposite shifts in the ER." Tate and Tanner's sister is sweet and beautiful. I can only imagine how she's managed to date with these two playing interference.

"I think she's good. She's been keeping to herself a lot lately." Tate takes a large bite of potatoes and gravy, and I dig back into my meal.

"How're you doing, Kat? I didn't get to see you much at the Halloween party."

I look up from my plate and notice he and Tanner are both grinning at me. Damn. They must've seen Nick carrying me off. "I'm good. Nothing new, really. I stay busy at work. And I volunteer once in a while. I have to deliver my route next week."

"Deliver?" Tanner's speech is garbled by the long green bean he's wrestling in his mouth. I can't help but laugh.

"Yeah, I deliver meals to shut-ins once or twice a month. I missed volunteering when I gave up riding with the rescue squad. It's a pretty easy gig. Most of them are older or handicapped in some way that inhibits easy access to meals. I have about ten older folks on my route. Some I have to heat their food for them, but most just meet me at the door. They're all really sweet. You can tell they're lonely and don't get many visitors. It's kinda sad to think of someone spending their golden years alone like that."

I suddenly take in the magnitude of what I've said and realize that's the very track I've been on. Why on Earth would I want to spend my days alone when I could take a chance at a relationship with someone like Nick? If it doesn't work out, sure, I might get hurt. But I won't be any worse off than I am now.

The guests have all left, and I'm trying to help Mel clean up the last remnants of the gathering. Melanie's parents took the kids home with them and are taking them to school in the morning so Melanie can sleep in.

"Kat, let's leave the rest for tomorrow. Jake can put away the tables and chairs tomorrow too." We both look over in his direction. He's sitting on the couch with his head back, feet propped up, rubbing his belly. "Go over and sit with Jake. I'll grab us some coffee drinks."

"At ten o'clock? Mel, did you forget I don't sleep well?"

Grinning, she answers, "Kit Kat, these are decaf and loaded with Bailey's and Kahlua. If anything, they should help you sleep."

"Ah, bring on the coffee." I plop down beside Jake and pat him on the leg. "You okay, big guy?"

"I'm so stuffed. Mel's going to have to just leave me here on the couch." I can't help but laugh. I pull my phone out to lazily scroll through social media for a bit as I wind down and notice there are new messages.

9:20 p.m.
Nick Barnes
Nick: Missing you.

9:37 p.m.
Nick Barnes
Nick: No pressure.
Just don't forget about me.

9:43 p.m.
Nick Barnes
Nick: I'll be the guy all alone over here thinking about the cutest little stray Kat I found at a Halloween party once.

"Hey, Kat, I meant to ask you." Mel hands a steamy cup of fragrant coffee in my direction, distracting me from my naughty pen pal. "Are you going to the Christmas party this year?"

"What, the hospital one? I don't usually go, why?"

"Well, they're having it at the science museum this year. I think it'll be cool. You should come."

"Don't fall for it, Kat. She's usually bored out of her mind. We get all dressed up, and all the doctors insist on talking shop while they're there, and she's usually rolling her eyes at me because she wants to dance."

"Wow, there's dancing?" I perk up.

"Not like you do it. There'll be no dirty librarians coming to the company Christmas party, Kat," Jake states, seeming much more alert than he was five minutes ago.

"Okay, okay. I can dance conservatively." I look to blank stares by both Jake and Mel. "What? I can. When is it again?"

"It's next weekend, December 1st. Oh, please say you'll come, Kat," Melanie pleads. "I'm sure I have a dress you can wear. You can come here and get dressed and ride with us. Spend the night afterward."

"I don't even know if I'm off next weekend."

"You're off." The two of them answer in unison.

"I asked Jake to make sure you were off so you could come. You worked Thanksgiving, and you never come to these. Please?" Mel steeples her hands together.

"Mel, I'm going to feel like a third wheel. Everyone will have dates there."

"No, they won't. A lot of people come alone or with work colleagues. I promise, if you're miserable, you can either take an Uber home, or we can bail early."

"Yes, please, Kat. Let's make a deal now. If you come, start complaining you want to leave about an hour in so we can leave early," Jake requests earnestly. He receives a jab in his side from Melanie for this. "What? I don't want to go anyway."

"You have to go. You're the Director of the ER. It'd look bad if you didn't go," Melanie whines.

"Yeah, yeah. You just want an excuse to get all dolled up and go out without the kids."

"That too." Melanie shrugs her shoulders and giggles over her coffee cocktail.

"Okay. I'll go. But you better have something phenomenal for me to wear, Mel. I don't have time this week to be worrying about a dress."

"Oh, thank you, Kat. I'm so excited. This is going to be so much more fun with you there."

"Sure, why not? What could happen?"

Chapter Nineteen

Kat

"Hey, Mel, I'm here." The week flew by, and I'm ready to get 'all dolled up,' as Jake put it. Melanie said she had the perfect dress for me. I just brought the shoes. They make me smile when I look at them, knowing what a fondness Nick has for them.

Nick. I miss him. He's sent sweet text messages almost daily. We haven't communicated as much as we've stayed connected. He seems to be honoring his word, giving me space to get things sorted. I meet with Dr. Miller in a few days, so that'll help. I feel like my romantic life has been such a mess. I need guidance from a professional now that I've learned zolpidem's effects on me.

"Kat, come on up. I have everything laid out to get us ready."

Walking into Melanie's room, I see she has various pieces of jewelry, hair clips, and nail polish on display. She also has two glasses of bubbly sitting atop her dresser. "Boy, you think of everything," I tell her.

"Well, you don't get to go to events like this often. I say make a night of it. Hell, we aren't driving." Coming closer, I pick up several small bottles of nail polish. "I knew you wouldn't get your nails done beforehand, so I'm going to do them. And pick out whatever jewelry you'd like to wear."

"Mel, can I see the dress?" I ask, rubbing my hands together excitedly. Mel has exquisite taste, so I'm not at all worried about what she's chosen. Grabbing my hand, she pulls me toward her overstuffed closet. Hanging from the door, I see it and gasp. "Mel. It's beautiful." The dress is a sapphire blue, full-length satin gown with small crystals along the bodice. It's a sheath column dress with off-the-shoulder cap sleeves. "It looks like it belongs on a runway."

"Kat, with your dark hair, it's going to look beautiful on you."

"Mel, I don't want to wear my hair down tonight," I quickly blurt out.

"It's okay. I thought you might say that. I found a partial updo that'll work. You'll have enough of it up that you won't feel conspicuous."

"Thanks, Mel. This is just gorgeous."

"Oh, I'm just so glad you're coming with us. Have you talked to Nick? Do you think he'll be there?" Mel asks, throwing me for a loop. I hadn't even considered this.

"We haven't talked. He sends occasional texts, and I respond, but nothing conversation-worthy. More like we're just checking in." It's odd. I haven't seen him at work at all lately. I think he's trying to give me the space I need. "Mel, he's a really good guy."

"That's what I've been trying to tell you. A good guy and looks like that? Girl, you better get that damn appointment with your psychologist soon. He's not going to be available for long."

I can feel my heart lurch a little at that proclamation. I know she's right. But I'm trying to do things the right way this time. He's been hurt before too. Seeing Dr. Miller to iron this stuff out and get his opinion will protect both of us.

～

"You girls ready?" I hear Jake out in the hall. "If we don't leave soon, there's no sense in going."

"Oh, cool your jets," Mel barks. She looks into the mirror to do one last cursory touch-up of her makeup. She looks stunning. She's wearing a deep red strapless gown that has a slit going up one leg. She has beautiful diamonds draped around her neck, her striking dark hair falling in soft waves down her back. Strappy black four-inch stilettos adorn her feet. She makes walking in those things look easy. Mine are thankfully not that tall, but I still feel like I'm a newborn foal walking on shaky legs in these heels. The reminder of my recent fall making me even more cautious.

We make our way to the car and settle in for the ride. My purse doesn't leave much room for anything beyond essentials. My phone, lipstick, and a couple of folded tissues.

As Jake pulls into the science museum parking lot, he drives up to the front and drops us off. I follow Melanie's lead on entering the venue, as attending galas such as this are not my forte. We check our coats and wait by the door for Jake to arrive before venturing on. The place is abuzz with party-goers. The large space is dimly lit, and elegant white lights are draped everywhere. There are various Christmas trees placed about the space and multiple red and white poinsettias on display.

"You girls ready?" Jake asks, placing an arm around each of us.

We head into the main ballroom and see there are easily several hundred guests in attendance. There are bar height tables scattered around the periphery draped in white linen, some with candles and others with small festive foliage in clear vases. Melanie walks toward an open table closest to us. "Jake, can you get us a drink? I just want to people watch for a while."

"Sure, Mel. Kat, you want a glass of wine?"

"Yes, that'd be great." Like Mel, I take in the scene. There's a variety of party wear on display. There are conservative, matronly frocks on the older women in attendance and flirty, almost prom-like dresses on the younger set. Of course, there are the dresses that appear painted on the women who want to stand out. Melanie points out a few attendees she refers to as trophy wives and a few others who are wannabe trophy wives.

"Mel, some might think you're a trophy wife. Look at you. You're stunning and married to a successful doctor."

"I never said I wasn't. Jake hit the jackpot when he found me." She winks, and we both laugh. Melanie is the most down-to-earth, non-judgmental person I know. Her antics are all in fun.

I look up to see Jake walking toward us with a young man behind him wearing a banquet uniform, balancing a scotch and two wine glasses on a tray. As they reach our table and hand off the beverages, Jake offers a toast, and we all clink glasses. As I take a sip from mine, I notice Jake lean into Melanie. At first, I think he's offering her a peck on the cheek until I catch the subtle change in Mel's facial expression. Watching her gaze shift behind me to the front doors, I can't help but turn around. As I do, I catch the sight of an attractive blonde that I recognize as an orthopedic physician assistant in Nick's practice standing beside none other than Nick Barnes himself. He's dressed in a black tux, with a crisp white shirt and black bowtie. I suddenly feel a lump in my throat. Turning back, so he doesn't catch me staring, I look at Mel.

"Maybe it's already too late."

Nick

Heading to pick up Ava, I wonder what I was thinking agreeing to go to this shindig. The last place I want to be is at some big hospital gala. Dr. Morgan convinced me to attend, as it's a good place to network, so I relented. Ava shared that she really wanted to attend, but her husband wouldn't be available until late in the evening. He apparently travels a lot for business, and she didn't expect he'd return in time to escort her to the party. I reluctantly offered to pick her up, as she has been a real asset since moving to St. Luke's.

I walk up the steps to Ava's door, and before I've reached the top step, she swings open the door to greet me. "Hey, Nick. Thanks so much for doing this."

"Sure, no problem. You look beautiful, Ava." Ava's a very pretty girl. She's petite and blonde. She has Nordic features, and the ice blue dress she's wearing complements her eyes. Her jewelry is radiant, much like her personality.

"You look fantastic." Ava blushes a little with the compliment.

"Why, thank you. Shall we?" I assist her with her wrap as we walk down the sidewalk to my car.

"I just got off of the phone with Mick. He should be landing at the airport in about an hour."

Once inside, she continues. "I know you weren't looking forward to attending tonight. But Dr. Morgan's right. It's a great way to mingle casually and get your name out there. Break the ice with the staff physicians. But if you decide to bail, Mick will be coming to pick me up. I'm fine to wait for him there."

"I hate to leave you alone."

"I won't be alone. I'm sure with as many people who attend this thing, I'll find someone to chat up while I wait. I just appreciate you bringing me. It's so awkward walking into something like this by yourself."

We pull into the science museum parking lot, and I quickly realize this is a massive affair. I decide to use the valet, so Ava won't have to walk half a block in those heels.

Exiting my car, we walk toward the entrance, and Ava's already making small talk with other guests in formal wear. She's worked at St. Luke's for several years and seems to know most everyone on staff there.

As we check our coats, we walk toward the main ballroom, and Ava immediately pulls me toward a tall, dark-haired gentleman.

"Nick, have you met Dr. Weston? He's a general surgeon at St. Luke's. He's worked there for quite some time."

"Watch it, Ava. You make me sound ancient." I watch as a slight blush crosses Ava's features. It's more significant on her, given her pale features. "Hi, I'm Broadie Weston." He reaches out a hand to shake. "I think I've seen you in the OR, but you look quite different in this outfit than the scrubs, surgical cap, and mask."

Laughing, I return his handshake. "Nick Barnes. I'm an orthopedist, new to the hospital. It's nice to meet you."

We continue to make very little headway into the venue as Ava stops every few steps to introduce me to someone new. But that's why I'm here, so might as well get to it early. I'm only allowing myself one drink tonight. Beyond the fact that I have to drive home, I have an early day with Dad tomorrow.

As I turn toward one of the banquet staff to ask for water, I catch a glimpse of a stunning creature dressed in deep blue. Her hair is down enough on one side that I'm almost certain it's Kat. I can feel my pulse pick up and pray she'll allow me to join her this evening. *God, I've missed her.* As I'm gazing in her direction, her back to me, I notice Melanie is standing across from her and Jake's approaching with drinks.

I turn to Ava to inform her I'm planning to head over to Kat's table to say hello. Instead of remaining with the older physician whose name I've already forgotten, she waves her goodbyes to come along with me. As I approach the table, I see Jake and Melanie look my way with a pensive smile.

"Hi. Don't know why it didn't dawn on me you guys might be here." I direct to the table. I walk around to where Jake is standing to offer my hand.

"Hey, Nick. Good to see you."

"Oh, I'm sorry. Have you all met, Ava?" I start to introduce Ava to Kat, as she's standing beside her, but then I recall Ava knows practically everyone who works at St. Luke's. I remember my manners and decide to introduce her to Melanie when I notice Ava is looking toward the front entrance. Waiting for her to break eye contact with whatever she's fixated on, I stand quietly, observing her for a second. Her stare doesn't waver, so I follow her line of vision to see what has her so fascinated.

As if someone has announced their arrival, I watch as all heads turn in the direction of Sebastian Lee and his stunning date as they enter the ballroom. It's as if their entrance is choreographed. They look like royalty as they approach. He's wearing a designer tuxedo with a black bow tie and looking as smug as ever. On his arm is a blonde, attracting the attention of men and women alike as she glides across the room. Her hair's been carefully woven into an artful chignon, displaying her long, delicate neck. Expensive diamonds draped about it reflect the lighting in the grand space. I feel my jaw tighten as they approach.

"Ah, if it isn't Dr. Nicholas Barnes. Fancy meeting you here." I observe as he takes in the people standing around the small cocktail table. "What, no date this evening, Nick?" I watch as he eyes Katarina, who's standing across from me, silently observing this spectacle next to Ava.

"Bas," I return, even more annoyed than usual at his interference in my life. I'm decidedly not dignifying his question with an answer.

"I believe you know my date?" Bas announces proudly.

Turning to the woman on his arm, I offer a clipped greeting. "Hello, Sophia."

Chapter Twenty

Nick

I knew it was only a matter of time before I'd be confronted with the two of them as a couple. I'm not sure why it never crossed my mind it could happen here. My thoughts of Katarina hadn't allowed room to contemplate anyone else. Obviously, I'm over Sophia. I'm more upset with him most days than her. Strange given *she* made vows to me, not Sebastian.

Realizing we've all been standing here silent, metaphorical crickets chirping at this uncomfortable situation, I decide to take myself out of the equation. "I'm headed to the bar. Excuse me." Making the briefest of eye contact with Kat before I depart, I turn and head into the crowd. *I need a fucking drink.*

I scan the area for a bar a safe distance from the museum's entrance. I don't need anyone coming after me to talk. Not Bas, not Sophia, not even Kat. I just need some space from this shitshow.

"Scotch?" The bartender quickly pours and slides the crystal tumbler in my direction. I take a sip before even stepping from the bar. I turn and take in the setting, trying to spot somewhere other than the men's room I can go to be alone. I notice someone coming in from a side door. It's probably the smoker's area, but who gives a fuck. Cold, smoky air beats the stench of this place.

Frigid air hits me as I walk toward the balcony railing. I take another sip of the amber liquid and enjoy the burn. Looking into the dark abyss of the night's sky, I see flashes of a time long ago, beginning medical school right down this very road. I started school with staunch determination. Nervous but driven, I rarely did anything social as my head was always in the books. I remained at the top of my class, with Sebastian always heavy on my heels.

At first, I didn't know what to make of the cocky, arrogant classmate who was born with a silver spoon in his mouth. He came from money and had no trouble flaunting it. I came from a very modest upbringing. This only spurred on my desire to be number one. There was an innate need to show money can't buy everything.

But as the years passed by, we realized we had more in common than we wanted to admit. We both craved a challenge. Our teen years hadn't gone as we'd hoped. I looked for solace in my grades and career, and Bas seemed to look for it in his independence. He was chasing a dream at the cost of his family's wealth and his inheritance.

By our senior year, we'd become as tight as college friends could be. We continued to compete against one another in almost every setting. It didn't matter. Darts, grades, girls. But it was all in fun. I knew he had my back, and I had his. I've never let anyone else in since Sebastian. Since that betrayal.

When I started dating Sophia, I suspected Sebastian was equally interested. I'm honestly not sure why she chose me, given he had more money. I think it was his reputation. Bas had always been a love 'em and leave 'em kinda guy. He was too focused on his future and making a name for himself to consider committing to someone else. Who's to say if a relationship with Sophia would've changed that, but for whatever reason, she seemed to be more interested in me at the time, and I wasn't complaining. She was and still is one of the most beautiful women I've ever met. Physically that is. Any man would be crazy not to find her attractive. Plus, she knows how to lay on the charm. After years of dating Sophia, I thought she'd make a good wife and mother. It was just the next step in this thing called life. But after meeting Kat, it's clear what I felt for Sophia is quite different than my current emotional turmoil. There was never the heart-wrenching need to be with Sophia. She certainly never gave me a panic attack, even when she was leaving. Any anxiety I felt was purely at the hands of her betrayal.

I take a larger sip from my glass, needing the scald of the liquor to distract from the sting of my past. I look into the expensive liquid and remember a time when Sophia and I barely had two pennies to rub together. I would've never guessed the relentlessly greedy bitch she'd become. Looking back, there were subtle signs along the way. I just didn't want to face it.

From the beginning, the wedding was over the top. Thankfully, her parents had prepared for her rich taste as my father didn't have that kind of money. I certainly wasn't taking out a loan for a wedding on top of my mounting medical school debt. Once we were married, she seemed to stay within a budget. Or so I thought. Then the credit card bills started arriving. Though this persisted, I decided it wasn't worth fighting about. I made a moderate salary as a resident and moonlighting at Urgent Care centers, but there were still bills to pay. I planned to pay off the debt once I was working full-time as a surgeon. I'd hoped to get her on a budget later. Plus, Sophia always seemed to support my long hours during residency. She never complained. In hindsight, I wondered if she preferred my absence.

I've realized over the last year, things seemed to change almost immediately following the wedding. The three of us still spent a great deal of time together, but Sophia didn't have the starry-eyed romanticism she'd displayed during our engagement. I could tell she was pulling away, but I assumed it was boredom or resentment as she spent so much time home alone. I'd frequently come home to find she'd already retired for the evening or a note saying she was out with the girls. We had a good sex life, or so I thought. I recognize now it isn't the hot, earth-shattering sex I have with Kat. But as I said, Sophia is stunning. I'm a man. Sex with a gorgeous woman was enough. I never suspected it was lacking. Maybe she did.

I question now whether those nights out with the girls were really *with the girls*. I've never had a formal confrontation with Sebastian regarding their affair. It was easier to just walk away from both of them. However, the betrayal by my friend and confidant was somehow worse than the woman who vowed to commit only to me. If she'd taken up with some random stranger, I don't think the divorce would've been nearly as painful. There were additional complex questions regarding their affair I knew I'd probably never have answers to. But that bitter pill was too big to swallow with this highball.

Polishing off the remainder of my drink, I chase the burn of the scotch with a deep inhale of the cool night air. I've sulked long enough. I'm not interested in participating in this meet and greet any longer. I need to give my goodbyes to Ava and try to soothe the ache of my past with a sweet smile from Kat before I depart.

Walking through the crowded space, I see Ava up ahead with Justin. I know he's no longer a fan of mine but decide to be polite and greet them and advise Ava I'm heading out. As I approach, I notice Jake and Melanie still standing at the bar table where I'd originally seen them. But Kat's no longer there. After giving Ava a quick goodbye, I head in their direction.

"Hey. Sorry, I had to step away like that. I didn't mean to be so rude."

"It's okay, man, we understand," Jake says, giving me an almost knowing swat about my upper arm.

"Is Kat out dancing?" I ask, knowing I'm probably not hiding my smile well.

"No. You just missed her," Melanie offers, looking forlorn.

"What? What do you mean?"

"I don't think she was interested in coming tonight. I pushed her to join us. She decided to head home."

Before I can consider how rude I'm being, I turn and run for the front door. I nearly collide with an older woman trying to hold onto the railing as she carefully takes one step at a time in her formal wear and sensible shoes. After a game of Frogger, trying to pass her and avoid colliding with oncoming guests, I fly through the front doors and jerk my head in both directions. Nothing. Running further out into the parking lot, I almost get run over by a damn car.

Stopping, I take in a shaky breath then continue at a slower pace. Walking a few steps further, my damn heart in my throat again, I give up, and head for the valet stand dejected. *Well, this night sucked balls.*

The thought has barely left my brain when I see Katarina laughing with the valet, her back to me. As usual, this enchanting vixen has me spellbound. My steps hasten automatically as if my feet are on autopilot. As I walk up behind her, I reach for her elbow.

"Kat," I pant.

"Oh, hi." She seems distant. There's a hint of concern on her face, but she certainly doesn't seem pleased to see me.

"You're leaving?"

"Yeah, I'm kinda over the whole evening."

"Are you waiting for your car?" I press on, still sounding out of breath.

"No. I called an Uber."

"What? No. Let me drive you home."

She looks at me pointedly. "Who'll drive Ava home?"

"Her husband!" I snap. I stand, wordlessly staring at her. How could one night get so fucked up?

Unable to control my irritation at the clusterfuck this night has turned into, I grab her arm. "Let's make this clear once and for all, Katarina. There's no one for me but you. Got that? No one." Realizing I'm probably grabbing her arm a little too tight in my frustration, I drop my hand, trying to rein in my irritation. "She only asked if I'd escort her here, so she didn't have to enter the gala alone. Her husband was running late from his job. I didn't think to tell you because it never dawned on me that it'd be an issue."

I stand in front of her, waiting for her eyes to connect with mine. I need to know she's absorbed what I've said. Looking at me, I can tell she understands.

"Kat? Please. This night has been total shit. Can I at least drive you home?"

"Yes. Okay," she quickly blurts. I watch as her face shifts from looking more relieved to empathetic. What's it going to take to convince her? Then I recall all the dickheads in her life. If they've treated her half as bad as the two who waltzed in from my past tonight, I get why she's always suspicious.

Kat cancels her Uber, and we walk silently to my car, which is apparently parked in another zip code. I look down at my feet to avoid wanting to pull her into me. The events of the evening are starting to catch up with me, and I'm in dire need of some comfort. Comfort that can't be poured out of a bottle. I suddenly notice she's wearing those shoes. Despite the evening's madness, my cock twitches at the memory of her lithe legs wrapped in black laces, standing atop those sexy tall heels.

"Is that it?"

"Um, what?" Recognizing I've completely zoned out, I turn and notice she's pointing toward my Audi.

"Oh, yes. Good eye, kitty." I see a small smile turn the corner of her mouth. I want to get us to somewhere pleasant this evening. Even if it's just a tender kiss goodbye. I need to know we're okay. It's agonizing giving her the space she needs when I want so much to go to her. I open the passenger door for her, and she lays her hand on my arm briefly as she lowers herself into the seat. That electric spark is still there, warming my skin as I walk to the driver's door.

I start the engine and adjust the temperature a bit before pulling out. Kat remains eerily quiet. I'm not sure what to expect from this girl tonight. She seems so aloof. I had hoped once we cleared the air about Ava, that'd no longer be the case.

"Nick?"

"Yes?"

"Was that?" she hesitates. I'm pretty sure I know where she's going with this conversation.

"Yes."

"Are they?"

I remain silent, hoping she'll drop it.

"Do you want to talk about it?"

"No." I know I need to talk to her about this at some point, but I don't have it in me tonight. I'm still agitated from seeing them together, looking like Prince William and Kate fucking Middleton.

Taking a breath, I assure her. "Kat, I'll tell you the whole story one day. I just can't handle it tonight."

"I understand." I feel her soft hand lie atop mine, and my whole body relaxes at her touch. I rotate to hold her hand as we make the remainder of the drive to her home in silence.

～

We pull into her drive about thirty minutes later. "Where's your car? Do you park in your garage?"

"No. I got dressed with Mel. I'll get her to drive it over tomorrow. I don't work until Monday."

"You and the Harris family have a pretty tight bond. That's nice."

"You have no idea. I don't know what I'd do without them."

I try to reach her door before she opens it, but she's already out of the car. I only asked to drive her home, so I try not to make her feel uncomfortable. Even if I'd give anything to be with her. "Let me just walk you to the door."

I notice she goes to the garage keypad, instead of the front door. I can't help but watch the digits she enters, wondering if she didn't bring her keys. I contemplate ways to prolong this time with her since I thought I'd at least have the time it would take to walk her to the front door. As the garage door opens, she turns to me. I guess this is goodbye then.

As I open my mouth to wish her a reluctant goodnight, she comes closer and slips her arms around my neck. Looking into her big brown eyes, I whisper, "Thank you. Driving you home is the best thing that's happened to me all day." My answer is sincere, and I think she knows it.

"Well, hopefully, it just got better." She smirks.

Before I can ask what she means, she's removed her arms from my neck and grabbed ahold of my hand, pulling me along behind her through the small garage. *Hell, yeah, it did*

Kat

This man. He's so patient and kind. He's continued to be by my side regardless of the turmoil my life has become. It's awful to see him hurting. Both by my accusation about Ava and from inquiring into the uncomfortable situation with Dr. Lee and his ex-wife. I can't help but wonder when exactly Dr. Lee and his ex-wife got together. But I certainly won't press.

As I walk inside the house, I turn and look up at Nick's handsome face. Reaching up, I cup his masculine jaw and stand up on tiptoes to kiss him. I've missed this man so. As I place soft, warm kisses on his mouth, I can feel his tongue begging entrance, and I open for him. His arms slide around my waist, and we continue to slowly kiss and hold each other, drowning out the ghosts of the evening.

"You wore my shoes," he murmurs against my mouth.

"Hmm? Oh, yeah. I did. I thought about you when I picked them out, actually."

He nuzzles my neck with his nose and nibbles on my ear. "I love picturing you in those shoes." I can feel his heavy exhale of warm breath against my ear. "I'll never forget the way you looked that night. In and out of the shoes."

"Well, I'm quite awestruck with the way you look in a tuxedo, Dr. Barnes. You look like you could be on the cover of a Menswear magazine." I pull back from him to take him in from head to toe. This man is literally the most attractive man I've ever met. The firm pecs and abs, the sexy smirk, the sharp edges of his stubbled jaw, and that heavenly hair.

"Thank you. But you... you took my breath away before you even turned around, Katarina. That is definitely your color. You look amazing. I'm sorry I didn't say it sooner. This night has done a real number on me."

Reaching up, I stroke the honey-colored scruff along his cheek and smile. "Can I offer you a drink?"

"No, I really shouldn't. I had one at the gala. I don't like to drink more than one if I'm driving."

"What if you weren't driving?" I ask coyly.

I notice his facial expression changes. He suddenly looks serious, not playful, and smiling as he did mere moments ago. *What on Earth did I say?*

"Kat? Are you serious?"

I stammer a bit. "What? Why?"

"I'd give anything if you were serious," he says earnestly.

"Anything?" Relieved, I waggle my brows and giggle, trying to break the tension in the air between us.

Crushing my body to his, lifting me off of the ground, he buries his face into my neck. "Anything, kitten. Name it."

"Nick. I've already got everything I need right here. Do you want that drink now?" I'm unable to stop giggling.

"No, you're all I want," he growls into my ear. I notice my panties are becoming wet. As he slides me down his body, returning me to the ground, there's a firm bulge in his tuxedo pants I don't recall from moments ago. Deciding to be bold, I reach over and run my hand along his obvious erection. A delicious groan tumbles from his sexy mouth.

"Would you like to get more comfortable?"

"Yes, ma'am." I watch as he slides his expensive black tuxedo jacket off and drapes it over the armchair. He bends down to slide off his shiny black shoes and places them neatly beneath the discarded jacket. As he reaches for his bow tie, I stretch my arm up to stop him. Running the pads of my fingers over the smooth material, I slowly untie the black fabric and drop it onto his suit jacket. Grabbing his hand, I lead him into the bedroom. There's no sense pretending where this night is going. I couldn't have asked for a better ending to this day.

I turn to him and start to unbutton the silver cufflinks. Slowly caressing the front of his starched shirt, I glide my hands up his torso to the top button. Distracted by his handsome face, I have to stop unbuttoning several times to place kisses on his big, beautiful lips. As I open the garment to display his strong pecs and rippled abdominals, I drift my hands up and down. "I love your body, Nick," I bashfully admit to him as he watches me silently.

He grabs the shirt and slides it off of him, and places it gingerly along the bench at the end of the bed. Walking closer, he folds his arms around me, and I can feel the zipper of my gown slowly descending. Once the cool air has hit my back, I sashay a step back, allowing the dress to pool at my feet. I watch him closely as he drinks me in, standing before him in my black lace bra and panties, wearing his favorite black heels with the thin black laces that course up my calves.

"Katarina." I hear my name fall quietly from his lips, like a whisper. *Does he even know he's said it?* I reach down to pick up the dress and lie it on the bench. I wouldn't want to tell Mel I'd damaged it because I was overcome with lust for this sexy surgeon, but somehow, I think she'd forgive me. As I turn back to him, there's a fire burning in his gaze. He drops to his knees in front of me and pulls me into him, burying his face in my belly. This incredible, adoring man. No one's ever touched me the way he has. I drag my hands through his thick, golden hair and pull. I'm having a hard time controlling my desire. He slowly peels my panties off, taking care around the sharp, pointy heels. Once he's done, he stands and removes my bra. Pulling back the sheets quickly, he lifts me in his arms and places me on the bed. I try not to feel embarrassed by his careful scrutiny, allowing him to take me in wearing only 'his shoes.' Thankfully, Nick starts to undo his belt without my having to beg. As he stands, his erection is so prominent the head is peeking out of the top of his boxers. This is a momentary sighting as he quickly removes them and joins me amongst the sheets.

"Kat?"

"Yes?"

"You've turned a hellish night into something spectacular. It wouldn't matter if we only laid here together. Seeing you like this, being close to you. It's all I've wanted lately."

Looking into his stunning hazel eyes, I see the admiration there. But I can't help teasing him a little. "You're so sweet, Nick. Okay, goodnight." I roll away from him, giggling.

"Oh no, you don't." He laughs, tugging my body into his. His erection is so large and hard, I consider whether it might be painful. As if that thought has me instinctively wanting to comfort him, I reach down to stroke the smooth skin along his rigid shaft. A loud moan escapes him. He drops his head into my chest and nuzzles my breasts.

"Oh, how I've missed you two." He caresses, licks, and sucks from my breasts and nipples adoringly as I chuckle beneath him.

Suddenly, I'm flipped on my stomach and feel him rubbing his hard cock against my backside. *Oh, I'm definitely not ready for that.* Quickly, he adjusts himself, and I can feel him gliding his thick shaft back and forth along my swollen, folds. Hearing the drawer to my nightstand open, he leans into me. "Kat? Is this okay?"

"Yes." I want to say, *try stopping now and see what happens.* But I settle for yes.

I hear the condom wrapper open and tremble in anticipation of what is to come. A whimper escapes me as he nudges the tip of his cock into me. There's more groaning behind me, and this makes me smile into my pillow. He pulls my hips up, so I'm on all fours, and slowly slides his engorged cock into me. I'll never get used to the amazing way he makes my body feel. So full, so exquisitely turned on. Reaching around me, he grabs ahold of my breast as he thrusts in and out of me.

"I need you to come for me, Kat. The sight of you in those fucking shoes already has me on the edge." He begins to rut into me more aggressively, groaning out his pleasure. "Fuck, my own little sex kitten. You're the stuff of fantasies in those shoes."

Oh god, I'm so wet, but he's that close already? Knowing my history, I try to encourage him. "Don't wait for me, Nick. It's okay."

Suddenly, he stills. *Thwack!*

"Oh!" I shout. I can feel my walls clench around him with the sting of his slap against my right butt cheek. Abruptly, my hair is pulled back, and I can feel his breath against my ear.

"Are you trying to insult me, kitten? You don't think I can make you come?"

"No, I—"

"Tsk, Tsk, Tsk. Just for that, I'm going to need you to come twice before I blow my load."

Panicking, I shudder as I feel him rubbing the now warm skin of my tender bottom. "But, I—"

Thwack!

"Ah!" *Holy heck. Who knew this would turn me on?* I can feel myself tighten around him with

each slap, and I can tell I'm wetter than I've ever been. He starts to ram into me even harder, my hair tightly in his grip. His right hand slinks around my waist, rubbing against my swollen clit. "Oh, Nick."

"That's it. Come for me," he growls.

I can feel myself grinding into him with each thrust of his hips, knowing I'm right on the edge when I hear him grunt.

"Are you holding out on me? I need it, Kat." He adjusts his stance, pulling his hand away from my aching sex. I can feel him pull my hair back a little tighter just as I feel his left hand slap my left buttock. I clench down on him right before he reaches around and slaps my pussy, sending me over the edge.

"Oh god." I cry out, unable to keep from shaking underneath him. My walls convulse around him, my entire body ablaze by his unexpected dominance. As I start to come back down, he withdraws, and I immediately wince at the loss. Placing a hand to my back, he pushes me down into the bed and rolls me over.

"Kat?"

"Yes," I pant.

"I want to eat you."

"No."

"What do you mean, no?"

Nick

I look down at this stunning creature, confused. "What do you mean, no? I've never known any woman who didn't want that."

"Well, first, don't lump me in with all of your other women," she glares, "and second, I'm not ready for that."

I give her a stern look. "Kat, I wasn't lumping you in. I'm sorry if that came out wrong. I honestly thought all women wanted that."

"Well, I wouldn't know. It's too intimate an act for me. I'd never be able to relax and enjoy it. I'd feel way too vulnerable." She looks as if she's trying to catch her breath. "Nick, isn't it enough you've finally allowed me to have an orgasm with someone? Can we not push it?"

Worrying I may have ruined the mood, I try to get us back on track. "Baby, I just want to make you feel good. That's all."

"I know." She reaches up to stroke my chest. "Obviously, you do. Maybe one day. I'm just not there yet."

Reaching down, I kiss her. Taking in her tempting body, I'm dying to be back inside her. I begin to stroke her sweet pussy, still wet and swollen. I rub the head of my dick along her folds, trying to reassure him his turn is getting closer. I lift her limber legs against my chest, dragging her pelvis closer to me. Caressing her supple calves, wrapped in the black silk laces, I deposit her feet clad in those fuck hot heels over my shoulders and slide my eager cock inside her wet heat. *Oh, I'm so deep like this.* I have to avoid looking down at her, or I'm going to look like a chump with my whole 'you need to come twice' routine.

"Oh god, I love how you make me feel, Nick." She moans out her pleasure as I slowly grind in and out of her, rubbing her swollen nub with my thumb. Deciding I need to amp her up a little, I wait for her to make eye contact with me and raise my right hand to my mouth. As she watches, I drag my tongue along the three middle fingers and then place the tips into my mouth. Dropping my hand to her pussy, I rub a little more aggressively as she undulates against me.

"Kat?"

"Yes."

"Is it all oral you want to avoid?"

Looking a bit alarmed, her eyes jerk up to mine. "What do you mean?"

"Well, I've been dying to see your pretty lips wrapped around my cock."

A look of relief washes over her face. *What the hell did she think I meant?* "No, I want to do that. Do you want me to do that now?"

Groaning, I shake my head. "No, I wouldn't last a minute now." I start to buck into her more fiercely as the thought of her hot wet mouth wrapped around my shaft dances behind my closed lids. I have to pull out of her for a minute and collect myself, or this is going to be over. I slowly withdraw and notice the look of disappointment on her face. I slide my fingers into her wet folds and use my thumb to rub her clit as I plunge my fingers in and out of her. As she starts to tighten around me, I curl my fingers forward as I slide them out and watch as her pelvis lurches in response. I know I've hit her sweet spot. Withdrawing my fingers, I slide back into her and grab ahold of both of her legs, using them as a fulcrum as I pound into her with more force.

"If I can't return the favor, make you come with my mouth. I need to know what else I can do for you." I pant. I'm probably leaving bruises on her thighs the way I'm digging my fingers into her as I drive into her sweet body. "Tell me what you want, Kat. What've you thought about me doing to you. What naughty little thing can I do to make you feel good?" I struggle for control, my thumb returning to her swollen clit, flicking it in time with my thrusts.

"Ohhh." She moans loudly. "I want you to come all over me." *Holy shit, this woman is going to be the death of me.* I'm so revved up now, I'm practically going to rip her in two with the aggressive way I'm thrusting into her, feeling those laces rubbing against my neck and face.

"Where, Kat? Where would you want it?" I'm almost manic now with the need to come.

Feeling her squeezing around my pulsating dick, I look down and see she's pointing to her pelvis. "Here." She moves her finger upward toward her sweet little navel. "Here." I'm picking up speed, praying I can hold on. I watch as her finger points to her tits. They are bouncing deliciously for me as I beat into her. "Here." God, I can feel that familiar sensation. My balls have received the signal, there's no holding back. She points her finger to her chin and then lays her fingertip along her lower lip. "And here." I'm done.

"Fuck, Kat!" I yell, lifting her pelvis higher as I thrust into her.

"Nick. Nick. Nick. Oh god." She cries out, and I look down to see her arms spread wide, hands clutching the sheets as she comes undone for me.

"Fuuuck." I let out a roar, unable to control the state I'm in. My pulse is roaring in my ears, my heart pounding in my chest as I empty into the condom. *Holy fuck, I'm going to have to be careful removing this rubber. I might have broken my dick with the sheer force of that climax.* Letting go of her right leg, I lean forward, bracing my arm against her headrest with my eyes closed. I continue to hear the loud thrum of my heartbeat pulsating in my ears, my breaths labored. White spots are dancing behind my eyes. Continuing to lean into the wall, slowly, my senses begin to calm. Gradually, I open my eyes. Looking down, the vision of her steals my breath.

Kat's hair is splayed around her, eyes shining, skin flushed. She's surrounded by her white sheets as if she's wearing a gown. I'm completely mesmerized by this beauty.

"I'm going to marry you."

Chapter Twenty-One

Nick

"Wha...?" Kat looks up at me, eyes wide in question.

'I'm going to marry you.' Shit. Did I really just say that out loud? I guess I'm all in now. Might as well keep digging this hole.

Chuckling, I lean down into her neck and whisper playfully. "Face it, kitten, I'm going to marry you. I'm going to marry you, and you're going to have all my babies." I can feel her body quake as she's giggling underneath me now.

"Oh yeah, Dr. Barnes? And how many babies are we having?"

"Ah, the way we fuck... lots!" I laugh and smother the side of her neck, jaw, and face with kisses. Suddenly, I notice she's quiet. Has the enormity of what I've said finally caught up with me? Is she questioning my sanity? Or maybe hers for being with me?

"Um, Nick?" I hear her soft, contemplative voice.

"Yes?"

"Could we go on a date before we get hitched?"

I snort with laughter, and she joins in, both of us rolling over together in her bed clutching each other. "Yes, ma'am. See the extremes I'll go to to get you to finally agree to go out with me. If only I'd known I had to threaten to marry and impregnate you to get a date." She catches me in the ribs with her pointy elbow. "Uh, watch it, naughty kitty. I might need to start the spankings up again." Smirking at her, I bend down to kiss the corner of her mouth.

"As much as I enjoyed that," I watch the blush across her cheeks as she continues, "you wore me out. I think I could actually sleep through them."

I hesitate briefly, making sure I phrase this the right way. "Kat? I know we've usually had quite the workout before we fall asleep when I'm with you, but you seem to sleep well when we're together."

I watch as a slow smile curls the corner of her mouth. "Yeah. I thought that myself the other day."

Stretching my chest wide, I declare with a bit of bravado, "Well, glad to be of service." She smacks my arm and buries her face in my neck, and for the first time, I think *we might just be okay*.

Kat

Waking to the sound of a dog barking outside, I stretch and roll toward my bedmate. My delicious bedmate. My delicious bedmate who is again not in my bed. I sit upright, deciding not to panic. The bathroom door is again open, revealing no occupant. There are no remnants of his clothing laid upon the bench at the end of the bed.

This man has been nothing but supportive and kind. I'm sure there's an explanation. Even if he always seems to be running.

I rub my hands up and down my arms, trying to displace the chill to my skin. I'm not used to waking completely naked, but with Nick Barnes sharing your bed, why wear clothes? I stand and walk to the bathroom, grabbing my robe and brushing my teeth. As I turn to walk down the hallway to my kitchen, I notice a piece of junk mail and a pen lying next to my coffee pot. I look at the back of the envelope, where a note is penned in masculine script.

Kat,
    I'm sorry I had to leave, but couldn't wake you. I have something pressing

*with my dad this morning. I may be busy most of the day, but you'll never be
far from my thoughts.*
    Nick
    Xo

Okay, how am I such a girl that the first thing I gushed over was the
xo? He left a note because he didn't want to wake me. I can't help but
sigh as I read it again.

Knock, Knock.

I walk toward the door and notice Melanie standing in front of the
window, dangling my car keys. It's ten o'clock, and I've enjoyed a
leisurely morning of coffee, a long steamy shower, relaxing in front of
the fire, and rereading my first love note. *I let out another dreamy sign
and laugh. What the hell is wrong with me?*

"Good morning, sunshine." Melanie strolls in carrying a cardboard
drink carrier with two Starbucks cups and a tempting brown paper
bakery bag.

"You are always coming to my rescue, Mel. What's in the bag?"

"I stopped for Starbucks, and they had the most delicious-looking
scones. I couldn't resist. Although I need to lay off the carbs after all
the grazing I did last night. Oh, Kat, you didn't eat anything before
you left, did you?" She quickly covers her mouth, realizing she may
have said something upsetting.

"No. But it all worked out fine. I wasn't really hungry. For food
anyway."

Melanie spins on her heel and gives me a raised eyebrow. "What
pray tell does that cryptic little statement mean? Kat, please tell me
that means you had a visitor."

"I did." My smile is about to pop teeth out of my face. I can't
control it. "Nick caught me while I was waiting on an Uber and drove
me home." Watching the glee on Mel's face, I wickedly decide to add,
"And once we got here... well, he continued to drive me home." I
cover my face, chuckling at my ridiculous pun.

"Oh. My. God. Are you serious? You should have seen that boy fly down the steps and run out the front door to look for you once I told him you'd decided to leave for the night. Jake and I just looked at each other and said, 'he's got it bad!' Kat, he really is a good guy. I hope you two can finally get things on the right track."

Taking a large white coffee cup in hand and sipping from the Columbian nectar, I exhale my joy. "I feel pretty good about it after last night. But I still want to meet with Dr. Miller to iron out everything with the pills and the texts from Mark. I need to figure out how to handle the Rohypnol test if it comes back positive. It's a lot to ask someone new to take on. I have enough past romantic life drama I don't need to give him any other demons to deal with."

"Well, speaking of drama. What was all that about with Dr. Lee? I'd never met him before. Holy crap, is he hot, by the way!" I just nod because there's no arguing that fact. The man looks like a model with that dark hair and blue eyes.

"Jake told me who he was. He said he's kind of a smug surgeon, and apparently, Dr. Lee and Nick have had run-ins before. Jake said Nick tried to warn him not to let Dr. Lee anywhere near you."

I almost choke on my coffee. "What?"

"Yeah. Nick told Jake Dr. Lee was a terrible player and didn't want you getting hurt by the likes of him."

"Oh." I cover my lips with my index finger, relishing in Nick's macho, overprotective ways. *It's kinda hot.* "I don't know much detail. And I don't ever want Nick to think I'm sharing his dirty laundry…"

"But…" Melanie prompts, hopefully.

"That blonde. She's Nick's ex-wife."

"Holy shit! No?"

"Yeah." I take another sip of my coffee. "He didn't want to talk about it, and I certainly understand that scenario. I don't completely understand their situation. He seems to not have any love lost for her, but the last time I saw her… well, she and Nick were hugging in front of Julio's restaurant."

"Wow. It's hard to imagine that after what I saw last night."

"I know. I don't completely get it either. I couldn't place her when I saw her with Dr. Lee. But once Nick addressed her, and I looked back and forth between the two of them, I remembered seeing them together. I hadn't known him long at the time."

"I wonder if Dr. Lee is the reason they broke up?" Mel adds, taking a slurp from her cup. We are starting to sound like two old hens. My curiosity is killing me, but he has been so respectful of my needs, I'm certainly not going to push him to share anything until he's ready. *But he needs to do it before the wedding.* I giggle.

"What's that laugh for?"

"Nothing. So, when are you opening those bags?"

An hour later, we've enjoyed good coffee, scones, and gossip worthy of a *Real Housewives* episode. I ask Melanie if she's ready for me to drive her home and grab my bag in response to her nod. We make idle chatter on the way to her home, but with each silence in the conversation my mind drifts back to Nick.

"Thanks for bringing my car. And the scones. You're the best," I shout out the open window as Melanie ascends her front steps.

"Yeah, I know," she bats her eyes playfully.

Heading for home, I listen to various love songs on the radio and bask in the glow of the evening before. A wild grin takes over my face at the recollection of his words. *"I'm going to marry you, and you're going to have all my babies."* How long I'd waited for someone to say something like that.

Suddenly, I feel my phone start to buzz in my pocket. A grin inhabits my face before I can even see my cell. I've missed Nick today. After last night, I just wanted to be reconnected somehow. Yet, I didn't want to impose on whatever he and his father had going on. As I bring the screen closer, I instantly realize this text is not from Nick.

11:42 a.m.
Unknown number
Unknown number: Image

There's no text, just a picture. A picture of me. A picture of me wearing that thong and those black boots, covering my naked breasts with my hands, dollar bills raining down upon me.

Nick

I walk up to Dad's front door and take in a deep, fortifying breath. This day is hard every year. We try to make it positive, but it's hard all the same. Dad is usually here with the door wide, waiting on me with each visit. But I know he's feeling as downtrodden as I am this morning. Even if he'll try to put a brave face to it.

Because of the solemn nature of the day and his recent pelvic fracture, I try the doorknob instead of knocking. It's open, as I'm sure he's expecting me. I don't see him in the den or the kitchen as I peek in. Turning, I head down the hall toward his bedroom and find his slumped form seated at the edge of the bed, face buried in his hands.

"Dad?"

"Oh, Nick. I'm sorry. I didn't realize the time." He attempts to wipe the tears away without my noticing. My heart squeezes in my chest at the site.

"You all right?"

"Yes, just chokes me up every year. But this is a day to celebrate Lydie, not mourn, right?"

"Sure, Dad, but we're human. It's okay to cry."

"You wouldn't think after twenty years there'd be any tears left."

"I don't know... I still get choked up when I think about her. My first love."

My dad pats me on the leg as another tear tumbles down his soft, wrinkly skin. "Yeah, we were lucky."

Every year since my mother died, my father has made a big to-do over her birthday. We choose not to remember the day she died, only the life she lived. We spend each year much the same. We start the day with a trip to the florist to pick out the perfect flowers for her graveside. We're often so inspired by the floral shop's selections we decide to stop by the local nursery to pick out a new rose bush to plant in the yard in her honor. I think every color of the rainbow is now well represented. We end our day with a big meal, prepared at home, followed by her favorite cake. Although she baked most of our celebration cakes by hand, her birthday cake was always a local grocery chain yellow-pound cake with buttercream icing. Nothing fancy, but extra sweet. Just like Mom.

The day progressed as it did most years, laughter mixed with a few tears. As the sun makes its descent I can tell my dad is exhausted, and quite honestly, so am I. It's been a long weekend, and I need some quiet time to get centered before beginning another busy week.

As I drive home, I reflect on the mix of emotions I've felt this weekend. Sebastian, Sophia, Kat, and my dad. It's been an emotional rollercoaster. I thank God for my dad and his ability to handle loss in such a graceful way. My misguided interpretation of his loss as emptiness, when in reality it's his utter devotion to the woman he loved. I admire Kat for taking a chance with me despite her past. And I decide I'm going to let go of my feelings of animosity toward Sophia and Sebastian. Hanging on to that hate is only hurting me. *Hell, they deserve each other. Why should I stand in their way?*

Walking into my home, I put both hands on my hips and take a good look around. That's it. I'm doing it. I'm selling this damn place. There may not be any memories of a happy home torturing me here, but I need a clean slate. I'm going to start looking for something else. With that decision made, I somehow feel lighter already. Closing out this weekend with a drink and some Sports Center is about all my brain can handle at this point.

Unless Kat was here. I don't have the mental energy to talk or text, but still wish she was here with me. I wonder what she's doing right now.

Chapter Twenty-Two

Kat

Sitting on my bed, knees pulled up against my chest, rocking back and forth, I contemplate what I'm going to do. My dreamy mood has shifted faster than Danica Patrick can change gears after receiving that text. Seeing that picture has me instantly alarmed and humiliated. *How is this my life?*

I turn to sit at the edge of the bed, my body trembling. I've taken a scalding hot shower and put on the ugliest pajama pants and shirt I own. To curb the shaking, I've donned a sweatshirt and put on a pot of tea. Nothing is helping. I hate to do it, but I think I'm going to have to wash my Benadryl down with a glass of wine. If I don't get my nerves under control, I'm going to go off the deep end. *But hey, I can watch the whole thing unfold on camera later if I do something else worthy of what? Blackmail?*

I'm certain the texts are coming from Mark. It's the only thing that makes sense. But why the unknown number? Is he protecting himself since he knows what he's doing is wrong?

I don't have time to worry about his criminal behavior. I've got enough of my own inappropriate actions to contend with. Has anyone else seen this photo? There's no doubt it's me. I'm standing tall in all my glory, wearing only that ridiculous thong, those damn knee-high boots, and a shocked expression. *Now I have proof. No need to use the Nanny cam to show I've lost my mind.*

Speaking of losing my mind, I have an appointment with Dr. Miller in two days. Thank heavens because I can't tell anyone else about this. I'm mortified.

Walking to my kitchen, I look for a bottle of wine. I couldn't care less what it tastes like. Heck, I'd drink cooking sherry if it'd help me to calm down. I simply need something to dull the quaking nerves until my Benadryl kicks in. I pour a glass of Pinot Grigio and sip the crisp, fruity beverage as I walk to my front door. I ensure the door is locked, and my front porch light is on. I double-check my garage door is closed, and the door into my home is locked. Lastly, I verify the back door is locked, and everything seems sound. I have no reason to think Mark would come and harm me, but then again, who would've ever thought him capable of this. And for what?

I return to my bedroom and decide to look through my phone's playlist to see if there's anything there to distract me. I jump, startled, as my phone buzzes unexpectedly.

10:50 p.m.
Unknown number
Unknown number: Only you've seen this picture, but don't tempt me.

11:01 p.m.
Unknown number
Unknown number: This phone is untraceable. Don't try.

The shaking is now ten times worse. I text back.

11:04 p.m.
Kat: Why are you doing this?

Throwing the phone across the bed, I bury my head in my hands and scream. I don't understand. He's my friend. How does he have this picture? Is it possible I was really there, dancing, in a strip club? And he was watching? How can this be happening? I can't even begin to ask him what it is he wants. Does he think he can blackmail me into dating him? Or is there something more he's interested in taking?

Running to the sink, I splash cold water onto my face. What am I supposed to do now? If I go to the police, he could leak this picture. There'd be no disputing it's me. If this came out, I'd have to move. I'd be too embarrassed to stay. I doubt people from outside of the area would care, but I've lived here my whole life. I couldn't face people, wondering if they'd seen it and what they thought of me. Every time I walked in to see a new patient, I'd wonder. *Holy heck, could I get fired for this? Jeez, of course I can.* Who'd believe my story? I'm sure they'll think I strip for fun.

I get up, taking my glass of wine with me, and head for the shower. I'm getting back in. Somehow the volume of tears doesn't seem as bad when I'm in there. It's my refuge from my own personal storm. It's a good thing I can't tolerate cold showers, or I'd probably drown in there.

I roll over to the sharp sting of sunlight. Checking my clock, it's 6:10 a.m. I'm working at 10:00 a.m. today, so I have plenty of time to get ready. I think I may have managed three hours of sleep which is surprising given that's about average for me. After last night, I'm surprised I slept at all.

I manage to sit up and grab my robe. At least I'm wearing the same thing I had on last night. *Don't need to watch the highlight reels on the Nanny cam.* I shuffle into the kitchen and start the coffee brewing. I need a clear head to plan how I'm going to manage until I see Dr. Miller tomorrow. Once I get through today, I'm not scheduled to work again until Thursday. Willing myself to handle this with more strength and courage than I actually possess, I head back to the shower. My water bill is going to be insane this month.

"Good morning, Kat," Dr. Street greets as he walks past the hallway. I've only been here ten minutes, but I'm already dreading the day in front of me.

"Hi, Marty."

"You okay, love? You don't seem yourself this morning," he asks with obvious concern.

"I'll be okay. Just have a lot on my mind," I offer up. "Is there anything I can help you with before I start picking up patients?"

"No. I'm good," he responds, apprehensive.

"Really, Marty, I'll be okay. It's the sleep thing, that's all."

"Okay, doll. Just get another cup of coffee or something.

"Probably not a bad idea on the coffee. I'll be back in a minute." I walk down the hall toward the physician's lounge and swipe my badge. The room is quiet, and I head for the industrial-sized coffee machine. Placing the cup in the dispenser, I try to focus on the scene in front of me. I must not let my mind wander. I will figure this out with Dr. Miller tomorrow afternoon.

"Hey, Kat." I jump, hearing my name. "Hey, steady there. You okay?" Dr. Lee asks.

"Yeah, I'm fine."

"You don't look fine." He places his hand on my back; I know he's innocently trying to comfort me. We've been here before, but somehow it feels awkward now, accepting consolation from him knowing what he's done to Nick. Like conspiring with the enemy.

"It's nothing, really."

"Well, I feel insulted," he responds flatly. I look up to see he appears terse. "You must think I'm stupid. Something is clearly wrong, Katarina. Is this like last time? Is someone bothering you?"

I look down, wringing my hands. I have to get my shit together, or I'll never make it through this day.

"If you won't tell me, is there someone else who can help you?" he pushes.

"I'm not sure anyone can help," I whisper. I don't want to insult this man who's only trying to help, but there's no way I can share my problems with him. "I appreciate you trying to help. I have to take care of this on my own. It'll be okay. But thank you." I swiftly grab my coffee, turn for the door, and head back to the emergency room before the conversation can continue any further.

This day couldn't go any slower. At least the patient volume has been steady, which has taken my mind off of things a bit. I continue to type my notes into the computer so I can leave on time.

"Hey, Kat." Again, I'm jumping like I'm in a damn haunted house.

"Hey, Jake."

"Marty said you haven't been yourself today. What's going on?"

"Nothing. It's nothing. I'll be fine. I see Dr. Miller tomorrow. I'll be fine. I just need to keep busy and get out of here." I feel him place his hand over mine, begging for my attention. As I look up from my computer where I've been spilling this word salad, I meet his concerned gaze."

"Kat, come with me."

I stand and follow him to the consult room. This is where families sit and await updates on their critical loved ones. Somehow, it's almost apropos I should be in here. I feel like my sanity needs life support.

"Okay, cut the crap, Kat. What's going on? You look like you didn't get an ounce of sleep, and you're jumpy. Mel said you were fine when she was with you yesterday. Did Mark text you again? Has he said something to you?" Jake looks at me with the concern of a big brother.

"No. I think everything's catching up with me. I couldn't sleep, and the questions about that night are getting to me. I have an appointment with Dr. Miller tomorrow. I'll get things sorted with him. In the meantime, please don't say anything to anyone about this. I know you're trying to help, but I need to handle this on my own. It's my fault for agreeing to go out with him. I don't want to disrupt the group over this."

"All right, if you say so. But would you please tell me if there's anything I can do? I hate to see you like this. Have you told Nick?"

"No!" I blurt. "And I know you two have talked about me before, but I need this kept between us. I don't want my baggage being handled by anyone but me. If there's a chance anything could work out between the two of us, I need to take care of this." I can feel my body starting to shake at the enormity of all of this.

"Okay, okay. I get it. I promise I won't tell him anything. But, Kat, that guy really cares about you. He'd want to know if something has happened."

"I don't care. I have to handle this on my own. He has his own issues. He didn't want to talk about his ex-wife and Dr. Lee. It's not tit for tat or anything, but I'm allowed to keep some things to myself until I'm ready to share. I see Dr. Miller tomorrow. I just need to focus on work the rest of the day, and I'll be fine. I'll work it out with him tomorrow."

"If you say so." He rubs my arm before pulling back and punching me lightly in the shoulder. So why are you bothering me with your personal drama? Get back to work," he teases.

As I walk out of the consult room behind Jake, I look up to see Nick coming down the hallway. I really can't handle that right now. I speed up a bit to get into the emergency room and busy myself. I care a lot about him, but I cannot handle seeing him today. He'll see right through me. Heck, everyone else has.

"Hi, Jake." I hear Nick's voice as I return to the ER. I'm praying my friend will make up some sort of excuse for why I wouldn't have time to talk to Nick right now. There are only a few more hours before I can go home and get ready for tomorrow. Dr. Miller will help me figure this out.

"Okay, so everything I tell you here is completely confidential, right?" I blurt, my ass barely in the chair before I give Dr. Miller the inquisition. Nothing like getting right to it.

"Good afternoon, Katarina. Yes, everything you share here is completely confidential. Has something else happened since the last time we spoke?" he asks, fingers steepled under his chin.

"So, I took the Rohypnol test to make sure Mark hadn't had any involvement in my memory loss the night of our date. I'm supposed to receive the results of that any day now."

"Well, that sounds like a wise decision. I'm glad you're trying to take control of your situation," he reassures.

"I don't know how much control I have. I got more texts from him last night. The number is still listed as unknown, but I know it's him. The first texts were warnings not to mention any of this to anyone, but then he sent a picture. There's no doubt anymore."

"What picture, Kat? No doubt about what?" Dr. Miller asks, confused.

"So, remember the weird dream I had where I was stripping at a club, and the following morning, I woke up wearing knee-high black boots I've never owned before?" I look to see Dr. Miller nodding in agreement. "Well, at the very end of the dream, I thought I recognized Mark being there. But it was a dream, so I didn't think any more of it." I reach for my bottled water as my tongue suddenly feels like sandpaper. "It appears it wasn't a dream. It must have really happened because he texted me a picture, and I'm wearing that thong and those black boots, attempting to cover the rest of my naked body with my hands," I cry out.

Trying to gather my composure before continuing, I take a deep breath and rub my sweaty palms over my jeans. "Not only have I been gallivanting about the town without any knowledge of my actions, but this asshole has it on film. Beyond the fact I'd be humiliated if the picture came out, I could potentially lose my job. Who wants some exhibitionist taking care of patients in their hospital?"

"So, remind me. This dream occurred before your date with Mark?" he asks, very serious now.

"Yes. I'd stopped taking those pills before my date with him. So, I'm sure it was before."

"Other than seeing him in the crowd, he had no other interaction with you? In the dream, I mean?"

"No. Not that I recall. But clearly, my mind is not reliable when I use sleeping pills." I pause and take a deep breath before continuing. "I'm certain it's the medication that caused me to act this way. It's been brought to my attention by someone that they saw me out one night, and I have no memory of it." Hearing myself say this out loud, I'm still as flabbergasted as I was the day Nick told me. "I haven't had any of that behavior since stopping the zolpidem."

"To be clear, Kat, you aren't having any more weird dreams or waking with things differently than you left them the night before."

"No, not since I stopped the drug. The night terrors are back. But they're different now. No ex-boyfriends. I just feel like I'm being watched or chased. But I wake up in my pajamas each morning. I'm pretty confident I haven't gone anywhere." I watch as Dr. Miller rubs his jawline and appears to consider all I've told him.

"When the pictures were sent to you… was there any threat? Did he insinuate what or if he planned to do something with them?"

"No. He texted again to tell me he hadn't shown them to anyone else and that he was using an untraceable phone. But when I asked why he was doing this, he didn't respond." My tears start up again, and I notice I'm clutching the armrests of this horrific green chair.

"Kat. I think you should consider going to the police."

"I can't. I have no idea what he wants. I can't risk making him mad, and then he plasters that picture everywhere," I shriek. "It was bad enough when I didn't understand what was happening, but if the whole world sees the shit I've been doing under the influence of that pill… well, I can't handle that, Dr. Miller."

"Have you confided in anyone about the new texts containing the photo?" he asks carefully. He can see I'm on the edge.

"No. And I won't."

"Kat. This is a huge cross to bear on your own. It's your choice whether you decide to go to the police. At the very least, I think you should get a restraining order. But if you decide you don't want to go that route, you need someone you can confide in. If nothing else, for safety. This guy sounds unhinged."

I consider his words carefully. I'm not getting the answers I'd hoped for with this visit. But there's only so much this miracle worker can do, I suppose. I can't tell Jake. He'll kill Mark. I can't tell Melanie. She will just tell Jake, who will then kill Mark. Maybe Olivia? *I need to go home and take another shower.*

"What's your plan, Katarina? How do you plan to proceed once you leave here? You should have some strategy in place to deal with this."

Staring at the floor, I try to come up with something concrete. "I'll reach out to a friend. There are actually two. I'll see if I can share enough, so they understand what I'm concerned about without having to give them the photo." I chew on my fingernail, trying to come up with anything else. "I'll think about the restraining order. I'm just not ready yet, and if I do, I'm not sure I can show the police that photo."

"I understand. I think that's a good start, Kat."

Thinking of Nick, the tears start to tumble again. "Dr. Miller. I started to get close to that man I told you about. The one I work with. I care for him a lot, and I'm pretty sure he feels the same. I've been holding back because of all of this mess. I don't want to begin dating with all of this hanging over me. This could be my first chance at a healthy relationship. I'm worried I'm going to lose him because I don't want to involve him in this." I sniffle and look up at his wise face.

"Kat. I don't think it's wise to begin a new relationship with someone when you're keeping things from them. If he's one of the two you're planning to share this with, then pursue things carefully. Let him know what's going on."

I can't do that. Beyond the total shame I'd feel if he found out, he'd probably do worse damage to Mark than Jake. I absolutely cannot let him get himself embroiled in this mess. I decide to keep this to myself. "Yes, Dr. Miller. That's probably wise."

Gathering my things, I head to the reception desk to make my next appointment. As I'm heading home, I consider reaching out to Olivia to see if she can come over so I can share the latest piece of this nightmare. I don't have anything except my volunteer job tomorrow, so I can stay home and try to figure this out. If I hear from Nick, I'll try to stay connected but let him know I'm still working out the sleeping aid situation. *That's not a lie, right?*

"Hey, Olivia. Any chance you might be able to come over tonight?" I recall she doesn't have a production until Thursday evening. "I could use a friend."

"Oh, Kat. Are you okay?"

"Not really." I sniffle, unable to keep the tears at bay. I've been home two hours, and even after my shower, I can't stop crying.

"I'll be over within the hour."

Thanking heaven above for dear friends, I hang up the phone and wipe my eyes. I'll put on some tea. While I'm waiting, I contemplate making one more call.

Nick

Things at work have been busy. I knew it would be, given sports are in full effect. I haven't had much of an opportunity to reach out to Kat. I wasn't in the right headspace for it on Sunday after my day with Dad. Seeing her from a distance Monday, I'd hoped to talk to her for a few moments, but Jake intercepted, and I got the feeling he was playing interference, so I let it go. She's asked me for time to handle this situation with the zolpidem, and I promised to give it to her. I just miss her.

Putting the dishes from dinner into the dishwasher, I decide to sit down and review some of the realtor's listings from their website. I want something small in town. I'm fortunate enough to have the finances to afford a small home near the hospital and a nicer home on the water. All of this despite Sophia's lawyers. I'll consider the lake house down the road but want to find a place in town I like so I can list this one in early spring.

Pouring one finger of scotch, I look down into my glass and remember the night of the gala. Boy, did that night end better than it started. My dad was right. I was fortunate to get out of that relationship with Sophia before kids came along. I laugh when I recall blurting out to Kat that I was going to marry her. Attempting to save face by joking about kids. She took it all in stride. But was I joking? There's absolutely no doubt in my mind she's it for me. I'm not daft. In just a few short months, I've fallen in love with her. In love with the beautifully tortured soul who appears more broken than I am.

Sipping from my scotch, I hold the cool glass to my throat as if it'll calm the burn of the liquid. I reflect on my prior decisions. To think I'd accepted my fate. A life alone to protect me from loss. Yet, the pain of losing Katarina would be just as great. I'll wait as long as she needs.

Kat

"Nate? Hey, it's Kat."

"Hey, girl. How've you been? God, I miss you."

Hearing his ever-present adoration dance across the phone line has me tearing up again.

"Kat? What's wrong?"

"Nate, I'm scared."

"Honey, what about?"

"Things are a mess, and I might need your help. But you have to promise me you will keep it between us. No matter what."

"Kat, you know I would. What's wrong?"

"I really should tell you this in person, but Olivia is on her way here. I'm going to tell her too. You're two of my closest friends, and I need both of you."

"I'm glad to be here. What's going on? Are you pregnant?"

"Ha!" I wish. I almost think that would be easier. "No. I…"

Knock, Knock, Knock.

"Oh lord, Nate. Olivia must've come over here like a speed demon. Can I call you back later?"

"Of course. I'm here doing a whole lotta nothing. Why don't you text me when Liv is heading out? I can come by then if you want."

"Okay. Maybe. Let me text or call you later."

I walk toward the door and see a very anxious starlet through the window. Opening the door, I beckon her in, "Come on in, Liv."

Grabbing my hand, she drags me down my hallway to the couch and sits down, pulling me with her. "What's going on? You've got me worried sick."

"Well, remember the weird stuff I was trying to sort out and the date with Mark?"

"Of course. What's happened now?"

"Well, I've pretty much figured out it's all related to the sleeping pill. I still don't have the Rohypnol test back, but someone confirmed they saw me out late one night when I'd taken the sleeping pill, and I don't recall being there."

I watch as Olivia gasps and covers her mouth. "Are they sure it was you?"

Not divulging all the dirty details here. "Uh, yeah. They're quite sure." I squirm in my seat a little. "What's more, the night that I told you I had weird dreams of being in a strip club and the next morning waking up in bizarre clothes..."

"Yes?" Liv's eyes are like saucers, watching me carefully.

"Well, that guy that I went on the date with, the one I'm waiting for the Rohypnol test to come back, he must've been there because he sent a picture of me on stage."

"Holy shit, Kat." She grabs for both of my hands, and I'm surprised to find I'm not crying. *Holy crap, I must be empty.* Or maybe I'm too numb to cry anymore.

"Why did he send you the picture? Did he know you were confused about what was happening?"

"No. I don't know why he sent it. His texts have been very cryptic. None of it makes any sense. I don't know if it's some type of blackmail or if he's retaliating because I told him I didn't want to date. My counselor thinks I should file a restraining order."

"Kat, I agree. This guy sounds scary."

"I know, but I can't risk making him angrier. What if I do, and he suddenly releases that picture on social media or something? It's not just my pride. Olivia, I could lose my job if a picture like that came out."

"I hadn't thought about that. What're you going to do?"

"I don't know. My counselor said I needed to involve a few people. If I wasn't going to the police. So, I had a plan in place if anything got worse."

"Well, I'll do anything to help, and so will Mac. Do you want to stay with us for a while?"

"I think I'll be okay. You two have so much going on with the wedding. I don't want to impose. But it'd make me feel better to know I had somewhere to turn if things got worse."

"Of course. You don't even have to ask. But Kat, can I ask you something?"

"Sure."

"Are you still seeing Nick?"

"Kind of. We aren't in any formal relationship or anything. But well... we keep hooking up." This brings a smile to my face. This emotion feels so foreign now. "I told him I needed time to work things out after it was confirmed I'd been doing things without my knowledge on the sleeping pill. He's so understanding, Liv. He's like no one I've ever been with."

"By a long shot."

"I have to admit, I'm worried I could lose him over this mess."

"Why would you say that?"

"My psychologist, Dr. Miller, advised it wouldn't be best to continue a relationship with him if I didn't tell him what was going on with Mark. But I don't want him dealing with any of my baggage. I want to get it right this time, Olivia. Plus, I couldn't live with myself if he went after Mark. I don't want him doing anything stupid on my account."

"I hadn't considered that. But I think Dr. Miller's right. It won't help to keep things from Nick, but I understand why you're conflicted. I wouldn't worry about losing him, though. You guys have been through a fair amount already, and he keeps coming back for more. I think it'd take a lot to run him off." Olivia beams comfortingly at me. "I'm going to use your restroom before I go. I'm really glad you called me, Kat. You have to stop handling everything in your life alone." My dear, sweet friend squeezes my hands in hers. "You're loved. Lean on us."

I sit, considering Olivia's words. I do feel better knowing she's aware of what's happening. I have nothing to be embarrassed about where she's concerned. She knows me. She knows I'd never behave the way I did without the influence of the sleeping pill. I'm a victim here. The more I ruminate on that statement, the angrier I get at Mark. That he's put me in this position.

Olivia walks toward me and looks a little pale. "Liv? You okay?"

"Yeah. Since we're both sharing all of our personal nitty-gritty. I need to let you know there's an issue with the wedding."

I instantly become alarmed. After all of these years, is Mac having cold feet?

Sitting up taller, I push, "What do you mean?"

"I'm pregnant. I don't want to walk down the aisle looking like a beached whale. So, we're moving it to Valentine's Day. Corny, huh?"

The shock of her statement finally settles in, and I burst into laughter. "That's not corny at all. It's amazing. The best news I've heard in so long." I grab her to my chest and squeeze her until I remember she isn't feeling well. "Oh, I'm sorry, Liv. The last thing you need is me grabbing at you."

"Don't be silly. What's a little puke between friends?"

Olivia heads home a short while later, and I decide to let Nate know I'm feeling better but wouldn't mind catching up in the morning if he's free. Between the counseling session with Dr. Miller, the multiple showers and crying fits, and now Olivia's visit, I might actually be able to sleep tonight.

I reach for my phone to call him and notice there's a new email notification. Clicking on the prompt, I see it's from the lab. As I hit the email in question, I wait for the attachment to load.

Rohypnol: positive

Chapter Twenty-Three

Kat

Knock, Knock.

I walk toward my front door and see my dear friend Nate through the window.

"Hey, come on in." I usher as a decadent aroma wafts in with him.

As he walks past, I notice coffee and donuts from Country Time Donuts, a beloved local confectionary institution.

"Oh my gosh, I love you!"

"You love me or my donuts?" Nate laughs.

I honestly didn't think anything could help my mood this morning. I didn't sleep at all last night. My feelings flipped from angry to fearful, betrayed to violated. I still can't get a handle on this. Sitting down at the kitchen table, I start to share the events of my life. All the humiliating events. I come to the portion of the conversation where I have to share my recent texts from Mark, and I stop.

"Nate. I'm sharing this with you because I desperately need your help. You mean the world to me, and I trust you. I was trying to manage this on my own, but my counselor convinced me to let a few people I trusted in. I trust Jake and Mel, but you can't tell Mel something and not expect it to get to Jake." I watch as Nate nods in agreement. "And I can't tell Jake because I'm certain he would try to kill Mark."

Nate suddenly looks shocked and a bit, angry? I tell him about the date with Mark, the questions that followed, and the texts that began appearing after I advised Mark I wasn't interested in dating. I disclose receiving a picture confirming he saw me at the strip club performing and that the purpose of said picture is still unknown. I leave out what I was wearing because this situation is degrading enough. Reaching over, I grab his arm. "Nate, I found out last night the Rohypnol test I took came back positive."

Nate jumps up from his chair, the wooden furnishing falling to the ground behind him with a loud thud. "Oh, hell no!" he yells into the air.

Jumping up to try and comfort him, I beg. "Nate. Please. I know you're upset. I am too, but I need you to stay calm. I don't want anyone doing anything to Mark. I have to figure all of this out. When I called you yesterday, I had no idea about the test results. I was just upset about that damn picture. My counselor wants me to go to the police."

"Yes, Kat. You need to go today. This isn't a joke. I don't know what he thought he was doing. Hell, you don't have any idea what he might've done to you!" he shouts.

"But, Nate, he could release that picture. Obviously, he has a screw loose. I need to figure this out before I do anything that'll set him off."

"I'm going to kill him!"

"No. This is bad enough. I can't have anyone else getting into trouble because of me. I'd never forgive myself. Please, Nate. I reached out to you because I thought you'd listen. Please. I need your help." I'm almost hysterical in my attempts to reason with him.

Suddenly, the strong, loving arms of my dear friend are wrapping around me. I can feel my body sway back in forth in his embrace. I sniffle into his shirt. "Kat, we'll figure this out. I'm going to try my best not to do or say anything to him, but I can't promise I won't lose it if I see him."

"Nate, please. I beg of you. I couldn't bear it if you hurt him, and he pressed charges. What if that happened, and then he released the photo? Where would that get us? I just need some time to figure out how to handle this."

My big, handsome friend cups my cheeks and looks directly into my eyes. "You're not alone, Katarina. We're going to figure this out. Do you want me to stay with you when I'm not at the station working?"

"I don't want to impose, but I wouldn't turn it down."

"Done. What does the rest of your week look like?"

"I have my volunteer meal delivery today. I'm looking forward to something normal for a few hours. Then I return to work tomorrow. As stressful as it is there, I'll feel safe. As long as Mark doesn't bring a patient in."

"I don't know if he's working tomorrow, but I can get his schedule easy enough. You might feel like you've got a little more control when you know he could potentially come in."

"You're right. That would be helpful."

I give Nate a hug, thanking him for his help. With another reassuring glance, he turns and heads to his car. It's just as well, as I need to be heading out so I can deliver my volunteer meal route. I've never been so excited to see a bunch of little old people in my life

Nick

I'm exhausted. This week at work has been almost as busy as the week following my dad's fall. I'm looking forward to the weekend. I have a soccer game Saturday, and Sunday I'm meeting the realtor to view a few homes.

Dr. Morgan referred an ER patient a few moments ago and although Dr. Morgan's on call, he believes this patient's issues are related to his rotator cuff which another shoulder specialist repaired before I arrived to St. Luke's. As I walk in that direction, I secretly hope to see Kat. I'm so tired of giving her space. Even if it's just a momentary visit, it'd make all the difference.

Arriving to the emergency department, I locate the patient in question and make quick work of evaluating him. I've given him a steroid injection, and encouraged him to follow up in the office. I haven't seen Katarina, but I know she's here. Her lab coat is hanging from her favorite computer chair. Deciding to enter my consult note in the ER versus my office, I sit in the chair next to hers. As if thinking of her has conjured her arrival, she whips by me in a whirlwind, muttering to herself.

"I don't know why I think he'll ever do anything himself. I have a thousand things to do, but 'Kat, can you put a staple in room ten's head? She only needs one.'" I try not to chuckle as she does a pretty impressive imitation of Dr. Silver. She continues to mumble, "If it only needs one, why do you need me to do it? Freaking douche canoe."

"Ha." I can't hold back any longer. Turning, I look directly at her and realize she's had this entire rant unaware anyone was sitting here. She must be in a bad way today.

"Oh, god. Sorry." She covers her mouth, giggling because it's me. At least, I hope that's why she's giggling. "I'm surprised you didn't 'Nice' me." She chuckles louder now.

"Nice." I guffaw. Before I can continue my jibe, Dr. Silver himself comes around the corner.

"Oh, Dr. Barnes. Just the guy I was looking for. I have an orthopedic patient here who will need a splint placement."

"Are you consulting me, Dr. Silver?"

"Yes, I guess I am." He responds with a questioning expression.

"Well, Dr. Morgan is actually on call. You need to contact the service. I was seeing a patient in the ER for Dr. Morgan as a courtesy. I have to get back to my office. I have a waiting room full of patients I need to return to."

"Ah, sure. Kat?" Dr. Silver now directs his attention toward her.

"I already did it. You can discharge her now." Kat answers abruptly, her eyes never leaving her computer screen.

"Oh, thank you. That was fast." I watch as Dr. Silver walks off, scratching his head.

Hoping to get one more smile from my girl, I mutter as she'd done just moments ago. "Asshat."

Through my periphery, I take her in as she covers her delectable mouth with her hand and chuckles into it. I stand from my seat and find I'm physically unable to restrain myself from taking her hand from her mouth and pulling it to mine. Placing a kiss there, I bend down and whisper, "See you later, kitten."

Kat

Pushing through my day, I'm amazed it's gone as well as it has. Nate providing me with Mark's schedule has helped. I don't have to worry about bumping into him today as he isn't working until tomorrow. From what Nate says, this rotating schedule should allow me to know when he's working well into the future. Hopefully, I can use it to ask Jake to give me those days off. I still cannot believe that son of a bitch drugged me. I'm choosing not to think about what he might've done. My underwear were still on in the morning. I had no marks on me. I'm not going there. There's nothing I can do about it now anyway.

As I finish placing a splint on the elderly patient in room eleven, I try not to laugh at the way Nick mocked Dr. Silver this morning. Walking back to my computer, I reflect on the moment of brevity, knowing he was doing it to lighten my mood. Oh, how I've missed that sexy smile. Rubbing the back of my hand against my cheek, I can still feel the electricity of his lips on my knuckles.

"Ouch," I blurt out. Speaking of electricity. There's a sharp, stabbing sensation in my right lower abdomen. The jolt of pain strikes again. "Ah." What the heck now? *I've probably got a urinary tract infection from holding my bladder so long working here.* I stand from my seat and decide walking a bit might help.

"Hey, Kat, you don't look so hot." I hear Jake greet. He's coming on shift for the evening as I'm treading water to the finish line.

"Yeah, I'm worried I have a urinary tract infection. I've been getting these pains, and it's getting worse."

"You look a little pale. And you feel clammy."

"I'm sure it's the pain. It's making me a little nauseated." I rub my right lower pelvis to attempt to ease the ache there.

"Kat? You still have your appendix?"

"Yeah. Heck, Jake, that can't be it."

"Why not?"

"Because I don't want that to be it," I whine. "I don't have any time for an appendectomy."

"Oh, yeah? What've you got to do? If it needs to come out, it needs to come out."

"Jake, you're getting all worked up for— ah!" I clutch my pelvis again.

"Kat, this is ridiculous. It's not that busy today. You need to get this checked out. You're never sick. I'll call someone in if we can't make it a few more hours without you. But you need to get some bloodwork, and they'll need to put in an IV to check your appendix."

"Oh, for god's sake. Ouch. All right."

It's been a little over an hour, and I'm sitting in this exam room, wearing a hospital gown, feeling like a complete dunce. I'm sure this is a urinary tract infection, and I've wasted an ER visit.

Jake strolls in and says, "Not a UTI."

"What? Really? I thought for sure that was it."

"Look at the bright side, at least you aren't pregnant."

I sneer at him for joking about such things.

"Your bloodwork is back. Everything there looks good, and you aren't running a fever. They should be coming soon to get you for your CT. Do you want me to call your mom and dad?"

"What? No. I'm sure this is a whole lotta nothing. I don't want to worry them. We can call them later after we figure it out. I'd say it was a pulled muscle, but I haven't done anything. Could it be a kidney stone?"

"Maybe. Has there been any blood in your urine?"

"Not that I recall. And I haven't had any pain over my kidney, but hopefully, that's it."

Two hours later, and I sit watching some mindless television show, waiting for the results of my CT scan. I can't believe this. *At least the*

medicine Jake gave me has helped that sharp stabby pain. As if he's heard his name called, he strolls in the door and shuts it behind him.

"So? What's the scoop? Am I having my appendix out?"

I watch as Jake carefully lowers himself to the bed. His features seem tense. *What the heck? Do I have cancer or something?*

"Kat. I've called the on-call Ob/Gyn."

"What? Why?"

"It appears you have an impressively large ovarian cyst on that side."

"Oh, whew. You had me worried. Ovarian cysts are no big deal." I notice Jake is stoic again.

"Kat, this one is big. The weight of it has caused it to rotate on the fallopian tube. You aren't getting any blood flow to that ovary."

Oh god. This isn't good.

"Try not to worry yet. Wait until the Ob/Gyn comes in and sees you. Maybe there's something they can do." Jake grabs my hand in his, but I already know. I can tell by the look on his face, he does too.

I awake hours later, in a different room than where I was last. Dr. Ryan had come in well after midnight to tell me the cyst had caused too much damage, and they were going to have to remove it. It, and my remaining ovary. I tried to hold my emotions together until I was alone. I didn't know Dr. Ryan beyond when I'd briefly watched him deliver Katrina's baby, Grace. I just nodded and listened as he made plans to take me to the operating room as soon as the on-call team could arrive. Looking about, I notice I'm in a regular room now, sunlight through the blinds alerting me it was a new day.

I roll onto my side and feel the tears start to fall. *What do you know? Guess I'm not empty anymore.* Funny how suddenly all the shit with Mark and the photo doesn't seem to be that big a deal anymore. My heart squeezes in my chest. I'm not sure why I'm crying.

I'd made choices after I was repeatedly hurt by the men in my life. I wasn't getting married, much less having children. So why is this so painful? Probably because it's no longer a choice. That coffin has been nailed shut. There won't be any babies for Katarina Kelly. Then the reality settles in. No one really wanted me before. Why on Earth would any man want me now?

Nick

It feels as if it's been a long day, but in reality, it's only 11:00 a.m. I came in early to take a patient to the OR who'd fallen the night before. She had an ugly, unstable ankle fracture, and I was thankful to get her in first thing this morning. Afterward, I'd gone to the office to see a few of my scheduled appointments before returning to check on her. She's a special case as she's thirty weeks pregnant.

As I complete charting her progress note in the computer, I look up to see Jake of all people coming out of a room. *That's odd. Maybe he's coming to check on one of his ER patients.*

I come around the nurses' station and slap him on the shoulder as he's standing by the door. "Hey, man, fancy seeing you up on the floor. I didn't think they ever let you out of the ER," I joke, but quickly notice anything but a jovial expression on his face.

Grabbing my arm, he starts to pull me down the hallway. "Hey, good to see you, Nick. Yeah, just heading back to where I belong."

I quickly gather his tone, and the strong grip on my bicep isn't friendly banter and turn quickly to see the name on the door: K. Kelly. "What the fuck, Jake?"

"Nick," he cautions.

"She's in the hospital, and you couldn't tell me? You were going to usher me away like she wasn't here?"

"Keep your voice down," Jake scolds. "You know good and well I can't tell you she's here unless she specifically asks me to tell you. I'm not breaking the hospital privacy laws or her personal privacy to tell you anything."

I stand staring at this man I thought I knew. I'm dumbfounded by this entire situation. I know he's right, but he knows how much I care about her.

"Nick. It's nothing personal. She doesn't want me to tell anyone but her parents she's here. I can't tell you anything, even if I wanted to. And you need to respect her privacy. Don't upset her."

I drop my voice and almost plead with him. "Is she okay?"

I watch in horror as his head drops. "I think she will be. Just give her some time, Nick. Okay? I have to go. I only ran up here to check on her because I was here when she had to be admitted. But I need to get back downstairs." He pats me on the shoulder, turns, and walks away.

Looking around, I notice there's no one around. No nurses, no techs, no other doctors. Fuck it, I can't help myself. I'd never invade her privacy by looking at her chart. But she can't expect me not to check on her. Turning quickly toward her door, I slowly push it open and find her lying on her side, her back to me. As I carefully walk toward her bed, I whisper her name.

"Kat?" I don't know if she's asleep, but she isn't answering me.

Unable to stop myself, I lower myself to the edge of the bed behind her and reach for her hand. An IV is taped to her soft skin, and I try to hold her delicate fingers so as not to hurt her.

"Kat. I don't know why you're here. I saw Jake leave your room, and I... well, I couldn't not check on you. I promise I won't pry into your condition. I just need you to know I'm here. That I..." *Holy fuck, man, get yourself together. Don't dump anything heavy on her right now.* "I'm here. If you need me. Just let a nurse know to call me or text me, and I'll be right here. Okay?" My heart feels like it's torn in two. I need to get out of here before I start blubbering like a schoolgirl. "I'm going to let you rest. But please let me help? Let me know if you need anything."

Kat

I feel Nick place my hand down onto the bed carefully, and a tear falls from my eye. I'm trying desperately not to make a sound, as I couldn't possibly handle seeing him right now. My heart is heavy, my dreams are dashed. My life was already a colossal joke, and now this.

I hear him leave, the door shutting behind him, and the dam breaks. My tears pour endlessly. The hollow feeling in my chest matches that of my pelvis. My body has betrayed me just as all the men in my life have. All but one. Listening to him speak to me, I could feel the genuine caring in his voice. Just as he has shown me time and time again. But he deserves much better than the likes of this broken girl. Every part of my world is fractured. My mind, my spirit, my heart, and now my womb. I wonder what I did in a past life to deserve all of this. But right now, I don't have the energy to think about it anymore. I close my eyes, trying to sleep through the tears.

Chapter Twenty-Four

Kat

I wake to find several multicolored vases of flowers scattered about my room. Sitting up a bit, I take them in. But no one but Jake knows I'm here. Oh, and Nick. As this reality returns, my focus becomes clearer, and I notice my sister, Rachel, sitting in the teal vinyl chair in the corner of the room.

"Rach?" My voice feels hoarse.

"Hi, Kat."

Confused as to how she knew I was here, I look at her in question.

"Jake called Mom and Dad and they called me. Mom just stepped out for a minute. Is it okay that I'm here?"

"Sure, Rach. It's okay," I answer, feeling completely devoid of feeling, drained from all of my crying.

"Kat, you can't handle everything alone." I watch as she stands and comes to sit on the side of my bed. Reaching out, she strokes my hair. Tears immediately begin to fall again. *Uh, when will I be empty again?* I realize the tears aren't just for my current situation, but her affection. I honestly cannot recall the last time she touched me. Our family isn't made that way.

I hear what sounds like a sniffle, and I look up at her angelic face. "Kat, I'm so sorry." She starts to cry a little harder now. "You never let me in, so I don't know why after all of these years, you don't have a man. You're so beautiful and smart and funny. I just figured you were so career-driven you didn't have time for men."

I wipe my tears, wanting to tell her the truth, but the words just won't come.

"Trust me. The whole marriage and kids thing, it's not what it's cracked up to be. I mean, I love Jenna and Luke but…"

My tears start to slow, and I watch her, unsure I understand what she's trying to tell me. Maybe this is just her awkward way of trying to empathize with me.

"Kat, I've been jealous of you for so long. You are so smart and so driven."

What? Am I still under the influence of heavy painkillers? How on Earth could this gorgeous girl who's had everything she's ever wanted be jealous of me?

"I know I should've told you a long time ago. My grades were a struggle. I had to charm friends to tutor me. My marks were okay, but it was hard for me. In hindsight, I should've asked for help. I really wanted to go to college. But I decided to just accept I wasn't meant to be an academic. I traded that dream for a family. I love kids and always wanted my own, so I started a little sooner than I planned." I watch as she shrugs her shoulders like she's trying to convince herself and me that what she's saying is true.

"Rach? What did you want to go to college to study?"

She looks at me, stunned. Like no one's ever dared ask her before. "I wanted to be a teacher. Not like high school science or anything. But a kindergarten teacher. I wanted to help the little ones who were just leaving home to learn the basics. It's dumb. I've got a good life. I'm only telling you this because you need to know how much I've admired you all of these years. For following your dreams. I'm so proud of you."

Cue the waterworks. I barely have a chance to reply, when the door opens, and my mother strolls in carrying another large vase of flowers. She walks over to the windowsill, deciding where to place them. After she finds the perfect spot for her vibrant wildflowers, she steps to the left and bends to inhale the pale pink roses sitting beside her vase.

"Who's Nick?"

I look up to see my mother and Rachel watching me in anticipation.

"Um, he's... he's someone I've been seeing."

"Really?" Rachel suddenly claps her hands and looks at me with optimism.

"It's not like that. We've only been seeing each other for a little while. It's nothing serious."

"Well, he has excellent taste in flowers," Mom says.

"Mom, he probably got his secretary to order them. You know how men are."

Rachel stands from her spot on the bed and states, "I need a cup of coffee. I'm going to run to the cafeteria. I'll be back in a bit. Can I get you anything, Kat?"

"No. I don't have much of an appetite. Thanks, though."

I watch Rachel grab her purse and head out the door as I try to adjust the oversized hospital gown I'm tangled in. My mother comes over to the bed and helps me adjust my sheets so I can lift myself to the edge of the bed for a minute. "I'm just going to use the restroom and wash my face," I tell her. She immediately comes to my side to help me up. This feels so strange. I can't remember her helping me with anything, even as a child. She was always so focused on Rachel.

Returning to the bed, I watch as she rushes back over to my side. I sit back down into the bed, and she covers me with the sheets. Sitting by my side, she grabs my hand and softly strokes it with her thumb.

"You okay, Katarina?" *Heck, I was 'til you held my hand and asked me that.* I can feel the tears start to well in my lids.

"I don't know. I'm okay if I don't think about it too much." And there they go, tumbling down my cheeks again. "Mom? Who's ever going to want me now?" I've moved on to full-blown sobs now.

Suddenly, my mouth drops open as I watch my mother climb onto the bed with me, pulling me into her side. She wraps her arms around me and gently rubs my back. *Am I having a stroke?*

"I don't know why this happened, Kat. I don't understand why some peoples' lives turn out the way they do, and others have to struggle." I can feel her hand move up to stroke my hair now. "From the day you were born, you seemed to be the most independent little girl. Not in a bad way. You never threw temper tantrums to get your way, but you always seemed to take care of things yourself. It was probably my fault. Having Rachel when you were a toddler stole all of my attention from you. She always seemed to need me more. I know I should've told you more, how proud I was of all you've accomplished through the years. I think I often held back because I didn't want Rachel to feel bad. She didn't have the drive you did. But I still should have told you."

Lying here, I can't believe all I'm hearing today. It's eye-opening.

"Kat, I know this is hard right now. But you're a special girl. The right man will come along. The only thing that'll matter to him is you. The two of you will figure the rest out."

I lie here with her, my tears slowing a bit, taking in her words. I try to find comfort in them. But I'm sure of one thing. Nick Barnes is meant to have children. He wants lots of babies. He's amazing with Seth and Ruby and went so far as to sign up to be a "big brother" to a kid in need. I can't ask him to give up his dreams for me. It'd be different if we were in some committed relationship. But we've been doomed from the start. Now I have this stuff with Mark to contend with. Granted, now that I'm dealing with life's newest blow, I barely feel bothered by Mark any longer. But I can't let any of this spill onto Nick's life. The last thing he needs after his wife's betrayal is to have some woman he's dating splattered all over social media in practically her birthday suit. A woman who can't even give him what he really wants.

I hear a knock at the door and look up to see Dr. Ryan. My mother sits up, trying to smooth her clothes with her hands, and stands by my bed.

"Hi, I'm Becket Ryan." He reaches out a hand to my mother. "How're you doing, Kat?" I can hear the sympathy in his voice. I'm sure in his line of work, he's used to doling out bad news.

"I'm okay. Considering."

"Well, I know it's been a lot.. I think physically you're well enough to go home if you'd like."

"Yes. I'd like that."

"The nurse will go over your post surgical care with you before you leave. Although, I'm sure you probably already know what to expect. I can't encourage you enough to reach out to your psychologist. I think things will catch up with you later once you're alone."

"No, you're right. I'll call him this afternoon." I watch as my mother looks at me questioningly. I'm sure I'll have to explain that later.

"Okay. Well, I'll get the discharge process started. Call me if you need anything."

"Thanks, Dr. Ryan."

~

Two hours later, and a volunteer has arrived with a large cart to carry my assorted flowers to the car. As I'm wheeled to the front doors of the hospital, I wrap my arms around myself in preparation for the December chill. My mother has the car pulled up, and Rachel is waiting for me by the front door.

As she reaches down to pick up a vase of flowers, she whispers, "Holy shit, Kat. Who's the hot doc?"

From the corner of my eye I see Nick looking at me from the elevator. I cannot handle that right now. I know I'll start crying if I make eye contact with him. I just need to get home and wallow in this. Without thinking, I answer, "That's Nick."

~

An hour later, my mother and Rachel have brought in my flowers and plastic hospital-issued water jug, and I'm settled in my bed. My mother puts on a pot of tea, and Rachel is busy fluffing pillows.

"Rach, I'm not dying of cancer. I'll be fine. I think my heart hurts more than my body."

I notice her sympathetic gaze. "I know, Kat."

"Can you do me a favor?"

"Sure, anything."

"Can you get Mom to go? I honestly just want to have a good cry and go to sleep."

"Okay. If you're sure. I'll tell her we can drop by with some food tomorrow. That'll get her out of here."

"Thanks."

"No problem, Kat. I'll tell her you're already asleep. I'm going to turn the light off and shut the door. Call me if you need anything."

"Okay. Thanks, Rach. For everything."

She gives me a knowing look and a sliver of a smile before shutting the door.

Utter exhaustion, mental and physical, has completely wrecked my body. But I can't shut out the events of the last week from my mind. I blink through tears most of the night, unable to get any sustained sleep at all. Confused by the time, I look at the clock. 8:20 a.m.. Looking back down at my phone, I notice I have missed messages from the evening before. I'm almost afraid to look. My tattered psyche cannot handle any more texts from Mark.

Holding my breath, I open the little green app.

7:40 p.m.
Nick Barnes
Nick: How are you?

8:25 p.m.
Nick Barnes
Nick: Can I get you anything?

I'm so torn. This sweet man, he's so kind and caring. But he doesn't deserve to be with an empty shell of a woman. I'm not going to make any decisions yet. I can't think clearly in my current state. But I know I'm not in a place to see anyone right now. I need some solitude. I just want to be alone. About to close out of the app and head to the kitchen for some coffee, I spot there's one more.

8:45 p.m.
Nick Barnes
Nick: Get some rest. Call me when you can. I just need to know you're
okay.

Okay? Am I ever going to be okay? As if on cue, the tears begin again. Good lord, how are there any still there? I'm trying to wean myself off of the showers, or I'll turn into a prune with legs. Wrapping my thick robe around me, I traipse into the kitchen to fill my coffee pot. I can barely see the top to fill it with water as my weeping is obscuring my vision.

Knock, Knock.

What? Who could be coming by here at this hour? I'm sure it's my mother. Jeez, I'll never hear the end of it. 'Katarina, clean yourself up. You're a fright.' Well, my whole life's a fucking fright. Might as well dress the part.

Knock, Knock, Knock.

Uh, I really don't want to see anyone today. I just want to be left alone. But the knocks are more persistent now, and I don't need her waking the whole neighborhood once she starts shouting my name. Attempting to wipe the tears from my eyes is useless, new ones simply take their place. As I round the small hallway toward my entryway, I can see flowers in the narrow window beside my door. They're beauti… Oh god. I move to the left so he can't see me. Turning my back to the front door, I feel my heart racing. What's he doing here? Doesn't he work today? Leaning to the left, I peek out again.

Standing in a suit, holding the largest bouquet of pink and white flowers I've ever seen down by his side, is my knight in shining armor. When exactly did he exchange his arrogant coat of arms for this benevolent one? My body is suddenly wracked with sobs, shuddering uncontrollably. I slide down the door until I'm crouched on the floor, no longer able to stand under the weight of the overwhelming feelings. I can't see him like this. I'm too emotional. Leaning my head back, I hit the door and wince, worried he'll have heard me. How can I possibly let him in? I need time. This man has already put up with so much, he doesn't deserve this. A girl who can't sleep and has pictures that could grace the internet any day of her doing god knows what. A girl who's receiving texts from someone who she thought was a friend, why? To threaten me? A girl who's now barren and will never be able to give him the life he wants. He deserves the world. He deserves so much more than what he'd get with me.

Thud. "Dammit."

I hear the sound right behind my head and turn to see the flowers are now lying on the porch by my window, his large hand wrapped around the base of them. He's sitting directly behind me, separated by the door. Covering my face with my hands, I attempt to stifle the blubbering that won't stop. Suddenly, there's shuffling behind me, and I sit up straighter. I lie my back against the cool door and listen. After what feels like an eternity, I hear his car start. Turning my head once again, I watch as he drives away. Probably for good this time.

It's been days. Days of this agonizing, gut-wrenching pain. My body has healed, but I doubt my heart ever will. I've managed to grab short naps along the way but have not had any sustained sleep... probably since I was under anesthesia. I feel like a zombie. I barely know the time of day, much less which day of the week it is. Looking out the window, I see it's dark out. This has to stop tonight. I know my fragile state is worse due to the lack of rest. I can't think clearly in this condition. I need to find some relief soon, or I'll never get back on my feet. I can't lose my job on top of everything else.

I've tried this on my own. Admitting defeat, I drag my weary body to the kitchen. I have to get some sleep. Nothing else matters at this point. I reach for a bottle of wine I have sitting on the counter. It's a red, doesn't need to be chilled. *Heck, I'm not drinking it for the taste anyway.* Grabbing the corkscrew, I open the bottle and look for a glass. I might have to finish the whole damn bottle, but I'm getting some sleep tonight come hell or high water.

Pouring the fragrant red Pinot Noir into my wine glass, I head back to my bedroom. I'm surprised I can smell at all as swollen as my face has become with crying for days on end. As I sip from my glass, I turn and see that book. Dr. Ryan had consulted a Psychiatrist who dropped by to see me before I was discharged. "Dealing with Infertility" stares back at me from the cover of the book. Suddenly dealing with a potential stalker and portions of my life only known to me through pictures and conversations with others didn't seem as daunting. *Could I go back there? Trade this nightmare for the previous version?*

Several hours later, I've consumed about half of the bottle of Pinot and taken a Benadryl. I still can't shut out the demons dancing in my mind. I try to meditate on something pleasant, but those thoughts turn to images of Nick holding flowers on my front porch, and I begin to cry again. After he left, I opened the door and found them lying on the front porch mat. Clutching them to my chest, I brought them inside. I had to put them in a vase, the paper wrapping was soaked in my tears. They were lovely. Just like the exquisite man who delivered them. Could this kind, adoring man love me despite my brokenness? If anyone could, I'm sure it would be him. But is it fair to ask that of him?

The tears start to fall again, and I realize I'm out of tissues. Gathering my wine and used limp tissues, I head for the bathroom. After depositing the tissues in the trash, I look under the sink for a new box and come up short. *Uh. Figures. I should own stock in Kleenex.* I sit down on the floor by my tub and reach for my toilet tissue, wiping my eyes and then my nose. Just as I think I'm getting myself together, I notice I've brought that damn book in here with me, and the tears begin again. "I'm so done with this!" I shout at no one. I need to shut this off and get some sleep. Without thinking, I turn and pull the cabinet door open and reach in the back. *I can almost feel them. There…*

Looking down, I inspect the little brown bottle. Desperate times call for desperate measures. I honestly don't care anymore what could happen. How could things possibly get any worse?

Chapter Twenty-Five

Kat

Popping the top off of the bottle, I pour the white pill into my hand and examine it momentarily. How could this little thing have caused so much damage? So desperate for relief, my past indiscretions under the influence of this chemical are not stopping me. I think to myself, *I have to do this. I need to sleep.* Swallowing the pill with my wine, I close my eyes in prayer. *Lord, I need something to change. I need help. I can't do this alone anymore.* Crying again, I beg, "Please, help me."

Pushing myself up off of the floor, I head back to the bed. I grab my phone and select a random song, putting on my headphones. The beginning chords of a Staind song begins, and I see a text has just popped onto my phone.

9:42 p.m.
Nick Barnes
Nick: Please talk to me

9:45 p.m.
Nick Barnes

Nick: Let me help, please.

Clutching the phone to my chest, I lie back onto the sheets. As Aaron Lewis belts out "Something to Remind You", I try to hold onto the phone like it's my lifeline. This song is tough to listen to on an average day, but today, even more so. Yet, I don't have the strength to choose a new tune. Praying it's the zolpidem kicking in, I relax into the song and hold onto the only connection with Nick I can handle right now.

Nick

10:20 p.m.
Kat Kelly
Kat: I'm done

What the hell does that mean? 'I'm done.' I pace around my kitchen, feeling unglued.

The last few days have been torture. I decided this morning I couldn't take it any longer and called Ava, asking if she could see any of the patients scheduled that didn't need me specifically. As always, she came to my rescue, and I drove the distance to the flower shop my dad and I always get Mom's flowers. I needed them to reflect how special Kat is to me. But I sat there like a chump on her front porch, turned away again. Yet, I can't blame her. Obviously, she's going through something monumental. I'm not walking away until the exit sign is flashing in my face.

Abruptly, I stop my pacing as a thought comes to me. Does she mean she's done with me? It didn't say we're done. It said I'm done.

I know I'm being melodramatic. I'm stewing in my own misery. Yet, I can't shake this feeling something is terribly wrong. Not just with her hospitalization and disappearing act, but the feeling is more ominous. What could be so bad she can't tell me? *Did she try to hurt herself?*

My stomach lurches at the thought. I refuse to believe she could've done anything of the sort. She's been through a lot. But I've never gotten the impression she's a quitter. And as caring as she is with her patients, I cannot fathom her doing anything like that. But then again, everyone has their limits.

I sit staring at my food. I ordered Thai as that usually helps when I'm down. Yet as I pick at the pad Thai, I finally push the plate away, knowing I just don't have any appetite. Dropping my head to my hands, I try to calm my nerves. I shouldn't continue to interfere. Her car was there this morning. I know she was home. She simply didn't want to see me.

Standing from the kitchen island, I walk to the couch where the realtor's listings beckon from the laptop. I try to flip through the images, but I can't concentrate. Returning to the phone, I reread her text as if the two little words on the screen aren't printed in English. *What the hell does this mean?*

I'm starting to lose it. This is crazy. I'm on-call tomorrow, but I can't sit idly by while she suffers. She's going to let me in this time. The neighbors can call the damn police for all I care. I'm banging that fucking door down if I have to.

Grabbing my keys, I head for the car. As the garage door opens, and I look out the rearview mirror, I notice it's raining. "Fitting," I mutter. Backing out, I try to focus. I'm rattled. It's beyond feeling like I've been shut out. I just can't figure out why this anxiety is suddenly hugging me like a glove. Am I starting to have another panic attack?

Focus on the road, Nick. The drive to Kat's house is only about twenty minutes from mine. Honestly, I've been spending a great deal of time looking for new homes in her area. She may not know it yet, but she will. She's going to be mine. I don't care what's happened. I need to make her understand.

As I drive the distance to her home, the rain pelts into the windshield. It's almost raining perpendicular to the ground due to the whipping wind. My Audi has always handled the elements well, but I have to be cautious of other drivers. As I pull into her neighborhood, my heart rate begins to hasten. I'm bracing for a storm, and I don't mean the one outside. As I pull into her drive, I realize her car isn't here. "Fuck." She doesn't usually park in her garage, and I can't imagine that's changed as she has things stored there, which wouldn't allow room for her SUV.

Hitting my steering wheel in frustration, I turn back toward my home. Maybe she's with Mel and Jake. Then why do I still have this portentous feeling? Perhaps this *is* the beginning of an anxiety attack.

Approximately ten minutes later, I approach a light. I can see a police officer down a side road with his blue lights flashing behind a car. Looking closer, I determine it isn't Kat's vehicle. The light turns green, and I carefully pull forward. The rain is really coming down now. I make it a few more blocks when I see something peculiar in the tree-lined street to my right. It's just behind a gas station, but the car appears to be off of the road with the headlights pointed in my direction. *That's odd.* I follow my ridiculous instinct that has so far led me on a wild goose chase and turn onto the side street connecting with the back of the gas station. *Fuck!*

I abruptly turn my car around and park in a space at the rear of the convenience store attached to the gas station. Running back to the car, I look into the driver's side window and see Katarina slumped over the steering wheel. Bang! Bang! Bang! I practically break the glass of the window, trying to get her attention. On a whim, I grab for her door and find it's unlocked. Shaking my swollen hand, I think, *should've started with that, you dumb ass.* I need to get a handle on myself. Lifting her chin, she appears to be unconscious. Is she hurt? Leaning in to check a pulse, I smell alcohol on her breath. *What? Kat doesn't drink like that.* Realizing that is a conversation for another day, I focus on the priorities.

"Oh." I hear her moan.

"Kat? Baby, it's me, Nick. Are you okay?"

"What?" I watch as she slowly opens her eyes, glassy and unfocused, and then closes them again. I've seen that look before. *Dammit.*

Trying to come up with a plan, I reach over and unbuckle her seatbelt. Running around the front of her car, I open the passenger side door and lean in on one knee. Grabbing her underneath her armpits, I drag her across the center console into the passenger seat. Once I'm able to pull her legs over, I rearrange her sitting forward. I notice her head lulls to the side as I try to place her legs into the floor of her car.

I stop for a moment, wiping her wet hair from her face. Looking down, I notice she's wearing... pajamas? I take my coat off and drape it around her. As I notice motion in my periphery, I glance down at her.

"I'm sorry, baby. Trust me, okay?"

It's then that I rip open her pajama top, baring her naked breasts, startling her. Her eyes fly wide as buttons snap against the solid surfaces of the car.

"What are you...?"

Chapter Twenty-Six

Nick

Watching the stunned expression on Kat's face, I realize I have no time to explain. I lay my body on top of her, wrap my hands around her sweet face and crush my mouth onto hers. This needs to look believable. *God, I've missed her mouth.* Kat opens her lips, deepening the kiss. She's making it easy for me.

Bang. Bang.

I look up to a blinding light shining in through the driver's side window. I knew I didn't have long. Observing Katarina's startled face, she stares up at me warily. Her shirt and her heart both ripped open and leaving her agonizingly vulnerable. I watch as she attempts to shield her eyes with her hand as the intense glare invades the dark space.

"Could you roll the window down, sir?" the stern officer asks.

"Yes, of course," I answer quickly, attempting to pull Kat's top over her breasts while the officer observes. *Dear God, please help us.* Almost on cue, I thankfully accept the lord's generous answer. "Hi. Tate, is it?"

A little quirk of a smile is noted as he takes in who's speaking, and his gaze drops to Kat. "It's Tanner, actually. Is everything okay here?"

Embarrassment shrouds my face, and I'm fully cognizant this emotion isn't part of the act. But play the part, I will. "Yeah. Sorry. We just got a little carried away."

"Kat, you okay?" Tanner asks.

"Yeah," she whispers and covers her face with her hands.

"I'm really sorry, Officer Manning. I thought it was better to find a dark spot to pull over than risk driving in the rain... well, in the state I was in." I look back to Kat, who, thankfully, still has her face covered. "She makes me a little crazy," I add. "But we're almost home. We'll try to behave a little better in the future. Right, Kat?"

I watch as she opens a narrow crevice between her hands to peek out at me. "Yep." Unable to stop myself, I bend down to kiss her nose. *Fuck it. Give me a damn ticket. I'll go to jail for this woman.*

Clearing his throat, Tanner begins to speak, a slight chuckle present in his voice. "Okay, you two just get home safe, okay?"

"Thanks, Tanner. I'm sorry to trouble you out in the rain like this." I reach over to shake his hand, and he does the same. As he starts to head back to his vehicle and shut off the brilliant blue lights swirling around us, I take in my little maniac. She's already back out. Face turned to the side, breathing heavy.

"What am I going to do with you?" I whisper. I make sure she's secure and close her door. As I walk to the driver's door, I climb in and have to adjust the seat to fit my legs. I take in the dash and various knobs to acquaint myself with her vehicle. Before I pull out, I turn off the headlights momentarily to compose myself. The earlier anxiety has started to subside. I don't know if this is because the threat of Katarina being arrested for driving in this state has passed or if it's simply because she's here with me.

Reaching over, I stroke her dark locks and run my thumb down her cheek. Her face seems puffy. *God, why won't you tell me what's going on? What could be this bad?* Why has she returned to taking those pills? The very pills which caused her to need space from me. Space to figure out what had been happening when she took them. Is she addicted? Had there been some sort of intervention?

I drop my hand from her soft face and lie my head against the headrest. Watching her, I contemplate my next move. I've got to get her home. I'll call an Uber to get back to my car eventually. I'm on call tomorrow, so I just need to be available by six. Fuck, I'll walk back to my car if I have to. But I'm not leaving her alone a moment longer. I'll grab my car, go home and shower, and return to her house. She has got to talk to me. I need to know what is going on if I'm going to help her. I'm not letting her push me away again.

Driving down the rain-soaked road, back to her home, I look over to my sleepy passenger. My heart squeezes at the sight of her. I grab her hand and kiss it gently, then cradle it against my leg. I remember a time not long ago, where I was in a similar position. Chuckling to myself, I recall there was no placing her hand on my leg that night.

Turning back to her, she's a very different girl than the temptress of that evening. There's no sexy cat costume or fuck me heels. This fractured angel sits slumped in the seat, hair soaked, shirt ripped open to expose the soft skin beneath. Normally, I'd be aroused by such a sight. Yet, at this moment, my heart aches for the pain she must be suffering to have found her in such a predicament. She was horrified to learn of what had happened while she was taking the sleeping pills. I knew that look in her eyes, the one from the night under the tree. For her to have returned to that, things must be bad. She probably hasn't slept for days.

Maroon 5 begins to play on her car stereo. "She Will be Loved." Yes. She will.

I pull into her drive and turn off the ignition. Grabbing the keys, I place them in my pocket and run around to Kat's door. The rain is pummeling me now in its intensity. I open the car door and reach in, scooping her up into my arms and closing the door with my foot. It dawns on me I'll never reach the keys now in my pocket, so I run with her to the garage keypad and attempt to enter the number I recalled her using. I give a silent prayer of thanks as it opens, and I'm able to enter.

Walking into her home, I head for the door that leads inside and shut the garage door behind me. As I take in the small space, I realize not much has changed since the last time I was here. I head for her bedroom and place her carefully on her disheveled bed. I'm surprised she hasn't budged with all the jostling and pelting rain.

I look down at her wet form and immediately look for something to dry her. I don't want her to start shivering like this. Darting into her bathroom, I grab a towel from the shelf and run back to her side. Placing the thick white towel about her damp skin, I attempt to sop the water lying atop her body. Her clothes are soaked. I hesitate momentarily, fearing she'll wake up and think I'm taking advantage of her. She's been through enough. Hell, I ripped her damn shirt open, trying to make it look like we were getting it on in the car. I'm surprised she didn't slap me then. Yet, I still don't want to risk her getting sick. I quickly rummage through her dresser for a dry change of clothes. Not sure where she keeps her sleep clothes, I settle for what appears to be an oversized shirt. I grab some boy shorts in her underwear drawer and return to her.

After wiping the excess water from her exposed skin, I carefully cover her with a towel so I can gently remove her top. She's not wearing a bra. Taking in the state of the room, I suspect she's been living in pajamas lately. There are multiple water glasses and used tissues lying on her nightstand. Her phone is on the floor beside the bed, the headphones connected. I look down to see Staind playing "Something to Remind You." Holy hell. That song's enough to want to off yourself. I grab her phone and click the forward button to move it to anything else. Great, "Broken" by Seether. My new theme song. Choosing not to think about that any longer, I return to removing her wet garments.

I gingerly slide her wet bottoms off of her legs, trying to undress her with dignity, keeping that damp towel on top of her. Once the clothes have been removed, I place them on the floor long enough to dry her skin completely before carefully placing the shirt over her head. I'm surprised how easy this is. Although sedated, she appears to help as I lift each arm into the sleeve. I cautiously drag her white cotton boy shorts up her legs until I feel I've reached the gentle slope of her hips. Looking down at my beauty, I exhale. Damn, her hair is still soaking wet. I need to get another towel to wring out her soaked strands.

Turning for the bathroom, I remember the discarded wet items on the floor. Bending down, I grab them as I hear an inaudible mumble escape her lips. I gently place a kiss atop her forehead before I return to the bathroom.

Walking in, I note another dry towel hanging over the tub. As I deposit her wet clothes into the tub, I glance about the space. There's a wine glass on the floor next to the porcelain tub. Beside it, that bottle of zolpidem, just as I suspected. Toilet tissue is littering the floor, resembling makeshift replacements for Kleenex.

It's then my heart stops. I force myself to take a lung full of air. "Dealing With Infertility." What is this? Moving quickly back to the bathroom door, I look over to my beautiful girl. My beautiful, beautiful girl. I can barely breathe. "Kat?"

Nick

I look back down at the book on Kat's bathroom floor, imagining the horror she's been dealing with on her own. *Fuck.*

Carrying the towel back over, I start to dry her hair. There's a lump in my throat. Now that I'm closer to her, her face really is swollen. She's probably cried from the moment this happened. I'm not going to let my mind wander to what caused her infertility, but I'm sure this has to be related to her hospital stay.

Recalling the retelling of my own mother's pregnancy story used to make me sad. Knowing how long they waited and had almost given up hope. But that's just it. They still had hope. Hope that was ripped away from Katarina.

I run her dark wet strands through the towel until it feels dry enough for her to sleep that way. I wonder if she braids it to sleep? *Hell, that's more than I can figure out on my own.* Getting up to take the towel back to the bathroom, I become conscious of the fact I'm a sopping mess. Once I hang her towel to dry, I start removing my clothes. I'll sleep with wet boxers. I'm not giving her any reason to feel uncomfortable. I'd never fit in one of her shirts, so I'm going to have to plead my innocence if she awakes.

Hearing the tail end of "Broken" lilting through her headphones, I curl into her. Caressing her arms and holding her close. I just need her to feel loved. I want this girl to feel safe. *Fuck it, we'll adopt if she wants kids.* There's no doubt she's it for me, and I'll do anything to make her happy.

As I hold her, I feel tears fall onto my arm. *Fucking hell, she even cries in her sleep.* I change my position a bit to make sure she's comfortable but not smothered as "lovely" by Billie Eilish and Khalid begins to play. I consider unplugging the headphones and letting the music play louder, but I don't want to do anything that will awaken her.

Kat

It's so peaceful here. I feel more at ease than I've felt for days. I'm not sure where I am, but the environment feels serene. The scene is painted in muted versions of white, ivory, and light pink, and I feel as if I'm lying amidst flowers. The wind occasionally catches my hair, as I can feel it moving against my skin. But there's no chill in the air.

As I look at the sky, the rain starts to fall. Or is it my tears again? I can't seem to escape them. So much loss. So much heartache. What lies in store for me? Me and my useless body?

Miraculously my tears dry, and I feel like I'm being rocked in someone's arms. I look up to find the face of my sweet Granny. I'm curled in her arms, gliding back and forth as if we're on an old porch swing. "I'm so happy to see you," I tell her. She looks down at me with her wise, loving eyes and smiles. There are no words, just the rocking in the breeze and the gentle stroke of my hair. "Gran, I really did it this time." We rock and rock. "Am I dead?" Clutching her, I begin to cry again. *There wasn't anything in this life for me anyway.*

Nick

Readjusting Kat, I hold her in my lap and rock her back and forth. I continue to gently rub her arm and her back and kiss the top of her head. Anything to soothe her weary soul. As I stroke her hair, I notice she continues to mumble inaudible things. But she doesn't appear scared. I don't think she's having a nightmare.

Looking at the clock, it reads 1:00 a.m. I return Kat to the position we were originally lying, as she's stopped crying, and I no longer hear any murmurs from her. I continue to keep my arms about her as she's clinging to my hand. Honestly, there's nowhere else I'd rather be.

I need to try and get at least a few hours of sleep. If I get called into an OR case, I can't risk being off my game. The alarm on my phone is already set. I left it right next to me so I can hopefully turn it off quickly in the morning, so I won't wake her.

Nuzzling her hair and asking for God's mercy on us, I close my eyes and pray for a better day tomorrow.

I somehow wake before the alarm and dress in my still wet clothing. I should've put these in her dryer, but I wasn't thinking straight last night. I've summoned a taxi as I couldn't get a timely response for an Uber. I decide to set up the coffee maker, so all she has to do is push the button. Looking about the kitchen to find paper to leave her a note, I find a notepad and pen and scribble a message instructing her the coffee pot is loaded and ready to go. I then write a brief note explaining what happened last night, on the off chance she doesn't recall my being here.

Taking a quick look around, I notice she has the flowers I left for her on the porch in an elegant vase on the kitchen table. I notice other floral arrangements scattered around the home, but my other large bouquet is in the center of the kitchen island. This makes me smile. I hope she knows how much she means to me. And if there's any doubt, I'll spend the rest of my life showing her.

Kat

I awake to bright sunlight and rub my eyes. Stretching, I realize I've finally gotten sleep. Almost as soon as the smile crosses my face, I notice I'm wearing a shirt I use to paint or do odd jobs around the house. I've never worn this to bed. I look around and don't notice anything else out of place, so I get up and head to the bathroom to brush my teeth. I've barely turned on the water before I see my pajamas lying in the bottom of the tub. They appear… wet?

Holy crap, not again. Standing over the tub, I try to remember anything about last night. Nope. I see the pill bottle and the wine glass, and it comes back to me. *What was I thinking?*

I run to the Nanny cam. I've never actually watched anything on here. I try to play with the device to figure out how to see footage from last night and accidentally hit a button that shows the black and white, grainy footage going quickly in reverse. I hit another button, and the video stops. Stops on Nick, carrying me into the bedroom and placing me on the bed.

Watching this footage, I cover my mouth with my hand. I'm stunned. Not only by the events of the evening but the great care he took of me. It isn't adding up. Why was he here? Why did he have to carry me in? Why was I wet? I watch carefully as he comes to the door of the bathroom and just, what? Stares?

Completely intrigued by this, I watch as he slowly comes to the bedside and slinks down to his knees, kissing my face. After he dries my hair, I watch as he leaves the view of the camera and returns in his boxer briefs, and joins me.

Fresh tears start to tumble down my face at his reverence. I watch as he strokes my hair and holds me. At one point, he gathers me into his lap and rocks me. This seems to go on for a while, so I decide to stop watching. My head is in a daze. How could I not remember anything that happened? Had I let him in? How had we both gotten so wet?

I head back to the bathroom to perform my usual morning routine and slide on my robe. I definitely need coffee. As I approach the coffee pot to fill it with water, I find a note.

It's all ready to go, kitten. Just push the on button. Kinda like you do to me. There's an actual smiley face drawn on the note. Nick Barnes drew me a smiley face.

I hit the button and turn and notice there is another note propped against the flowers he'd sent to the hospital.

Kat,

I'm not sure if you recall last night. I promise to fill in the blanks when I see you. You must've taken a sleeping pill. I came to see you, and you weren't here. I found you safe, but you were soaked by the rain. I need you to promise you won't take those pills again. I couldn't bear it if I lost you. I'm on call this morning. I didn't want to leave. I'll see you soon.

We've got this, Kat

Nick

xo

Chapter Twenty-Seven

Kat

Returning to my room, I carry Nick's sweet note and place it on my bedside table. I pick up my phone, realize the battery's dead, and plug it into the charger. In contrast, I feel more energized than I've been in days. It's amazing how a little sleep can help. As the thought crosses my mind, I ponder how I'll be able to continue finding respite without the sleeping pills. Nick's right. I can't continue to use the little white pills. They're far too dangerous. Beyond the chance of committing any further misdeeds, not to mention those acts potentially being discovered by others, I could've hurt someone. I was desperate. It's my only excuse. But I have to find some other way.

Looking down, I observe my phone has come back to life, and it's still open to my music app. "Breathe Me" by Sia is cued. Removing the headphones, I hit play. As the haunting melody begins, I take in the opening line of the song. *'Help, I have done it again.'* More and more, my life seems to imitate art. And not in a good way.

I lie back down onto my pillow, rolling away from the light of the world outside. As I do, I can smell Nick's manly scent on the linens next to me. I still cannot tell if it's his cologne, aftershave, body wash, or just him. There's a musky undercoat, topped with a layer of lust. I clutch it to me and remember the image of him on my Nanny cam, caring for me in my altered state. So many unanswered questions. How is it fair to chain a man like this to a wreck like me? I jerk at the sensation of the phone buzzing, interrupting Sia's evocative melody.

"Hello?"

"Hi, baby. It's me. I needed to check on you."

"I'm good."

"You sure?"

"I don't know, Nick. I'm just overwhelmed by whatever took place last night. I'm sorry I took that pill. I was desperate. I hadn't slept in so long."

"I know, kitten. But we're going to come up with another way. I'm throwing those things out today."

"No. You're right. Wait, what do you mean you're throwing them out?"

"Open the door, Kat."

Startled, I jump up and look down at myself. I'm wearing an oversized shirt I use on dirty chore days, boy shorts, and a robe. I certainly don't have any makeup on, and my hair is a fright.

"Kat. Please open the door. You aren't shutting me out anymore."

"But I look—"

"Beautiful, Kat. You always look beautiful. I found you in your pajamas last night, and you never looked lovelier." I hear a chuckle on the line, and this breaks my hysteria.

"Yeah, I'll bet. A drugged-out fanatic in flannel. Okay. I'll be right there." Walking toward the front door, I take a quick detour into the bathroom to clean up a little. I only take a minute as I know it's freezing outside, but *good god, I'm a freaking mess.*

Swinging the door open, I greet my gallant knight. I can't control the smile that takes over my face as I take him in. He's clad in charcoal suit pants, a white button-down shirt and light grey tie, a dark grey wool overcoat, and carrying the largest bouquet of roses I've ever seen.

"Hi." I welcome him as I move aside to allow for the outlandish floral spray he's carrying. I watch as he places a vase the size of a Volkswagen Beetle onto the kitchen table and moves the wilting flowers previously in this location next to the trash can. He turns to me and smiles tentatively, keeping his distance.

"Can I hold you, Kat?"

I just nod, overcome with emotion for this amazing man.

Pulling me into him, I shiver at the cold still attached to his garments. "I'm sorry, let me take this frigid thing off."

He removes his coat and drapes it over the armchair in my den. Turning back to me, he grabs my arm and pulls me back in for another hug. Whispering into my ear, he states, "I'm on-call until six tomorrow morning. I have everything I need in the car if I have to go in. Can I stay here with you?"

"What? Really?" I peer up into his dreamy hazel eyes, astounded by his continued desire to care for me in spite of all of my whacked-out behavior.

"Yes. I don't have any office patients." He trails his finger along my forehead, playing with the fine stray hairs that have escaped the bun sitting atop my head. "I usually work on office stuff, but there's nothing pressing. I've only gotten one call so far, and it was something Ava could handle."

I nuzzle his neck with my face, trying to warm his skin with mine. "I'd love it if you stayed. But can you fill in those blanks while you're here? I don't want any more time lost."

"Of course."

Hours later, and Nick's connected all of the dots from the night before. *Holy crap. I owe this man so much.* I could've ended up in jail. Or dead. I'm definitely flushing those pills today. There's nothing that could tempt me to use those hallucinogenic white tablets again.

Nick also shared finding the book. There's no hiding my infertility. He's aware and he's still here.

After finally excusing myself to clean up and change, I return to put on a pot of soup. Nick gathers things to make grilled cheese sandwiches. You'd think we were an old married couple. This thought triggers my memory.

"Nick?"

"Yeah?"

"Once things are better, are you still going to take me on a date?"

Chuckling, he answers, "Ah. I haven't figured out the details, but I'd love to take you on a date, Ms. Kelly."

"Not any time soon." I correct. "I'm still trying to deal with, well…"

"Kat, I understand. This was a major life event. I don't pretend to understand what you've had to endure… how you're feeling. But you aren't doing it alone anymore. I'm not going anywhere."

I can't help but sniffle at this statement. He knows I'm unable to have kids, and he's still here. He knows what a hot mess I am yet refuses to leave my side. I don't understand it, but for now, I'm simply grateful. I watch as Nick places the ingredients by the stove and comes closer to where I'm standing. He cups my face with his hands and waits for me to look up into his mesmerizing eyes. They look so serious.

"This is a process. Healing is a process. I hope you take as much time as you need from work and focus on yourself. See your counselor and take care of yourself. I don't want you alone at night right now. I'll sleep in your guest room if you want." He pauses briefly to kiss me before resuming. "I don't want you to think I'm taking over your life, but I need to know you're okay. If you want to spend time with your family or friends, I'll be here when they can't. But you aren't pushing me away anymore. We'll worry about dates once we can focus on each other. For now, *I'm* focusing on you." He stresses the *I'm*, kissing me on the nose as he finishes speaking.

A tear trickles down my cheek, but this one, I don't mind. It's not the prelude to agonizing sobs but the acknowledgment of Nick's tender heart and kind words. He bends down to kiss my wet cheek and lifts to kiss my temple before returning to making our sandwiches as if this is just another day for us. As if he didn't just arrive to painstakingly heal my tattered heart.

"Nick, thank you. For putting me back together."

"Ah, kitten. I'm good at fixing the broken, I just never thought you'd be the one to heal me," he replies tenderly.

"You?"

"Kat," he exhales, "I was an angry, controlling loner until you came flying into that parking space. I fought it tooth and nail, but there was no staying focused on work and my ordered, routine life once I got a glimpse of you." I watch as he runs his hand through his now tousled hair, demonstrating the seriousness of his words. "Hell, I avoided visiting my dad because I couldn't handle seeing how losing my mom had made him so detached. Yet, I was turning into the very thing I despised. I shut myself off from the world so I wouldn't get hurt. But I was living an irritable, isolated existence. I thought I could continue to live that way until you came along."

I try to absorb his words, my mind reeling. It's hard to grasp someone as genuinely caring as Nick could've been living a life similar to mine. It seems unfathomable. You never know if someone else is suffering in silence.

We spend the next half hour eating and chatting about less serious topics until Nick receives a call from his service about a consult. As I open the door for him, he bends to kiss me and says he'll be back when he can. I lean against the doorframe, watching him walk to his car. The wind is whipping his overcoat as he struggles to open the door. As he backs out of the drive, he gives me a tender smile before turning the car and driving up the road. I suddenly feel more content than I can remember as I twist on my heel to head back inside.

As I start to close the front door, I notice the return of that black Ford F150 parked by the curb. It's sitting closer to my house than the last time I spotted it. I still find its presence odd, as I'd never seen it here before. Looking toward the windshield for the gray-haired gentleman who was driving it last, all I see is smoke. It appears the driver has lit a cigarette. As I scold myself for being a busy body, I notice the driver's side window must have been lowered a crack because the smoke is starting to trail out of the car. Just as I'm about to close the narrow opening of the front door, the air within the car clears enough that I make direct eye contact with the driver, Mark Snow.

Quickly locking the door, I walk back to my bedroom to calm my nerves. Why is he here? Did someone tell him what happened? Jake wouldn't dare share my situation with anyone at the fire department without asking me. Unless he and Mel said something to Huggie, who let it slip? Is he here to check on me? *Heck, I can't handle a visit from him to my home.* Especially now that I know the Rohypnol test came back positive. If he comes to the door, I'm staying right here. I'll call 911 if I have to.

Bzzz. Bzzz.

I jump at the sensation of the vibrating phone. Picking up the device, I open the message app.

5:25 p.m.
Nick Barnes
Nick: I'll call when I'm on the way back. I can bring a late dinner.

Holy cow, I thought that was going to be Mark. I don't afford myself the luxury of relishing in his sweet text. Impulsively, I walk to the front of the house, looking out the window toward the street. He's gone. Thank god. But gone or not, I'm completely frazzled. I hastily walk from one door to the next, verifying all are locked. I then go to the kitchen to put on some hot tea to calm my nerves. If this doesn't work, another shower is in my future. I was so relaxed a few short moments ago, and now... well, now I just want Nick back.

Sitting curled up on the couch with my mug of hot tea, I try to center my thoughts. *I will not let him rattle me.* But what if, on top of dealing with my now infertile state, Mark decides to release that photo? What if seeing Nick here has made him mad enough to destroy my reputation. Why is this happening? Because I wouldn't go out with him? He's never had a dearth of women. He could easily find someone else. *Has he done this before?*

I make a choice. I've got to handle this without including Nick. He's already volunteering to deal with my fertility crisis, as well as the fact I almost got arrested for driving under the influence. *I can't even remember the first time we had sex, for god's sake.* He doesn't need any more of my dirty laundry to convince him I'm not worth it. Plus, I couldn't bear it if he got into it with Mark and something happened to him. I won't push him away again, but I have to keep this part of my nightmare to myself.

I practically finished the entire pot of tea and ran the hot shower until the water turned cold. I'm a little calmer than before but still on edge. I decide to just get in the bed and hope Nick returns as he said he would. But at 9:40 p.m., it's already later than I expected he'd be. *I wonder if he had to take someone to the OR?*

Bzzz. Bzzz.

Again, flinching at the sudden intrusion into the stillness, I grab my phone relieved Nick is finally texting he's on his way.

9:42 p.m.
Unknown number
Unknown number: Not dating, huh?

Dammit. There's no doubt who's texting from this unknown number now. Sure, I said I wasn't dating. But technically, I'm not. Nick is offering to care for a friend. What business is it of Mark's anyway? Why the hell am I having to defend myself?

I refuse to get out of this bed to check the street again. I'll only make myself crazier than I already am. Sinking into my sheets, I pull the covers up to my neck as I try to relax. *Breathe in through your nose and out through your mouth, Kat. Nick will be back soon.*

And back he came. Stripping down to his boxers, he climbs into bed behind me, curling his warm body around mine. Completely unaware of the time, I relax into him as he holds me. I've never been so thankful for anyone to be by my side. Feeling his strong limbs wrap tightly around me isn't sexual but sensitive. Not romantic but reassuring. His choice to stay an ever-present, compassionate reminder of his desire to take care of me, and himself, by allowing someone in. With him by my side, I can handle this. I honestly think I can handle anything.

Night after night, Nick would return. He'd sweetly ask permission to visit or stay. He's always respectful not to push for something sexual. My body and my heart have to heal before I can return to anything physical. Some nights we cuddle on the couch and watch mindless television or sports. Other nights he just drags his weary body in after a long day, showers, and we go to bed. At times we talk into the early hours before sleep claims us, others, we comfort each other silently as we drift off. It's becoming more and more evident Nick is all the medicine I need, for there's never an issue with sleep when he's near.

Occasionally, I stay with Nate. I even stayed with Rachel one evening when Steven was away on business. I have a lot of mending to do with my family. I'm not sure how we lost our way, but if there's a silver lining in my loss, it's gaining their love and affection.

Walking to the mailbox, I wrap my arms around me to combat the frigid air. I hadn't realized how much the temperature had changed. I haven't left the house much in the last few weeks. Between Amazon, grocery delivery services, and Nick, I haven't had to venture out. As I get closer to the mailbox, I see a delivery van pull up.

Opening my mailbox to grab a few small business envelopes, I greet him. "Hi, Bernie."

"Hi, Kat."

"What do you have for me today?"

He chuckles. "Uh, roses. Like every day."

I can't help but giggle back. "Ha, you're right. But they're all different."

"He's going to run out of colors soon."

"Well, I'm sure he'll come up with something when you guys have to break the news to him," I share, reaching over to grab the delicate vase with a dozen pale peach roses nestled inside. "Bern, can you come to the porch? I didn't expect you to come pulling up."

"Kat, you'll go broke tipping me every time I come. You're too generous." He starts to laugh. "But if you really want to, just double up tomorrow." Winking at me, he gets back into his van and waves goodbye. This kind young man of about twenty has been to my home nearly every day for weeks. His deliveries always come with a smile and add to the opulence that now decorates my home. I've seen more of Bernie and Nick than anyone else lately. I'd asked everyone I knew to give me some space. They were hesitant until I shared Nick would be with me, and then they suddenly agreed, wanting me to have the time I needed with a man they respected.

As I walk through my front door, I start to look about my small home. Where is there left to put these?

"Hey, beautiful." I hear as someone sneaks up beside me and wince, not at the voice but the statement. I'll never be able to shake its connection to Gabe. It was his typical greeting, both in person and over the phone, and knowing how insincere it was, unconsciously makes me cringe. I look up to see Nick staring down at me with a myriad of emotions painting his handsome face.

"It's starting to look like a funeral parlor in here." I laugh.

"No. It looks like a rose garden."

I briefly gaze up at this generous, over-the-top man before returning to my hunt. "Ah." I sigh, having found a spot on a small library table near the fireplace to place his latest fragrant gift. I feel him come up behind me, wrapping his arms around me.

"I love seeing you surrounded by them. It reminds me of my mom and dad."

Surprised at the statement, I rotate in his strong arms so I can see his stunning face. "What do you mean?"

"Mom loved roses. She had a beautiful rose garden. You could always find her there. It was like her special place." He leans down to kiss me on the head. "My dad said there was nothing more beautiful in all the world than my mother surrounded by her roses."

"Oh, Nick, that's so sweet."

"Kitten?"

"Yes?

"What was that look for?"

"What look?"

"Earlier, when I first came in. Have I done something?"

Clutching this thoughtful, insightful man tighter, I place gentle kisses on his throat. "Of course not." I take his hand and walk him to the couch. "Nick, my ex was a real tool. Well, all of them were, but he took the prize by a mile. We were together for years. He was always super charismatic, but I found out it was all for show. He was cheating on me the entire time, right under my nose. He'd lie straight to my face, having been with someone right before coming to me. Anyway, that was his standard greeting for years. I know you aren't him, but whenever I hear it, well…"

Swiping my hair from my face, Nick lifts my chin with his thumb and forefinger. "Kat, we both deserved better than what we got. I'll try not to say it again. But it'll be tough." He moves his hand to stroke my hair. "How am I supposed to tell you how beautiful you are if I can't say it?"

"You show me every day, Nick. Trust me." I lean into him, wrapping my arms around his muscular torso. "Besides, it's just that phrase 'Hey, beautiful' I can't stand. I've never minded when you called me beautiful girl or any of the other ways you've said it."

"Good to know." We sit, holding each other. It honestly feels like a dream. Or something from an over-the-top Hallmark movie. Resting in his strong arms, listening to his adoring words, surrounded by what seems like thousands of roses in a variety of colors and presentations. Some are in full bloom, while others have tight buds. There are tiny rose bushes and single stem vases.

"You know you can't keep this up, right?"

Pulling back from me, he looks into my face. "What?"

"The flowers. You can't keep this up. I'll either run out of room, or they'll run out of roses." I can't help but snicker at this conversation.

"Ah, Ms. Kelly. No one has informed you. I'm the last person you want to challenge on anything. It'll be my personal mission to see to it that I keep this up. We'll just have to start transplanting them into your yard." He winks. Bending down, he places a kiss on the corner of my mouth. "Now, get up and make me some lunch, woman. I have to get back to work."

"Hey, I know we still have a few weeks, but Christmas is coming. Have you thought about what you want to do?" Nick asks as we scroll through Hallmark Christmas movies on Prime. It's the weekend, and he has elected to spend it with me around a quick lunch date with his dad and Gavin for pizza tomorrow.

"I'm not really in the holiday spirit."

"I know, Kat, but things are getting better day by day."

I take a fortifying breath, put down the remote, and turn to him. "Nick. I need to tell you something."

I observe his relaxed facial features become taught.

"December isn't my favorite month. A few years ago, I somehow became pregnant despite using the pill and condoms. I not only lost the baby, but that's how I lost my first ovary. I had an ectopic pregnancy, and they tried but just couldn't save my ovary.

"Kat." He exhales, tucking my hair behind my ear.

"Remember 'Hey, beautiful'? Yeah, he was a real asshole. After losing the baby, I confirmed he'd been cheating on me pretty much the whole three years we were together. He actually took out one of the nurses while I was in the freaking hospital." I watch as Nick's expression turns monstrous and try to calm him as best I can by stroking his chest and arms. "It isn't worth it to get upset by the jerk. It's in the past. But tomorrow is the anniversary of that horrible day." I'm surprised no tears come with this declaration. "I decided today I'm going back to work. I need to start embracing some normal again. But I'm not ready for anything Christmassy beyond the television."

I play with the fringe of the wrap I'm bundled in as I continue to speak. "I might visit my family. They surprised me when I was in the hospital. We've always been there for each other but not affectionate or open with our feelings. They stepped out of their comfort zones for me when I really needed it. I feel like I need to repay the favor."

"Wow, Katarina. I had no idea. I'm sure this has been harder than I ever realized. Are you ready to go back to work?"

"I'm not sure I'll ever feel ready. I just want to stay in my cocoon with you." I stop to run the back of my hand down his stubbly cheek and offer a warm smile to this man I adore more than life itself. "I need to get back to it, though, or I'll wallow in this too long. I'm going to offer to work on Christmas Eve. The day will be slower. Easier to manage. I'll go to my family's Christmas morning and watch my niece and nephew open gifts and come back here to recover. It'll all work out. What about you? What were you thinking?"

"Well, I was hoping to take you to my dad's. But I understand. Once you're ready, I'd like you to meet him. We'll probably do as we did for Thanksgiving and invite Gavin and his mother over. They don't have family nearby, and Dad's really grown close to Gavin. He's been good for both of us, really."

"I've never told you, but I think it's amazing what you're doing with Gavin."

"Yeah, it's odd. People say that, but I don't feel like I'm doing anything. He's a great kid under all the snark. It's been good for me."

"What's his mom like?"

"Can't get much of a read on her. She's my age. She seems to love Gavin but doesn't spend much time with him. She's busy with work. I'm sure it isn't easy being a single parent." He appears to have an odd expression on his face when he's speaking of her.

"Wow, I didn't realize she was that young."

"Yeah, me either."

I sit quietly, not knowing how I feel about all of this. Both of them invested in this young man. I recall her appearing attractive when I saw her at the soccer field the day she dropped off Gavin. Suddenly, I feel fingers tickling my ribs. "What're you doing?" I shriek.

"You jealous, kitten?"

"No."

"Ah, oh, well." He stops teasing.

"Okay, maybe a little," I reply, watching a proud smirk cross his face. He grabs me, pulling me into his body to snuggle as he takes the remote from me.

Settling on something, he says, "Hmm. How about *Holidate*? This looks good."

∾

Christmas Eve morning arrives and I'm getting myself together to head to work. Nick left early to get to the office as they have a short day scheduled. He seemed to be quite happy about this fact, announcing, "I'm a man. Christmas Eve is when real men get our shopping done." He blew me a kiss and promised to see me when I was done for the day.

Nick arrives late in the evening, after I've made it home following my first shift back. As far as the ER goes, it wasn't too bad. Most people had deferred a trip to the ER unless it was a true emergency, given the sacredness of the day.

"What time do you head to your family's house tomorrow?" Nick whispers into the back of my neck, wrapped around me like a second layer of skin.

"I have to get up early. The kids are anxious to open things. Rachel lets them open their stocking and gifts from Santa, but they wait on the rest of us for everything else. I'm sure there's only so much 'how much longer' Rachel and Steven can take." I laugh and feel a rumble along my back from Nick's chest as he joins in. I can't help but feel a little forlorn thinking of other people watching their kids open things on Christmas morning.

"What about you?" I ask. "When do you head out?"

"We're doing ours a little later. Picking up Gav and Shelly at about eleven so we can have lunch together at my dad's. The gifts aren't as big a deal at our house."

We lie quietly together, and I start to wonder if he's fallen asleep.

"Kat?"

"Yeah?"

"You're all the gift I want."

"Now you've done it. You've gone and made me cry again." I reach back to playfully smack his arm. "And I'd made it the whole day."

Christmas day is a whirlwind of watching kids rip open neatly ornamented gifts, chatter amongst family, and way too much food. I can tell my family members are treading carefully with each conversation. I'll be relieved when this monumental life event has become a thing in my past, and people don't walk on eggshells around me any longer. However, my mother and sister have never really treated me with kid gloves, so I appreciate the gesture all the same.

Later that evening, I sit curled up on my couch, continuing to reopen my phone app awaiting word from Nick on when he's heading home. *Home? What the heck, Kat? Don't get ahead of yourself.* You've never even had a proper date with him. He's been staying here to be kind. There've been no declarations of love.

Maybe he decided to stay with his dad for the evening. Maybe he's doing something with Gavin and Shelly. This thought makes my heart clench a little.

Nick and I left the house simultaneously this morning. Nick decided to shower and change at his house before leaving for his dad's, and so we wished each other Merry Christmas and went our separate ways. There was never any discussion regarding plans to get together this evening. I just assumed he'd return. I was proud of how I'd handled the day, trying to focus on the positive more than the negative. However, I'm admittedly becoming sad at the prospect of spending Christmas night without my Saint Nick.

Suddenly, there's a knock at the door, and I find myself running before I can stop to consider what I look like. Sliding on the hardwood flooring to the front door in my socked feet, 'this is my Hallmark Christmas movie wearing shirt' and leggings, hair in twin braids, I grab the door and swing it wide. My handsome man is standing in a black leather jacket, dark jeans, and a white button-down, holding a bottle of wine and a small wrapped gift box. Unable to control myself, I fling myself in his direction and almost knock him to the ground.

"Well, Merry Christmas to me." I hear him chuckle in my ear.

"I was worried you wouldn't make it back. I missed you." I kiss his cheek, all scruffy and cold.

"Kitten, nothing could keep me from spending Christmas with you." I feel him squeeze me tighter, lifting me off of the ground. "Let's get inside. It's so cold."

Nick enters, lowers me to the ground, and sheds the cold leather jacket. Following me to the den, he joins me on the floor in front of the fire. I can't help but rub my hands up and down his sleeves in an attempt to warm him. As he smiles at me, I remember his gift. Reaching up onto the couch beside me, I grab ahold of the small box I have waiting for him.

"Merry Christmas," I say, handing the small wrapped package to him, filled with delight for the special gift I'd chosen. He opens the wrap slowly and carefully.

"Kat, you didn't have to. I told you, I already have the perfect gift," he says, winking at me. He snaps open the lid of the box, revealing the watch I'd selected. I'd found a Movado Gunmetal watch online that screamed Dr. Nicholas Barnes. "Kitten, I love it." Bending forward, he kisses me softly on the mouth. "I'll think of you every time I look at it." I beam at him as he pulls the watch from the box, replacing the one he'd been wearing. Holding his arm out, admiring it exaggeratedly, he grins with apparent pride. "I love it."

"Open yours. I was going to get you flowers." He chuckles. A loud guffaw escapes before I can stop it with my hand. Carefully tearing the beautifully wrapped paper, I find a Tiffany blue box hidden underneath. As I slowly crack open the jewelry box, I admire the beautiful white gold key pendant, the top of the key shaped like a heart. I stroke it gently with my fingertips, my mouth agape. It's the most incredible thing any man has ever bought me. "You hold the key to my heart, Kat. Too lame?"

Again, I charge this beautiful man, knocking us both to the floor. I cannot stop placing kisses all over his face, neck, and jaw. "Thank you. Leave it to you to give me the best Christmas ever, in spite of everything that's happened."

We spend the remainder of the evening watching Hallmark movies with the wine Nick brought and bask in the glow of a healthy relationship in the making. It's the best gift I could've ever asked for and never thought I'd receive. Better than flowers or jewelry. As the holiday comes to a close, I'm well aware I've fallen in love with Nick. For however long this lasts, I'll be eternally grateful for having him in my life when I needed him most.

～

Several mornings later, I walk toward the kitchen to find Nick's ridiculous coffee station taking up half of my small kitchen counter. He insisted on bringing it over once he started spending so many nights here. Other than its size, I'm not complaining. It really does make incredible coffee, and we wake to the rich aroma each morning, beckoning us to rise and shine. Nick had to leave early this morning for work after receiving a call from the service about a post-op patient on the orthopedic floor who wasn't doing well. He was lucky to have the holiday off from working and taking call. However, as the newest physician in his practice, the tradeoff was being on call for much of the week following Christmas so the others could spend time with their families.

As I grab a mug from the cupboard and head toward "the Cadillac," as Nick refers to it, I notice there's a note beside it.

Katarina,

Now that the holidays are over, I'd like for you to do something for me. Please have your coffee, take a shower, and try to eat something. Then, I need you to go and do something for someone today. Anyone. You have such a giving heart. It'll help you heal to focus on someone else. There are people who need you. (Besides me)

Nick

xo

Chapter Twenty-Eight

Nick

The last week of the year is kicking my tail. I'm on-call more days than I'm not, but after having off for Christmas Eve and Christmas Day, it's hard to complain. I'm looking forward to getting past the holiday season to take that stress off of Kat's shoulders. Maybe she can face the world again if things are a little more normal.

I worry I may have pushed her with my note this morning. The last few days, she's seemed so downtrodden. I didn't want her to revert to where she'd been. She always seems so serene when she speaks of her volunteer job and when I watch her care for others in the ER. Maybe if she can focus her attention elsewhere, the other pain may lessen.

I'm fighting my own internal struggle right now. I miss my sexy vixen. I wouldn't want to be anywhere else, and I'll try to remain patient, but it's tough lying next to her and not being able to make love to her. I'm not sure how long after her surgery she's been advised to wait, but hopefully, she'll get clearance to return to a normal sex life after her next checkup. Now, if only her heart and head will give her the go-ahead.

As I try to focus on typing progress notes in the computer, my mind continues to wander. Maybe after our 'date.' Maybe that's how we can change gears and return to the hot-blooded relationship we had before. I need to come up with something special. I want this date to be perfect. To show her how much she means to me. To finally tell her I'm in love with her.

My nerves are starting to get to me, worrying I've upset her with my note encouraging her to do something for someone else today. She's barely left the house in weeks except to work on Christmas Eve and visit her family for a few hours on Christmas Day. I'm not sure when she's due to return to work full time.

Pulling out my phone, I decide to shoot her a text.

11:48 a.m.
Nick Barnes
Nick: Hey, whatcha doin? I miss you.

Okay, Nick, now that's out of the way. Type your damn progress note on this patient.

11:55 a.m.
Kat Kelly
Kat: I'm about to go visit Katrina and the baby.

This makes me happier than it should. I'm so proud of her. Not only did she choose to visit someone she seems to care about, someone less fortunate than herself, but this woman who's been told she can no longer have children is going to comfort another who didn't realize she was pregnant. Recalling the story Kat shared, I shake my head. I don't entirely understand the relationship that Katarina has formed with this young woman. Sounds like this girl is a bit of a mystery.

As I sit here attempting to focus on the task at hand, it dawns on me Katarina may have bitten off more than she can chew. At my insistence, she's visiting a young woman with a baby in the NICU. What if it's too much for her. I start to panic. *Fuck. What was I thinking pushing her?*

12:10 p.m.
Nick Barnes
Nick: Are you going to be okay? If it gets you upset, please call me.
I'll come and meet you.

12:14 p.m.
Kat Kelly
Kat: I'll be okay. I've got this, Saint Nick.

12:18 p.m.
Nick Barnes
Nick: No, we've got this.
Call me if you need me.

Hell, I almost told her I loved her over a text message. We need to have that date night soon, or I'm likely to blurt it out in my sleep. I want it to be special when I tell her. Because as far as I'm concerned, she's the last woman I'll ever say it to.

Kat

I pull up to the hospital and take a deep breath. I've got this. I hadn't considered I was walking into a room full of babies when I decided to visit Katrina. When Nick encouraged me to do something for someone today, she was the first person I thought of.

I'd been working on a little outfit for Grace when I was home alone. I made a little skirt out of tulle. Given how tiny Grace is, it didn't require much fabric. The alternating red and yellow tulle was tied around a red ribbon, creating a tutu for the bottom of the costume. I'd found a superman preemie onesie for the top. Sewing a little scrap of red silk fabric to the onesie, it looked as if there was a cape. If anyone had superhero powers, it was this little girl. She'd fought the good fight since the day she popped out.

Walking the cold, sterile hallway toward the NICU, I keep the outfit tucked in a bag under my arm. As I approach the nurses' station, I can see Katrina in her yellow gown, rocking little Grace in a wooden rocking chair. The nurses recognize me from prior visits and advise I can wash up and don my yellow gown and join Katrina when I'm ready.

"Hey, Katrina. Merry Christmas. Sorry I didn't make it before today. I've had some personal things to attend to." I grimace as I say this, realizing Nick's right. I need to focus on someone else.

"Hi, Kat. I understand. I'm always glad to see you." I notice she doesn't appear glad. Her expression appears flat today. She's normally over the moon to see me. Strange given I've had no relationship with her outside of the hospital. She seemed to simply latch on to me somehow. But she doesn't seem herself today.

"Katrina? What's wrong? Is this all getting to you?"

"I don't know. I think the closer I get to taking her home, the more scared I get. Kat, what if I can't do this?"

I stoop down, so I can see her at eye level as she rocks little Gracie in the chair. "Katrina, do you want to do this?"

"Yes, of course. I love her so much." I feel a lump in my throat as I observe how distressed she seems. "She deserves so much better than me."

I can't hold back any longer. I place my hand on her arm and try to console her. "Katrina. Grace knows you love her. I'm sure she can feel it. You've been here tirelessly for her, day in and day out. Whatever you decide to do, she'll know she was loved. I'm sure of it." I hope this offers her some comfort, as I can't imagine what she's feeling right now. I'm certain if I wasn't sure where my next meal was coming from, I'd be worried about raising a baby too.

I try to change the subject. "Did your sister and brother have a nice Christmas?" I gulp, suddenly worried I've made a huge mistake with this line of questioning almost as soon as the question has come out of my mouth. *What are you thinking, Kat? If they didn't, do you want to rub her nose in it?*

"Yes. They probably had the best Christmas they've ever had. I was able to fill out a form for the Angel Tree. The Salvation Army collected stuff for them. They got clothes and toys and even got a bike each. They were thrilled."

"Oh, Katrina, that's great."

I notice she's now crying. "Kat, can you take her for a minute?"

"What?" I start to panic a bit. How can I possibly hold this infant without losing it in here? I'll be a blubbering mess.

"Please?"

Oh, for god's sake. Woman up, Kelly. This poor girl needs help. I stand up, not wanting to risk falling over with this frail infant in my arms. Extending my arms to her, I watch as Katrina places little Gracie in my arms.

"Thanks, Kat. I just need a minute. I'll be right back."

"Wha—?"

Katrina is gone in a flash, and I'm standing here holding this beautiful, innocent little angel. Looking down at her, eyes closed, she's the epitome of peace. As I gently sway her to and fro, her little fingers wrap around mine. I try to stay focused on the little miracle I'm watching and not my own grief. I don't know how Katrina's done it day after day. It has to be terrifying, wondering each day if it could be Grace's last. They've come a long way with modern medicine, but these preemies are so small. There are no guarantees.

After what seems like hours, Katrina comes back. Her face puffy, red blotches staining her cheeks.

"You okay?" I whisper.

"Yeah. This seems to happen a lot lately. I'm just so overwhelmed. But you're right. I have to believe she knows how much I love her. So long as I continue to pray and do the best I can... well, that's all there is, really. It's going to have to be enough."

As I hand the little bundle off to her mother, she rocks her briefly and then lowers Grace back into the incubator.

"I just fed her before you got here. She'll sleep for hours now."

"Are you getting any sleep, Katrina?"

"Yeah. I hang out in the waiting room. I catch naps in there. Everyone here's been really nice to me. I go and take a shower and get clean clothes when Grace sleeps."

"Any idea when she'll come home?"

"She still has some weight to gain." Shrugging her shoulders, she continues, "I just hope I'm ready before she is."

The two of us walk out of the NICU together, and as I turn to her, she grabs me in a firm embrace. Her small frame barely coming to my chin. She really is a tiny thing. I look down at her hopeful brown eyes and suddenly can feel tears start to collect in my own. This amazing, brave young woman is facing her biggest fears for her daughter. She holds her head up and faces each day with prayer, putting her best foot forward.

Abruptly, as if I no longer control my own faculties, I grab this young girl and clutch her petite body to mine. "Kat? You okay?" I hear Katrina's voice, muffled against my chest.

"Oh, I'm sorry, Katrina. I'm just so proud of you. You inspire me."

Looking shocked, she almost yells, "Me?"

"Yes, you! Don't ever doubt yourself. You've been here every moment for Grace. You're facing the unknown because of your love for her. I'm so impressed with your determination. I know this isn't easy." I have a lot to learn from this young woman.

"Thanks, Kat. I've got a long way to go, but I'm going to try even harder because of you."

"Oh, I almost forgot. I made this for Grace. It's a little Super Girl outfit. It's not much. But I think I should have made a Wonder Woman one for you too."

"Oh, Kat. It's so cute. I can't wait to put it on her. Thank you."

Waving goodbye, I head back toward my car. The entire way home, I reflect on Katrina and what a brave young woman she is. If this girl who has nothing can fight for her and her daughter's future, why can't I? *Grow up, Katarina! It's time to stop sulking.*

I drive home from visiting Katrina and make myself a cup of tea to reflect on my day. After what seems like hours of introspection and prayer, I head to the shower. This time I'm not there to cry my eyes out but to start anew. I feel the need to wash away my past and embrace a new dawn. I turn on the spray and then circle back to look for my phone. Connecting the Bluetooth speaker, I choose a song that embodies the way I'm currently feeling. Putting "What I've Done" by Linkin Park on repeat, I start to undress and enter the steamy shower.

As the hot water and suds run down my body, I grow more and more determined. How could I have let this happen? How could I let anything steal my worth? I don't understand why these things have befallen me, but I'm not letting any of it take me down again. I'm so tired of living this way. Feeling defeated. Feeling unworthy.

I exit the shower and quickly dry off. Wrapping my hair in a towel like a turban, I head to the dresser for a black bra and panties and put them on. I return to the bath to unwrap my hair and sit on the bathroom stool to begin blowing my locks dry. Flipping my hair over, I continue to apply the warm billowing air to the roots. Once it's done, I toss my hair back over my shoulders to brush quickly before placing it in a solitary braid. Looking in the mirror, determined eyes shine back at me. Pulling out my makeup drawer, I locate the items I need. I apply natural liquid foundation, some mascara, and dark eyeliner before placing a light stain on my cheeks. Finally, I locate the bold red lipstick I wore for Halloween.

Exiting the bath, I pick up a pair of thick black leggings and a black tunic. After dressing, I drape my cross-body bag over my chest. Sitting on the small ottoman in my closet, I don my socks and begin to reach for short black ankle-high boots, and that's when I notice them. Smirking at myself, I discard the ankle boots and reach for the boots that caught my eye. Bending down, I put one foot in at a time, then stand to look in the full-length mirror. With my dark clothes and those damn black knee-high boots, I look like Lara fucking Croft in *Tomb Raider*! I feel empowered. But something's still not quite right. As I stare into the mirror, the lead singer from Linkin Park still belting out about facing himself, I take in my reflection. I agree with this song. Today this ends!

Reaching up to my braid, I pull the tiny nylon ponytail holder from the end and run my fingers through the strands. Still not feeling free enough, I bend and shake my head before flipping my hair back. I look back into the mirror and speak to the girl in front of me. "Yes, today this ends."

Spinning on my heels, I head down the hall. Grabbing my keys and a coat, I get into the car. My heart is racing. I can do this. I refuse to let anything take me down. I'm getting my life back. I deserve nothing less.

Driving down the road, it's early evening but darkness has already started to descend. Porch lights, Christmas lights, and headlights all dance around me as I make my way toward my destination. As I arrive, I find a space and park. Grabbing my coat, I slide my jacket on and step out of my car. I suddenly feel free. I thrust my right arm into the air, hand fisted just like Judd Nelson at the end of *The Breakfast Club*. The air whips around me, tossing my hair like a tornado.

As I approach the steps, the lights along the street bright against the night's sky, I stand tall and take a deep breath. Fuck it if someone sees me in these damn boots. Fuck it if anyone ever sees that picture. I start to climb the steps with renewed determination.

Flinging open the metal door, I walk down the marble foyer toward glass doors. Grabbing ahold of the long shiny handle, I open it and step toward the counter. Initially, no one approaches, and I have a minute to consider turning and heading back home. But I silently encourage myself, *today this ends*!

"Yes, Miss. Sorry to keep you waiting. Can I help you?"

"Yes. I need to file a restraining order."

Thank you for reading

Stay tuned for the continuation of Kat and Nick's story in the third book in The Deprivation Trilogy: Stronger

Keep reading for an excerpt of Book Three.

It has been my dream to share the many characters, taking up residence in my mind. I hope you enjoy their adventures as much as I have enjoyed putting them to paper. Without you, I could not continue to live this dream.

To obtain more information on my current books, upcoming work, and special offers
please visit my webpage:
www.authorlmfox.com
While you are there, subscribe to my newsletter to read more of Ava's story in a free copy of **Moon Shot**.

Visit me on Facebook at AuthorLMFox and my readers' group, Layla's Fox Den, as well as on Instagram, Twitter, and TikTok @authorlmfox

PLAY LIST

Sweet but Psycho, Ava Max
For You, Staind
Pump It, The Black Eyed Peas
Butterfly, Crazy Town
Close, Nick Jonas
Wow, Post Malone
Scream, Usher
Only Girl, Rihanna
lovely, Billie Eilish & Khalid
My Songs Know What You Did In the Dark, Fall Out Boy
Broken, Seether
Bad at Love, Halsey
Numb, Linkin Park
Something to Remind You, Staind
Drive, Incubus
Secret, Maroon 5
She Will be Loved, Maroon 5
Stay, Rihanna
Breathe Me, Sia
What I've Done, Linkin Park

Acknowledgments

I again want to thank TL Swan for starting me on this journey. As with book one, she continued to help guide and inspire me and many other grateful fledgeling authors every step of the way. And she did this while continually writing and trying to meet deadlines. Thank you from the bottom of my heart. (Your best selling books are my reward and motivation.)

Thank you to my team! I wouldn't have been able to complete this book without the amazing work of my editors/formatter Kelly, Cheree, and Shari. Your diligence and hard work are so appreciated. And I remain so thankful to Wander Aguiar for the art of his photography and Hang Le for creating my incredible covers. Your work is second to none! Jo, thank you and Give Me Books for your tireless efforts to help get my books out there. Linda, you continue to give me constant direction and encouragement. I don't know where I'd be without you. Thank you!

Thank you so much to my beta and ARC readers! You were the first I trusted to share my thoughts on paper and I so appreciate your time, patience, and encouragement. Denise, Laura, and Siri have been my rock from the beginning. I can truly say this would've never made it to print without you. I treasure your feedback and most of all your friendship! Patricia came along later and I'm so grateful for your support. And to my ARC readers: I cannot thank you enough for your willingness to read my work. I'm so blessed and grateful.

I want to send a special note of thanks to all of the Fox Cubs in Layla's Fox Den, my Facebook Author group, as well as the followers on my Facebook, Instagram, Twitter, and TikTok pages. Your continued support encourages me to continued creating stories. You are so motivating and I appreciate each and every one of you.

I'd like to thank my boys. I lost two little ones during late-stage pregnancy. While I did not suffer with infertility, I feared trying again after all we'd lost. I love and miss Logan and Mason as much today as the day they were born, two Decembers, a year apart, many years ago. My heart goes out to every mother who has lost a child, during pregnancy, after birth, or the loss of the dream of children due to infertility. It's a heartbreak I wish on no one. I wrote this book in the loving memory of my children and yours'.

Most of all, I have to thank my family for their continued unconditional love. Working full time in the Emergency Room was hard enough on my family. The stress, the time away, the holidays spent at the hospital instead of with them. Thank you for continuing to love and support me through the madness. I love you so much.

An Excerpt from Stronger

Bzzz. Bzzz.

Looking down at my phone, I notice an incoming text.

11:50 p.m.
Nick Barnes
Nick: What are you doing?

11:51 p.m.
Kat: I'm working. What are you doing?

11:53 p.m.
Nick Barnes
Nick: I know that you cornball. Are you in the middle of anything?

11:54 p.m.
Kat: No. Just discharged a patient.

11:56 p.m.
Nick Barnes

Nick: Good. Get your ass to the doctors' lounge. You've got four minutes. Chop chop.

"Marty, I'm running down to the doctors' lounge for some water. You want anything?" I yell, hoping he says no.

"No, I'm good."

I practically sprint down the hall, knowing what awaits me. I slide my badge along the electronic lock to grant access and push open the door to find... nothing. I walk around the small area, noting I'm all alone. I swiftly turn, wondering if he's playing some trick on me, and collide into the familiar hard chest of Dr. G. Nicholas Barnes.

"Good lord. What an entrance," I laugh, smacking his chest.

He grabs my hand and tugs me into the adjoining room which contains various tables and chairs, computer stations, and a tv mounted on the wall which is showing Times Square. The streets are swarmed with people who are all cheering. The announcer advises the ball is about to descend as he counts down from ten.

I suddenly feel my heart rate speed up as I look at my beautiful companion. I watch as he slides his strong hands along my jawline, his thumbs stroking my cheeks. The look in his eyes is both intense and blissful.

"Two, one—," I hear the announcer say as Nick's mouth comes crashing onto mine, and I hear cheers and the chords of 'Auld Lang Syne' begin to play. His kiss is hungry, demanding as he wraps his arms tighter around my waist and pulls me into him. His tongue teases my lips and I instantly open for him, yearning for the taste and feel of his wet kiss. Our tongues dance to the chorus of the well-known New Year's Eve tune which encourages party-goers to drink to days gone by. I only want to toast to the days ahead, as I pray for many more with this endearing, fiercely passionate man. He pulls away from me, resting his forehead against mine.

My head is spinning, overwhelmed by my obvious love for him. There's no doubt about it. I'd give anything if a life with Nick was in the cards for me. "Nick," I exhale against his mouth.

"Oh, Kitten. What I'd give to take you into that tiny little bathroom and ring in the new year with my cock in your tight little body."

I feel my cheeks burn with the heat of his words. "I—"

"It's okay. Two more days and I get a hot date with the prettiest girl I know. I've got it all planned out. There'll be dinner and dancing, so prepare to be romanced, Miss Kelly."

Returning to the ER, Nick follows along before saying goodbye. I have less than an hour left in my shift, so I need to finish up whatever charting I have left and make sure Marty Street doesn't have anything pressing he needs help with. As we walk toward the main physicians' workstation, I stop dead in my tracks. Thirty feet in front of me, typing into his EMS laptop is Mark Snow. As our eyes meet, the asshole winks at me. I see Marty coming in my direction and simultaneously watch as Nick approaches Mark to shake hands and wish him a happy New Year. This is what I get for trying to handle the stalker Mark situation on my own. Closing my eyes at the irony of this circumstance, I feel a hand on my arm.

"Hey, Kat. You okay?" Marty asks. "You don't look too good."

Preorder STRONGER Here

Additional Titles by LM Fox

The Deprivation Trilogy, Book One

Deprivation

The Deprivation Trilogy, Book Three

Stronger

Due early November, 2021

Preorder STRONGER Here

Moon Shot

(free with a subscription to my newsletter):

www.authorlmfox.com

Upcoming Titles:

The Bitter Rival

(Anticipated release: late 2021)

My Best Shot

(Anticipated release: spring 2022)

The Deprivation Trilogy, The Epilogue

(Anticipated release: 2022)

About the Author

Born and raised in Virginia, LM Fox currently lives in a suburb of Richmond with her husband, three kids, and a chocolate lab.

Her pastimes are traveling to new and favorite places, trying new foods, a swoony book with either a good cup of tea or coffee, margaritas on special occasions, and watching her kids participate in a variety of sports.

She has spent the majority of her adult life working in emergency medicine and her books are written in this setting. Her main characters are typically in the medical field, EMS, fire, and/or law enforcement. She enjoys writing angsty, contemporary romance about headstrong, independent heroines you can't help but love and the hot alpha men who fall hard for them.

www.authorlmfox.com

Printed in Great Britain
by Amazon

84139763R00181